Rogue
Oracle

Alayna Williams

POCKET BOOKS

New York   London   Toronto   Sydney

Pocket Books
A Division of Simon & Schuster, Inc.
1230 Avenue of the Americas
New York, NY 10020

This book is a work of fiction. Names, characters, places, and incidents either are products of the author's imagination or are used fictitiously. Any resemblance to actual events or locales or persons, living or dead, is entirely coincidental.

Copyright © 2011 by Laura Mailloux

All rights reserved, including the right to reproduce this book or portions thereof in any form whatsoever. For information address Pocket Books Subsidiary Rights Department, 1230 Avenue of the Americas, New York, NY 10020.

First Juno Books/Pocket Books paperback edition March 2011

JUNO BOOKS and colophon are trademarks of Wildside Press LLC used under license by Simon & Schuster, Inc., the publisher of this work.

POCKET and colophon are registered trademarks of Simon & Schuster, Inc.

For information about special discounts for bulk purchases, please contact Simon & Schuster Special Sales at 1-866-506-1949 or business@simonandschuster.com.

The Simon & Schuster Speakers Bureau can bring authors to your live event. For more information or to book an event contact the Simon & Schuster Speakers Bureau at 1-866-248-3049 or visit our website at www.simonspeakers.com.

Cover illustration by Don Sipley

Manufactured in the United States of America

10 9 8 7 6 5 4 3 2 1

ISBN: 978–1–4391–8281–9
ISBN 978–1–4391–8283–3 (ebook)

Acknowledgments

THANKS TO my fabulous editor, Paula, and the wonderful ladies of the Ohio Writers Network: Linda, Michelle, Rachel, Melissa, Emily, and Faith. And thanks to Gloria for the game theory.

Thanks to Jason, who always suffers through "muse duty" with aplomb.

PROLOGUE

H E'D DO anything to hear those voices again.

Galen's head was too silent. The other voices in his skull had drained away, leaving him alone. He pressed his cold hands over his ears so that he could hear his own blood and breath thundering, like the ocean in a shell. It was a bit less like being alone. He peered into the darkness, waiting. Waiting for the next voice to fill his thoughts and his dreams.

Through the pulse of his hands, he could hear the whir of an air conditioner and the creak of roof beams cooling overhead as sunlight drained from the day. The orange strip of light shining underneath the closet door thinned and faded. Galen brought his knees up against his chest, and a dress brushed against his cheek. The jasmine scent of his quarry's perfume on his clothes mingled with the smell of shoe leather.

A car crunched in the driveway, followed by footfalls

and the rattle of a key in the lock downstairs. Keys and purse jangled as they were cast on a hall table, and he heard the *thunk* of shoes kicked off on the slate tiles of the entryway. The shuffle of mail sounded like a deck of playing cards.

Galen's breath quickened, and he dug his fingertips into his close-cropped hair. Not long. Not long, now.

Stocking feet padded into the kitchen. He heard the refrigerator door open, then close. A microwave whirred, and a bell chimed. Galen's nose wrinkled. Reheated rubber chicken from a trendy bistro, with tomato sauce. A television droned, comforting voices rising up through the floor. He leaned his head back against the wall of the closet. The television voices nattered on about Middle East peace talks, of a terrorism suspect captured, of the latest results from a television game show.

A fork clattered in the kitchen's stainless steel sink. The television was turned off, plunging the house into false silence. Footsteps climbed the stairs to the second floor. Galen could hear the polyester *zing* of stockings on the plush carpet as his quarry walked past the closet. Light spilled under the closet door.

He held his breath.

The footsteps swished into the bathroom, opened the bathtub tap. Pipes creaked behind the closet wall. Galen smelled bath salts and citrus soap, heard the squeak of flesh against the bottom of the enameled tub. A plastic bottle belched its last quantity of shampoo before it was tossed away into a trash can.

Elbows resting on his knees, Galen waited.

Like the rest of his prey, he'd never met her. This one's name was Lena. He'd been led to her by the memories of others. Those voices burned bright in his mind for a few weeks and faded quickly, like a bruise. They left behind vacant space, space meant for another to occupy. And another. His last victim, Carl, had remembered Lena. Through Carl's eyes, Galen had seen Lena in all her fearless beauty: Lena, walking across Red Square with her lustrous dark hair covered by a scarf. Lena, dressed in a gown with a plunging neckline, her throat glittering with jewels—paste jewels that contained smuggled microchips in the settings. Lena, methodically taking apart a gun in a hotel room and wiping it clean of prints.

If he'd ever really bothered to admit it to himself, Lena had been the love of Carl's life. Carl may not have seen it, but when Galen had taken possession of Carl's memories, he could see it. Carl's memories were twenty years old. But Galen wanted to see Lena, as Carl had. Though Carl's voice had stopped ringing in Galen's head, some of that feeling remained. Carl, the old spy, had carried a torch for Lena, right up until the time Galen had killed him. Galen possessed few feelings of his own. Like a voyeur, he savored the emotions of his victims.

The light under the closet door winked out. Galen heard Lena pull back the bedspread and climb into bed. He heard her punch the pillows and rearrange the covers. After a half hour, all Galen could hear was the soft hiss of her breathing, moving in time with his own breath.

Galen nudged the closet door open. His muscles creaked as he unfolded his lanky frame. He caught his breath, certain Lena could hear him. But the form stretched on its side in the bed remained motionless.

Galen approached the bed. Dim light from the street filtered through the curtains, illuminating Lena's features. Age had softened her face, sketching new lines that hadn't existed in Carl's memory. Her dark hair was streaked with silver, brushed over a shoulder that was rounder than Carl remembered. Her right hand curled loosely over the pillow, and a ring glittered behind a swollen joint. Galen recognized it: it was one that Carl had given her, many years ago, in a spontaneous fit of affection.

Galen peeled back a corner of the covers and slipped into the bed behind Lena. His arms wrapped around her waist, fingers ripping her nightgown. Lena awoke with a jerk, struggling against him. She howled and bit the hand he clamped around her mouth, drawing blood.

Galen could hear her. He could hear her swearing at him, screaming. The scream softened as he slipped his hand around her throat and squeezed. He felt the delicate hyoid bone in her throat shatter as his grip dug deeper, into her flesh. His own skin had grown porous and elastic, thumb reaching up into her jaw. Lena's eyes rolled back in panic. She wheezed as Galen pressed his chest to her back. He could feel her warm flesh against his cold body, felt the cells in his skin growing plastic, reaching out. One of Lena's white teeth glinted in his thumb. It disappeared as his hand lost its shape and flowed into her mouth. In his other hand, he could feel his fingers splitting apart Lena's ribs, feeling the fluttering of her heart like a sparrow in a cage. His hand unfolded and fused with her heart, and he could feel his pulse pumping in time with hers.

Galen heard Lena whimper as she became part of him, trapped in his embrace, melting into his flesh. He could feel her disintegrating, her skin losing surface tension as his body began its parasitic devouring of every vessel and cell, like a snake digesting its prey. But this digestion was external: a slow dissolving of Lena's body. Galen was conscious of the sharp point of Lena's elbow somewhere near his lung, of the contraction of her fingers around his ribs.

And he could hear her. The whisper of Lena's memories suffused his head, as Carl's had. Whispers tumbled over each other, shards of memory cutting deep in his head where they intersected with Carl's fading thoughts.

Galen smiled.

He wouldn't be alone . . . for as long as Lena's voice lasted. Afterward, just as Carl's memories had led Galen to her, Lena's secrets would lead him to others.

Chapter One

"THE WARDEN calls you a monster."

Tara Sheridan stared over the edge of a manila file folder at the man in an orange jumpsuit, wrists fettered to his waist with a belly chain. He looked back at her with contempt over a battered stainless steel table. As she paged through the psych reports conducted by other profilers, she was inclined to agree with the warden's assessment. Zahar Mouda was an accused terrorist. He'd been caught by campus police at a large Midwestern university attempting to drag a drum of solvents out of the chemistry lab. He'd been unsuccessful in convincing the campus cops that he was dragging a keg to a frat house. Subsequent investigation had discovered other missing material that could be used to make bombs. Lots of them.

Zahar shrugged, the movement restricted by the rattle of the chain. For all the dire warnings in the reports before

Tara, he looked very young to Tara: thin, gangly build, large brown eyes framed by square-rimmed glasses. His file said he was twenty-two. She watched his fingers fidget with his restraints, watched him chew his lip.

"Do you think I'm a monster?" he challenged.

"I don't know. But the Bureau of Prisons would like me to find out."

"What do you know about monsters?" Zahar snorted.

"Plenty," Tara told him.

He stared at her, but his gaze faltered as it snagged on a white scar that crept up from the collar of Tara's suit jacket, curling up around her neck to her jaw. Tara didn't flinch, didn't bother to hide it. Perhaps it wouldn't hurt Zahar to know that Tara had faced much greater monsters than him. Monsters that had nearly killed her.

Tara leaned forward, pressing her elbows to the battered table, resting her chin in her hand. A wisp of chestnut hair from the chignon at the base of her neck pulled free, tickling the raised skin of the scar. She ignored it. "What were you doing with those chemicals?"

Zahar rolled his eyes. "Look, I was just trying to make some money. It was just little stuff, at first. First the guy asked for a departmental phone book, then a few sample slides, then . . ." He shook his head. "It was a few bucks, here and there. For dumb shit."

Tara's mouth thinned. This was how traitors were groomed. Small, inconsequential requests snowballed into larger favors. Before long, the victim had given up too much and was too indebted to his handler to climb out of the trap.

"You took the money. Why?"

"I'm trying to save up to bring my sister over here. She wants to study pharmacy."

"Who offered you the money?"

"Some guy at the student union."

"You got a name?". She regarded him with ink-blue eyes, measuring to see if he told the truth.

"Masozi. I already told the cops."

Tara tapped her pen on her notepad, keeping her face carefully neutral. The Federal Bureau of Prisons had asked her to develop a profile on Zahar, to determine how dangerous he truly was. "How much?"

"Ten thousand per shipment."

"That's more than enough money to get your sister over here."

"Stuff's expensive."

Zahar leaned back in his chair, and Tara could sense he was shutting down. She tried a different tactic: "Tell me about your sister."

Zahar licked his lips, and his eyes darted away. Not a good sign . . . His body language indicated he was buying time, fabricating. Or else weighing what to tell Tara. When he spoke, though, his voice was soft. Almost vulnerable. "You don't understand. I had to buy my sister back."

Tara's pen stilled. "Buy her back?" she echoed.

"She's married. Third wife of one of my father's colleagues. He's not really fond of her. Slaps her around." Zahar looked away, and Tara watched his Adam's apple bob as he swallowed. "He agreed to allow her to apply for a visa, but wanted money. Fifty thousand in U.S. dollars."

"What about student loans?"

Zahar shook his head. "I'm on fellowship. My tuition's waived, and I get a monthly stipend. Seven hundred fifty dollars, after taxes." His mouth turned down, and he pushed his glasses up his nose with his shoulder. "And let's face it, nobody wants to see a male chemistry nerd do fifty thousand dollars' worth of exotic dancing down at the strip club."

Tara cracked a smile. "Tell me about when you were children."

Zahar didn't miss a beat. "Asha's three years younger than me. Takes after our mother. She did great in school. She got through her first year of college before she met my father's business associate when she was home on break. The guy took an immediate shine to her." His fists balled at his waist. "I wanted to kick his ass."

"What was her favorite toy?"

"A doll my grandmother made for her. She named it Rahma."

"Tell me about when you fought." This was a trick question. All siblings fought. She wanted to gauge how honest Zahar was with her.

"Our worst fight was when we were little . . . She was probably seven. I found a bird egg in a tree and broke it over her head. She ran crying to our mother, and we both got punished."

"Did you feel bad about that?"

"About getting my sister in trouble? Not really."

"No." She paused. "About breaking the egg."

He blinked quizzically at Tara. "I don't know what you mean."

A knock rang against the metal door behind Tara, and a guard's voice filtered through: "Five minutes, Dr. Sheridan."

"Thank you," Tara called. She scribbled some notes on her notepad. The Bureau of Prisons had guaranteed her a secure room without observation cameras for her interview with Zahar. She was heartened to see that someone had eventually bothered to check in on them.

Zahar stared at Tara. "Well, what did you decide?"

"What do you mean?"

"Did you decide whether or not I'm a monster?" His mouth twitched around the word.

"I haven't made any decisions, yet."

"But your opinion is one that matters."

Tara's mouth thinned. "Your psychological profile will make a great deal of difference in this investigation. But mine isn't the only opinion you need to fear."

"Will it make any difference in how I'm treated?" Zahar's fingers knotted in the chain. "Am I going to get deported?"

"That's not up to me."

The door behind Tara swung open, and two federal prison guards crowded into the tiny room. They unlocked the belly chain from the metal chair, and marched the prisoner back through the door. Zahar's plastic inmate flip-flops slapped on the concrete floor.

One of the guards held the door open. "You coming, ma'am?"

"Can you give me fifteen more minutes?" Tara said. "I'd like to jot down my notes while they're fresh."

"See you in fifteen." The door clanged shut, and Tara was left in the tiny room with the fluorescent light buzzing overhead.

She stacked the contents of her file up neatly and placed it in the file folder. She shoved the folder aside, placed her purse on the table. She rooted around in the bottom of her purse for a pack of cigarettes. Tara didn't smoke, but the cigarette pack attracted little notice on the metal detectors at the prison or in the quick manual search of her bags. Tara flipped off the lid of the pack and pulled out a deck of cards.

The backs of the cards were decorated in an Art Nouveau pattern of stars on a background of midnight blue, edged in silver. These Tarot cards had been a gift to replace the deck her mother had given her, long ago. They'd been a peace offering, of sorts—Tara's lover had given them to her, though he was uneasy with what they represented. Tara's original deck had been destroyed. These still felt too crisp to her, the cardstock stiff and shiny-new. She hadn't quite yet bonded with this deck. Each deck had its own quirks, even a limited personality, and this one seemed determined to surprise Tara at each turn.

She moved to Zahar's still-warm seat, wanting to occupy his physical space. She blew out her breath and shuffled the cards. The sharp cardstock cut her thumb as she shuffled, and she popped her thumb in her mouth as she wiped a droplet of blood from the edge of the deck.

"Tell me about Zahar," she breathed at the cards, ignoring the paper cut. "Tell me about his heart, mind, and spirit."

She pulled three cards and placed them, facedown, on the table. Tara's fingers fogged the scratched stainless steel, and she turned the first one over.

The Fool, the first card in the deck, confronted her in a riot of clear watercolors. The ancestor of the joker in the modern playing card deck, the Fool depicted a young man skipping through a green field, toward the edge of a cliff. The Fool held a bundle over his shoulder, and gazed up at birds in a blue sky. The Fool, one of the Major Arcana cards, represented archetypes at play, suggested the broad strokes of destiny.

Tara steepled her fingers before her, brushing her lower lip. The Fool was a card of innocence and reckless-ness. It spoke of youth. Where Zahar was concerned, it might reflect the idea that Zahar had been carelessly going down the path of the traitor without watching where he was going. At heart, he might be more innocent than she'd thought.

She turned over the second card, the Seven of Cups. Cups were one of the four Minor Arcana suits, and rep-resented choices and reactions to destiny. As a suit, cups represented emotions. In her three-card spread, this signi-fied what had gone on in Zahar's mind. The card depicted a man gazing at a pyramid of seven cups, from which fan-tastical creatures and images crawled: dragons, golden fish, a jewel-encrusted sword, a snake, a castle, a griffin, and a veiled woman. This was a card of illusions. Zahar's head was filled with lies, perhaps from his handler, perhaps from his sister's husband. Zahar may have started out innocent, as the Fool, but he'd made a choice to be deceived.

The last card in the spread represented spirit. Tara was most eager to see what Zahar really was, deep down. She flipped over the Three of Wands, which depicted a man staring out over the sea at a ship, surrounded by three staves. The Minor Arcana suit of wands represented fire, movement, and creation. But the Three of Wands was reversed, suggesting treachery and ulterior motives. Tara's brow wrinkled. Zahar's handler may have been lying to him, and Zahar might have even been deceiving himself. But, with this card, she was also certain that Zahar was lying to her.

She blew out her breath. She cleared the three cards from the table, shuffled them back into the deck. She felt the whir of the rigid cards in her hands as she whispered to them: "What else do I need to know?"

Tara cut the deck three times and drew the first card from the top of the reshuffled deck. Her brow creased as she turned it over.

The Lovers. The Major Arcana card depicted a man and a woman tangled in an embrace. It was difficult for her to tell where one ended and the other began. A voyeuristic angel watched over them from a cloud.

Stymied, Tara rested her head in her hand. She didn't yet fully trust this new deck, and it seemed that this card had nothing whatsoever to do with Zahar's situation. She tapped the picture with her fingers, let her mind rove around the image. She didn't like where free-associating led her: to her own personal life. To Harry Li. Harry had given her this deck, and it seemed to be intent upon reminding her of him.

Her fingertips crawled up her collar to the scars lacing her throat, remembering Harry's kisses upon them. She hadn't seen Harry for months. As an agent for the Special Projects Division of the Department of Justice, he'd been sent out several times—destinations classified—on various assignments, making a relationship difficult. Tara understood; years ago, she'd been an agent for Special Projects. Special Projects took, but rarely gave anything back.

Her fingers hesitated on her scars. Special Projects had taken a great deal from her. Working for them, she'd fallen under the tender mercies of the Gardener, a serial killer who buried women in his greenhouses. She'd survived, barely, and called it quits. She only hoped that Harry wouldn't be subjected to similar dangers.

The latch on the consultation room door ratcheted back, and the door opened. Tara scrambled to shovel her cards into her purse. Looking up with a scowl, she expected to see one of the guards.

"You're back early—" she snapped, but her breath snagged in her throat.

Harry Li stood in the doorway, his hand on the knob. He was almost exactly as she'd remembered him from months ago: sharply creased charcoal suit, polished shoes, black hair precisely parted. But there were circles beneath his almond-shaped eyes.

"Hi, Tara." He let the door clang shut behind him.

"I . . . oh. I thought you were the guard." She finished scooping the cards into her purse, but her heart hammered.

Harry inclined his chin at the disappearing cards. "Still reading?"

"Yeah." She zipped her purse shut and folded her hands over it. "How did you find me?" she asked, but what she really wanted to ask was: *Why here, and why now?*

"When you said you were getting back to work, I figured that you wouldn't stray too far from your forensic psychology roots."

Tara's mouth turned down. "Just contract work. Some pro bono stuff for psychiatric hospitals. That kind of thing." She'd dipped her toe back into work, gingerly. So far, it seemed to be going well, in those measured small doses. Her work with Zahar was filling in for a government psychologist away on maternity leave.

An awkward silence stretched.

Harry stuffed his hands in his pockets, jingled loose change. He did that when he was nervous. "I missed you."

Tara glanced up at him. His face was open, tired, and she felt a jab of sympathy for him. Her fingers knotted in her purse strap. She was fighting the urge to stand up and kiss him. "I missed you, too."

His eyes crinkled when he smiled, and he dropped into the other chair on the opposite side of the table. Exhaustion was palpable in the broken line of his shoulders. "Special Projects is killing me."

Tara reached across the table for his hand. His fingers folded around hers so tightly that she couldn't tell where hers ended and his began.

"I've been there," she said, without irony.

"I know." His mouth flattened. "That's why I came to ask for your help."

Tara's hand froze. She had hoped that he'd come to see *her*. Not for work. "Oh." She looked down at her fuzzy reflection in the table.

Harry reached across the table and crooked a finger under her chin. "Hey. That's not what I mean. I wanted to see you, and—"

Tara withdrew her hand and pulled her chair back, drawing her professional mantle tightly about her. "Tell me about your case, Harry."

Harry stared down at his empty hand, closed it. "A half dozen Cold War–era intelligence operatives have disappeared. We've got evidence that specialized intel connected to them is being sold internationally, to the highest bidder. Most of it has to do with uranium stockpiles, leftover pieces of weapons from Soviet Russia. Tehran has been all over it."

"That sounds like a military issue. Or an NSA problem." Tara crossed her arms over her chest.

"You would think. But the disappearances are . . . unusual. These men and women have been vanishing without a trace. No bodies, no evidence of struggles."

Tara shrugged. "Maybe they defected. Maybe they're having a beach party in Tehran."

"Homeland Security hasn't caught any of them trying to move outside the country. Some of them have literally walked off surveillance footage and were never seen again. It's like the fucking Rapture—they leave their clothes, jewelry, even cell phones behind, and vanish."

He smirked, mouth turning up flirtatiously. "Of course, there's also the fact that there are no beaches in Tehran."

Tara lifted an eyebrow, intrigued at both the case and the flirtation. "What's their connection to each other?"

"All of them were associated with something called Project Rogue Angel in the 1990s. It involved cataloguing and tracking the disposal of nukes in the former USSR."

"That sounds like a thankless job."

"Wasn't as successful as one might hope." Harry rubbed the bridge of his nose. "I think somebody got to these people. I can't prove it. But I need help in figuring out who's behind the disappearances. You're the best damn profiler Special Projects has ever seen, and we need you."

Tara considered him. Harry wasn't the type of man who would readily ask for help, and he'd done so in a clumsy way. She was reluctant to become involved with Special Projects again, to be their tool. But she owed him.

He looked at her, eyes red with too little sleep. "I need you."

She reached forward and took his hand. She couldn't say no to him.

CHAPTER **TWO**

GETTING AWAY from work would be easy. With the piecemeal jobs she'd been working as a forensic psychologist, Tara was certain that no one would notice if she disappeared for a couple of weeks.

Getting away from her secret life as an oracle would be difficult.

Tara dragged her battered suitcase down from the top shelf of her bedroom closet. She chucked it on the butterfly-print bedspread that smelled like lavender. An aggrieved yowl emanated from the bed, and a gray tabby cat rocketed from under the quilt.

"Sorry, Oscar." Tara winced. The fat cat could flatten his substantial mass into disappearing shapes that would defy Stephen Hawking to describe on the quantum level.

Oscar looked up at her and twitched his whiskers. He yawned dramatically, then stalked into the open closet to root among Tara's shoes. Tara reached to the top shelf for a battered pistol box, containing a Ruger SP-101 revolver. Tara opened the barrel, forgetting whether or not she'd cleaned it after the last use. Fortunately, the stainless steel was shiny and smooth, smelling of mineral oil. She placed the pistol and a box of bullets beside the suitcase.

The suitcase sported an address sticker from years ago, and Tara ripped it off. She'd fill out a new one—reflecting her current address at a Tennessee farmhouse —at the airport. Her tenancy had been intended to be temporary, but it had already stretched into several months. It wasn't home, but it was where she needed to be.

It was where Delphi's Daughters were gathered.

Through the open window, feminine laughter echoed over the buzz of the cicadas and the bass notes of the bullfrogs. A bonfire blossomed in the backyard under a huge yellow-cheese moon, and the shadowy silhouettes of women passed before the flames. The bell-like sounds of zills rang into the darkness. Tara's nose twitched. She smelled marshmallows and incense. A woman cast sparkling dust into the fire, while the others *oohed* and *ahhed*. Another, a little tipsy, got up to do the funky chicken dance to rowdy cries of "Opa!" and "Shake it!" The dancer kicked high, and a flip-flop soared into the bonfire.

Delphi's Daughters were just that: a contradiction. They'd existed since the beginning of recorded time, just behind the scenes, foretelling and nudging the courses of world events to suit their liking. By day, they were soccer moms, actuaries, and soldiers. By night, they told the future according to unique gifts. Some dealt in dreams, others in the reflection of the moon on water. Some could tell the future by listening to the calls of birds or swishing the albumen of eggs around at breakfast time. Most of them found some time during the year to gather at the farmhouse, under the guise of conferences or visiting distant relatives.

Tara was the only living cartomancer in the group—not that she was officially a member. She had mixed feelings about their work and their message, but she'd forged an uneasy peace with them to watch over the youngest of Delphi's Daughters, Cassie Magnusson. She was Cassie's self-appointed guardian and protector, and Delphi's Daughters seemed to respect that.

Most of the time.

"Hey, do you know where the bottle openers are?"

Tara's door swung open without a knock. Cassie Magnusson, a young woman in her early twenties, stood holding a bag of marshmallows. She was dressed in shorts and a T-shirt, barefoot, with grass clinging to her pale legs. Her dark hair was tied back in a ponytail, and on her head perched a silvery headband with alien antennae topped with wobbly stars. Glitter from the stars had fallen on her cheeks, giving her an ethereal, if somewhat sticky, glow. A chubby Labrador retriever waddled behind her, claws clacking on the hardwood floors.

Cassie paused, taking in the suitcase and gun. "Where are you going?" she accused.

"Nice headgear," Tara said. "Is that part of your training—receiving signals from space?" Against Tara's better judgment, Cassie was being groomed to be the next

Pythia, the most powerful of oracles and leader of Delphi's Daughters.

"No. The Pythia gave 'em to me as a prize for passing my last astrology test. And don't change the subject." Cassie parked herself on the bed beside the suitcase, and the Labrador lay down at her feet with a sigh. "Here, Maggie." She dropped a marshmallow on the floor, and the dog gobbled it. Oscar waddled out of the closet to sniff the bag of marshmallows. Cassie dropped another on the floor. He batted it under the bed and disappeared. "Where are you going?"

Tara sighed and sat next to Cassie on the bed. "Harry came to see me today."

Cassie's face brightened. "How's Harry?"

"Busy with work."

"That's what you keep saying."

"Yeah, well . . . Harry's line of work is like that. It's nothing personal."

"That's what you keep saying."

Tara wrinkled her nose at Cassie. "Harry needs my help on a case."

"Sure. He wants your *brain*." Cassie arched her eyebrow, and her antennae wobbled.

Tara reached out to pat Cassie's shoulder. "I won't be gone long."

Cassie looked sidelong at her, and the girl's fingers fidgeted in the plastic bag of marshmallows. "Promise?"

"Promise."

As she hugged the girl, anxiety twitched through Tara. She knew Cassie picked up on her unease with leaving her alone with Delphi's Daughters. She realized Cassie had overheard the furiously whispered arguments Tara had with the Pythia, late at night, about her training. Tara wanted Cassie to lead as normal a life as possible.

But there was no normalcy in a house full of oracles.

Tara put her arm around the girl's shoulders. "You have the cell phone I gave you, right?"

"Yeah. It's under the floorboards in my room."

"You call me whenever you need me, or if you just want to talk, okay?"

"Okay." Cassie's antennae drooped.

"You're gonna be okay." Tara squeezed her shoulders, and the antennae nodded in agreement. Oscar peered out from under the bed skirt. "You'll have Oscar to watch over you. And Maggie." The dog's tail slapped on the floor, and she whined for another treat.

"Yeah," Cassie said, clutching the bag of marshmallows close to her chest. "I guess I should go find that bottle opener."

Tara smiled bravely as the girl left the room, Maggie following behind. Her smile faltered when they left, and she stared down at Oscar.

"Keep an eye on her, will you?"

Oscar blinked his golden eyes and rolled onto his back for Tara to scratch his belly. Tara took that to be assent. She might be uneasy around the other oracles, but she trusted Oscar and Maggie entirely.

Tara finished packing and zipped up the suitcase. Its wheels made squeaking sounds down the hallway, following her down the steps with a series of *ka-thunks*.

She rolled it into the dark kitchen, keys in hand. Dried herbs hung in fragrant bunches, strung by pieces of string from a lace-curtained window through which moonlight streamed. The moonlight picked out the dishes soaking in the sink and the cheese trays on the scarred butcher-block countertop. The only other illumination in the room was the dim blue light from the pilot light in the stove . . . and a red light bobbing in the corner.

Tara's nostrils flared, smelling a familiar cigarette. "Hello, Pythia."

A dragon of smoke blew across the window, and the Pythia stepped into the weak light. The short woman jingled softly when she walked, her swaying hips strung with a scarf covered in coins; she'd been dancing. She paused before the sink to tap her cigarette into an ashtray. A curtain of dark hair fell over her face, strands of silver glinting in the moonlight.

"Going somewhere?" Her musical, softly accented voice wrapped around a steely inflection. She gestured with her chin to Tara's suitcase.

"Harry's asked me to help him with a case."

"Harry's good for you. You should go."

Tara gritted her teeth. "I don't need your permission to leave the house, Amira." She rarely used the Pythia's real name; it was a sign of too much familiarity or disrespect. "I'm not one of Delphi's Daughters."

The Pythia shrugged. "You can say what you want, but your actions prove otherwise."

"Leaving proves your influence over me? I don't follow."

"No. Coming back just might, though." The Pythia's white teeth shone in the darkness when she smiled.

"You know that I'd come back for Cassie. That's all."

"Yes. I know that you wouldn't leave her for long. Heaven only knows what we would teach her, in your absence. But you serve us, and our patterns, whether you want to, or not."

Tara bristled. She'd been estranged from Delphi's Daughters for years, at her own insistence. She chafed under the idea of surrendering herself to their control, of giving in to her roots, rather than forging her own way in the world. She wasn't going to be anyone's tool. Not the government's, and not Delphi's Daughters'. "More of the idea that free will is an illusion?"

"Free will isn't an illusion. Free will can nudge destiny off its tracks."

"I know that," Tara said, in irritation. The Pythia was old enough to be her mother, and somehow always managed to make Tara sound like a petulant child. "And I'm exercising my free will to help Harry."

The Pythia stepped over to the stove, hip scarf chiming in time with her steps. She switched on the gas stove burner with a click and a *whoosh,* cranked the blue flame up high. The light cast her shadow long across the kitchen floor, and the Pythia squinted at the fire.

Tara crossed her arms. The Pythia's talent was pyromancy. She could see the future in something as mundane as a match spark or as devastating as a house fire. The gas flames twitched yellow, curling in on each other.

"Interesting," the Pythia said.

"What?" Tara couldn't resist asking.

The Pythia abruptly switched off the burner. "Beware the Chimera."

"What does that mean?"

The Pythia shrugged, took a drag on her cigarette. "I don't know yet. That's just what the fire said to me."

Tara rolled her eyes and dragged her suitcase to the kitchen door. The Pythia called after her, cheerfully: "Call when you need us."

Tara banged the screen door shut behind her, muttering under her breath: "Not fucking likely."

Tara always loved traveling at night, especially by plane. There was something about the dimness of the cabin lights, the lack of crowds, and the glitter of lights in the darkness below that made her feel apart and insulated from the problems of the world.

The commercial red-eye flight Harry had booked for them was nearly deserted. A group of hungover college girls was already asleep in coach, sprawled across empty seats. A salesman hunched over his laptop computer, sweat stains spreading underneath his arms. A mother held a sleeping infant on her lap, staring out the window. But Tara and Harry had business class all to themselves.

The silence was awkward.

For the first part of the flight, Tara busied herself with paging through Harry's summary file of the case. Three former operatives had vanished, under odd circumstances. As Harry had said, they had all worked in various capacities for a project called Rogue Angel. The details of the project itself had been heavily redacted in black marker, but Tara gathered that the project's goal had been to track inventories of nuclear components in the early 1990s. The project had met with little success, and had been scrapped in 1994.

All of the missing had worked for Rogue Angel. But it was there the similarities ended.

The first lost operative had been a retired CIA agent, Gerald Frost. His file photo showed him as a tanned, athletic, balding man. Gerald had spent a great deal of time traveling the countryside of the former USSR in the course of his work, and had apparently never gotten the bug out of his system. As a retiree, he'd returned to many of his old haunts as a tourist. An online travel agency had booked him on trips to Moscow, St. Petersburg, and Ukraine two years ago. Somewhere en route to Kiev, he'd vanished. His train ticket hadn't been used. His cell phone and credit cards were later found, sold and resold on the black market. The State Department had assumed that he'd met with modern day highwaymen, and had not been able to trace his actual point of disappearance.

One incident might be a fluke. But the others drew more attention. Frost's former administrative assistant, Carrie Kirkman, disappeared six months later from her Las Vegas real estate office. She was recorded walking into the building by a security camera on a Friday morning, and never emerged. On Monday, her clothes and jewelry were found locked in her office.

The pattern had repeated with the next victims. A retired intelligence agent, Carl Starkweather, vanished from a parking garage of a casino, with his clothes left in his trunk. Foul play was immediately suspected, but the ex-agent owed no one any money. His wife had taken out sizable life insurance policies on him, but she had an airtight alibi.

And secrets were filtering back through the intelligence community. Old secrets, but marketable ones. CIA chatter had caught snippets of information about degraded uranium sold to Iran. And Russian patrols had caught a group of Taliban sympathizers digging around old mines in Siberia. When the men had been arrested, the patrol found a half-exhumed nuclear warhead.

Tara closed the file. There was only so much the official reports could tell her. She gazed at Harry. He'd fallen asleep, his chin resting against his shoulder. She allowed herself the luxury of looking at his face for a moment, then reached down for her handbag.

She pulled her cards out of her purse and lowered the tray table. Glancing around, she confirmed she was out of the other passengers' line of sight. Tara thought of the disappearances of the operatives as she shuffled, then drew her cards. She laid them down on the table in a familiar order: six cards arranged in a cross, two cards in the center and four more surrounding them, with the cross flanked by four in a straight line on the right. The tray table was small, and this was a large spread, so the edges of the cards overlapped.

"What do your cards say?"

Tara started. Harry was awake, looking over her shoulder. He blinked away sleep, gesturing at the spread.

She pursed her lips. She didn't like reading in front of others. But Harry knew who and what she was. He knew about Delphi's Daughters. Though he was a practical man, a man of science and the physical world, she appreciated that he attempted to suspend his disbelief, on occasion, to enter her world.

"I don't know, yet."

"You mind if I watch?" Harry asked. "I mean, I could leave you alone . . ." He gestured to the other empty seats in the dim cabin.

She shook her head. "No. It's all right. I'm just not used to the idea of reading around just anybody." Not that Harry was "just anybody." She bit her lip. "You know what I mean."

"Okay," Harry said. He folded his hands in his lap. Though he wasn't given to hocus-pocus, he seemed to be genuinely trying to understand how she worked. To understand *her*.

Tara gestured to the cards. "This is what's called a Celtic Cross spread. It's one of the most commonly used spreads in Tarot. It's intended to give a bird's-eye view of the situation, past, present, and future. This part"—she gestured to the left side of the arrangement—"is the Cross. And the right side often symbolizes a staff."

She touched the card in the center of the Cross. "This is the card that represents the heart of the question, or the questioner." She turned it over, revealing a figure dressed as a woman, standing in the middle of a laurel wreath. Surrounding her were a man, bird, ox, and lion. "This is the World. It represents completion, victory, synthesis, and eternal life. It's the end of a journey or the hero's quest."

"Like in fairy tales?"

"Joseph Campbell popularized the idea of the hero's journey as an eternal theme, populated with archetypes found in every culture. Many scholars believe that the Major Arcana cards of the Tarot also speak to that journey. The Major Arcana begins with the Fool, who passes through trials and wisdom, and finishes with the World."

Harry squinted at the card. "That's a pretty manly looking chick in a dress."

Tara laughed. "That's the Sacred Androgyne, a perfect creature that unites the male and female."

"Hm. Hermaphrodites in Tarot. Who knew?"

"The card is really about union of everything . . . men, beasts, the four elements." Tara flipped over the card turned crosswise over it. "This card crosses the question. This represents the obstacles facing the subject of the reading." The Five of Cups depicted a man staring somberly at spilled chalices of wine. "This is a card of regret. If there's a single person or group behind these disappearances, I'd hazard a guess that there's a great deal of regret or grappling with conscience going on."

"A guilty hermaphrodite, okay." Harry fidgeted in his chair.

"Harry . . ." she began.

He raised his hands. "Okay, okay. I'm trying to learn."

She plucked up the card above the World. "This crowns the question, represents the subject's highest aim." She flipped it over, showed him the Lovers. "Before you make any jokes about hermaphroditic love, this card means more than that. It's about fusion, union, trust. Could mean that whoever's behind this is missing some feeling of belonging. Or he or she could literally be missing a lover." Tara tried to ignore the possibility that her own feelings could be clouding the reading. "The subject may be afraid of being alone."

She put the card back on the table without meeting Harry's eyes, and moved to the card below the World. "This card represents the foundation of the situation." Tara picked up the card beneath the World. "This goes to underlying motivations, events in the past that are still reaching into the present and influencing the question." The Tower showed two people falling from a structure hit by lightning. "The Tower is a card of catastrophe, of natural disasters, storms, and general destruction of an old way of life." Tara's fingers walked upward to the Lovers card. "In the Tower, we see the Lovers falling to earth. I'm guessing that whoever's behind your disappearances may have experienced an estrangement in the past, one he or she is still trying to correct.

"In this reading, we're seeing three Major Arcana cards in a row: the Lovers, the World, and the Tower. It suggests that the past is strongly affecting the ambitions of the person who's behind these disappearances."

"Especially since whoever's doing this is dealing in old secrets."

"Good point." Her fingers rested on the card to the right of the World. "This card is behind the questioner, representing the recent past. Here, we have the Nine of

Swords. The crying woman sitting up in her bed with nine swords hanging over it represents sleeplessness, worry. Swords represent the element of air, ideas."

Tara turned over the last card in the Cross, to the left of the World. "This is the immediate future influence, the Emperor." The card showed a severe man crowned with laurel leaves, sitting on a throne. "A man involved with the rule of law is going to become involved in the situation. Someone who embodies the Apollo-like ideals of reason."

Tara turned to the staff, the row of cards to the right of the Cross. She turned over the bottom card, and her mouth turned down. "This card symbolizes the questioner." It showed Strength, a woman serenely closing the jaws of a lion. Crimson drops of blood welled over her collarbone, where the lion had clawed her. This was a card Tara had, in the past, drawn to represent herself. Her hands self-consciously flitted to her throat.

"That's me," was all she said. "The next card shows the environment around the question." She turned over a card showing a knight holding a golden disk with a star engraved on it. He gazed at it pensively. "This is the Knight of Pentacles. He's a practical, methodical person. Well grounded. Pentacles are associated with the stable element of earth."

"Does this relate to our subject?"

"Unlikely. This is a card I associate with you." She said it matter-of-factly, but wondered if the admission made his skin crawl.

"You have a card for me?"

"Not intentionally. It just sort of happened, over time." She plunged ahead to the next card up. "This represents the inner emotions of our subject, his secret wishes and fears." The Nine of Wands showed a wounded warrior leaning on a staff. He seemed to be scanning the horizon for the next threat. Wands were associated with fire. "This is a card of obstacles and adversity. Vigilance is recommended."

She turned over the last card. "This is the outcome, the Eight of Cups. See the figure fleeing in the night from the treasure of the eight stacked cups? This means that your subject is fleeing. He might abandon the effort of his own accord, or he might simply be one step ahead of you."

"Great."

Tara rested her elbows on the tray table. "Overall, I'd say that you're dealing with a person who's out for revenge for past wrongs. Someone who's survived a great deal of calamity—perhaps a natural disaster, maybe something like 9/11. Some event that really made an indelible mark on the world stage. Your subject is feeling isolated, and is searching for completion. That could be in a relationship, like a lost love, or it could be as part of an organization. Maybe a terrorist one. The Nine of Wands suggests to me that he knows how to wait, and the Eight of Cups tells me he knows when to run. The World, with the Sacred Androgyne, indicates he may be able to disguise himself, or at least that he's well traveled. He may not be a U.S. citizen.

"From a numerology standpoint, the presence of two eights—Strength is the eighth card in the Major Arcana, and we have the Eight of Cups—brings up the underlying theme of karma, of mastery. He's doing what he's doing because of something in the past, perhaps as retribution.

"The two nines in the spread imply your subject has issues with completion and attainment. He feels incomplete, unworthy. That may be something you can use to bait him."

Tara trailed off, lost in thought. Her mind churned, seeking connections between these symbols and others in the physical world.

"Damn," Harry said, quietly.

She blinked, looked at him. Her face flamed, and she instantly regretted sharing the experience with him. "What?"

"The more I learn about how you think, the more I wonder . . ." He shook his head. "It's like the rest of us see light in the visible spectrum, and you see infrared and ultraviolet."

Hearing the rattle of the refreshment cart coming, Tara scooped up her cards and stowed them in her purse. "Growing up, as an oracle, I never had to explain. And the rest of the time, I hid it . . . so . . . I realize it doesn't make much sense."

Harry shook his head. "It doesn't need to make sense to me. It just needs to work."

Tara stared at her ghostly reflection in the window. She hoped that she could do this for him. He'd never asked her for anything, and she'd do everything in her power not to let him down.

Chapter Three

S PECIAL PROJECTS was not as she'd remembered it.

When Tara had been an agent, Special Projects had worked out of backrooms of nondescript office buildings in a dozen cities. Special Projects had kept a low profile then, making do with mismatched office furniture and scavenged equipment. SP HQ in Washington had been a redheaded bureaucratic stepchild, housed in the sub-subbasement of the Library of Congress in downtown Washington. The space had once been used for archives, but a pipe leak rendered it unusable for document storage. The place always smelled of mildew, and the supply cabinet was prone to pillaging by rogue librarians. Tara remembered being chased from the copy machine three floors up by an archivist wielding a heavy-duty stapler. He'd been a good shot, had dented the elevator door with the stapler he'd hurled at Tara's head before she escaped.

The building was familiar, the same one SP HQ had been in when she'd been an agent. There was more security at the door now; despite Harry's creds, Tara had still been subjected to a full search and fingerprinting to get a temporary ID. She'd been impressed at the instant background check station behind the security desk, and with the screens showing surveillance camera footage from more than two dozen angles within the building.

Standing in an elevator with Harry as it descended below street level, Tara adjusted the still-warm laminated badge on her lapel. "Do they still call Special Projects the 'Little Shop of Horrors'?"

Harry blinked. "No. I've never heard that."

Tara stared at her shoes. "Sorry. That's what we called it when I worked here."

His face split open into a grin. "It fits."

"Are there still turf wars with the librarians?"

"Yeah." Harry sighed. "They stole our refrigerator a couple of weeks ago."

"Did you get even?"

"Sort of. They didn't realize that there was a severed head a forensics tech left in the fridge until they got it upstairs. We assembled a raiding party and took it back. In the process, we swiped a really sweet espresso machine."

Tara smothered a laugh with the back of her hand. "Some things never change."

The elevator doors opened to reveal a glass fishbowl, full of dark-suited fish swimming in blue light. Flat-screen computer monitors glowed on stainless steel desks, the hum of servers indistinguishable from the overhead fluorescent shop lights. Desks were clustered together like a newsroom bullpen. Glass partitions muffled sound and gave the illusion of privacy. Filched archival shelving lined the walls, stacked with evidence boxes. Cords had been duct-taped to the concrete floor to prevent tripping, and coffee was burning, somewhere. Underneath it all, Tara could still smell the old, pervasive scent of mildew.

"You guys got some new toys," Tara remarked.

"Three cheers for the Homeland Security budget." Harry jabbed a thumb at a glass-walled office. "Even paid for a sweet flat-screen TV for the boss to monitor the cable news."

"Who's the new division chief?" The previous division chief had met a bad end. The official reports had said that he'd died in the performance of his duties, but Tara knew better.

"Ron Aquila, from U.S. Marshals. You know him?"

"No. Is he ex-Secret Service?"

"Yeah. Seems okay, so far. A stand-up guy." Harry pursed his mouth, and Tara reminded herself to ask Harry for more details, later.

A short Hispanic man in the glass-walled office passed in front of the television, tapped on the glass, and beckoned to Harry.

"Is that Aquila?"

"Yeah. Come meet the boss."

Tara followed in Harry's wake to the office, smoothing the front of her suit jacket. Returning to Special Projects made her nervous. It was like falling into an old pattern of the past all over again, one she'd tried to forget.

Aquila circled around his desk to greet her. Tara noticed the desk did not match the steel and glass of the rest of the décor. It was an old, polished, wooden desk. Tara guessed it had come with him from Treasury. It suggested Aquila could be sentimental . . . or was simply intolerant of waste. It also suggested that he didn't care much for what others thought, which was a good start.

"Chief Aquila, this is Dr. Sheridan." Harry made the introductions.

Aquila shook Tara's hand briskly. "I've read your work, Dr. Sheridan. I'm pleased that Agent Li brought you in to consult."

"It's good to be back," Tara lied. She bit back her mixed feelings about being thrust back into Special Projects' work. She'd promised herself she'd be more cautious, this time.

"Please, have a seat." Aquila gestured to chairs opposite his desk. "We can chat while we're waiting for the rest of the team to arrive."

Tara's brow wrinkled. Working around Harry's sensibilities was difficult enough. If she was to be working with others, she'd have to go to greater lengths to conceal her methods. "You've assembled a task force?"

Aquila nodded. He laced his hands before him on his blotter. Tara noticed that the blotter was full of notes—an indicator that he didn't fully trust the sleek computer sitting on his desk. One of his square hands was adorned with a wedding ring, and his red tie was the only bright spot of color in the room. There were no photographs of his wife and family to watch him. Tara could understand his desire to shield his family from his work. "NSA, the National Counterterrorism Center, and CIA have their fingers wound into this investigation."

"They haven't provided us with much to go on," Harry groused. "Everything they give us is redacted to the point of uselessness."

Aquila held up his hand. "I know. Which is why I asked them to assign someone to us. Hopefully, that will enhance the flow of information." He turned his attention to Tara. "Would you like some coffee, Dr. Sheridan? Tea?"

"Coffee would be wonderful," Tara said. She was missing too much sleep to go for long without caffeine.

"Certainly." Aquila pushed out of his chair and walked out of his office.

Tara blinked. She'd never seen a man at his level go get his own coffee. That boded well—Aquila wouldn't ask his staff to do anything he wouldn't do himself.

Harry nodded in approval. "It's a nice change from Corvus's leadership."

"I can see that."

Tara's gaze roved around the office. Aquila kept bookshelves of law books, a locked file cabinet, and an impersonal potted plant. She turned around in her seat, expecting to see what she'd see in any other executive office: framed commendations and degrees on a trophy wall. There would maybe be a framed document replica; Tara figured it was a toss-up between whether it would be the Constitution or the Gettysburg Address.

But her breath caught in her throat.

Aquila kept a trophy wall, but it wasn't the kind she'd expected. Instead of a wall devoted to his own laurels, Aquila kept a wall of the Division's accomplishments. She recognized most of the souvenirs from her days as a profiler. A letter from a child who'd been abducted and rescued was rendered in crayon and kept pristine behind glass. A piece of a foundation from a haunted house, where excavation had revealed twelve suspected yakuza members buried in the foundation. The faded toe shoes of a murderous ballerina. A piece of a satellite that had fallen out of orbit. A disarmed necklace bomb that had been tied around the neck of an activist nun in South America. And a relic from Tara's most famous case: the Gardener's curved knife, a Japanese weeding blade called a Hori-Hori.

Reflexively, Tara's fingers wrapped around her ribs. She remembered the feel of that weapon cutting into her flesh, the sound of it spreading dirt over her near-lifeless body. Even here, sanitized and cleaned, it was still a shock. It was a tangible reminder of the hold Special Projects had once held over her life, the power of life and death.

Harry's hand grasped her sleeve. "Hey. You okay?"

She nodded. "Sure."

But when Aquila returned with the coffee, she had to concentrate to keep the liquid from sloshing beyond the rim of the mug as her hand shook. She focused on keeping her hands still, balancing the cup against her knee.

"I'll be honest. Special Projects is out of its level with this case." Aquila settled behind his desk and dunked a tea bag in his cup.

Beside her, Tara could feel Harry bristle.

"That's saying a great deal," Tara said neutrally. "Special Projects is the catchall for the cases that are out of everyone else's level."

"Yes. We're the 'Little Shop of Horrors.'" Aquila grimaced and took a sip from his tea. Tara wondered if he'd been surveilling her elevator conversation with Harry, or whether he'd known the nickname before he'd taken the post.

A knock banged on the glass door, rescuing Tara from commenting. Without asking permission, a man pulled it open and stuck his head inside. "Sorry I'm late."

Aquila stared over his cup. Tara had the sense that Aquila wasn't a man who brooked breaches in etiquette. The interloper barged in and dragged up a chair beside Harry. He was easily a decade older than Tara, but was attempting to give the illusion of youth with a tan, European-cut dress shirt, hair product that smelled like limes, and a bleached smile. This was a guy trying very hard to be relevant. He leaned over Harry to shake Tara's hand.

"Sam Veriss, National Counterterrorism Center."

"Mr. Veriss is an intelligence analyst," Aquila said, placing his cup and saucer down on his desk. Tara noticed that he didn't offer Veriss any coffee when he made introductions.

"Actually, I'm an economist, by training."

"Economics. That's interesting," Harry said. "But I'm not sure how this impacts the case." He lifted a questioning eyebrow to Aquila. Tara could see he instinctively disliked Veriss. Harry had a low threshold for artifice, and a lower threshold for uselessness.

"My specialties are in network theory, and I dabble quite a bit in game theory." Veriss plunged onward. "I've been working on analyzing terrorism networks and predicting terrorist movements using various computer algorithms. Most of it's derived from intelligence chatter, but I've got some pretty good working models that have predicted some fairly significant events over the last few years."

"Such as?" Harry challenged him.

Veriss grinned. "Well, my model predicted the last three suicide bombings in Afghanistan within a radius of four hundred feet."

"Great. They were stopped, then?"

Veriss's face darkened. "Well, no. The input data wasn't specific enough to predict the event with that much precision as far as timing. But the model is improving."

"What kind of data do you use, Mr. Veriss?" Tara asked, attempting to be polite. Her thoughts flashed back to the Emperor card from her reading. The Emperor was the avatar of science, the embodiment of masculine logic. Veriss seemed wedded to that worldview . . . which might make him a useful ally, or a source of conflict with Tara's intuitive way of working.

"All kinds of sources. Everything from the movement of currency to the results of elections to stock market fluctuations. It's amazing what can feed into an individual— or group—decision to mount an attack. Lately, I've added cell phone traffic to the model, and—"

Harry glanced at Aquila with a look that said: *Why is this jackass sitting here, pissing in my swimming pool?*

"Folks," Aquila interrupted. "I expect you to work together under Agent Li's direction. I want you to determine who's behind these disappearances and the information leaks. I don't care whether it's a terrorist group, an individual, or a cluster of suicides. Figure it out, and put a stop to it. Any questions?"

Tara shook her head.

"All the resources of Special Projects are at your disposal. Use them."

Tara bit her tongue, trying not to burst out laughing at the idea that those resources involved staplers stolen from the Library of Congress.

The phone on Aquila's desk rang. Aquila snatched it up, and his expression darkened immediately. Oblivious to Aquila's reaction, Veriss was chattering at Harry about available server space for his data analysis tools. But Tara watched as Aquila's face hardened, and his finger massaged his temple. He set the phone down without saying a word.

"There's been another disappearance," he announced, cutting off Veriss's list of electronic storage demands.

"Great! Another data point to add to the model . . ." Veriss chirped.

"Shit," said Harry.

Tara was inclined to agree with Harry.

LENA IVANOVA WAS NOT THE KIND OF WOMAN WHO WOULD have disappeared in the night.

At least, not without packing some really expensive shoes.

Tara pawed through the missing woman's closet with latex-gloved hands. She flipped through matching hangers holding a wardrobe of designer clothes, much of it silk and leather. The closet was ordered according to type—blouses, jackets, skirts, and pants—then ordered by season and color. The woman had an enviable collection of shoes lined up at the bottom, arranged by heel height and color. Empty luggage was stacked neatly on the top shelves. Scuff marks on the bottoms suggested she traveled frequently.

Tara squatted down to peer at the shoes. The almost obsessively neat line of shoes had been disturbed, kicked aside. She knelt and shone her flashlight on the floor of the closet.

Interesting.

On hands and knees, she crawled into the closet and turned around, careful not to disturb the shoes. The closet smelled like leather and jasmine perfume. The shoes had been shoved aside in a pattern that suggested someone had been inside the closet. Someone had been sitting here and hadn't wanted to have a stiletto boot jammed up his ass.

"You hiding from Veriss in there?"

Tara peered at Harry's dress slacks, then up. His arms were crossed, and he was staring down at her with a smile playing around his lips.

"Maybe."

The drone of Veriss's voice could be heard downstairs, and Harry rolled his eyes. "Is there room for me?"

"Probably. But I think someone was waiting in here for Lena." Tara gestured to the scattered shoes, which looked like the leavings of a centipede. "I'm guessing that whoever was in here stayed here for a long time. Maybe hours."

"That fits." Harry frowned. "Lena Ivanova was last seen three days ago. She owns a local art gallery. She left work after meeting with a client, and hasn't been seen since. Her car's still in the driveway. Her housekeeper came in to work, expected her to come by to pay her. When Lena didn't show, the housekeeper called the police."

"This is where she was taken. I'm sure of it." Tara crawled out of the closet, and Harry offered her a hand up. She scanned the bedroom, taking in the elegant furnishings. An antique four-poster bed dominated the room, surrounded by abstract watercolor paintings in vivid jewel tones. The bed was made, and the adjoining bathroom smelled of lemon cleaner.

Tara glanced sidelong at Harry. "How long had the housekeeper been here before she called the cops?"

Harry pinched the bridge of his nose. "Two days. And the local PD took their sweet time declaring the victim to be a missing person. They're still convinced she might have taken off to Bora Bora on a whim. The housekeeper's been busy cleaning the house. For two days."

"And destroying evidence for two days."

"You got it. Forensics is going through the laundry now, and having a tantrum."

Downstairs, Tara could hear the musical sound of the

maid's voice, interrupted over and over by Veriss. She tried to ignore it. She could hear muttered swearing from the forensic technicians who were trying to get prints from the freshly scrubbed windows. There had been no obvious signs of entry. And whatever evidence they would find would be so compromised by the maid's actions that it would never stand up in court.

Tara crossed the plush carpet to the bed. The pile was covered in precise vacuum cleaner tracks, and she was certain that some poor forensic tech would have the task of taking the machine apart to look for unusual fibers. The bed had been crisply made with hospital corners, a jacquard and velvet comforter stretched so perfectly over it that it looked like a page from a catalog.

Not so much as a speck of dust had settled into the posters of the bed. Tara squinted at the carving on the upper posts. What she first took to be scrollwork actually resolved into a pattern of wings . . . reminding her of the Lovers card from her Tarot readings. In the card, an angel watched the Lovers from on high. What had these wooden angels witnessed?

Tara peeled back the covers, pulling them loose from the pile of decorative pillows. She ran her gloved hands over the cool, plum-colored sheets. The mattress was dented in the center of the bed, suggesting that Lena usually slept alone. But her mind kept tracking back to the Lovers card from her Tarot reading. She turned over the pillows carefully, wondering if the housekeeper had washed them recently.

"Harry," she said. "Look at this."

She pointed to a slightly darker stain on the underside of a pillow. It was almost imperceptible against the darkness of the fabric, a small smear scarcely larger than a finger.

"Looks like blood," he said, squinting at it. "Could be anything. Could be from a nosebleed, given the placement on the bed."

"Or it could come from our abductor."

"I'll get forensics in here to look at it. This will be the most fun they'll have all day." Harry left Tara alone in the room. She could hear the clatter of coins in his pockets as he jogged down the steps. He was frustrated. But Tara knew that she could still trust him to be methodical. He was, after all, her Knight of Pentacles. Whether he still wanted to be, or not.

She spun on her heel, thinking. Lena's bedroom looked very much like a showplace. There was little here to suggest any personality . . . no photographs of family or friends on the dresser. Everything here fit precisely into a design scheme, and felt oddly impersonal. In some ways, it reminded her of Aquila's office: no personal life on display.

Except for one thing. On the dresser was a painted Russian doll, a matryoshka. Tara picked it up. The delicate hand painting depicted a woman with dark hair in a kerchief, holding a basket of roses. She turned it over, seeing a legend scribbled on the bottom: *For my Matryoshka, my darling of many faces. Love, Carl.*

Tara's intuition prickled. Was this a gift from Carl Starkweather, who had also served on the Rogue Angel project? She opened the doll, unscrewing it at the waist.

Any other matryoshka Tara had seen had been the same: six or eight successively smaller nested dolls, all depicting idyllic country girls in cheerful colors. But this was not a doll like that. The doll inside was a bear ... and not a teddy bear. The bear's jaws were parted in a ferocious expression, golden paint glittering on its claws.

The next doll was equally strange. A wolf was painted in silvery gray stripes, looking down its long snout at Tara. A pink tongue lolled from between its teeth.

Curious, Tara continued to open the dolls. Next was a girl, dressed like Red Riding Hood with a crimson cloak and picnic basket. Then, a red fox, its tail wrapped around its feet. A gray tabby was next, smiling like the Cheshire cat. Tara involuntarily thought of Oscar. Underneath its paw was a feather. The smallest doll was a bird ... a dove, holding a piece of olive branch in its mouth.

Tara arranged the shapeshifting matryoshka in order. Something in her subconscious tickled her, and she thought of the World Tarot card. The woman in the center of the card was surrounded by beasts, and she was not what she seemed. Tara made a mental note to go over Lena's personnel record. From what little she'd gleaned on the ride over, she'd been told that Lena had been associated with Rogue Angel. She might have been anything from a secretary to a spook ... and Tara would be curious to see what her relationship with Carl was, what had caused Lena to keep the only sentimental artifact in the whole room.

A wheeled cart dragged through the carpet, towed by a forensic technician. The tech was a young woman with her blonde hair tied back in a French braid, swimming in a too-large windbreaker with the name ANDERSON embroidered on the front. "Agent Li said there was some blood stain evidence here?"

"I think it might be blood, but that's your call." Tara showed her the spot on the pillow. The tech photographed the location from several angles, then unfolded a large paper bag from her cart to hold the pillow. She handled the evidence with exceptional care, sealing the bag with tape and filling out the evidence tag.

"This may be a good lead," Anderson said. "We weren't able to isolate much unique DNA in the last case."

"What do you mean?" Tara leaned against the dresser.

The tech's mouth turned downward. "Our lab took DNA swabs in the Carl Starkweather disappearance. Unfortunately, the DNA was contaminated."

Tara's brows tugged together. "Was there a chain of custody issue?"

Anderson shook her head. "Not that we were able to determine. All the slides that the lab prepared showed multiple DNA markers."

"That's good, right? More suspects?" Tara's thoughts raced around the possibility that there might be a group behind the disappearances. Her gut told her that wasn't the case, but if the evidence pointed there . . .

"Not what we ended up with. We got garbage . . . It was like somebody put samples from a roomful of people in a blender." Anderson shook her head. "We're still trying to straighten it out. But it'll be useless in court. The guy who collected the samples got suspended."

"I'm sorry."

Anderson shrugged. "Aquila has been breathing down our necks on this, and it sucks not to have any answers." She finished filling out the evidence tag, scanned the room. "And this scene looks like it's gonna be a bust, too."

"Yeah. I hear the maid got a bit overzealous."

Anderson shook her head. "Not really her fault. She was just doing her job. But this . . . this may just be one of those unlucky investigations that's one clusterfuck after another."

HE WASN'T ALONE, NOT ANYMORE.

Galen lay curled up on his side in the bed of his rented room, listening to Lena's voice in his head. Wrapped up in a sheet, he scribbled through notebook after notebook, committing Lena's voice to paper. Her secrets and memories flowed across the page, interspersed with sketches of people and places, maps, bits of remembered passwords and codes. As he filled each notebook by the meager light from the bedside lamp, he cast them aside to a heap with hundreds of other notebooks beside the radiator. Those were Carl's memories. And Carrie's and Gerald's.

Galen flexed his fingers, feeling his hand cramp. Like a molting snake, his skin flaked away, and he absently scratched at it. His attention was seized by a lump on his left ring finger, and he dug more deeply at it. The skin sloughed away, revealing Lena's ring, embedded in his finger, just below the last knuckle. He gave it an experimental tug, but it would not pull free. Not yet.

Galen padded, naked, to the bathroom. He stretched, and a few extra vertebrae in his back popped. He knew this stage was temporary. After he'd consumed Lena, it would take some time to finish digesting her. His fingers roved over the planes of his face, grown a bit lopsided in the mirror, like wax too close to a flame. He was reminded of the Dali painting of the melting watches, running out of time.

He ran his hands over his scalp. A few strands of Lena's long hair clung to it. It smelled like jasmine. He pulled it across his nose to enjoy the fragrance before reaching for the electric clippers. The buzz of the blades against his skull scythed through the bits of Lena's hair, leaving Galen with a bald, lumpy scalp and a nest of hair in the sink.

He looked more human when he was finished. Not like himself, yet. But less like Lena.

He turned on the shower, let the hot water beat upon his flesh. He grasped a stiff bristle brush and scrubbed at his body. Skin sloughed away in parchment-thin flecks, circling the drain. He scrubbed until his skin was raw and pink, until he could see the glitter of Lena's gold ring more clearly.

He wrapped a towel around his body, dug around under the sink. The ring was an inorganic compound. He wouldn't be able to digest it. It would have to come off.

Galen slapped his hand down on the edge of the sink. He grasped the edges of the ring with a pair of pliers and pulled. The ring shifted a bit, but wouldn't budge over the shiny red knuckle. He'd waited too long; he could feel it grown into the bone.

He grasped the pliers again, with more determination, feeling the bite of them against the circle of metal. With all his strength, he twisted and pulled. He could feel his knuckle split, and warm, red blood seeped down over the pliers. He cast the bent ring into the sink with a clatter.

Wrapping his bleeding hand in a towel, Galen picked up the ring. Lena remembered it. She remembered when Carl had given it to her in Red Square. Carl had said it was a promise, but Carl had forgotten.

But Galen wouldn't. Resolutely, he turned back to the nest of papers on his bed. He picked up his pen, determined to write everything Lena knew down, before her bones dissolved into his and her memory faded.

Before he was alone, again.

Chapter **Four**

Tara always found it difficult to assimilate into an investigation already underway. There was always a good deal of playing catch-up, and she hated being at a disadvantage. Sometimes, all she could do was retrace the steps of the previous investigators. She knew from the file that Carl had been married, with four children. The Lovers card had appeared in her reading, and she suspected that there was more to Carl and Lena than it first appeared. Had they run away together?

The only way to find out would be to see for herself.

She stood outside the Starkweather house, a nice house in a suburban Falls Church neighborhood. The house was a bit too big for the tiny lot, but each one of the other houses on the cul-de-sac had been built that way. She guessed this was a neighborhood populated by government workers, imagined that nobody could speak much about what they did at block parties. They probably talked more about the shiny, late-model cars in the garages and the kids pedaling their tricycles in the driveway than what anyone actually did for a living.

The pansies lining the walkway were a carefully mulched blend of violet, white, and red that grew in a riot of color. Tara wondered if gardening was Mrs. Starkweather's hobby, or if they had a gardener. The front walk had been freshly power-washed, and the grass clipped short in diagonal furrows across the lawn. Whether she was doing the work herself or overseeing it, Mrs. Starkweather had been keeping busy.

Tara rang the doorbell and waited. She heard the mincing *tap-tap* of impractical shoes on the inside floors. Eventually, the front door opened. A tanned, blonde woman in cropped pants and a pink tank top looked at her. She was easily a decade younger than Carl, very beautiful, in a California beach girl way. Nothing like Lena. "Yes?"

"Mrs. Starkweather? I'm Tara Sheridan, from the Department of Justice, Special Projects. I'm investigating your husband's disappearance."

"Oh." Her well-manicured nails flexed on the door handle. "You people were just here."

"We just have some additional questions."

Carl's wife nodded, opened the door. "Please give me a moment to send the kids out to play."

"Of course."

Tara stepped into the foyer. The travertine floors had been freshly waxed, and Tara could smell lemon cleaning solution. Mrs. Starkweather rousted two children out of a kitchen shiny with stainless steel appliances. The kids were about nine and twelve. The kids clomped down the hall, and Mrs. Starkweather gestured for Tara to take a seat at the kitchen barstool. She scrubbed at a sticky mess left by the kids with a dishcloth. Her left hand was heavy with a diamond setting the size of a bottle cap.

"Your children are beautiful," Tara said.

Mrs. Starkweather beamed. "I'm glad I'm not the only one who thinks so. The house feels a bit empty, now that Jamie's off to summer school and Mark's a college student working an internship in New York this summer . . ." She trailed off, continued to scrub at the stain on the granite before it set up.

"Thank you for talking with me, Mrs. Starkweather. I really appreciate it."

She grimaced. "Mrs. Starkweather sounds like Carl's mother. Please call me Suzanne."

"Suzanne, can you tell me the last time you saw Carl?"

Suzanne rinsed the dishrag out in the spotless sink. "Two weeks ago, he said he was going to Vegas with some of his old friends. I dropped him off at the airport." Tears welled in her eyes, and she savagely wrung out the dishrag. "I kissed him good-bye, and he took his suitcase and went into the terminal."

"Did Carl travel often?"

Suzanne nodded. "He was always prone . . . to a kind of wanderlust, I guess." She carefully arranged the dishcloth over the faucet so that it would dry out. "It's just the way he is. After he retired, he got restless. I guess he was used to always being on the go." She looked up at Tara.

"Would you like something to drink?" She wandered over to the refrigerator. "I have juice, milk, regular and diet pop, iced tea . . ."

Tara felt some sympathy for her. She had the impression that Suzanne tried hard to make things perfect for Carl, keeping the perfect house and watching over the children. Her body was well toned and tanned, her hair expertly highlighted. She did her best to make him happy, to support him, and now he was gone. Not by an assassin's bullet on the job, in a hero's fall and folded flag. He was simply gone, with no explanation. "Thanks. An iced tea would be great."

Suzanne pulled a glass out of the cabinet and filled it with ice from the refrigerator door. The iced tea pitcher was full of lemon slices. Tara smiled when she tasted it. It was perfect, sweet but not too sweet, just enough lemon.

"We're looking into a number of disappearances of people who have worked with Carl," she said, reaching into her attaché case. "I'm wondering if you know any of them?" She fanned out pictures of Gerald Frost, Carrie Kirkman, and Lena Ivanova. Tara watched how Suzanne's gaze lingered on Lena's picture, and how her jaw tightened.

"Carl golfed with Gerald every Sunday, before he went overseas. Carl said he vanished, but suspected he found some Russian girl to keep him company in his old age." Her collagen-enhanced lips thinned. "I don't know her." She pointed at Carrie's photo.

"What about this one?" Tara slid Lena's photo across the granite to Suzanne. It wasn't very current, but still showed the flush of Lena's exotic beauty, ten years ago.

Suzanne wouldn't touch it. "She worked with Carl."

"She's gone missing, too." Tara watched the play of emotions crossing Suzanne's chemically frozen brow.

"That son of a bitch." Suzanne's well-manicured hands balled into fists. "Did he run away with her?"

"I don't know. Were they—?"

Suzanne glared at the photo. "I told him that I never wanted him to have anything to do with her again. I heard all the excuses. He was half a world away, he was lonely . . ." She shook her head. "I told him that if he dared divorce me, I'd take everything. And I meant it." Tears glistened on her eyelashes. "I did everything for him. Everything."

Tara impulsively reached across the counter to pat Suzanne's hand. Starkweather had been consumed by his career, to the exclusion of his personal life. Tara didn't wish that on Suzanne. "We don't know anything for certain."

Suzanne dabbed at her eyes. "Have you ever been married, Ms. Sheridan?"

"No. No, I haven't."

Suzanne's mouth was set in a hard line. "Don't get involved with a man who works in shady government business, who works with secrets. You'll wind up being alone. You do everything alone—fixing the furnace, making sure the kids' report cards get signed, taking them to the emergency room." She shook her head. "It'll only bring you suffering."

Tara dozed in Harry's car. It had been almost two days since she'd snatched more than an hour or two of sleep, and it had begun to drag at her. She'd wrapped her arms in her jacket, feeling the warm night air blowing on her face, when Harry spoke over the click of the turn signal:

"Um. So, do you want to stay with me while you're in town?"

Tara opened one blue eye. Illuminated by the green dash lights, she could see a shadow of worry over Harry's eye. This was awkward for him. And her. It had been months since they'd been together, and it felt like they were renegotiating boundaries all over again.

"I mean, you don't have to." His words tumbled over each other. "Special Projects will put you up at a hotel. I just thought . . ." He trailed off, floundering, as he changed lanes on the freeway.

"Sure," she said, winding her fingers in her sleeves. "Thanks."

She'd often wondered where Harry lived. She wondered if he lived in a posh neighborhood with nightlife, like Old Town Alexandria, with a view of the Watergate lights playing on the Potomac. Or did he find a place near a college, like in Georgetown? On the phone, he'd never really talked about where he'd moved to.

Harry exited south of DC, just over the line into Virginia. He wound down some residential side streets, past a donut shop, a nondescript grocery store, and several fast-food places, and into an apartment complex with tan vinyl siding, a pool, and a freshly paved parking lot under yellow streetlamps.

"It's not fancy," he said, shutting off the engine in a numbered parking spot. "But, as far as short-term leases go, it was a good deal."

"Why the short-term lease?" she asked, keeping her voice neutral.

Harry lifted Tara's suitcase from the trunk. "I don't know what's in store for me at Special . . . at the Little Shop of Horrors. I'm still on temporary transfer. No telling where they'll send me next." He slammed the trunk and frowned. Tara left it alone.

Harry led her up the steps to a second-floor apartment. His keys jingled in the lock, and he opened the door. "Home, sweet home."

The light clicked on to reveal a living room with plush tan carpet. The vanilla paint on the walls still smelled new. A black leather couch was pushed up under the living room window, tags still dangling from the back, facing a flat-screen television. Cardboard boxes stacked neatly up against the walls, along the line of the living room wall into the galley kitchen.

Harry rubbed the back of his neck. "Yeah, I haven't really unpacked."

Tara nodded. "No worries." Deep down, she suspected what Harry did: that he wouldn't be here very long. "It's a nice place."

"Thanks. I call the décor 'Overworked Federal Agent.'" He bent down to pick up the mail scattered on the floor that had accumulated through the mail slot.

"It's attractive. I especially like the clock." Tara gestured to the clock hanging on the kitchen wall. It was shaped like a black-and-white cat, and the eyes moved right and left in time with the switch of the pendulum tail. It looked over the kitchen sink, where a lonely coffee cup stood.

Harry rolled his eyes. "Yeah. Pops sent that to me."

"It's cute," she insisted. Harry's adoptive father had an odd sense of humor.

"He also sent me a banana hammock as a housewarming gift."

Tara blinked. "He sent you a *what?*" Perhaps Harry had been having more of a wild time in DC than the solitary coffee mug suggested.

Harry plucked an item off the counter to show her, a sheepish expression on his face. It was a C-shaped device on a wooden base with a hook at the terminus of the C. "You hang a bunch of bananas on it to keep 'em from bruising. Pops calls it a banana hammock."

Tara laughed out loud. It felt good to be in the small, warm circle of light in Harry's modest kitchen, with the cat clicking time over them. It felt almost like the way things had been, months ago. "I can honestly say that I've never seen a banana hammock before," she kidded him, with an arch glance.

"Pops will be thrilled."

Harry brought her suitcase to the only bedroom, set it on the bed. Tara followed with her hands clasped behind her back, but her heart thudded under her tongue. Harry stepped away, hands in his pockets, jingling the change in them nervously.

"I'll take the couch. Make yourself comfortable, and uh . . . let me know if you need anything."

Tara nodded, swallowed, smiled. "Thanks." But she wanted to say: *It's okay. You don't have to sleep on the couch.*

Harry closed the door behind him, leaving her alone.

Again. She sighed, turning back to her suitcase. She unzipped it and began pulling out her clothes. She opened Harry's closet to hang her suits, and noticed a hole in the wall beside the closet.

She frowned, running her fingers over the chalky dent. It was at her shoulder level, the perfect crater of a fist. She wondered at it, worried at the kind of stress Harry was under that would drive him to take it out on his walls. She'd never known Harry to be needlessly violent. That . . . that was out of character for him. Was Special Projects devouring him, causing stress fractures in his personality as it gnawed through him? She would hate to see it chew Harry up and spit him out, as it had done with her.

She turned her attention back to the closet. Harry's closet was nearly bare. His suits and shirts hung on the left side, shoes lined up below. Tara hung her clothes beside his, but gave them a respectful distance, so they weren't touching. She turned on her heel, taking in the sparse room. Some part of her wondered if Harry always slept in his bed alone. The boxes stacked in the corner made her wonder if the memory of her was packed away with the rest of his past, not urgent enough to unpack in the present. If there was someone else, she didn't really blame him. And she didn't really want to know.

She took off her watch and placed it on a dresser, the only other piece of furniture in the room. Even the bedside lamp sat on the floor. Aside from the kitchen implements, Harry's dresser was the only other place in the apartment that showed any evidence of his personality. A glass peanut butter jar held coins, probably dug out of his pockets at the end of the day. A framed picture beside it showed Harry and his adoptive father, Martin, holding fishing poles. On the mirror above the dresser was tacked a scrap of paper. Tara reached for it, and her heart skipped.

It was a Tarot card, Strength. Ragged and torn, it depicted a woman holding closed the jaws of a lion. It was Tara's card, from the deck she'd inherited from her mother, long ago. The deck had been destroyed, and this had been the only part of it that remained. Tara fingered the grimy, faded inks. It still smelled like earth, where Harry had found it, months before.

A smile touched her lips, and some of the tension drained out of her shoulders. She knew that Harry had not forgotten her.

She undressed quickly, averting her eyes from the mirror. A Jack Frost pattern of white scars crossed down her throat, over her abdomen, ending over her right hip. Stipples of scars puckered over her right arm, under her left breast, and onto one thigh. Gifts from the Gardener. Tara was self-conscious enough about them not to want her gaze to linger. She shrugged quickly into her black knit pajamas: wide-legged pants and a long-sleeved top that covered most of them. She didn't need the reminders when trying to sleep . . . or work.

Tara reached for her cell phone and climbed into bed. She dialed the number for the farmhouse. She picked her cards out of her purse and laid them on her lap. As the phone rang, she shuffled the cards. She plucked one from the deck, turned it faceup: the Priestess. A woman in heavy robes and headdress in the shape of a crescent moon gazed serenely back at her. Tara made a face. This was the guardian of esoteric mysteries, the card of intuition. It was also the card she associated with the Pythia.

"Hello, Tara." The Pythia answered. Tara didn't know if she knew who was calling because she was squinting into her cigarette lighter, or whether she was using caller ID.

"Hello. Is Cassie awake?"

"Just a moment." The phone was placed down, and Tara heard footsteps and the murmur of voices. Tara had no doubt that Delphi's Daughters would be listening in to the conversation. She plucked another card from the deck, the Star. It depicted a young woman pouring water into a stream with a bright yellow star shining overhead. It was the card of hope, of the future. It was the card she associated most with Cassie.

"Hi, Tara." Cassie's voice sounded tinny over the connection.

"Cassie. How are you?"

"Good. How was your trip?"

"Tiring. Got some sleep on the plane, but it's been nonstop running since I got here."

"How's Harry?"

"Good. I think."

Tara could hear Cassie's smile over the phone. "You don't know?"

"Things are complicated."

"They always are, with you two."

Tara took a deep breath. "Hey, it looks like I might be here longer than I thought."

"Oh." There was a pause.

Tara pulled another card: the Four of Wands, reversed. It showed four garlanded wands and four maidens celebrating underneath, with a castle in the background. Reversed, it suggested insecurity. "Everything okay there?" Tara kept the tone of her voice light, but she worried about the girl. The cards were the only means she had of gauging the true situation back at the farmhouse, an oracle's lie detector.

"Things are fine. The Pythia is going to start some new training with me tomorrow."

Tara's eyebrows crawled up. "More astrology?"

"She didn't say. Just said that this was more 'practical training,'"

"Hmmm." That could be anything from cooking to martial arts.

"But I'll tell you all about it tomorrow. You're going to call tomorrow, right?"

"Of course, sweetie. I'll call you tomorrow."

"Okay. Good night, Tara."

"Snuggle up to Maggie and Oscar. Good night."

The phone line clicked silent. Tara shuffled her cards back into the deck. She wasn't happy about leaving Cassie alone with Delphi's Daughters. But in light of this case, she couldn't go rushing back. Her uneasiness—and Cassie's—would have to wait.

Tara bent down to click on the lamp on the floor. She spread out Lena's file before her. Like the others, it had been heavily redacted. But from what Tara had gathered, Lena had been Carl's interpreter for Project Rogue Angel. She'd traveled with him throughout Europe, searching for forgotten equipment and trying to broker deals for scientists to stay. At that time, brain drain had been severely affecting the former Soviet republics. Many scientists had gone to the highest bidder. Or gone missing.

Tara shuffled her deck. "Tell me about Lena," she breathed to it. A card skipped out of the orderly shuffle, and she pulled it.

The Queen of Pentacles stood in a lush garden, holding a star. Her dark, braided hair hung over her richly embroidered robes. The Queen of Pentacles was an earthy, practical, and sensuous woman. She was a hard worker, a woman who accomplished what she set out to do. And she had no difficulty enjoying the rewards.

"Tell me about her colleague, Carl," she asked the cards. She cut the deck three times and drew the King of Pentacles, holding a five-pointed star and the reins of a sorrel horse. These two were meant to be together. The King was the master of practical matters, of status, and negotiations.

"Tell me about their relationship." To confirm her suspicion, she laid a third card between them. She drew the Six of Cups, showing two children drinking from the same chalice. This card suggested that these two were living too much in the past, attached to a love affair that had long ended.

Tara flipped back through Carl's file. His photos showed a fit, gray-haired man. He'd been married at the time he'd been working in Russia. Tara flipped through photos of Suzanne and the kids. The wife was a perfectly beautiful woman, and the children took after her. But Carl's true love had been Lena.

Tara suspended judgment. She was simply a voyeur, looking from the outside in. The less she judged, the more she might be able to understand.

She yawned. She might be able to understand more, but not tonight . . . at least, not while she was awake. She shuffled her cards and pulled a random one from the deck: the World. Tara tucked the card under the pillow and switched off the light. This was an old technique her mother had taught her. Leaving a card in mind, whether to meditate upon, or dream upon, sometimes gave up some interesting insights.

She pulled up the comforter around her chin. It smelled of Harry, like soap and aftershave that smelled faintly of sandalwood. A lump rose in her throat at being in Harry's bed without him. As she fell asleep, she blinked back tears.

TARA DREAMED, BUT SHE DREAMED OF MORE THAN THE WORLD.

She smelled blood, and opened her eyes. At first, she thought she was reliving the nightmare of the Gardener. But the details were different. She wasn't in a box, bleeding out in a shallow grave; she was standing upright and feeling sun on her face. She was wearing a blue dress, the bodice smeared in crimson. Her fingers fluttered to her throat. The neckline of the dress was torn, and she could feel seeping wounds on her collar. Her hands were covered in gloves, and the sticky redness stained the leather.

Something bumped her side. She looked down, and gasped.

A lion, tawny and massive, looked up at her with unblinking golden eyes. His tail smacked the back of her legs. The muscles in his back rippled languidly as he circled her, and Tara held her breath. The lion sat down and began to lick blood off his massive paws. Her blood.

"Holy shit," she breathed. In this world, in the world of Tarot, she was the avatar of Strength. The avatar of Strength could close the jaws of the lion. Could she?

She knelt before the lion and reached out her hand, as if the lion was a dog in a park she was trying to make friends with. He sniffed disinterestedly at her. Tentatively, she reached out for the top of his head. His mane was coarse and thick, but warm. His skull was larger than her chest, and her fingers easily disappeared in the short fur behind his ears. He made no move to harm her, keeping his teeth firmly hidden behind his whiskers. Whatever altercation she'd had with the lion was lost on Tara, but she kept her guard up. As tame as he seemed, he was still a wild animal.

Tara looked over his ears at the landscape. Wind whipped desert sand through the red light of sunset, casting her shadow before her. The wind had carved grooves in the sand, like the tracks of a sidewinder.

But another shadow crossed over the ripples of dunes. She and the lion were not alone.

A woman walked across the sand some yards distant, the hem of her velvet dress dragging in the sand like the wing of a broken bird. Tara recognized the Queen of Pentacles, with a moonlike face, carved with high cheekbones. Dark eyes swept over the landscape.

"Lena?" Tara cupped her hands over her mouth to shout.

She turned toward Tara. The wind whistled through her heavy sleeves, tearing at her hair.

Another figure appeared behind the Queen, casting a long shadow in the setting sun. Tara shaded her eyes with her hand, straining to see an androgynous figure clothed in a sheet that rattled like the sails of a ship in the wind. Long blond hair streamed over the figure's shoulder, but Tara couldn't tell whether the figure was male or female. Laurel leaves were bound in the figure's hair, ripped free by the wind. Blue eyes burned in hooded sockets.

The lion at her side growled. His claws flexed in the sand.

"The World," Tara breathed.

"Lena, come here." The World spoke to the Queen in a man's voice, beckoned her with an open hand. Lena's head turned to the voice. The World's hand caught her sleeve, dragged her into a crushing embrace.

"No!" Tara ran toward Lena and the World, sand sucking at her feet.

But she was too late. The World enveloped Lena in his white sheet. For a moment, their limbs were twined together like the Lovers. But the violet brocade of Lena's dress disappeared. When the World opened his hands, Lena was gone.

Only the howl of the wind rattled through his hands.

Tara met his gaze, but they were not the blue eyes of the World. Not anymore. They were Lena's brown ones, staring back at her.

Harry stared at the ceiling, hands laced behind his head. Streetlight striped the walls through the blinds, and the insomniac cat clock kept watch, ticking out the time with each switch of its tail.

His thoughts chased Tara. He wished he had some of her gift of insight, to know what she was thinking. The world always seemed so transparent to her, but she seemed opaque to him, now. Closed. He blamed himself for his absence, for leaving. He hadn't wanted it that way. Time just stretched out, and he couldn't find his way back.

He didn't know what he expected from her. He had no right to expect anything, really. But he knew what he wanted: when he first saw her in the prison meeting room, he'd wanted to take her beautiful face in his hands and kiss her until she couldn't breathe. He needed her that much.

But she . . . she probably didn't need anything. Anyone, least of all him. She seemed so distant and self-contained . . . and he was afraid that too much time had passed between them, that they wouldn't be able to pick up where they'd left off.

It made no sense, him and her. She lived in an entirely different world, in the shadowy world of Delphi's Daughters. She lived in magick, finding signs and portents in everything she saw. Based on the few glimpses he'd had into her world, Harry suspected that mundane reality didn't really exist for her at all, that it had fallen away bit by bit in the process of becoming an oracle. Harry wondered if she would always be able to keep a foot in the everyday world, or if she would eventually be absorbed by Delphi's Daughters, no matter how much she resisted.

He turned over, hearing the couch leather squeak beneath him. He existed in a hidden world, too . . . the world of the Little Shop of Horrors. And that set him so far apart from daily life he wondered if he'd ever be able to go civilian again. He was armed every hour of every day, even when he went to the grocery store. He jumped when cars backfired on the street. He suspected child abuse every time a mother scolded her child at the store. He couldn't eat out when he was seated with his back to the door. He couldn't remember the last time he'd been out in public just wearing a T-shirt and jeans . . . He always had to find a way to conceal the holster and his creds. Just once, he'd love to stretch out on some grass or sand and feel the sun on his bare chest. He had to content himself with the cold streetlight streaming in from the window when he slept. Alone.

Harry slid from the couch and padded across the floor. The cat clock gave him a sidelong glance as he walked noiselessly down the hall to the bedroom. His hand hesitated on the doorknob. He turned it softly, pulled it open.

Illuminated by the weak streetlight pouring in from the window, Tara lay on her side. The thick fringe of her eyelashes cast shadows across her cheeks, and her hair tangled over her shoulder, rising and falling steadily in sleep.

Harry noiselessly crossed to the bed. He reached out, wanting to caress that pale cheek, but his hand dropped away. His fingers twitched, sensing some chill that he wished he could erase.

Sadly, he walked away, closing the door behind him.

In her sleep, Tara exhaled. When she breathed out, her breath steamed like the cold fog of a breath on a winter's day, taking the shape of the World consuming Lena.

Chapter **Five**

T ARA HAD been able to shake the dream when she'd awoken, but not the chill.

"You're not getting sick or something, are you?" Harry asked over coffee.

Tara shook her head, though she'd wrapped her hands around the coffee mug and was holding it close to her chest. She'd drained the hot water out of the apartment water heater, and was still cold. She couldn't explain it, but it was a chill that had seeped deep into her bones. Like winter. "No. I'm okay."

Harry reached across the tiny kitchen table and pressed his hand to her forehead. "You're cold." His touch lingered for a beat longer than necessary, and Tara covered the flush in her cheeks by taking a sip of her coffee.

Unlike the dream, this morning felt like a very odd domesticity. Very normal. Tara had never known much about *normal,* and it felt really nice to be reading the paper at a kitchen table without oracles running underfoot, flinging rose petals or falling into trances.

"It's summer. It won't last," she said. She hoped. She'd never experienced a dream as vivid as the one last night, even when she'd meditated on cards before. They'd seemed less real, more like academic exercises. Tara wished that her mother was still alive, that she could ask her what this strange change in her powers meant.

Harry frowned, took his cup to the sink to rinse it. "I warn you, lady, I'll be watching you," he said, in mock seriousness.

"I think we've got more serious things to worry about." Tara stood to collect her purse and attaché case.

"Yeah. Like keeping Veriss busy."

"He's under your skin that much already?"

Harry made a face and stared at his cell phone. "Yeah. He's sent two text messages this morning about a briefing first thing. I've got the feeling that's gonna be two hours of my life I'm not gonna get back."

"Maybe it won't be that bad," Tara said, following Harry out the door.

"I bet he has fucking slides to show us."

"If he has slides to show us, I'll buy you dinner."

Harry grinned. "You're on."

Tara lost the bet. There were slides. Lots and lots of slides.

"This is worse than when Pops goes on vacation," Harry whispered to Tara when Veriss had his back turned.

Tara rolled her eyes and shifted in her chair. Her butt was already numb, and she looked at her watch. They'd been listening to Veriss natter on about his research methods for over an hour, and there were no signs of abating. Aquila had already ducked out to respond to a phone call, and hadn't returned.

". . . as I mentioned, I'm combining elements of chaos theory and game theory to create predictive models for human behavior. Chaos theory assumes systems that react to small errors in initial conditions, yielding larger effects." Veriss drifted before the projector in the dim conference room. Differential equations were displayed behind him. Christ, he even had a laser pointer.

"Yeah," Harry said. "We got that, already. The Butterfly Effect. A butterfly flaps its wings and causes a hurricane halfway across the world."

"Well, that's an overly simplified way of putting it. And I'm applying it to social systems, not physical ones. And instead of the topological mixing assumed in physics, I'm assuming social contagion from the social sciences, using network theory."

"What about periodic orbits?" Tara asked. Veriss had spent the last hour talking down to them, and she was beginning to get irritated. "In classical chaos theory, materials move in dense periodical orbits. Do you have a parallel assumption for human systems?"

"Actually, Ms. Sheridan—"

"That's Dr. Sheridan, Dr. Verris." Veriss had insisted that everyone address him by title. Tara felt it was fair to request the same consideration.

"Dr. Sheridan." Veriss chewed on the inside of his lip. "I account for that by mapping social interactions using an evolution function. Would you like for me to show you?" He tugged a whiteboard closer to him and brandished a dry-erase marker.

Harry kicked Tara under the table. His expression said: *Don't egg him on.*

"Not necessary. Just trying to keep you honest, Dr. Veriss," Tara said primly.

Veriss cleared his throat. "As I was saying, I also use elements of game theory. I treat the commission of crime as a strategic situation in which the choice to commit a crime is dependent on the behavior of others. For example, a criminal may choose to offend against a victim who, by his own choice, places himself in the offender's sights."

"Yeah," Harry said. "The better bait hypothesis."

Veriss capped his marker and cocked his head. "I'm not sure I've heard of that one."

"Criminals take the easiest mark. It's a no-brainer."

"It's much more complex than that, in the aggregate." Veriss switched slides. "It's really a simultaneous game in which decisions are made by both parties along a time continuum . . ."

Harry rolled his eyes. "Professor,"—Harry refused to call Veriss "Doctor"—"this is all very interesting, but do you have a working model for the crimes we're dealing with?"

Veriss clicked to another slide. "This is what I have so far for a working model . . . subject to revision, of course. These data points show disappearances of all intelligence personnel in the U.S. for the last fifty years. The assumption is that these patterns would hold true for our current cases. Ranked in order of prevalence, the disappearances were accounted for by line-of-duty deaths, defection, personal mental breakdown, unrelated random crime events, accidents, and unknown causes.

"I've added some other factors to the model, such as economic opportunity and absolute value of the intelligence held by the operative."

"You're assuming that some intelligence is more marketable than the rest." Tara crossed her arms over her chest. She glanced beside her and noticed that Harry was drawing pictures of devils on his notepad.

"Yes. And I determine this by the addition of several factors in world upheaval. With the ending of the Cold War, for example, there's just not that much market for mind control techniques anymore. There wasn't much market for nuclear secrets until the current situations with Iran and North Korea. That's caused the value of that intelligence to skyrocket."

"So, you're suggesting defection?" Harry asked, continuing to color in the goatee of his cartoon devil. "That they're all, I don't know, having a beach party in Tehran?" Harry grinned and kicked Tara under the table.

"That comes out at the top of my model. And there are no beaches in Tehran."

The door to the conference room cracked open, admitting a blinding wash of light. Tara and Harry's heads swung toward the door like starved sunflowers kept in a darkroom.

"Agent Li? Forensics would like you to take a look at some of their results." The office manager's voice was like a salvation from a benign god.

Harry was already on his feet. "We'll continue this later, Professor."

Tara snatched up her notebook and followed Harry out the door before Veriss could protest.

"Jesus Christ," Harry muttered. "Where do they find those guys?"

"Does he know about the marauding librarians?"

"Not yet. But I hope one of them steals that fucking projector."

Tara smirked. She was certain Veriss meant well, but she knew from experience that Harry had little respect for esoteric methods until they produced results. She suspected that applied to differential equations as much as it applied to Tarot cards.

The forensics department was a partitioned-off corner of the former archive. Steel curtains and fume hoods kept the chemicals away from the rest of the unit, but the concrete floors were still the same. When Tara had been an agent, they'd had to send most of their evidence out to the DOJ labs. She was impressed that Special Projects now had their own gas spectrometer and electron telescopes, perched on stainless steel counters. In the back, she heard the muffled report of guns, suggesting that they'd acquired their own ballistics tank, too. Swanky.

"Agent Li, Dr. Sheridan." Anderson, the tech Tara recognized from Lena's house, greeted them. "I've got bad news."

Harry passed his hands over his eyes. "Please tell me that no one fucked up the evidence."

"I can't say that, sir. As you know, the evidence was compromised by the time we got there . . ."

"Just show me what you've got."

Anderson flipped over pages in her clipboard. "The stain that Dr. Sheridan found was indeed blood. Blood pattern analysis indicates that it's a drip stain. Based on the positioning, our best guess is that it dripped from the victim's mouth. Problem is, we can't identify it."

"It's not Lena Ivanova's blood?"

"It is. And it isn't," Anderson said. "We did find her DNA in the blood. But we also found three other sets of DNA. One unknown. One matched Carl Starkweather. And the other matched Carrie Kirkman."

"How the hell is that possible?" Harry's brow wrinkled. "Did a group of ex-spooks show up to kidnap Lena?"

"Without cross-contamination, it's not really possible. I'm sorry—"

"Wait a minute." Tara shook her head. Her mind rifled through the possibilities. Had Carl shown up and convinced Lena to come away with him after a night of passion? It didn't quite ring true to her, but she couldn't say why. "The blood cells in the sample. Can you tell how fresh they are? Have they degraded?"

Anderson nodded. "We did perform an HPLC analysis on the blood. It's all the same age. We don't think it's a case of a stain of one type of blood drying on another stain." She blew out her breath in frustration. "It's bizarre. An extraction from one part of the slide shows one set of

DNA, and another set in another part of the slide. That just doesn't occur in nature, except in chimeras."

Tara thought of the Pythia's warning: *Beware the Chimera*.

Harry blinked. "What do mythological beasts have to do with this?"

"In mythology, the chimera was a combination of a lion, a goat, and a snake," Tara said. "But, in genetics, a chimera has two or more sets of DNA."

"But that's exceptionally rare," said Anderson. "In humans, a chimera occurs when one fraternal twin fuses with another in utero. In that case, the subject may have, say, a liver with one set of DNA, and skin with another."

"We know that Lena, Carl, and Carrie weren't chimeras," Harry said. "Their CIA physicals would have shown that, right?"

"Maybe, maybe not." Anderson's mouth twisted in thought. "Most chimeras have no idea. And it's extremely statistically improbable. But we could find out. Carl had children, and we might be able to trace DNA abnormalities through them. Lena also left traces of her DNA around . . . hairbrushes, old blood tests for CIA. We might not be able to say with one hundred percent authority, but we could get close to finding out if one of them was genetically abnormal."

"Or, perhaps it's our assailant who's abnormal," Tara said.

"We'll get a geneticist in here and tear those samples apart, molecule from molecule," Anderson promised. "If there's a scientific reason why, we'll find it."

Tara nodded, but she wasn't quite ready to place her full faith in science.

"AN ORACLE MUST NOT ONLY BE PREPARED TO SEE THE future. She must also know how to fight it."

Cassie stared skeptically at the Pythia. The Pythia stood out in the field behind the farmhouse, a shotgun planted on her hip. The weapon looked vaguely ridiculous next to the petite woman wearing a red peasant dress. Two of the other Daughters of Delphi ranged around, holding guns, hearing protectors, and boxes of ammunition. They were in jeans and T-shirts; slightly less incongruous, but this still wasn't a hobby Cassie had imagined for them. Soap-making, maybe growing a little pot, but not weaponry.

"I thought the Daughters of Delphi were women of peace," Cassie said.

"We are. And we prefer to work behind the scenes to positively influence the destiny of humankind. But we must also know how to defend ourselves and protect what is ours."

Four scarecrows made of straw and baling wire were assembled across from them, ten yards distant. They looked pretty limp and defenseless to Cassie.

"Your gift is astrology," said the Pythia. "While it's a useful talent, it won't help you to defend yourself. At least, not at this time. All our gifts evolve over time, and we will see where yours unfold."

"I thought the point in being able to see the future was being able to head danger off at the pass." Cassie stared down at her feet in the tall grasses, hoping she wasn't going to be eaten alive by ticks.

The Pythia smiled. "Sometimes, the future unfolds too quickly for you to stop it."

She turned and blew a kiss at one of the scarecrows. When she brought her hand to her mouth, a spark fell from her lips, and was exhaled across her fingertips. Cassie felt the heat of it against her face. She involuntarily stepped back. The fire rushed across the distance to the scarecrows, flashed over the first one in a plume of orange. Straw crackled and smoked. The scarecrow went up like a dry Christmas tree. The other two Daughters of Delphi dragged a garden hose to the scarecrow and began to put it out.

Cassie swallowed. She knew that the Pythia's talent was pyromancy— seeing the future in fire. She didn't know that fire would respond to her whim like that.

The Pythia smiled in satisfaction at the damage. "This is what I mean by evolution of your gifts. I couldn't control fire at your age. And there's no telling how your talents will develop. But for now, you must learn more practical ways to protect yourself."

The Pythia gestured to the guns arranged on a weathered picnic table. "Pick your weapon."

Cassie leaned over the table. Most of the guns looked quite complicated; a couple were machine guns. Cassie chose the simplest-looking gun in the group: a revolver.

"Good. Pick it up."

Cassie picked the gun up by the wood grips, awkwardly.

"That's a Smith & Wesson Model sixty-six." The Pythia reached behind her, popped out the revolver barrel to show Cassie. "It holds six shots, either thirty-eight or three fifty-seven."

"It looks like a Dirty Harry gun," Cassie said.

"No. Clint Eastwood had a Model twenty-nine. I'll show you how to load it." The Pythia plucked bullets from a brick-shaped box and handed them to Cassie. "Put one in at a time. Keep it pointed downrange, or at the ground."

Cassie fitted the bullets into place. "Okay. Now what?"

"This gun is double-action. That means that you can shoot it by pulling the trigger, or by cocking the hammer and then pulling the trigger. There's no safety."

"What's the difference?"

"Takes less force to pull the trigger after you've cocked it. I'll show you."

The Pythia put her hearing protection ear guards over her head and fitted Cassie's over her ears. They were like giant stereo headphones that muffled the outside sound, but amplified the sound of Cassie's breathing.

"First, make sure there's no one downrange," the Pythia told her. The rest of Delphi's Daughters had put out the fire and milled behind them. "Next, hold the gun before you."

Cassie did as she was told, but the Pythia shook her head. "Spread your feet about shoulder-width apart. Good. Lift the gun to shoulder level, and straighten your arms. No. Don't lock them." The Pythia fussed over her stance. "Now put the heels of your hands together on the back of the grips. That will absorb the shock."

The Pythia stood on tiptoe to look over Cassie's shoulder. "Now, sight in. See those two orange marks? Line those up just at your target . . . lower . . . there."

Cassie swallowed. This felt very foreign to her.

"Good. Now, breathe out so that you don't shake your aim. Take your first shot when you're ready."

Cassie squinted over the sight and squeezed the trigger.

She'd expected it to be like firing a water pistol. But the gun had a mind of its own. When she squeezed the trigger, the gun bucked in her hands with a loud report, kicking her arms up over her head. Cassie managed to hold on to the gun, but the sound and movement rattled her.

She opened her eyes. "Did I hit anything?"

The Pythia laughed. "You missed. Try again."

Cassie set her jaw, took aim, and fired again. This time, she was better prepared for the reaction. A bit of straw was knocked from the arm of the scarecrow.

"Good. Try again."

Bang.

"Again."

Bang.

"Again."

Cassie shot until the gun clicked empty.

"Very good," said the Pythia. "You didn't flinch when you ran out of bullets."

"What does that mean?"

"That means you're not afraid of the gun." The Pythia took the gun back to the picnic table and reloaded it. Cassie wiped her hands on her jeans. They were sweaty and smelled like gunpowder.

"This is what we will show you how to do today." She gestured with her chin at one of Delphi's Daughters, who now had the shotgun aimed at the straw man Cassie had been plinking away at.

The woman took aim with the shotgun and fired. The gun reported so loudly that Cassie jumped. The woman advanced upon the straw man, ejecting shells and rapid-firing thunder until the straw man was sheared in half. His ragged head and torso bowed in front of the woman.

"Wow," said Cassie, thunder still ringing in her ears. "I don't think I can do that." It scarcely seemed the other Daughter had time to aim, but she'd destroyed the scarecrow in seconds.

The Pythia shook her head. "You will."

Cassie swallowed. She didn't think she had much choice in the matter.

GALEN SAT ON THE STEPS OF THE LINCOLN MEMORIAL, watching the tourists mill around the reflecting pond. A hazy blue summer sky shimmered in the pool, and sun beat down on the visitors with their summer clothes and cameras.

Galen leaned back in the shade. He wore jeans, sunglasses, and a long-sleeved black T-shirt. He'd mostly healed from devouring Lena, but didn't want to call attention to the fading assimilation marks in his skin. He understood that this look wouldn't draw undue attention; it was simply considered "emo" in America. His close-cropped hair had begun to grow back over his smooth skull. There was nothing remarkable about his face any longer. It was symmetrical, as near-perfect as it had ever been.

Another man sat down beside him. He was not "emo." He was more what Americans would consider to be a "yuppie": he was dressed in chinos and a collared shirt, with a blue sport coat and flashy watch. He unwrapped a sandwich, began eating it.

"What kind of sandwich is that?" Galen asked. As much as he tried to lose the accent, a trace of Russian still crept in.

"It's a turkey club."

"Ah. I prefer pastrami."

"You can get the best pastrami in Oradea, in the old country."

"So I've heard." The buyer had given the correct code word. Galen bent down to unzip the backpack at his feet and pulled out a spiral-bound notebook to hand to the buyer.

The buyer dusted crumbs from his fingers. Galen studied the buyer as he paged through the book. He didn't know who the buyer worked for. It could be Iran. It could be China. Or Pakistan. He didn't really care. Truth be told, he didn't care much about the money, either.

The buyer nodded. "Latitudes and longitudes. Exactly as described."

Galen didn't say anything. From Lena's memory, he'd just given this man directions to a buried cache of degrading weapons-grade uranium.

The buyer pulled out his BlackBerry, began punching buttons. "I'll make the transfer now."

Galen nodded. Within seconds, his own phone in his jeans pocket began to vibrate. He took it out, peered at the screen. The alert confirmed to him a bank transfer of two million U.S. dollars to an offshore account. "Got it."

"Good doing business with you." The buyer tucked the notebook under his arm, stood, and walked away with his sandwich in hand. He disappeared quickly in the throng of tourists.

Galen leaned back in the shade, feeling a stab of satisfaction at his accomplishment. Whoever had purchased the information would doubtlessly manage to stir up some chaos with it.

And chaos was his primary goal. It was as close as he could get to getting even with a world that had chewed him up and spat him out, molecule by molecule.

He was a monster, he knew it.

And he would make sure the world suffered for it.

Chapter Six

I'D LIKE the number 185."

Harry handed the menu back to the waiter at China Palace. The waiter looked over his notepad. "Sha Cha Beef?"

"Yes, please."

The waiter lifted his eyebrow, scribbled down the order, and walked away.

Harry shrugged at Tara. "Wait until you see the look I get when I ask for a fork."

Tara rested her chin in her hand. Soft red light from paper lanterns made translucent circles on the white tablecloth, and a breeze slid through wind chimes on the patio. Harry was jealously transfixed by a strand of hair that had wound free of her chignon and tickled the scar on her shoulder. "Pops never taught you to use chopsticks?"

"Nope. And I don't speak a bit of Chinese. It's occasionally socially awkward."

"Do you think you missed out?"

"Probably." Harry poked at the chopsticks on his place mat. "I missed out on a lot. Probably as much as you did when you lost your mom."

Tara's mouth thinned. "Yeah. Though I had her long enough to learn a lot from her. About the Tarot. About life."

"You said that she belonged to Delphi's Daughters."

"She did. She was the right hand of the Pythia. And the Pythia wasn't happy when I left them. I blamed them for her death, but . . ." Tara sighed. "It was just cancer. There's really no blame there."

"Yeah. I spent most of my teens blaming everyone in sight for the car crash that killed my parents. But I was lucky. I had Pops to look after me."

"Your Pops is a helluva man." Tara had met Harry's adoptive father months ago. She wished she'd had a man like that in her life, growing up: warm, wise, and brave.

"Thanks. I don't know what I'd do without him. He's . . ." Harry sighed, looked away down the street. The isolation he felt was hard to articulate. ". . . he's one of the few people I feel at home with."

Tara nodded. "I guess home is wherever we find ourselves." Her gaze was faraway, and Harry wondered where home was for her.

The waiter returned with their food. Without Harry asking, he brought forks.

Harry raised his glass. "To orphans."

Tara clinked hers against his. "To orphans."

Harry pushed his food around with his fork. "Speaking of orphans . . . how long are you going to stay at the farm with Cassie?"

"I don't know," she admitted. "I don't like leaving her alone there."

"You still don't trust the Pythia?"

"No." Tara savagely sliced a piece of pepper in half. "The Pythia is never what she seems. She serves her own purposes."

"And you've said that the Pythia has plans for her."

"Yeah. She wants Cassie to be her successor, the next Pythia. And I don't want to see Cassie turning out like that."

"Cassie will be her own girl," Harry said. "She's stronger than you think. Don't underestimate the kid."

Tara's shoulders slumped. "I know. I just . . . feel like I should be protecting her. When I was her age, I had my mother to ask about being an oracle. She deserves someone who will tell her the good and the bad."

"And you will."

Tara shoved her rice around. "I wish my mother was still around. God knows I still have questions."

"Questions about being an oracle? I thought you already had that down pat." Harry looked at her quizzically. Tara was the most self-possessed person he knew.

"Yeah. It's not like someone hits you with a wand one day and—boom—you're an oracle." Tara shook her head. "It evolves. It changes. And now that my deck has changed, I'm . . . renegotiating my relationship with those cards."

Harry frowned. "Look, if they're not working out, I won't be hurt if you want to get another set . . ." When Tara had lost her mother's deck, it had seemed only right that he replaced it. Now, he felt like he'd fucked up. Given her a chopstick when she needed a fork.

Tara shook her head. She reached across the table and grabbed his hand. "No. I love this deck." Her voice was impassioned, and she blushed, pulling away. But Harry trapped her hand with his.

"How about I show you where I got them?" Harry said. "They came from a bookstore just a few blocks from here."

Tara hesitated. "I'm keeping the deck, but . . ."

"But?"

Curiosity glittered in her blue eyes. "You know, I would really like to see where they came from."

"How did you find this place?"

Tara stared up at the façade of the colonial brick row house that had been converted into a shop. The front store window was crowded with a display of books, and a wooden sign above the front door depicted a black cat and a moon, bearing the legend: ARIADNE'S WEB OF BOOKS. Red geraniums bloomed in window boxes, beside a pair of concrete lions. Tara's hand lingered on a lion, still warm from the day. Darkness had fallen, and stray fireflies swam through an evergreen hedge, trying to hide from the threat of rain.

"I was getting deposed here in Washington, after we met." Harry stood with his hands in his pockets, jingling change. "I was out for lunch, and just started walking." He shrugged. "I ended up here."

Tara climbed the front steps and opened the door, a screen door left open to the summer night. She smelled incense, and a bell jangled overhead to announce their arrival.

Polished wooden floors supported floor-to-ceiling bookcases lining the walls and aisles. The interior floors of the house had been gutted, she realized, to make room for an iron spiral staircase that looked as if it had been torn from a ship. Upper floors of steel and wood curved around the cavernous space, lit by amber glass pendulum lights suspended from the uppermost rafters. A breeze blowing from the open windows on the upper floors trickled through wind chimes.

The shelves didn't hold only books, though there were thousands of them, new and used, smelling of dust and incense. Knickknacks of various vintages dotted the shelves: jars of herbs, bells, glass bottles of stones. Tara ran her finger down the spine of the wired skeleton of a lizard guarding a shelf of herbalism books.

"Can I help you?" Footsteps padded across the polished floor. Tara turned to see a middle-aged woman with platinum-blond hair braided around her head. She wore a long gray dress embroidered with leaves and black ballet slippers. *This must be Ariadne,* Tara supposed.

"Yes." Harry said. "I came in here a few months ago, and—"

"I remember you." The woman's face split into a smile. "You're the fellow who bought the Tarot cards."

"You have a good memory."

"I have a good memory for unusual sales." The woman moved behind a glass counter that held a cash register and peered through her bifocals. "What can I do for you?"

Tara pulled the deck from her purse. She was reluctant to allow another person to handle them, since she wanted the deck to imprint fully upon her. "What can you tell me about these, about where they came from?"

Ariadne peered through her glasses at the deck. "Ah. Those. I've never seen another deck like them." Her fingers hovered above the deck, but she didn't touch. That made Tara think she knew more about cards than an ordinary book or antiques dealer.

"Me, either."

"If I remember . . ." She dug through a file cabinet. "Those were sold on consignment. Let's see . . ." Ariadne smoothed out a yellow form that had wrinkled around the edges. "Those were from Tennessee."

"May I see that, please?" Tara asked, and Ariadne turned the page around. The seller's address was the farmhouse Tara had been living at. Her mouth tightened.

The cards had come from the Pythia.

Tara's gaze flicked up to Ariadne. "Do you know Amira?"

"I don't know anyone by that name. But I do know that these are supposed to be yours." Ariadne smiled at her. "You might say that I have a knack for matching up books with the right reader . . . and tools with the right practitioner."

"Thank you." Tara dropped the cards into her purse and backed away, thoughts churning. She knew that Delphi's Daughters routinely nudged world events. Putting a deck of cards back in her hands would be a relatively small feat.

Harry followed Tara down the steps and out to the street. "Hey, you okay?"

"I'm fine," Tara said. "I just—" Her phone buzzed. "Excuse me." She dug her phone out of her pocket. Her face brightened, but her brow furrowed. "Hi, Cassie. Are you okay?"

"Yeah. Sure."

"How was the Pythia's practical magic lesson today?"

"Different. We shot guns all day."

Tara's eyebrow crawled up into her hairline. "Oh, really?"

"Yeah. I suck with the MP-5. But she tells me I'll get better."

"Machine guns already?" Tara struggled to keep her voice neutral.

"I think I'm gonna have a bruise on my shoulder, though."

"Take some ibuprofen before you go to bed."

"I will. What are you up to?"

"Harry and I are walking downtown."

"Cool. Can I say hi to Harry?"

"Sure." Tara handed the phone to Harry.

Harry smiled into the receiver. "Hey, kiddo. How's things?" He nodded and laughed, and his gaze flicked to Tara. "Yeah. Yeah, I will. I promise." He passed the phone back to Tara.

Tara cradled the receiver between her shoulder and her ear. "Sleep well, Cassie."

"Okay."

"Can you put the Pythia on the line when you go?"

"Sure. G'night."

"Good night."

Tara could hear Cassie's footfalls scurrying away, then the even tread of the Pythia's jingling step on the floorboards.

"Hello, Tara," the accented contralto voice answered.

Tara gritted her teeth. "Listen to me, you bitch. You keep Cassie out of harm's way. None of that sophomoric hazing shit. Do you hear me?"

The Pythia laughed. "Cassie is perfectly safe. She's to be the next Pythia. I'd never allow anything to happen to her."

"Mark my words, Amira. Your crazy flock of followers may be too afraid to lift a hand to you, but I'm not."

"I won't hurt her. I swear."

"You'd better not." Tara switched off the phone, blew out her breath.

Harry reached for her elbow. "Hey, what was that about?"

Tara blinked at him. "The Pythia's got her playing with machine guns the instant I step out of the house."

"Cassie's a big girl. She can handle herself around guns."

"That's not what I'm worried about. I know Cassie can hold her own." Tara shook her head. It was hard to explain. "The Pythia can get into some very ugly training with Delphi's Daughters, if you leave her to her own devices."

"What do you mean?" Harry's hands balled into fists. Tara knew that he'd rip limb from limb anyone who hurt Cassie.

"Psychological shit. I remember being sixteen and taken on what she called an 'orienteering' course." Tara shook her head. "They dumped me in the middle of the woods and expected me to find my way out. It took me two days."

"Let's go get her," Harry said. He stood opposite her on the pavement, blocking her. He grasped her wrist. "Now."

"No. I know they were watching me the whole time, that no harm would actually come to me. But . . . it's disconcerting. And I haven't been able to explain this shit to her." Tara shook her head. "The Pythia's just trying to see how far she can push since I'm not there —" Her eyes widened as she looked over Harry's shoulder. "Harry, look out!"

A shadowy figure slipped up the sidewalk, a man wearing a ball cap pulled low over his brow and a denim jacket. He pulled a gun behind Harry's head, clicked back the hammer. "You. Hands up."

Harry's eyes narrowed, and Tara could see the wrath shimmering off him, like heat from the pavement on a summer afternoon. Slowly, he lifted his hands.

Don't do anything stupid, Tara thought.

But the thought was directed at Harry, not the would-be mugger.

"The lady gives me her purse, first."

Harry's heart thudded under his tongue. His body was

between Tara and that fucking punk behind him. He saw Tara reach into her purse, saw the glint of metal. He knew she'd talk the mugger down if given half a chance, would have the guy eating birdseed out of her hand and apologizing, if Harry would let her.

But Harry was having none of it. He'd had too many weeks of putting up with too much shit. Too much time on the outside, looking in. And he was tired of the world trying to fuck with him when he was trying to be the hero and save it. Something in him snapped.

He heard the punk's sneakers take two steps behind him. Harry guessed the gun should be about a foot behind his right ear.

Harry pivoted on his right foot, putting all his weight into his right forearm to knock the gun across the attacker's body. He flipped his arm out in a hold, grasping the gunman's arm as he kicked his feet out from under him. The punk yelped, and Harry bent his wrist back. The gun clattered to the pavement.

The gunman's wrist shattered under the torque of the impossible angle. Harry didn't hear him howl, just heard the blood pounding in his own ears. Harry's shoe slammed into the punk's ribs over and over.

"Who the fuck do you think you are?" he could hear himself yelling.

The mugger was on his side on the ground now, and Harry slugged him. That felt so good that he balled up his fist and struck him again. The hat fell to the sidewalk, and red spattered on the pavement. Like loose gravel, a tooth rattled away.

"*Who—*"

Harry kept hitting him.

"*—the fuck—*"

He couldn't stop himself.

"*—do you think you are?*"

Didn't want to.

But Tara wanted to stop him. He felt her hands winding around his shoulder, dragging him off the punk. Harry staggered back, breathing heavily. His hands were covered in blood, and the punk was spitting out teeth into the shrubs.

"Harry, let's go."

"His gun—" Harry gasped.

"I've got it. Let's go."

She dragged him down the street. The humidity in the summer air finally broke, and it began to rain. Harry looked back over his shoulder. The punk stumbled off into an alley. Only Tara's hands tangled in his jacket kept Harry from going back to beat him into the ground.

Tara flagged down a cab, shoved him inside. Harry sat, dripping on the ancient leather interior, his bloody hands before him. But he could only see the blood when streetlights flashed past overhead. When he looked at his hands, they shook. But only when he looked at them.

Tara overpaid the cabbie in cash and shoveled Harry out of the cab a couple of blocks from his apartment. Dimly, he knew that if the punk filed an assault report or showed up in the ER, they didn't want to be easily found.

Rain rinsed the blood from his hands as they walked in the darkness, without comment. Tara took his hand in hers, fiercely tight, and wouldn't let it go, even though it was sticky.

He tried three times to get the key in the lock before she took it from him and did it herself. He let her pull him into the apartment, into the bathroom with that harsh bluish light.

She wiped the specks of blood off his face with a washcloth without saying a word. He'd expected her to be disgusted with him, to pack her suitcase in the face of that brutality and leave him alone. But she didn't. She tenderly washed his hands and dressed a cut on his knuckle. He thought she'd leave when she undressed him and pushed him into the shower. He strained to hear the sound of the door closing over the hiss of the water.

But she was still there when he got out. She took his face in her hands and said: "What the hell happened to you?"

He shook his head wordlessly. He couldn't explain what these last months at the Little Shop of Horrors had done, what the years of chasing killers and living in unreality had created. He felt it chewing at him, gnawing at the edge of his consciousness. Until something broke.

He just shook his head. "I don't know."

But she knew. She'd been there before. She'd let Special Projects literally chew her up and spit her out. And she didn't ask any more questions.

She put him to bed, spooned up behind him. He sighed, feeling her hands wrapped around his chest.

And slept.

TARA DREAMED OF THAT TWILIGHT WORLD AGAIN, THE WORLD of the Tarot.

Her boots sank deep into the sand as she walked, and the lion walked before her, the sinewy muscles of his back undulating like the ripples in the desert surface. Their tracks ran together in the sand, footprints and paw prints sinking together. Tara was no longer afraid of the lion. She knew he was leading her. Once or twice, he looked back with his golden eyes, as if to make sure that she followed.

Tara knew she was searching for something. For someone.

There. In the sunset, she saw something shining. A figure in golden armor stumbled across the landscape, dragging a heavy golden pentacle behind him in the sand. It was lashed around the knight's throat, strangling him. A tattered red cape streamed behind him like the banner of a defeated army.

Tara recognized the figure. Her Knight of Pentacles. She began to run toward him.

The knight collapsed to his knees, fell over in the sand in a magnificent glittering heap, with a sound like pots crashing to the floor.

Tara fell to her knees beside him, struggling to remove the noose from around his neck. The sand was soft and sucking, and the knight's armor was scorchingly hot from the sun, dented and scarred as if from a terrible battle. The heavy pentacle, large as a millstone, was dragging the knight down. He was limp when she touched him, his helmeted head lolling to the side. The armor burned her hands. She succeeded in freeing the rope around his neck, but the sand tugged at him, dragging him down into the hot belly of the desert.

She cast about desperately. She could feel the sand trap blistering in, hear the hiss of sand as the grains fell in on themselves, like the well of an hourglass. The lion stood at the edge of the trap, growling.

Tara wrestled with the rope holding the pentacle, succeeded in unfastening it. The pentacle disappeared below the surface of the sand. Tara awkwardly cast the rope to the lion. It landed short, disappeared under the surface of the sand. The lion roared in frustration.

With one arm, she tried to keep the knight's scorching head above the sand. She reeled the rope back in, flung it out again. This time, it slapped down beside the lion.

The lion knew what to do. He grasped the rope in his powerful jaws. Tara tied the other end of the rope under the knight's arms. He'd half-disappeared in the quicksand, limp as a rag doll dressed in tin cans. She wrapped her hands around his neck, shouted at the lion.

The lion pulled, trotting away with his end of the rope, as effortlessly as if he were tearing a leg from a gazelle. With a sucking sound, Tara and the knight were dragged free of the sand pit, landing in a filthy heap on more solid ground.

Exhausted, Tara lay on her back staring up at the blazing sky. She rubbed sand from her eyes. A shadow fell over her. The lion. He dipped his head and began licking the sand off her face with a tongue as rough as a cheese grater. Her cheek was burned where it had come into contact with the knight's searing breastplate, but she didn't want to offend the lion by pushing him away.

"Thank you," she told the lion. He sat back on his

haunches as she sat up, and began batting at the end of the rope.

Tara struggled to get the rope disentangled from the knight. She got it off him, then turned her attention to the golden helmet obscuring his face. The red feathers on the top of the helmet had been destroyed by sand, broken like the plumage of a dead bird.

She pulled the helmet away, as carefully as she might pour the yolk from a cracked egg.

Harry's battered face was under the helmet. She pressed her hand to his hot cheek. He was unconscious, but she could feel the movement of breath across his cracked lips.

How had this happened to him? What terrible enemy had chewed him up? Her tears sizzled on his breastplate. She bent her head to kiss him. His eyelids fluttered, and his fingers twitched, but he did not come to.

Tara turned to the lion. "I need to take him to water."

The lion padded over to Harry, nudged him with his nose. He lay down beside the fallen knight. Tara thought she understood. She dragged Harry over the lion's back. As effortlessly as if he carried a kitten, the lion stood up and began to walk east.

Tara wound her fingers to pick up her skirts to follow.

The lion would lead them to water. She was certain of it.

Tara woke to feel someone shaking her.

At first, she thought it was the lion, that she'd stumbled somewhere along the journey, and that he was nudging her awake.

But it was Harry.

"Tara, wake up."

Her eyes fluttered open to find that Harry had grasped her arms and was shaking the dream out of her head. A twinge of fear flickered through her, seeing the concerned expression on his face. The bedside lamp was on, and Harry's hair was mussed from sleep.

"I—I'm awake." She shivered. She was suddenly cold, and when she spoke, her breath made ghosts in the air.

"Are you all right? You were mumbling in your sleep and kicking the covers like they were trying to eat you." Harry bundled the blankets around her. "You're freezing."

"I was dreaming," she said, allowing Harry to wrap the covers around her and turn out the light. He curled up behind her, wrapping his arms around her to keep her warm.

"You want to tell me about it?"

"I've been dreaming about the Tarot," she said. She felt guilty burdening Harry with these . . . visions. Especially when she hadn't fully digested them herself. She sensed that her relationship with the cards was changing, and that it wasn't just this deck. Something deep inside her was stirring . . . She could feel it uncoiling like a snake. "I'll tell you tomorrow."

"Promise?"

"I swear."

For the moment, Tara allowed herself the luxury of the warmth of Harry's arms, of feeling his heart beating against her back.

Harry had enough problems of his own. Her dreams were right—he was the one in need of saving. Not her.

This new twist in her power, these vivid dreams . . . This was something she'd have to work out on her own.

SOMETIMES, GALEN DREAMED OF SLEEPING IN THE ARMS OF A woman.

He wasn't alone in those dreams.

He wondered what it would have been like, to fall asleep beside a woman and wake up to find her still there. Rifling through the memories of Carl and Lena, he had the sense of the two of them whispering in the darkness of train cars, desolate landscapes rushing by outside. They lay twined together like snakes on a caduceus, finding some kind of healing and solace over those foreign miles.

Galen longed for that, too. That warmth of another human being, connected but separate from his experience. But, to him, the lines always seemed to blur.

He remembered when he was a teenager, hitchhiking through Belarus. He'd asked to be let out of the car when he'd seen a girl walking through the streets of a muddy town. She was walking down the street in a gray wool coat, long blonde hair loose over her shoulders in waves. Her hat was pulled low over her ears to ward off the early spring chill, but there was something about those eyes when she looked past the car. They were steel-gray, haunted.

Galen knew that look, that emptiness.

He slogged through the mud, trying to catch up with her. "Hey!"

She turned, the mud sucking at her shiny black boots.

Her eyebrow lifted at him. His heart leapt. Maybe she saw the same thing he saw in her. A spark of something kindred. Something that would keep him warm.

Galen spread his best smile on his face. "Can I buy you a drink?"

She looked him up and down, doubtful at the sight of his shabby coat. "You have money for a drink?"

"Yes." His fingers clutched a roll of bills in his pocket. He'd robbed the last person who'd given him a ride. "I've got plenty of money."

She leaned forward, and her breath steamed in his face. It smelled like cinnamon. "You don't need to buy me a drink."

That was okay with him. He wanted warmth. He wanted companionship. Just this once. Even if he had to pay for it.

The girl led him back to her tiny flat. Galen stood awkwardly inside the threshold, watching her kick the radiator. The paint was peeling off the walls. But everything was orderly. The futon in the center of the room had a newish looking bedspread on it, and the dishes in the broken cabinet were all clean.

"It'll warm up in a minute," she said, sticking her hands under her arms to make small talk. "Where are you from?"

"Nowhere."

The girl's crimson lips smiled. "Me, too."

Heat had begun to creep out of the radiator, plinking as the hot water began to circulate. The girl pulled off her hat and coat. She began to unbutton her blouse. When she turned around, Galen could see that her shoulders were a bit uneven, that the vertebrae of her spine didn't line up straight. His mouth thinned. She was indeed like him, from nowhere.

"What's your name?" he asked.

"I'm Yeva." She crossed the room to him in her bra and skirt. Her fingers fluttered up to unfasten his coat. She opened the first two buttons, skipped the missing third, and continued on to the fourth before he answered: "Galen."

She looked up at him through her eyelashes. "That's an odd name."

"It was the name of a famous healer." He felt his mouth turn downward. "My mother had great hopes for me."

"You are a doctor, then?"

"No." He shook his head. "I'm not anything."

She stood up on her tiptoes, pressed her finger to his mouth. "Never say that," she said, fiercely. "We are all someone."

She kissed him then, and she tasted like mulled spices. He sank into the kiss, felt Yeva tugging off his clothes and drawing him down to the futon. His fingers wound in her hair, and he relished the sensation of her warm mouth on his, her breasts pressed against his chest. His heart hammered in his chest as she straddled him, drew him inside her. As she rocked back and forth, he moaned.

He rolled over, pinning her to the futon. He felt whole, moving inside her, part of some tenuous connection to someone else. For that moment, his entire world was the young prostitute wrapped around him. His fingers wound in her hair as his excitement drove him over the edge.

Then, it happened. He heard her cry out, thought it part of the game. She turned her head away, and he thought he was tangled in her hair. He began to mutter an apology, but his ardor faded when he realized that his fingers weren't tangled in her hair . . . they were enmeshed in it. He pulled, couldn't free himself.

"Don't be rough." Yeva placed her hands on his chest to move him off her, but he wouldn't let her go.

Couldn't.

He felt himself flowing into her. It was beyond a simple orgasm. This ecstatic state was more. It was deeper, more meaningful. Yeva squirmed beneath him, began to shout for help.

He put his hand over her mouth. But his fingers dissolved into her lips and nose, melting like hot glass. Horrified, he tried to pull away, but couldn't. The orgasm and the heady feeling of wholeness rushed over his senses, dulling the panic and fear.

She tried to scream, wise gray eyes wide and rolling. She struck at him in panic, clawing at him. But he couldn't pull away. He felt himself sinking into her as she struggled. He felt her ribs opening and wrapping around his, felt her heart beating in his chest for a few moments after she stopped breathing, suffocating under his hand dissolving down her throat. He could feel it dripping, like wax. He felt her . . . all of her. All of Yeva's memories, her life drained into him. He could taste the cinnamon in his mouth, feel the curve forming in his spine.

The radiator ticked in the darkness, and he was wound around her like the snakes in the caduceus.

Yeva had been right. She had been somebody.

She'd been his first.

Chapter Seven

Tara didn't bring up last night.

Neither did Harry.

They stood on the elevator, descending into the Little Shop of Horrors. The only sign of last night's fight was a Band-Aid on Harry's right knuckle. That, and they stood together with shoulders touching.

The elevator stopped a few floors above Special Projects. A breathless woman in tan coveralls hopped on. Tara glanced at her. She wore a name badge on a beaded lanyard that identified her as Library of Congress staff. Under her arm, she held a projector that looked suspiciously like the one Veriss had been using in his presentations. Her gaze flicked sidelong at Tara and Harry, widened when she saw their badges. Harry, preoccupied with his thoughts, stared at the glowing buttons.

Tara could guess the woman's thoughts: *Busted.*

The librarian clutched the projector like a squirrel with a golden nut, and her cheeks flamed.

Tara gave her a short nod of acknowledgement, then pointedly ignored her.

The librarian's shoulders settled, and she sighed. When she got off at the next floor, she returned the curt nod to Tara before she scurried away.

Tara smiled. Perhaps, after all this time, she owed the Library of Congress a peace offering.

The doors finally opened onto the dungeon of Special Projects. Harry seemed to come back to himself a bit, though he self-consciously tucked his wounded hand in his jacket pocket to fiddle with loose change.

"Agent Li." Veriss rushed up to them, breathless, extending a sheaf of paper. "I have your data." He nearly tripped over himself in his excitement.

"Thanks, Veriss." Harry flipped through the pages, full of single-spaced names. "Is this all of 'em?"

"These are all the personnel who were associated with Project Rogue Angel. Everyone from the motor pool to the high-level spooks."

"Good," Harry said. "I've got another project for you."

"What's that?" Veriss bounced on the balls of his feet like a puppy expecting a bone.

"Use your forecasting model to help predict who's next on this list . . . who's most likely to defect."

"I'm working on that. I'm arranging them in a network graph, looking at strong and weak ties—"

"Good. Tara and I will start tracking folks down to get them into protective custody or surveillance."

"But . . ." Veriss's brow crinkled. "You can't put all those people into protective custody. There are one hundred thirty-one people on that list . . ."

"We're going to do our best," Harry said, firmly. He walked away from Veriss, and Tara drifted in his wake. He paused before Aquila's door, tapped the glass.

Aquila looked up from his desk and gestured for them to enter.

"Agent Li, Dr. Sheridan." He folded his hands over his blotter. "Good morning."

Without preamble, Harry said, "Boss, I need a favor. I need to rely on your connections with the Marshals . . . I need to put some people into protective custody. And we don't have the staff to do it ourselves."

Aquila frowned. "How many people?"

Harry looked at the list. "One hundred thirty-one. Some of them will be dead, some won't be able to be found. And some will refuse. But I need a place to put several dozen ex-agents while we figure out who's after them."

Aquila sat back in his throne-like chair, considering. "All right. I'll see what I can do. Just be aware that on short notice, the accommodations won't be posh."

"Understood." Harry turned to leave.

"I've received word about a new intelligence leak." Aquila's voice arrested him. "Two hundred pounds of weapons-grade uranium was just excavated in southern Georgia."

"Where is it now?"

"We think it's on its way to Tehran. CIA is scrambling

to find it. It should be hot enough to shine under night vision from unmanned drones. If it's there, we'll find it."

Harry's shoulders slumped. "How did the deal go down? Can we find a way to contact the seller of the info?"

"Data Services is working on it. So far, they've got nothing."

"We've gotta figure out how this guy is selling this intel." Harry clenched his fist, and Tara could see blood leaking through the Band-Aid on his knuckle.

Aquila glanced at Tara. "You think this is the work of a lone individual?"

Tara nodded. "Yes. My profile's still in flux, but I believe it's the work of one person. I don't think it's the Taliban or some organized group. It's all too quiet for that . . . Someone would have leaked some information by now, ratted somebody out. That hasn't happened. I think we're dealing with a determined guy who's got a personal axe to grind."

"The money would be a motivator," Aquila said. "Why not just the cash?"

"Well," Tara said, "CIA's not seeing any unusual influxes of cash in the usual networks. Nobody's buying any more guns or desert islands than usual. Whoever's getting paid for this is just sitting on the cash . . . It doesn't mean enough to him to spend it."

Aquila gestured to the list. "You'd better get those people corralled, and soon. Leave the hotel accommodations up to me."

"Yessir."

"Thank you, sir."

Harry and Tara filed out of Aquila's office. Harry stared ruefully at the list. "There's no telling who's next. It's gonna take time for the Marshals to round these people up."

"Can I see it?" Tara asked. He handed her the papers, and she thumbed through them. "There might be another way. Can I use your conference room?"

"Sure." He ushered her to the room that Veriss had used for his presentations.

Tara pulled the blinds, obscuring the view from the outside, and closed the door. "This room isn't on camera?"

"Not that I know of."

"Good enough." Tara placed the list on the conference room table before her and sat down. She pulled her cards out of her purse.

Harry pulled up a chair opposite her. "What are you doing?"

"Inviting a hunch." Tara counted the pages of the report. There were seven pages of roughly twenty names on each page. She took the deck and began to shuffle. "We can't interview all of these people at once. We need to zero in on the person who can give us the most information."

Tara drew a card from the deck, the Three of Cups. She turned to the third page in the report.

She concentrated and shuffled the deck again. She pulled the Hierophant, the fifth card in the Major Arcana. She counted down to the fifth name on the list.

"Our winner is Norman S. Lockley."

Harry pushed away from the desk. "Okay. Let's go interview Mr. Lockley."

Tara was amazed at the ease with which he trusted her. Months ago, he would have harangued her about making decisions with the cards, about using them as a crutch. Maybe he'd changed.

Or maybe he was just too worn out to argue with her.

Tara flipped over another card, wondering who Norman Lockley was. She picked the Moon, a card of illusions and deception. Half of a woman's face gazed from a pale moon, the rest of her visage obscured by shadow. A dog howled at the moon, and a crayfish had crawled out of the ocean, stretching its claws toward her. Black and white pillars in the distance suggested a choice: between good and evil, order and chaos, or some other pair of opposites.

The door to the conference room swung open. Harry elbowed his way in front of the door to give Tara time to stuff her cards back into her purse.

"Professor. Can I help you?"

"Yes." Veriss looked over Harry's shoulder with a disturbed expression. "Have you seen my projector? I thought it was in here, somewhere . . ."

"Haven't seen it," Tara said.

"Conference room is yours, Professor," Harry said. "We were just leaving."

Tara smothered a grin as she followed Harry out the door. She knew that Veriss would never see his projector again, not if the Library of Congress had anything to say about it.

ASTROLOGY WASN'T PARTICLE PHYSICS.

But it still required some degree of concentration.

Cassie tapped her pencil eraser on the kitchen table. Her charts and calculations were spread out before her in precise stacks. Her mind kept wandering from the stars and sacred geometry, but she was glad not to be on the makeshift rifle range today. Absently, she reached up to rub the bruise the shotgun had impressed upon her right shoulder.

She missed Tara. She'd always felt the tension between Tara and the Pythia regarding her upbringing. And she knew that the Pythia had plans for her, to groom her to walk in her footsteps. But Delphi's Daughters had introduced her to a variety of arcane subjects, from the domestic arts of baking and candlemaking to combat and astrology. An ever-changing cast of Delphi's Daughters entered and left the house, teaching her something new while Tara watched from a distance. Her new studies were a far cry from her beginnings as a physics graduate student, following in her father's intellectual footsteps. But she had nowhere else to go, and this place was more interesting than most.

Cassie rubbed her forehead, erased a mark. The Pythia had decided that Cassie's primary oracular talents lay in astrology. Initially, the thought had opposed everything she'd embraced about rational science. But she couldn't deny the irrational pull she felt, looking up at the sky at night, how she intuitively grasped the precession of the equinoxes, could sense the planets in the night sky as they passed along the ecliptic, through the houses of the Zodiac. The Pythia said that she was still flexible, too young to be wedded to any dogma—scientific or otherwise.

And so, Cassie, being a scientist at heart, undertook her studies as an experiment. She jotted down her observations and predictions, compared them to the statistical outcomes she might expect as a result of random chance. To her surprise, she was much better than chance. She amused herself predicting stock market fluctuations, playing with penny stocks. Her accuracy rates climbed, and she began to trust her results more and more.

But what she saw in her charts now troubled her, made her second-guess her intuition.

Cassie had been working with what the Pythia called "mundane astrology"—though it was anything but. The Pythia had explained that *mundane* came from the Latin word for *the world*. This branch of astrology was used to explain historical events and predict new world events. It involved casting a chart for a nation or group of people.

Cassie frowned at her chart for the U.S. She'd cast it for a few days into the future, with Washington, DC as the location. When she'd cast it, she kept showing Pluto in retrograde. Pluto governed power, nuclear energy, finance, crime, and catastrophes. The sun and Mars opposed Pluto, suggesting strife and instability. The chart also showed the moon in Scorpio. The moon governed agriculture, national security, populations of people and animals. And Scorpio was the eighth house, reflecting secrets, foreign relations, and crime.

She reached for her laptop to double-check her work. Against the Pythia's wishes, she'd built a computer program that would generate astrological charts and compare them. She entered in the latitude, longitude, and time, and let it generate another wheel-shaped map of the heavens.

She drummed her fingers on the table. Same result. The planets and houses clotted together at disturbing angles three days from now.

"Are you cheating again?"

Cassie jumped in her chair. The Pythia drifted into the kitchen, holding a cigarette. She was always able to sneak up on Cassie . . . Maybe it was the bare feet. Cassie had rarely seen the woman in a pair of shoes. Today, she wore a red caftan that smelled like sandalwood.

"It's not cheating if it produces the same result, and it's more efficient."

The Pythia harrumphed. "You need to learn to do it by hand."

"Yeah. And I did." Cassie held up her eraser-torn paper.

"What if you find yourself someplace with no electricity?"

"Then I'm camping. And I probably don't give a rat's ass about homework, then."

"Watch your mouth, young lady. An oracle never swears."

Cassie made a face. She still didn't understand why it was okay to play with machine guns, but not to swear. The Pythia insisted that Delphi's Daughters act like ladies, even when murdering scarecrows. "I don't see why not."

The Pythia put a hand on her hip. "Oracles affect the future more than ordinary people do. A curse from an oracle is exactly that . . . a curse. And it can affect the world."

Cassie rolled her eyes. "Okay. Whatever."

The Pythia took Cassie's homework from her, scanned it with eyes dark as sloes. Her fingers sketched out the Midheaven and the conjuncts. "Interesting."

"I don't understand what Pluto in retrograde means. Not that Pluto's a real planet, anyway."

"Pluto *is* a real planet. Always has been."

"Not anymore."

The Pythia snorted, waved her hand dismissively. "Politics. It will be again." She leaned over Cassie's shoulder at the computer-generated chart. Cassie tried not to be smug when she showed the same outcome.

"So . . . what does it mean?"

The Pythia took a drag on her cigarette. She stared intently at the lit end, and Cassie wondered what she saw in the ember. The Pythia had forced Cassie to try pyromancy, once. Cassie had stared at a candle until she fell asleep, and had a dream about marshmallows. The Pythia decided she had no talent for that art, and moved on.

"What do you see?" Cassie asked.

The Pythia stubbed out her cigarette in an ashtray beside the sink. Her hair fell over her face in a curtain, obscuring her expression. But when she spoke, her voice was dark: "Nothing good." She gestured to Cassie's computer. "Your machine . . . can it search for similar charts over time?"

Cassie shrugged. "Yeah, sure. I can ask it to search for any other charts that might meet the same description . . . planets in those houses, fixed stars."

The Pythia nodded. "Please ask it to search for similar patterns."

"We won't find an exact match . . . The outer planets move too slowly to make some configurations possible for hundreds of years."

"Just narrow it down to the last fifty years or so."

"No sweat." Cassie punched a few keys, and the processor in her laptop began to whir. She kicked back, waiting for it to compile. The Pythia didn't even like using the digital egg timer. She treated electronics as if they had a painful miasma to be avoided. On more than one occasion, Cassie had caught her trying to smudge the television with burning sage, or opening a window when someone was running a microwave. The woman had an unnatural dislike for magnetic fields.

The computer kicked up a chart on the screen. "Found a chart similar to our transiting planets," Cassie said triumphantly. "April 26, 1986, 9:23 Greenwich Mean Time. Latitude 51°17'N, longitude 30°15'E. Pluto was in Scorpio then, but still retrograde. And the moon was in Scorpio, the sun and Mars opposed it, and we have the same void from the Midheaven to the Descendent . . ." Cassie punched a few keys, and the current transiting map overlaid the historical mundane one. It was a nearly perfect match.

The Pythia read over Cassie's shoulder. She was very quiet, and Cassie looked back at her. The glow of the screen was reflected in her eyes.

"Does that mean anything to you?"

The Pythia's frown deepened. "That was the date and time of the Chernobyl disaster."

Cassie bit back a curse. "I guess that counts as 'nothing good.'"

Ex-spymasters shouldn't own garden gnomes.

Tara stared distractedly at the brightly colored creatures dotting the walkway to Norman Lockley's house. They were spaced at regular intervals amid pink begonias, cheerfully standing guard over the walkway like orange traffic cones on a highway. Lockley lived in Virginia; perhaps all that time in DC had caused him to miss the long summer road construction season.

"Weird," Harry said. He hit the doorbell of the white-sided cottage house. A dog barked, and the door opened. Tara noticed that the screen door remained locked. The voice emanated just to the left of the door, out of direct firing line, forcing Tara to squint into the shade of the house. Old spy habits apparently died hard.

"Norman Lockley?"

"Yes," a craggy voice answered. Somewhere behind the screen, the dog continued to bark. Tara jumped when a German shepherd slammed against the screen. She was instantly reminded of the dog depicted in the Moon card. The man behind the screen grabbed the dog's collar, muttering: "Down, Diana. That's not the postman." Diana whined.

"My name's Harry Li, and this is Tara Sheridan," Harry continued. "We're from the Special Projects Division of DOJ. We were wondering if you had a moment to answer a few questions for us."

"Let me see your creds."

Harry opened his wallet with his ID and badge and pressed it against the screen. Tara did the same with her temporary ID.

The man behind the screen snorted. "Ah. Zookeepers from the Little Shop of Horrors. Come on in." Special Projects' reputation had preceded them in spy world. He reached up to unlatch the screen door, motioned for them to come inside.

Lockley's house was cool shade compared to the summer heat outside. Tara could feel the wall of air conditioning striking her as soon as she stepped onto the parquet flooring.

Lockley was not what she had expected. He was a small, balding man sitting in a wheelchair. A striped golf shirt stretched over a bit of a paunch, and khaki pants were covered in dog hair from the German shepherd straining in his grip. A pair of bifocals had wandered down his nose as he struggled with the dog.

"Don't worry. She doesn't bite anyone but the postman. And she only does that because he's an SOB."

Tara leaned down and let the dog smell her open palm. The dog vigorously snooted her hand, including the scar that crept out from under her jacket sleeve. Lockley bumped the door shut, ratcheted the deadbolt, and let go of Diana. The dog wagged her tail and turned her attention to Harry, sniffing his shoes.

"What can I do for you folks?" Lockley crossed his arms across his chest.

"We're investigating the disappearances of some of your former colleagues. We were hoping you'd be able to provide us with some background information."

A bemused smile flitted across Lockley's wrinkled face, and he shook his head.

"What's so funny?"

"You have to understand," Lockley said, "it was my business to make people disappear. So . . . these things generally don't worry me much."

Harry looked him up and down, blurted: "You don't strike me as a sniper. Or an assassin."

Lockley laughed and shook his head. "No. I wasn't either of those. I was a disguise master." He gestured to Harry and Tara. "C'mon. I'll show you."

Lockley led them through a military-neat living room and a kitchen with a gleaming blank table. It was an ordinary bit of suburbia, befitting a lifelong bachelor: no frilly curtains, flower arrangements, or botanical chintz. Tara guessed that Lockley's dog was his only roommate. A sliding glass door provided a view to a patio where birdfeeders were staged. Goldfinches crunched thistle seeds and perched on the screen. Tara figured that was primarily for the dog's amusement, as Diana lay down on the tile in front of the door to watch the colorful show.

Lockley opened a door to the garage, clicked on a light, wheeled his chair down a ramp. Tara and Harry followed him.

"Welcome to my office."

What had once been a two-car garage had been converted into a laboratory for evil scientists. Faces hung, deflated, from hooks on pegboards. Jars held flesh-colored substances and paints. Workbenches were strewn with body parts: ears, fingers, noses. Pictures of faces, hands, and eyes were suspended by clothespins from a clothesline that ran along the walls. A dismembered leg lay on a tarp beside an airbrush machine, toes splayed. Eyeballs were held in egg cartons beside paintbrushes and molds. Tara reached out and touched an ear. Some kind of soft plastic, maybe latex.

"What is all this stuff?" Harry asked.

"My disguise shop. I'm retired, but I still take some contract work. Some for the Feds and private industry, but a lot of it for the movies. Keeps me out of trouble. This is what I'm working on." Lockley wheeled to a table, picked up a hand. "It's going to be part of a data security test." He passed it to Tara.

Tara ran her fingers over the rubbery material. The detail was amazing . . . Individual pores had been punched into the "skin," with fine hairs added. Veins had been sketched below the surface. Even nails made from a semi-opaque plastic had been imbedded in the ersatz flesh. It was indistinguishable from the real thing, even up close. Upon close inspection, fingerprints had been engraved in it.

"This is amazing work," Tara said.

"This is a prototype, modeled after a real hand. The fingerprints are real, too . . . We want to see whether it can fool a standard biometric scanner. If so, the client wants to work on developing scanners that can also rely on skin conductivity."

"Impressive." It made sense to her, now, the Moon card: Lockley had used his talents for deception his whole career. Judging by the modest state of his house, Tara guessed that he wasn't charging much. Or else, he was good at squirreling it away. She felt a little sad for Lockley, though . . . In his retirement, all he had was his work. The old man was clearly still proud of it, and eager to show it off to company.

"Eh. Retirement bored me," he said modestly.

Harry squinted at a photo of Lockley strung up on the clothesline. Below the photo was a wigmaker's dummy with a half-finished mask draped over it. Lockley's features were shown in sleepy relief. "What are you working on here?"

"Ah, that's gonna be my Halloween costume." Lockley's chair squeaked beside Harry. "I play a starring role at my local haunted house. Took a cast of my face, but I'm going to make myself a zombie . . . add some fake teeth, blood, decomposing flesh. The kids like that kind of thing." Lockley folded his hands in his lap. "But this isn't what you came here for."

"Right," Harry said, distracted by a cobalt-blue eyeball in an egg cup. "Four people who worked on Project Rogue Angel have disappeared."

Lockley's eyes clouded. "Who?"

"Gerald Frost, Carrie Kirkman, Carl Starkweather, and Lena Ivanova. Did you know them?"

Lockley sighed. "I knew Gerald and Carl well. We kept in touch after retirement." He took his glasses off and rubbed under his eyes. "What happened?"

"We're not sure. Frost vanished on a trip to Russia. He got on a train, and disappeared. Kirkman disappeared from her real estate office. Carl's car was found at a Vegas casino, and we think Lena disappeared from her house."

"You got any theories?" Lockley was waiting to see what they had, before he tipped his hand.

"Some intel has been sold. Information that only the Rogue Angel team had access to." Harry didn't elaborate.

Lockley frowned. "Gerald and Carl were not the type of men who go rogue and sell secrets. I spoke to Gerald about six months ago. He was planning a trip to Ukraine, to Belarus, St. Petersburg. He never forgot that place. It grew on him too much. It wouldn't have surprised me to hear that he took up with a Ukrainian girl, found himself a nice little dacha in the countryside . . . but Gerald would not have spilled any secrets. He'd put too much effort into trying to make sure that no one got hurt in the debris of the Soviet empire to sell out now. Gerald was a sentimental man."

Tara leaned forward. "How about Carl? Or Lena?"

"Carl was assigned to offer cash to former Soviet scientists to keep them from defecting. He was trustworthy enough for the shop to trust him with millions of dollars. Not a cent of it ever went missing.

"He and Lena . . ." Lockley paused, and started over. "He and Lena were star-crossed from the get-go. I was the one who helped recruit Lena, so I feel partly responsible. She was assigned to be his interpreter. But, if you knew her, you couldn't help but fall for her. She was that luminous." Lockley folded his hands in his lap. "Poor Carl didn't have a chance."

"I thought Carl was married," Harry said.

"He is. But he'll never have as much in common with

his wife as he did with Lena. Once you've faced life and death together, traveled across the world to exotic places, well . . ." Lockley waved his hands at them. "You can imagine."

"But he went back to his wife and kids?"

"Carl always took his duties pretty damn seriously. He had kids, and he wasn't going to leave them without a father. And Lena was the impetuous sort—I don't think she would have waited for him."

Tara thought back on the matryoshka on Lena's dresser. Perhaps, in some way, on some level, she had still been waiting for him. "Our working theory is that these operatives were taken against their will . . . We haven't worked out the how or why of it, yet. Can you suggest any enemies or groups that might have wanted to see this happen?"

Lockley closed his eyes. "I don't want to imagine my old cohorts abducted and tortured for their information. But I can't see any other way that this could happen. Rogue Angel made enemies, to be certain. But I have to believe that most of those people are dead and gone."

"People like who?"

"The remains of the KGB always believed that they could handle their own affairs, without our interference. I often felt they were one step ahead of us. God knows where they all are now."

Harry crossed his arms. "Mr. Lockley, we'd like to take you into protective custody until we figure out what's going on, who's behind this."

Lockley shook his head. "I'm not going anywhere. This is my home."

"But you'll be safer with the Marshals."

"No. I'm staying here. You can put surveillance on me, all you want," the old man replied, stubborn as if someone had suggested putting him in a nursing home. "But I'm not leaving home."

"Okay." Harry sighed, resigned. "I'll get a Marshal out here to watch the house."

"I'll give 'em all the coffee they can stand and let 'em use the bathroom. But no one's sleeping in my house."

Harry fished his cell phone out of his pocket, turned away to make the call. Tara watched him, wondering if all the rest of the operatives on the list were going to be this stubborn.

Lockley leaned forward. Tara saw his gaze following the scars on the back of her hand and the ones peeking out from her collar. "Let me see your hand, kid."

Tara's brows drew together. "Why?"

"Professional interest."

Reluctantly, Tara extended her right hand to him. The old man gently turned her hand over, ran his fingers over the raised white scar.

"Could you roll up your sleeve for me, please?"

Tara decided to humor the old man. She rolled her jacket and blouse sleeve up to her elbow. Lockley invited her to sit on a stool, placed her arm on the table before him. He clicked on the fluorescent light, examining the frost-like patterns. "I've never seen anything like this before. Do you mind me asking?"

"No." Tara squirmed. "They're from a Japanese spade, a Hori-Hori."

"Ah. I can see that, now . . . the curve and the skip of the cut." He peered through his glasses. "May I ask how you got them?"

She swallowed. She didn't like talking about this, but she supposed the curiosity was natural. "I was the agent who found the Gardener."

"I've read about him. He was the killer who locked women in boxes, bled them out to feed his plants." Admiration glinted in Lockley's gaze. "And you were a survivor."

Tara nodded, unwilling to speak further on it.

Lockley reached for a pot of flesh-colored powder. "May I?" he asked, poising his brush above the pot.

"Um. Okay."

She felt the whisk of Lockley's brush across her skin as he worked the pigment into the white scars. "You're very much like them, you know."

"Who?"

"Lena and Carl." Lockley didn't look up from his work. "But different." Tara sat, flummoxed, as the soft brush continued working over her skin. He continued talking: "I'm not ordinarily a fatalist, but Carl and Lena were supposed to be together."

"How do you figure that?"

"People like us need other people like us. That's why I never married."

He turned Tara's hand over. "See what you think."

She blinked, looking at her blank, scarless skin. She brushed the line of a scar that she knew was there, felt the numb, stiff ridge of it under her touch, but couldn't see it. "You do excellent work, Mr. Lockley."

He dropped his brushes into a laundry sink and turned on the tap. "If you ever decide that you want to be well and truly rid of those scars, I know a plastic surgeon who works miracles, did a lot of shop work for us."

Tara stared down at her curiously blank flesh. It was tempting. But she'd grown accustomed to the tough feel of them lacing over her body, like the strings of a corset. Without them, she was afraid, on a visceral level, that her flesh would simply fall apart. She hesitated, but she was accustomed to them. No illusion cast by the disguise master or a surgeon would erase the past. She was learning to own it, own her roots: not as a victim, but as a survivor.

"Thanks, Mr. Lockley." She smiled at him. "But . . . I think I'm all right as I am."

It sounded strange to hear herself saying that, but it felt true, for the first time in years.

Chapter Eight

U NLIKE THE memories of his victims, Galen never wrote down his own memories. He could fill volumes detailing what he'd seen and heard, independent of the other voices in his head. But he had no desire to record them. Reliving them was almost too much to bear, and he sought to crowd out his own recollections with the memories of others.

But the new memories faded too quickly, like weak perfume. He could already feel Lena's jasmine scent leaving him. On some level, he hated her for leaving him. Everyone left, eventually.

Galen lay on his bed, staring up at the fan turning on the ceiling, stirring hot breeze from the open window like a spoon in soup. Sweat prickled his skin, and he could feel it dripping between his shoulder blades. When he closed his eyes, he could imagine it trickling down his face, like a cold spring rain that tasted like metal. Rain always brought change to him, sometimes unwanted, but always powerful. He'd always loved the rain.

He'd met Gerald Frost in a late spring rain, in Pripyat. No one lived in Pripyat anymore. The little Ukrainian town had been abandoned, fenced in, and forgotten. The chain-link fences and stout gates were intended to keep looters away, but they didn't deter the owls nesting in the rusting Ferris wheel, the birds that had overtaken the apartment buildings, or the foxes that peered behind tall tassels of grass poking up from cracks in the pavement.

And those security measures didn't deter Galen. He'd slipped behind a peeled-back portion of fence to wander the streets. They were different than he remembered as a child: stained and disintegrating. Square apartment buildings had begun to shift on their foundations, gutters drizzling rain into the gravel-strewn ground. Forgotten bits of scrap metal, paint flakes, and broken glass crackled underfoot.

Galen paused before one abandoned apartment building, remembering. He knew this place, once upon a time. A rusting padlock held the front door shut. Galen kicked the wooden door from its hinges, and the sound of it falling into the darkness beyond sounded like an explosion. Birds scattered within, and he could hear mice scurrying in the dust.

Galen walked up the sagging steps. These Soviet buildings had not been made to be pretty, and they had not been when they had been in use. But something about the decay was aesthetically appealing: the moss that grew around the windows where water had leached; the mildew speckling the walls. It was as if Nature herself were reaching out to reclaim this place.

Galen paused before an apartment door, placed his hands and forehead on its cold surface. It smelled like metal and mold, like nothing living. The warped wood splintered away easily.

The apartment was smaller than he remembered. A mildewed couch sagged in the center of the floor. Dishes still sat in the galley kitchen sink, with a dishtowel disintegrating on the edge of the water-swollen counter. Water tapped steadily down the walls from a leak in the roof, and dribbled down the window frame. Galen stepped over the shattered remains of a lamp and curling tiles on the floor. He stopped for a moment to pick up a blackened piece of metal in the wreckage: a toy truck. His fingers rubbed carbon off the blistered red paint. Clutching the toy to his chest, he crossed to the window.

He stared down at the small, overgrown courtyard with empty swings. This was where he remembered playing in the black rain as a child, where he tasted the hot metallic water running down his lips,. He could still hear the ringing of the children's shouts in his ears as they splashed through the puddles formed in the ruts below the swings. He remembered his white shirt stained black in the rain, how the water prickled, like pins and needles, as it sank into his skin. It buzzed, almost like a living thing, as it ran down his neck.

Now, this place was empty, empty of everything but memory.

Galen heard the crunch of gravel through the broken window, and his gray eyes narrowed. He pocketed the toy truck, slipped back out of the apartment. He suspected that one of the stalkers had come, one of the unlucky workers whose job it was to monitor radiation levels. They wandered about in their canvas suits, as if the thin material would protect them by force of pure symbolism. But Galen didn't want to be caught here, accused of being a looter. He slipped down the apartment stairs, stood in the shadow of the door, watching.

The man who walked down the street was no stalker. He was an old man, gray and paunchy, in flannels and jeans and good-quality boots . . . a Westerner trying to blend in. An expensive camera was slung around his neck. Down the street, at the main gate, Galen could see a late-model rental car. He appeared to be alone. And he probably had money. Probably one of those journalists who popped up from time to time, clucking in sympathy while they sucked money out of the tragedy.

Galen slid out of the shadows, stuck his hands in his thin coat pockets. He approached the old man, heart hammering. Rain tapped on his skull, nearly shaven entirely of hair. That camera alone would fetch a nice price. And those boots . . .

"Hello," the intruder greeted Galen in clumsy Russian.

"Hello," Galen answered, speaking slowly for the old man's benefit. He gestured with his chin to the camera. "Are you a journalist?"

"No." The intruder shook his head. "I'm . . . I guess

you could say I'm a tourist. I came through here many years ago."

"A tourist," Galen repeated, attempting to conceal his contempt. A voyeur.

"And you? Do you work here? Are you one of the stalkers?" The old man raised his camera, as if to take Galen's picture.

Galen shook his head. "No. Not a stalker. A survivor."

Galen lashed out and struck the old man in the face. The old man stumbled back, the camera slamming against his chest. To Galen's surprise, he swung back though his nose gushed blood down his face. Maybe the old man was ex-military. But he was still an old man.

Galen blocked, slugged his opponent in the ribs. The wind was expelled out of the old man's lungs in an exhalation of red on Galen's shoulder. Galen let him fall to the ground, wheezing. He ripped the camera strap over the old man's head. Looming over the old man, he kicked him, over and over, until he felt the crunch of bone and the old man lay still.

Galen rolled him over by his belt, reaching into his pockets. He found money. Lots of it, loose in his pockets, with the keys to the rental car. The old man's American passport identified him as Gerald Frost. Frost had a lot of stamps . . . looked like he'd been everywhere from Japan to Spain. Galen flipped through it, calculating if the passport could be doctored. He jammed it into his coat, along with the money. He found the fat wallet molded to the shape of the old man's rump in Frost's back pocket. He flipped open the soft leather, finding an

American driver's license, three credit cards, and CIA credentials.

Galen's brow wrinkled. Interesting. He'd beaten the shit out of an old spy.

He wanted to know more.

He grasped the old man by the feet and dragged him through the broken pavement and grass to the old apartment building. Frost was still breathing, but Galen chucked him in the entryway, well out of sight. He turned his attention to the rental car.

Stalkers came by once every few days. It wouldn't do for it to be found before Galen got some use out of it. Galen popped open the door, climbed behind the wheel. He drove it around the edge of the gate to a secluded thicket. The car would be hidden from casual inspection, almost as if Gerald Frost had never been there.

Galen returned to the apartment building. He slung the old man over his shoulder, carried him up the creaking steps to his old home. Uninceremoniously, he dumped the old man on the soggy couch. Startled by the squeak of springs, a rat scurried out from beneath it.

Fucking voyeur. He'd show him something of the tragedy, firsthand.

Galen sat beside the old man on the couch. Blood dripped from Frost's nose and mouth. Galen took the old man's skull in his hands. He felt his fingers digging into the liver spots on the old man's flesh, sinking through skin and bone. Frost's eyes rolled back in his head. He gasped and screamed.

But there was no one here to hear him. No one at all,

no one but the rats and the sparrows, as Galen dug into his flesh and his mind, engulfing his skin and his memories. He learned all that the old man had known, how he'd come to Chernobyl many years ago to account for missing fuel rods. How the place had been indelibly stamped upon his memory, such that he'd returned like a haunting ghost many years later.

And that had been Frost's undoing.

After killing Frost, Galen took his time digesting him over several days. He watched the play of dim light on the ceiling from the sun, the wash of the stalkers' flashlights over the courtyard. He remained in the shell of his home, listening to Frost's voice in his head and watching the fingers of Frost's ribs dissolve into his chest, melting like ice in summer. He was now the vessel of all Frost's memories . . . and all his opportunities.

Galen jammed all that remained of Frost in the frame of the couch: his clothes, wallet, and a handful of metal fillings that Galen spat out. He kept the boots, the camera, and all of Frost's papers. And his knowledge.

Like a ghost, Galen let himself out of the ruined town, walked through the puddles toward the car. Frost had not only given him precious knowledge; he'd given him keys to freedom.

TARA WATCHED AS THE WATER RINSED AWAY THE MAKEUP ON her arm, like rain eroding the façade of a building. The familiar scars emerged from beneath the camouflage as the illusion dissipated. She felt a pang of regret, but she reminded herself it wasn't real. Even if she went to the plastic surgeon Lockley had recommended, the scars would always remain, below the surface. And she wasn't ready to let them go.

She dried off the water with one of Harry's bathroom towels and rolled down her sleeve. Outside the door, she heard the murmur of Harry's low voice on the phone. After last night, he'd seemed . . . shocked to her, too quiet. And she wondered what she could do for him.

She dried off the vanity and pulled her cards out of her purse. She picked the Knight of Pentacles out, Harry's card, and placed it on the white imitation marble to focus the reading. Closing her eyes, she shuffled, imagining the solid, unwavering Harry she knew . . . not the man who'd nearly beaten the mugger to death last night.

She plucked out three cards and laid them above the significator card. The first card she drew represented Harry's physical needs, the body. She flipped it over, revealing the Four of Swords. A knight lay in effigy on top of a sarcophagus, holding a sword on his chest. Light streamed in from a stained glass window, playing multicolored shadows on his armor. This was a card of rest: Harry needed a decent night's sleep and the chance to recover from the stress he'd been laboring under.

The second card represented what was on Harry's mind. Tara turned over the Devil, reversed. It depicted a beastly demon with a man and a woman chained to his feet. The card suggested bondage, perhaps bondage to ideals or repression of instincts. Reversed, the card suggested the need to be free of restriction.

The third card suggested what Harry's spirit needed: Temperance. Temperance showed a woman standing knee-deep in a stream that reflected the stars of the Milky Way. She poured the dark, starlit water from one cup to the other, and not a drop was spilled. The angel represented synthesis, the blending of opposites. Tara frowned at the placid angel. Bringing Harry around to tranquility might be almost as difficult as catching the person responsible for the Rogue Angel disappearances.

She let that thought linger, Rogue Angel and the angel of Temperance. The goal of the Rogue Angel project had been the moderation of unchecked power. Perhaps, in the same way, her impetuous partner would need to learn to balance and synthesize his own judgments. She was reminded that Temperance always followed the Devil in the sequence of the Major Arcana, suggesting evolution. This was just something that Harry would have to get through, in his own time.

She whispered at her deck: "What is the best that I can do for him, now?" She fanned the cards out and picked one. The Two of Cups depicted a man and woman gazing into a chalice, their fingers intertwined on the stem. Above them, a caduceus and a winged lion watched. The caduceus was a symbol of healing, and the card spoke to her of alliances, of a balanced partnership. Tara would just have to be there for him, help him carry the burden of the chalice wherever she could.

Tara's cell phone rang. She squinted at the caller ID and flipped it open. "Hi, Cassie."

"Hi, yourself. Everything okay in the big city?"

Though the girl was forcing her tone to sound light, Tara could detect an undertone of worry.

"As well as can be expected for chasing monsters," Tara answered. "What did the Pythia teach you today?"

"Well . . . I wanted to talk to you about that."

Tara froze, suspicion prickling the back of her neck. Was that bitch teaching Cassie how to rip out still-beating hearts? "She better not have—"

"No, no. No more guns," Cassie hastily told her. "We're back to astrology."

"Oh, okay." Tara relaxed slightly, but not much. She didn't trust the Pythia any further than she could throw her.

"I saw something strange when I was plotting my charts. Sort of a weird coincidence."

"There are no weird coincidences. Just synchronicity."

"But this was beyond strange . . . I did a natal chart for the U.S., but picked today's date and Washington for the location for the transiting planets. I got Pluto in retrograde, plus a whole lotta other badness."

Tara's eyes narrowed. "I don't know much about astrology, but that doesn't sound good."

"No. But I did a data search to find any similar charts using that computer program I built. And I found a really close match: Chernobyl in Ukraine."

Tara's thoughts raced to make the connections: Rogue Angel, loose and unaccounted-for nuclear matter . . . and Chernobyl. She plucked a card from her deck; it was one from her very first Celtic Cross reading on the case: the Tower. The Tower was a sign of total destruction, and it had been in the foundation position in her previous reading. Whatever was driving this case had come from there, from Chernobyl.

"Tara, you still there?"

"Yeah. Can you put the Pythia on?"

"She's right here."

Not surprising, Tara thought. She was certain that there was very little that went on in that house that the Pythia didn't eavesdrop on.

"Tara," the Pythia's musical voice filled her ear. "This thing . . . whatever it is you're working on, is much bigger than you expected."

Tara was reluctant to divulge much information, but it seemed that the Pythia would have clearer sight than most, in this case. She sketched the case in general terms. "Several government operatives who were sent to track and recover nuclear materials in the former USSR have gone missing, and their secrets have been sold."

Without skipping a beat, the Pythia told her: "You must stop this. Or there will be a repeat of Chernobyl. Here."

Tara's knuckles whitened on the phone. "I'm trying."

"I know that you are. Your cards—"

"These don't seem to be my cards," Tara said coldly, "are they? You went to a great effort to put these into my hands."

There was a pause. "Those cards were meant to be yours."

"Where did they come from?"

"It doesn't matter. All you need to know is that you'd better learn to control them before it's too late."

The Pythia hung up.

"Bitch," Tara breathed into dead air.

She scooped up her cards, and went to join Harry in the living room, which looked like a disaster zone. File folders with open papers were spread all over the couch and floor, circling an empty pizza box. Harry sat on the couch, his elbows resting on his knees and his hands dangling slack into space. His tie hung loose around his neck, shirt rumpled, and he stared unblinkingly at his cell phone on the makeshift coffee table of boxes.

Tara sat beside him on the couch, touched his knee. "Harry, what is it?"

He swallowed, stared blankly at the phone. "I've been . . . I've been thinking about last night. About that mugger. Called the local hospitals, just to make sure that nobody matching that description turned up dead. I couldn't live with myself if . . . if . . ." He rested his forehead in his hands. "I got a call from the morgue."

Tara's heart stopped in her chest.

He couldn't say anything else, blew out a shaky breath.

All she said was: "I'll go with you."

He didn't refuse. He just silently gathered his keys and left for the car. Tara followed him, watching. He said nothing as he drove, his knuckles white on the steering wheel. All blood had drained from his face, and Tara couldn't imagine what he was going through. Harry had always been an exacting perfectionist, had always demanded the best of himself and others. Now, he'd failed. He'd taken one step outside the lines, with disastrous consequences.

The DC medical examiner's office was tucked away in a complex of brick buildings across the street from a dilapidated block of row houses and an STD clinic. Harry parked the car in a no-parking space, and tossed his DOJ parking placard in the window, as if daring someone to tow the car. Tara followed him through the glass doors to the ME's office. He rang the service bell, and Tara waited beside him as he showed his creds to the night staff.

"I need to take a look at a body that was brought in early today," he said. "This is the case number." He shoved a scrap of paper through the window for the on-duty assistant to look at.

"Sign in here, please." The morgue assistant shoved a clipboard back at them to sign.

Once the clipboard had been returned, the assistant buzzed them in through an airlock-like set of double doors. Tara wrinkled her nose at the smell and hot air. Rumor had it that the DC morgue's air conditioners were plagued by gremlins; she believed it.

She followed Harry and the assistant down a long corridor with faded green industrial tile. The soles of her shoes felt tacky; she hoped that it was simply wax, but she doubted it. She smelled too much sour bile, piss, and blood.

"Wait here. I'll get it out of the freezer." The assistant left Harry and Tara in the main examination room. A radio somewhere played alternative rock music. Plastic buckets and steel cabinets lined the walls. The aluminum coroner's slabs were full of figures covered in white sheets and plastic. An assistant was washing the body of an old woman with what looked like an industrial-grade vegetable sprayer. Tara realized that the music she heard came from the earbuds tucked under the woman's hairnet and mask; she could see the wire trickling out of her collar and extending to her pocket. She picked up a bucket and sloshed away down the hall, leaving Harry and Tara alone with the bodies.

Harry stared at the floor. Tara reached for his hand, and it was cold and clammy, like stone.

The clatter of wheels echoed down the hallway, sounding like a shopping cart at the supermarket. The assistant wheeled in a flat cart containing a body wrapped in plastic. The assistant peered at the toe tag. "This one's a John Doe. Inova Alexandria Hospital sent him down. Cops picked him up in an alley. Our guess on the cause of death is blunt force trauma. Somebody beat the living shit out of him."

Harry winced. That hospital was the nearest one to Ariadne's Web of Books.

Tara watched as the assistant cut the twine surrounding the plastic and opened the body's head and torso up to the air, like someone unpeeling a sandwich from a wrapper. The body was badly swollen, face a black and blue mass with its eyes swollen shut. Blood was crusted on the body's crumpled nose. Tara saw no Y-incision crossing the chest, indicating that the ME had not yet performed an autopsy.

She glanced sidelong at Harry, who was steadfastly refusing to look at the body, staring off into space.

"Can we have a minute?" Tara asked the assistant.

"Yeah, sure. Come back to the front when you're ready." The assistant left.

Harry turned his attention to the body on the table. He stared at the swollen face, puffed up beyond any recognition. Tara could feel his hand shaking in hers.

"Is that him?" he whispered. "Jesus, he's busted up so bad that I can't tell if it's fucking him." He leaned over the cart, staring at the body, eyes devouring the wounds on his face. It had been dark, the guy had been wearing a hat, and the attack had lasted only moments. Even under the best of conditions, an ID would be difficult. But this was too much of a coincidence . . . "It's him. It has to be him."

Tara looked under the cart. A brown paper bag was stapled shut. Had to be his property. She snagged some latex gloves from a nearby counter. She reached for the bag, pulled at the staples.

"It's him. It's fucking him." Harry punched one of the metal cabinets, denting it. A fly, startled by the bang, flew off the surface. *"It's him."*

Tara dumped the contents of the bag on the plastic wrapper. Her hands danced over the items: a pair of shiny black shoes, a white dress shirt speckled with blood and cut apart, an empty wallet, black pants, and a crusty brown tweed jacket. The ruins of a tie were stuck to the bottom of the bag, and she had to peel it out.

"It's him," Harry was mumbling over and over. His eyes were squeezed shut, and he leaned against the wall, pinching the bridge of his nose. "I fucking beat a thug to death."

Tara snapped off her gloves. She spun Harry around, grabbed him by his collar. *"It is not him,"* she hissed, dragging him back to the cart. "This guy was mugged. His wallet's empty. He was dressed in business clothes . . . Those shoes cost more than you make in a month. He's not a petty thief. It's not him."

Harry blinked, staring at the corpse.

"It's not him," she repeated, more gently, as Harry sagged against her.

He closed his eyes, muttered: "Oh, shit."

THE LANDSCAPE OF TARA'S DREAMS HAD SHIFTED.

The sun had lowered on the horizon of the desert, allowing blue shadows to creep beyond the dunes. Stars were beginning to prickle through the violet sky, and the full moon had risen in the east. She and her lion were walking along the sand, tracks intermingling. Strange, how she had become used to his presence, like her shadow. She wondered if this was what it meant to have a familiar. The lion's eyes glowed in the darkness, holding captured sunshine, and his fur still retained the heat of the day. Her skirts swished along her ankles, blurring her tracks in the sand with sidewinder marks.

Something broke the soft line of the sand ahead, something man-made. A ruin of a structure was nearly obscured in the sand. It was without a roof, staggered, crumbling walls open to the ceiling of stars. Broken lintels suggested that there had once been windows. And the door had been destroyed long ago. All that remained was space and open stone, half-buried in the sand and dark.

Tara picked up her skirts and stepped over the stones, into the footprint of the small, crumbling building. Inside, she could make out stones that might have been benches, before erosion had toppled them and sand had swallowed them. Perhaps this place had been a church, in some other time and place. A monument to someone's belief. Moonlight poured in through the open windows. The lion, seeming disinterested in the place, padded back to the door. He lay across the ruined doorway, staring into the night like a guard with his shining golden eyes.

Her gaze roved to the far side, where an altar would have stood. Sand skimmed around a raised structure, the size of a table, half sunken in the sand. A snake swished away, startled at her approach. She scooped sand away with her hands, and her heart hammered.

This was no altar. It was a sarcophagus. A knight lay in effigy on top of the sarcophagus, his eyes closed, clutching a sword to his chest. He was cast in stone, bits of rust streaking his armor. It was the image of the Four of Swords.

Harry. Her fingers skimmed over the familiar planes of his face.

Tears sprang to Tara's eyes. She leaned forward, her hair brushing away the sand from his chest, and kissed his unyielding lips.

The stone was cool under her mouth, but warmed under her breath and her touch and her tears. She felt something shifting, something warm and alive, if only she could awaken it. The stone began to yield, melt. She kept her eyes closed, daring to hope that somehow she could break the spell he'd been under . . .

. . . until she felt Harry's breath on her face.

She drew back.

Harry's eyes fluttered open. He was no longer hewn of stone, but of real flesh and blood. He reached up for her with fingers tangled in her hair and kissed her with a mouth as warm as sunshine.

SHE WOKE UP, FREEZING, WITH HARRY'S HANDS STILL TANgled in her hair.

"Tara, wake up."

She shivered violently, curling involuntarily against the warmth of Harry's chest. Her fingers and toes ached from the cold, stiff as talons. Her ear throbbed against the thunder of Harry's chest as it began to warm. She was wrapped in blankets up to her chin, but she felt as if she'd been walking outdoors in January, not asleep in Harry's bed in summer.

"You're sick," Harry concluded. "There's an urgent care clinic just down the street. They should still be open." There was something reassuring about that decisiveness in his voice; he sounded like the old Harry.

Tara shook her head. "No. I'm okay."

"You're not. 'Okay' does not include shallow respiration, a drop in body temperature, and a pulse like a rabbit."

"It's not . . ." Tara took a deep breath that seemed to pull warm summer air into her lungs. "I don't think I'm sick. It's something to do with the cards. I . . ." She shook her head, struggling to explain. "I'm feeling them more intensely, dreaming about them. It's like . . . stepping into another world."

Harry looked at her suspiciously. "You're telling me this is a . . . trance of some kind?"

She nodded. "I think so. The information is very vivid, experiential."

"I didn't think your, uh, talents worked that way. I thought you free-associated with the card images . . . something about that collective unconscious."

"They don't. At least, they never have, before." She bit her lip. "I think my power is changing."

"Is it supposed to do that?"

"It's not unheard of. Power doesn't remain static over an oracle's lifetime. It waxes and wanes, depending on experience and circumstances. But it's not something that's predictable."

"Coming from an oracle, that's a strange statement."

"That's my best guess."

Harry gathered Tara's cold fingers in his hands and blew on them. Her fingers brushed his lips, and his warm breath traveled down her wrists, stirring blood that had lain cold for months. She looked away, but it rose in her cheeks. She could feel them flaming in the darkness, hoped he couldn't see.

With one hand, Harry pressed Tara's hands to his chest. The other pushed her hair away from her face, and he tenderly pressed his lips to her forehead, to the bridge of her nose. Where he kissed her, the heat followed: from her temple, to her upper lip, the point of her chin. His hand on the back of her neck felt like sunlight on a summer's day.

She wanted more of that light, that heat. Like him, she was drowning in her own darkness. Tara felt herself losing touch with the real world through her dream-visions, as much as Harry lost touch with his humanity through his work. She tipped her head forward and kissed him back. Harry's mouth chased the chill from hers.

Her fingers wound in his T-shirt as his kisses drifted down her shoulder over the exposed scar on her collar. She didn't fear Harry's judgment; he'd seen these marks before. He brushed her hair away, fingers sketching the scars between her ribs.

Like a cloak, Harry and the bedspread enveloped her. Her cold hands traced over his spine and the hard muscles of his back. Their clothes tangled in the bedspread, kicked to the bottom of the sheets. Tara sighed, feeling the blissful heat of his bare skin down the length of her body, skimming her hands across his chest.

"God, I missed you," he murmured into her shoulder. He reached down to part her legs, slipped his hand between them. She moaned, arching her back, as his fingers teased heat from her body. He pressed swollen and heavy against her inner thigh. Harry teased her until her nipples scraped his chest and she grabbed his buttocks to pull him inside her.

He wrapped his arms tightly around her as he thrust into her, grasping her hips. With a nearly violent crush of flesh, he drove into her over and over, thrust her up against the wall behind the bed. Tara clung to him with both arms wrapped around his neck, crying out as the orgasm overtook her. And it overtook Harry. His hands clutched her hips as he plunged into her one last time, growling as he came.

Tara slid back down the wall, her knees gone weak and gelatinous.

"Are you all right?" Harry had come back to himself, and his eyes were wide with worry that he'd lost control again.

"Yes. Are you?"

He took a deep breath, seemed to consider it. "Yeah. I am, now."

He kissed her soundly, wrapping her in his arms and the blankets. She pressed her ear to his warm chest, feeling it rise and fall and his heartbeat settle into sleep. When she looked up at him, he was as she'd seen him in desert effigy: a knight at rest in the darkness. This was the first peacefulness she'd seen in him in months

She laid her head back down, slipped into a dream of the desert. In her dream, Strength and the Knight of Pentacles, stripped of his armor, slept twined together on a sarcophagus while a lion kept watch over them.

Chapter Nine

As much as he hated to admit it, he needed her.

Harry shuffled through the papers on his desk while he was on hold with the U.S. Marshals. Though the Marshals had some irritating on-hold music that sounded like a tortured xylophone version of "Muskrat Love," he felt calmer this morning than he had in a long time, as if he'd sworn off caffeine. He glanced over at Tara, scribbling notes at a nearby desk filched from the Library of Congress. The stolen chair squeaked relentlessly, but she didn't complain, absorbed in her work. Harry had been mysteriously unable to procure a desk for Veriss, who was wearing a hole in the carpet in the conference room, pacing before a whiteboard. Harry liked him better over there, behind soundproof glass like a fish in a bowl.

Maybe Lockley was right. Maybe only people like them understood other people like them, could fathom what it was like to have the underlying tension of a more important mission every day. A duty that was more important than desire, love, or friendship. Lives were always at stake in their line of work, and everything else had to be sublimated to it. No one else would understand, no one but Tara.

Anderson from Forensics wound her way through the bullpen, making a beeline for Harry's desk. She was dressed in a white Tyvek hazmat suit, clutching a clipboard stuffed full of papers. Only too relieved to be free of the Marshals' "Muskrat Love," Harry hung up.

"Anderson, what's up? And is it Halloween already?"

Anderson's eyes glowed in excitement. "We've found something new. Something interesting."

Tara squeaked her chair around to face them, winced at the sound. "Did you re-run the DNA from Lena's disappearance?"

"Yes. And the previous samples. We consulted with a genetics expert at the University of Virginia, and he's very excited." Anderson grinned. "We didn't screw up the lab results, after all. The expert thinks that we have a chimera—of sorts—on our hands. There is more than one genetically distinct type of cell, but this isn't anything that anyone's ever seen before."

"How is that possible?" Harry leaned forward in his chair. "The DNA is from people that we know to be distinct . . . separate entities."

"We don't know. The DNA strands are all tangled together. But the strands are degrading at different rates. Look." Anderson perched on the edge of Tara's desk and showed them a printout. The first page showed three staccato lines. "In the first DNA samples taken from Carrie Kirkman's disappearance, we found three sets of DNA: Gerald Frost's, Carrie's, and an unknown. Gerald's DNA had degraded." She pulled out another page, including four lines. "In the samples taken from Carl's disappearance, we found four sets: Gerald's, Carrie's, Carl's, and the same unknown. Carrie's and Gerald's had degraded, though." She pointed out broken and faint third and fourth lines and flipped to the next page. "In Lena's disappearance, we found four sets of DNA: the unknown, Carrie's, Carl's, and Lena's." She pointed to two faint lines. "Carrie's DNA has degraded to the point that it's almost unrecognizable, and Carl's is dissolving, too. We think Gerald's degraded to the point that it no longer exists."

"What would cause that kind of degradation?" Harry asked, his eyes tracing the multicolored lines.

"Only one thing would cause degradation in this way. Serious radiation exposure."

Tara leaned forward. "Did you find radiation in the samples?"

"Once we looked for it, yes. Loads." Anderson inclined her head to the lab. "We found thirty microroentgens per hour in the lab, and are decontaminating it now. That's more than five times the normal background levels of radiation. Lena's house is soaked in cesium-137, iodine-131, and strontium-90 particles, and so is the evidence from Carl's car. We've stuck that in a lead-lined box. Nobody's seen residual levels of that type since—"

"Since Chernobyl," Tara finished.

"Yeah. Exactly." Anderson seemed stunned at Tara's intuitive leap. "We'd expect someone with this degree of residual radiation to have experienced serious physical damage: thyroid cancer, serious deformities, and invasive cancers. But whoever our unknown subject is, he's apparently well enough to be skulking around in the shadows."

"Are the levels enough to cause harm to you guys, or people working the case?" Harry asked, envisioning somebody somewhere suing him for something.

Anderson shook her head. "Unlikely that you'd get thyroid cancer from one-time vicarious exposure. But I'd advise anyone who worked those scenes to turn their clothes in for proper disposal. If any new crime scenes emerge, we've got more moon suits on order."

Harry drummed his fingers on his desk. "Where the hell did this come from? Is our kidnapper sitting on a stockpile of dirty bombs?"

Before Anderson could answer, Tara said, "No. Our subject is from Chernobyl."

Anderson blinked. "Damn, you're good. We don't know for sure, but the combination of radioactive materials is fairly specific. You could be dealing with a refugee, with someone who was bombarded with radiation for a long period of time."

"But why would a victim of the worst nuclear disaster in history be selling secrets to cause more destruction?" Harry wondered. "Is he doing this for the money?"

Veriss had swum out of his fishbowl and wormed his way into the conversation. Harry groaned inwardly. "Economic advantage is the single most powerful motivator in my models. I don't see why someone *wouldn't* sell those secrets."

Harry stared at Veriss. Hard.

Veriss backed up. "Absent any internalized societal norms to the contrary, of course. And being tried for treason might have an additional deterrent effect."

Tara shook her head. "I don't think our subject is in it sheerly for the money. I think it's about revenge."

Harry frowned. "What do you mean?"

She rolled forward, and her chair squeaked. "I think our subject has experienced hell. And he wants the rest of us to know what it's like."

Harry picked up the phone. "Get me Homeland Security. I need them to sweep every major airport with Geiger counters. We need to figure out where this guy got in."

TARA'S HELL WAS DIFFERENT FROM HER UNKNOWN SUBJECT'S hell.

And she felt it would serve her best if she could understand it.

The elevator up to the Library of Congress grated slowly on its cables. Tara looked at the flashing lights, notebook tucked under one arm, and a coffeemaker under the other. The Little Shop of Horrors had filched it from LOC, despite the LOC inventory sticker on the bottom. She hoped that if she brought it back, as a peace offering, she might be able to dig up some information.

Maybe.

The elevator doors opened on one of LOC's long-term storage areas. Rows and rows of moveable bookshelves stretched back as far as the eye could see—which wasn't far. The lighting here was on motion detectors to save energy and keep the documents from fading; a light flicked on when she stepped out of the elevator. They lit up as she wandered down the long, spotless corridors of documents that stretched into darkness that was air-conditioned and humidity-controlled.

"Hello?" Tara called into the stacks.

A light flickered on in the distance. Overhead lights winked on as someone approached; Tara could hear heels clicking on the concrete.

A young woman wearing a paper jumpsuit and pink latex gloves rounded the corner. Tara recognized her from the elevator; she'd been the one to filch Veriss's projector. Her eyes narrowed in suspicion upon seeing Tara.

Tara held up the coffeepot. "I, uh, found something of yours. I thought I'd bring it back."

The woman's head cocked to the side, and her light brown hair licked her cheek. A pair of safety goggles was perched on top of her head. "You're bringing it *back*?" This was not how the game was played.

"Yeah." Tara held it out to her. "It's yours."

"What did you do to it?" Suspicion turned the corner of her mouth.

"Nothing. I swear."

"Does it still work?"

"Yeah."

Fast as a cobra striking, the woman snatched the coffeepot from Tara's hands and held it to her chest. "Um. Thanks."

"You're welcome."

The woman examined the coffeepot for tampering, then looked back at Tara over the white plastic brim. "Is this a bribe? What do you really want?"

"I could use some help," Tara admitted. "Research help."

The woman's shoulders relaxed a bit. "Oh. What on?"

"Chernobyl. I'm looking for information about survivors, about radiation exposure and health effects." Tara looked at the white suit the woman was wearing. "Looks like you're the expert."

She shook her head. "No. I'm just an archivist. Cleaning some fragile silver nitrate photograph plates. Can't get dust on them. And they do have the tendency to corrode, if not stored properly." She paused awkwardly. "But I think I can help you, anyway."

"Thanks." Tara gingerly extended her hand in truce. "By the way, I'm Tara."

The woman grasped her hand with her pink glove. "Jenny. Let me get this gear stowed away, and I'll see what I can dig up for you."

Tara followed Jenny down the corridor to a back room with a locked keycard entry. Jenny swiped her badge to let them into a brightly lit space covered with workbenches and computer terminals. Under a flame hood and Plexiglass box, Jenny's silver nitrate plates glistened, smelling sharply of chemicals as they dried.

Jenny set the coffeemaker down on a table. She snapped off her gloves and unzipped her protective suit, stepped out of it, and stuffed the gear into a wastebasket. Underneath her suit, she wore a simple T-shirt and jeans—items that wouldn't require dry cleaning. They made her look very young, like a teenager playing dress up. She perched on a stool, watching Tara, probably guessing that Tara would run off to steal something when her back was turned.

"EPA has some files on Chernobyl. I know they've been over there several times on fact-finding missions." Jenny hooked her feet in the bottom rungs of the stool and turned to a computer terminal. Her fingers flitted over the keyboard. "Some of them are public record. Some are not."

Tara didn't figure her security clearance would get her very far. "What would it take to get access to those?" She leaned on a workbench, arms crossed.

Jenny's mouth turned upward. "You *could* file a request up your chain of command. It would probably take a few weeks."

"What if . . . what if I brought you a gift?" Tara was feeling out the parameters of the new game; it was like bringing treasure to the dragon, in the hopes the dragon would spill its secrets.

Jenny gestured to the coffeemaker. "I think that's an even trade. For now."

Tara lifted an eyebrow, wondering what other petty thefts she might need to turn a blind eye to.

Jenny's fingers flickered over the keys. "The EPA reports are used often enough that they've been digitized. You don't need the originals, do you? That would take some doing."

Tara shook her head. "No. Digital is fine."

Jenny slid from the stool. "I can't let you take any of this stuff with you, so you'll have to read at the terminal. I'll ignore any notes you take, though."

"Thanks." Tara slid into the stool and began to scan the files. In her peripheral vision, she saw Jenny fussing with the settings on the overhead vapor hood. She figured the archivist would probably hover around to make sure Tara wouldn't steal anything. Tara could live with that. She hunched over the terminal and began to read.

Her knowledge of the accident at Chernobyl was probably comparable to most people in the West: she knew a reactor in Ukraine had exploded, causing serious health and ecological damage. No one had known the true radiation levels at the time. Safety protocols and information from radiation detectors had been disregarded, though the true levels were twenty thousand roentgens per hour, well exceeding the lethal dose of five hundred roentgens. The area around the reactor plant had been cordoned off with a thirty kilometer Exclusion Zone, where no one was permitted to enter. The Exclusion Zone included the nearby city of Pripyat and the reactor buildings, which were not evacuated until more than a day later. But contamination had reached into Ukraine, Russia, and Belarus following the accident, which had been caused by an experimental shutdown of the Chernobyl plant by engineers. Of the four reactors at the Chernobyl site, not all were closed until 1999.

More than a half-million people had been involved in immediate efforts to stop the spread of contamination. These people, known as "liquidators," were given very little information about the effects of the radiation. They and firefighters were sent to drop sand and pour concrete on the lava-like reactor fuel still seething at the site, to haul away debris, to put out fires with water, and to seed the skies for rain that would precipitate volatile cesium from the atmosphere, resulting in black rain that poured down on an unevacuated populace. A temporary structure, known as the Sarcophagus, was built over the ruined fourth reactor to assist in containing the radioactive debris. But, in the intervening years since the disaster, the Sarcophagus was crumbling, allowing daylight and radiation to seep through.

These were facts. But she wanted to experience it. She wanted to see the pictures.

Pictures taken immediately after the disaster were mostly black and white, grainy in their quality. Tara assumed these pictures had belonged to the Soviets. They were surreal, showing the massive reactor shell ripped apart. Aerial views showed a black hole in the ground that smoked in daylight. Reactor fuel had poured into the foundations of the building, seething hot and unstoppable. It had cooled to a ceramic state, but descriptions indicated that it had flowed like magma. Photographs from space showed a glowing ember in the darkness that was the reactor melting down for days.

She clicked through photos of broken concrete and foam spraying that had been ineffectual, or had even made things worse. Massive bags of sand and boron had been dropped from the sky to muffle the radiation, but the magma-like mixture of reactor fuel and concrete burned through the reactor floor, threatening another explosion if the mixture reached underground water in a flooded cooling pool. Volunteers entered the ruined reactor to drain the pool, keeping the magma-like fuel from connecting with water beneath the reactor, successfully preventing a second explosion. But the ruined core had to burn itself out. There was nothing stopping a force as fearsome and unnatural as that.

She flipped through photographs of the Sarcophagus being built, with cranes and hasty welds. Workers described the sensation of the radiation as being like pins and needles on their bare skin. Some of the workers' and firefighters' skin turned black days later, and they died of radiation sickness. A morgue photo showed a man burnt to a black husk; Tara couldn't tell if it was from fire or from the radiation, as she couldn't read the original caption in Cyrillic.

With her heart in her mouth, she turned her attention to photographs from the hospitals, asylums, and children's homes for orphans. Some were children who had been alive at the time of the disaster; others were born after. Her vision blurred as she viewed a photo of a bald girl with thyroid cancer, sitting up in a bed staring out a window with heartbreakingly alert eyes. She knew. She knew what had happened to her. Children with horrific deformities, missing and misshapen limbs, lay on the floor of a children's home while nurses spoon-fed them. They would never walk. A boy with his brain growing in a pocket of skin outside of his skull was cradled by a nurse in a black-and-white photo. A boy in a wheelchair was captured in a frozen scream in a photo at the asylum. The American photographer, a worker from the Nuclear Regulatory Commission, had included the comment that the boy screamed every moment he was awake for his mother, who had abandoned him.

Tara pressed her knuckles to her mouth to keep from sobbing. These were the most horrible things she'd ever seen. More horrible than any of the cases she'd worked. Even more terrible than being cut up at the hands of the Gardener. The amount of human suffering was palpable, even through these flat, two-dimensional images.

She shuddered to imagine how they would invade her dreams. She couldn't imagine the dreams of the man who'd lived through it. And she didn't want him to share that dream with anyone else.

Cassie's sleep had been interrupted by troubling dreams. She'd tossed and turned, ejecting Oscar out of bed more than once. Maggie had stuck her cold Labrador nose in her face to check on her, whimpering. She'd finally crept out of her own bed in the early hours of the morning to sleep in Tara's room. She pulled Tara's quilt up around her chin and watched the stars revolve around the pole star until they faded at dawn. Only when the stars dimmed did she manage to fall asleep, waking only when the sun was high above the eaves.

She'd plodded down to the kitchen for coffee, bleary-eyed and barefoot. She wondered at the silence of the house, found a scrawled note in the Pythia's hand on the counter: *Went out for supplies. Be back at dusk.*

Cassie frowned as she plugged in the coffeepot. Hard to tell what supplies the Pythia had gone out for. Could be anything from bullets to bread to begonias. The Pythia was probably pissed at her for not being up bright and early for her next lesson. She swore the Pythia rarely slept; she always seemed to be creeping around with that inscrutably Pythia-like expression on her face.

She leaned over the kitchen sink to peer out the window, and saw no cars in the gravel driveway.

Cassie smiled. For the first time, she had the house entirely to herself. No Pythia. No Delphi's Daughters. Only Oscar, who stared at her suspiciously from the bottom step. He mewed. Cassie was certain that, in his language, he was warning her that curiosity had bumped off more than one of his kind.

Cassie patted him on the head, climbed back up the stairs to dig around in the secrets of Delphi's Daughters.

Like many houses, the farmhouse kept certain public areas open to company: the kitchen and sitting rooms on the first floor held little evidence that the house was a nest for oracles. There were maybe a few too many herbs drying above the sink, and perhaps an abnormally large amount of ashes in the fireplace for summertime. But there was little other sign of magick. Delphi's Daughters tended to keep their personal magick to themselves.

Cassie's footsteps creaked on the steps, and she padded through the upstairs hallway. The farmhouse had six bedrooms, variously occupied by whichever Delphi's Daughters were in residence at the time. Cassie didn't know how many total members were in Delphi's

Daughters. Tara said that she didn't know, either. But she told Cassie that they likely numbered in the hundreds, even thousands.

Cassie bypassed Tara's room. There was nothing there that she didn't already know about. Tara kept her personal possessions to a minimum. Cassie thought that was perhaps on purpose, to keep the Pythia out of her head. Only a photograph of Tara as a child with her mother stood on the dresser. Cassie knew Tara's mother was dead, that she had been one of Delphi's Daughters. But Tara had been less obedient than her mother. Tara would understand Cassie's desire to jiggle the glass doorknobs in the hallway, to investigate the company she found herself in.

None of the doors were locked. Most rooms were painted soft pastel colors, with rag rugs and quilts piled high on old iron bedsteads. Cassie peered into closed drawers, pawing through sock drawers and medicines arranged on dresser tops. One of Delphi's Daughters, a botanomancer, was on enough lithium to fell a dinosaur. Interesting. Another had a really impressive set of crystals arranged in a battered silverware box. She knew better than to touch, just let her eyes rove over the shiny surfaces. She admired the handbags one of the women had hanging on a hook. Expensive stuff.

But these things didn't interest Cassie nearly as much as the door at the end of the hall, where she knew the Pythia slept. *When* she slept. Cassie turned the glass doorknob and let herself in, heart hammering at her daring.

The Pythia's room wasn't like the others. The others were temporary abodes, places for women who were passing through on oracle business to sleep for the night. This room, however, was unmistakably the Pythia's. The walls were painted a deep cinnamon red, and the smell of frankincense and myrrh incense clung to the velvet drapes. Heavy Persian carpets covered the hardwood floors. A four-poster bed took up half the room, veiled in long, sheer violet curtains and gold tassels.

Cassie emitted a low whistle. It was like something out of *Arabian Nights*.

From the doorway, Oscar sat and gave her a disapproving mew. Even he wouldn't cross the threshold to the Pythia's realm.

Cassie's gaze roved over dozens of glass perfume bottles on the dresser, interspersed with half-melted candles. She headed for the closet, opened the louvered door to peer at the riot of silk costumes bursting from the too-small space. They were beautifully embroidered blouses, full circle skirts, bra-like tops and scarves adorned with bells and coins that jingled when the Pythia walked.

That, she expected. But the Pythia's closet held a few surprises. In the back hung two somber black business suits like those in Tara's closet. Two pairs of handmade Italian shoes. Cassie lifted her eyebrows in amusement. She'd never seen the Pythia in heels. A set of camouflage coveralls, like Cassie would expect to see in a hunting supply catalogue, only tailored for the Pythia's diminutive height. And what looked like a black flight suit, covered in pockets, but with no military emblem on it. Matching boots were in the back of the closet, tiny compared to Cassie's feet, but crusted in mud.

Cassie turned her attention to the Pythia's dresser. The Pythia's jewelry box was full of gorgeous gold bracelets, earrings, and necklaces. Cassie opened a locket that showed a black-and-white picture of a woman who strongly resembled the Pythia. She was dressed like Amelia Earhart, in a khaki jumpsuit and scarf. Her mother, perhaps?

The top two drawers held predictably slinky things that Cassie didn't want to picture the Pythia wearing, along with bath salts and soaps that smelled like amber. The next one held some disintegrating books written in Arabic. Paging through them, Cassie thought she recognized some of the Arabic names for stars: Al-'Adhara, Al-Firq, Al-Ka's. But the rest was a puzzle to her. She put them back and opened the last drawer.

This was where the Pythia kept her weapons. A knife with a jeweled hilt glittered in a tooled leather sheath. Cassie found a ring in a box and wondered at it until it popped open, and she could see a void beneath the stone that might hold poison. A handgun, exactly like the .357 the Pythia had taught her to shoot two days ago, rested in a holster. It was very Wild West, with mother-of-pearl grips and a worn holster. Cassie imagined the Pythia as a cowboy, standing in a dusty street at high noon, and giggled in spite of herself.

Through the open window, she heard the crunch of gravel. She froze. Shit. The Pythia was back. She slammed the drawer shut and peered out the window.

That wasn't the Pythia's car.

At first, Cassie thought perhaps it belonged to a new member of the rotating Daughters-in-residence program.

The nondescript sedan pulled up to the house, and she could hear Maggie barking. The man who stepped out was dressed in jeans and a T-shirt, staring at the house with an appraising look that Cassie didn't like. Instinctively, she knew he didn't belong here.

She heard his boots clomping on the porch a floor below her, heard the ring of the doorbell. Instinctively, Cassie reached back into the Pythia's goodie drawer. With shaking hands, she checked to make sure the gun was loaded, and padded down the hallway. Oscar zoomed into Tara's room and hid underneath the bed skirt.

She waited. From here, she had a clear view down the steps at the kitchen door. Maggie was lunging against the door, barking and snapping.

The doorbell hadn't brought a response. Cassie hoped the man would go away. Perhaps he was just lost, or selling something. Either way, she wanted him gone.

The doorbell stopped ringing, and Cassie blew out her breath . . . until she heard the thump of his boots on the porch, heard the jiggle of someone trying to get in the kitchen window. Maggie lunged at the kitchen counter, barking.

Cassie's fingers whitened on the gun. Maybe she could scare the guy off, keep him out of the house and not have to call the cops. Cassie considered the idea of summoning them and discarded it. The nearest law enforcement was thirty minutes away. They might as well not exist.

Cassie slipped down the stairs, hearing the creak of her steps and wincing. In a clear voice, she shouted, "Get away. I'm armed."

The jiggling at the window paused, died. Cassie's heart hammered. Good. Maybe that had frightened him away. She waited for minutes, her back pressed to the wall, waiting, but she didn't hear the engine of his car start back up. She mentally ran through all the first floor windows, didn't know which were left open and which were shut.

She jumped and squeaked when she heard the living room window screen crash inward and glass splinter on the floor.

Cassie clambered down the steps to escape, reached out for the handle of the kitchen door. She fumbled at the lock with shaking hands, conscious of Maggie snapping and growling beside her. From the corner of her eye, she saw the intruder barreling through the sitting room. He kicked Maggie aside with a yelp, sending the dog sliding limp across the hardwood floor, and advanced upon Cassie.

Fury lit in Cassie's chest, and she leveled the gun at him, snarling, "Don't you dare hurt my dog."

The intruder didn't pause, kept storming toward her in the glitter and crunch of ruined glass, like a foreign juggernaut in the safe space of the Pythia's parlor.

He didn't belong here.

She squeezed the trigger. The gun roared and kicked back over her head. The intruder paused, staring down at the blossom of red in his belly. His expression was disbelieving, as if he didn't comprehend that she really would kill him.

She forced the gun down, shot again, like the Pythia had taught her.

And again.

And again.

She fired until the chamber clicked empty. She couldn't hear the click, only felt it reverberating in her finger. She dropped the gun, as if it was hot, saw it bounce on the floor.

The intruder lay on the threshold of the parlor, twitching in a spreading slick of red. Cassie backed away from him, ran to Maggie. Maggie cowered at the foot of the stairs, tail between her legs. Cassie ran her fingers over the dog's ribs, crooning to her in a voice she couldn't hear over the ringing in her ears.

She looked over the dog's ears, pressed her fist to her mouth. It smelled like sweat and gunpowder. "What've I done?"

She stared intently at the body seeping blood on the floor. She couldn't detect any rise and fall in his chest, and he'd stopped twitching. On her hands and knees, she crawled to the man, touched his wrist with shaking fingers. She had to focus them to remain still, try to see if she felt a pulse.

But she felt nothing, nothing but the panic welling up in her throat.

Who was this man? What did he want?

She'd been chased by the military, months back. They'd wanted her dead father's secrets, but Delphi's Daughters had hidden her. Had they found her, at last?

She shook. Shook so hard she could barely put one foot in front of the other. She clambered up the steps. The gunfire had deafened her, and she could only hear her own ragged breath ringing in her ears. She grabbed her backpack, her cell phone, peeked under the bed to check for Oscar. His golden eyes were wide as moons. She saw him open his mouth, but couldn't hear him meowing. She dragged him out by the scruff of his neck, jammed him into her backpack. She stuffed her laptop computer under her arm, stumbled down the stairs with the squirming backpack over her arm and Maggie glued to her side.

She had to get out of there. Whoever this man was, whatever he had wanted, it wasn't safe.

She ran down the porch steps to the intruder's car, uttering a prayer under her breath that the keys were in the ignition and not in his pockets. The door opened, and she found them dangling from the ignition. She opened the passenger door for Maggie, put Oscar in the backseat with the computer.

She cranked the engine to life, threw the car into reverse. Every fiber in her being was telling her to flee. Fear of the intruder, what he represented, mingled in her mind with fear of the Pythia's wrath.

But she'd be long gone by the time the Pythia discovered the body on her parlor floor.

Far away, someplace where no one—not even Delphi's Daughters—could find her.

Chapter Ten

SOMETHING WAS wrong. Tara could feel it pulsing behind her eyes, like a half-formed headache. When she dug in her purse for a pen, her pack of cards tumbled out on the Special Projects conference room table among Veriss's network charts and Anderson's DNA printouts.

Tara hesitated, her fingers pressed against the surface of the pack obscured in the cigarette wrapper. Harry had sent Veriss out to pick up lunch, much to the analyst's irritation, leaving her alone with Harry and a mountain of data they were trying to decipher. She opened the pack and spread her cards out before her on the glossy table.

Across the table, Harry looked up from his files to watch her shuffle and draw. "Maybe you should give the cards a rest for a while, after that trance stuff," he said, fidgeting and glancing at the closed door.

She shook her head. "Something's not right." Harry might be concerned about her playing cards in Special Projects and getting caught, but she couldn't ignore the nagging feeling prickling at the base of her skull.

"This whole case is fucked up."

"Yeah. But this feels . . . different."

Tara shuffled the cards, and one slipped through her fingers to the cluttered surface of the table. She frowned. Jumping cards often contained urgent information. The Star showed a maiden bathing in a creek, looking up at the sky. She was the picture of innocence.

And that was the card she associated with Cassie. Her heart leapt in her throat, and she glanced at her watch. She didn't expect to hear from Cassie until late tonight, but that wouldn't stop her from checking in early. She picked up her cell phone, dialed the number to the farmhouse. It rang and rang, with no answer.

She looked down at the card, drumming her fingers on its margins. It was possible that Delphi's Daughters were out frolicking in the yard. Or that they'd driven to one of the neighboring towns for pizza. It was possible.

She tried calling Cassie's cell. It was shut off, rolled immediately over to voice mail.

She shuffled the cards again, and another card dropped to the table, beside the Star. The Ten of Swords showed a man lying on the ground, his back pierced with ten swords plunged into the rocky earth.

Without a word, Tara snatched up her cards and jammed them back into her purse. She grabbed her holster and made for the door.

"Hey, what's going on?" Harry asked.

"It's Cassie," Tara said. "She's in danger. There's no answer at the farmhouse or her cell."

Harry stood, reaching for his jacket. "I'll go with you."

She shook her head. "No." She kissed him soundly on the mouth. "Stay here, in case she finds her way back here."

Harry's mouth was set in a grim line, and he caught her elbow. Cassie was like a little sister to the both of them. "If something's happened to her—"

"There won't be anything you can do. This is a matter for Delphi's Daughters." She blew out her breath. "And if I find out that the Pythia's done something to her, so help me, I'll make sure that conniving witch has no future to predict."

The old man knew he was being watched.

Galen could see it in the way he tightly closed his blinds and shut his lights off after dark. The old man must be moving through his house through sheer touch and familiarity with the floor plan. Once in a while, streetlights would pick out a shimmer of metal inside, behind the glass. Whether it was a weapon or the shine on his wheelchair, Galen couldn't tell.

The old man had been warned.

For certain, the old man knew he was being watched by the two men in the sedan with U.S. Government plates sitting across the street. They stuck out like a sore thumb in the quiet suburban neighborhood, swilling their coffee, yakking on their cell phones, and flipping their newspapers. Neighbors kept peeking out behind their curtains to see what the men were up to. Galen was certain they were here primarily for deterrent effect.

And that would've worked for most people. An ordinary burglar would have simply passed by. But Galen wanted Norman Lockley. He wanted what was rattling around in his brain. That beautiful chaos he could sell, unleash upon the unsuspecting world.

Galen crouched in the shadow of Norman's bird feeders, listening for sounds within the house. He heard the jingle of chain and a dish scraping around inside. A dog. Eventually, Norman's wheelchair creaked into the back of the house, and Galen could hear the old man wheezing as he dragged himself out of the chair and into his bed. Bedsprings groaned as the old man made himself comfortable. A television droned in the background.

Galen crossed around the back of the house, his step stealthy. With a pair of wire cutters, he snipped the phone line leading into the basement of the house. He left the cable television line alone; no point in alarming the old man unnecessarily. He crept around to the back garage. A door opened out into the backyard, but it was locked.

No matter. Galen had learned a few simple criminal tricks in his time in Ukraine and Belarus. He'd learned many more from Gerald, Carl, and the others. He pulled a CO_2 fire extinguisher from his backpack, aimed it at the knob lock, and squeezed the trigger. The cold foam enveloped the brass knob, and Galen waited until the metal began to crackle and sweat. He withdrew a hammer from his bag and a bath towel to muffle the sound. He wrapped the towel around the knob. With one swift motion, he struck the knob with the hammer. The blow severed the knob from its stem, shattering it with nary a sound.

Gently, he opened the door, stepped down two steps into the garage. He allowed his eyes to adjust to the thicker darkness. Streetlights filtering in from the high windows showed him work tables full of disguises, of half-completed masks and bits of limbs. It seemed to be a dollmaker's studio, devoted to the simulation of life. Galen reached out to brush the back of his hand against the silicone flesh of a mask. He would use this information.

But later.

He stepped up a wheelchair ramp to the door leading to the kitchen. This door was a simple interior lock, easily dispatched with a credit card. The old man should've known better, but time had made him complacent.

Galen slipped across the kitchen, worked his way to the back of the house. Flickering shapes from Lockley's television played in the hallway. He thought he was being silent, but the dog found him halfway down the hall.

The dog, perhaps thirsty for her bowl of water, ambled sleepily into his path. Galen saw she was glossy and fat. Complacent, like Lockley. She blinked and crouched down when she saw Galen, pulling her lips back from her teeth in a growl.

Galen pulled his jacket sleeves down across his knuckles, holding his arms across his body to protect his chest.

"Diana, what is it?" The old man's voice rumbled in the back room.

The dog lunged, teeth digging into Galen's arm. He thrashed the dog against the wall, his free arm twisting into her collar. In his panic, he didn't let go soon enough. He felt his fingers digging into her jaw, the whine of the dog as she let go of his arm. She tried to squirm free, snapping and biting. She sank her teeth into his thigh, and he felt hot blood welling there. But she couldn't pull her teeth free of him. She was like a shark with a piece of meat, only the meat was devouring her. She began to foam at the mouth, thrashing like a fish on a line. A heady swirl of scents and colors invaded Galen's brain. He smelled meat, fear, sweat . . .

Galen stumbled into the bedroom, the dog flailing at his leg. The old man sat up in bed, fumbling in his nightstand for a gun. He lifted it, but didn't have time to aim.

"What do you want?" The old man's hand shook.

"I want what's in your head." Saliva oozed down Galen's chin in a string, and his tongue was too thick to speak around.

Galen slapped the old man's arm away. He grasped his wrist, and the gun clattered to the floor. Norman began to yell. Salivating, Galen reached for the man's throat, possessed by an instinctive urge to rip it out. His fingers plunged into Lockley's flesh, crushing the fragile larynx and wrapping around the tongue that pulsed behind his teeth. His head was suffused by Norman's fear and Diana's terror. It felt like his brain was being trapped in one of Lockley's grotesque, half-finished masks.

Galen bared his teeth and growled.

• • • •

TARA DROVE HOURS TO GET TO THE FARMHOUSE, ARRIVING when the moon had climbed high in the sky. Cassie's cell phone and the line at the farmhouse still rang unanswered. She was infuriated to see lights on at the house and cars parked in the yard when she pulled up the gravel driveway.

She snatched the keys from the ignition, slammed the car door, and stomped up the porch steps into the house. To her right, she saw one of Delphi's Daughters scrubbing the wooden floor and another one repairing a screen. Whispers could be heard in the back room.

"Where is she?" Tara demanded.

The Daughter scrubbing the floor looked down, didn't answer. Tara reached down and grabbed her sleeve, forcing her to look up. "I said, *where is she?*"

"Cassie's gone," the woman said.

When Tara looked down into her scrub bucket, she saw the rusty tinge of blood on the soap bubbles. She smelled spent gunpowder. "Where's the Pythia?"

She smelled the familiar scent of clove cigarettes. Tara wheeled to see the Pythia standing at the foot of the stairs with a cigarette in her hand. She wasn't dressed in her usual feminine skirt and blouse; she was clad in cargo pants and a T-shirt. Her boots were streaked with mud. She smelled like a fresh grave.

"What the hell's going on?" Tara released the woman scrubbing the floor and advanced on the Pythia.

The Pythia regarded her coolly, but Tara could see the worry mark deepening between her eyes. "She's gone. We can't find the cat or the dog, either."

Tara pointed to the stained floor. "What's all that?"

"Cassie shot an intruder. We found him dead on the floor."

Tara's heart hammered. "Where is he now?"

The Pythia shook her head. "He's been taken care of. Buried. No one will ever find him."

Tara believed it. She'd seen Delphi's Daughters dispose of bodies before. "What was he? Military? How did they find her?"

The Pythia shook her head. "It wasn't the military. I sent him here, as a test."

"You *what*?" Tara's eyes were round in incredulity.

The Pythia's red mouth turned downward. "The new Pythia must be capable. She must be strong enough to do what needs to be done."

"You dumped me in the woods when I was twelve to navigate my way out. Was that not test enough for her? You had to see if . . . if she was capable of killing?"

"Yes." The Pythia stared at her cigarette, seeming both cold and weary. "She passed."

Tara doubled up her fist and struck the Pythia in the face. The Pythia didn't flinch, turned back to Tara like some creature from a Terminator movie, not even spitting out her cigarette. Tara could see the swelling already beginning around that meticulously kohled eye. Two of Delphi's Daughters grabbed Tara from behind, keeping her from throwing a second blow.

"Where is she now?" Tara snarled. Damn, that felt good.

The Pythia shook her head. "We don't know."

"How can you not fucking know? You're the god-damn Oracle of Delphi. She's your protégé."

The Pythia's eye was beginning to blacken. One of the Daughters handed her a washcloth full of ice, and the Pythia pressed it to her face. "She hasn't made up her mind, yet." The Pythia sighed. "Tara, I'm truly sorry for this. It didn't come off as I planned. He was a serial child molester. He didn't deserve to live."

"That's not your call."

"Society failed to contain him. I did."

Tara shook her head. There was no arguing about guilt or innocence with the Pythia. "You just planned for her to kill this guy and stick around to tell you about it?"

The Pythia looked at her with her one good eye. "We're searching for her now. I can only ask . . . I can only ask that you help us."

Tara shook herself free of Delphi's Daughters. "I'll look for her. But I'm not going to bring her back to you to turn her into a monster."

The Pythia whispered after her: "My dear, you have no choice in it."

Tara turned on her heel and stomped off down the steps. She slammed into the car, cranked over the engine, and backed out of the driveway at top speed.

What had she been thinking, leaving Cassie alone with that witch? Her knuckles were white on the steering wheel. Cassie had trusted her, and Tara had left her in the care of that . . . that monster. The Pythia had become a myopic slave to her own ends, losing her humanity in the process.

Miles of two-lane country road flashed past before Tara found a place to pull off. This far from civilization, her only company was the sound of crickets and tree frogs, and the quarter moon rising high in the darkness. A forest spread to her left, and a meadow to her right, containing a small pond as still as a forgotten mirror. Fireflies drifted across the landscape.

She stepped from the car, climbed over the guardrail. Tall grasses lashed her legs as she descended down the embankment to the pond reflecting the moon and stars. It was water, a landscape as close as she could find to the one depicted in Cassie's card, the Star.

Tara descended to the edge of the pond. Algae crowded the banks, and bullfrogs sang in the cattails. She started when one launched itself into the water, shattering the surface of the mirror. Tara stomped down some of the tall grasses to make a place to sit at the edge of the pond. Sitting on the scratchy grasses, she arranged herself facing the pond. By the moon and Polaris, she determined that she was facing north. She took out her cards, rifled through them for the Star to focus the reading.

She placed the Star before her, focused all her energy and thoughts on it. "Where's Cassie?"

She took four cards out of the deck, arranging them at the cardinal directions around the significator card. The suits of the cards themselves possessed elemental correspondences: cups were tied to the emotional currents of water, wands to the creative spark of fire, pentacles to the grounding forces of earth, and swords to the intellectual powers of air. Those correspondences were classically tied to the cardinal directions: water to the west, fire to the south, pentacles to the north, and swords to the east.

Perhaps the cards could show her where to start looking.

She turned over the Eight of Wands, depicting a quiver of wands soaring through the air at great speed. It was a card of progress, and it lay in the southern quadrant. The Five of Swords showed a man collecting swords from his defeated and fleeing opponents, and this card was in the east. The Ten of Swords, depicting a woman sitting awake in bed with nightmares and ten swords hanging over her head, was in the west, and the Three of Swords was in the north. It depicted a bloody heart pierced by three swords.

Tara stared at the cards. Cassie was distraught, heartbroken, and was moving quickly. The predominance of swords suggested that she was heading East, and the Eight of Wands suggested that she might be moving a bit south.

Tara touched the Star in the center of the spread. She wished there was some way that she could communicate to Cassie, tell her that she'd been set up, that she could come to Tara. Her fingers tingled.

She thought of the dream-trances she'd experienced while sleeping. Was there a way she might be able to activate that intuition while awake? Tara bit her lip, wished there was someone she could ask about technique. Her mother was dead, and the Pythia was not to be trusted. As always, she was flying by the seat of her pants, hoping not to crash to the ground.

But it was worth trying. Tara crossed her legs before her and placed her hands, palms up, on her knees. She gazed at the Star, feeling the warm summer wind whistling through the grass around her. Slowly, she felt the adrenaline begin to settle out of her veins, and some of the tension in her shoulders slackened. Her eyes began to drift shut, and she focused all her will on finding the Star.

When Tara opened her eyes, she was staring up at the jewel box of stars in the sky.

She'd expected to find herself in the desert, as she had in her previous visions. But there was no soft sand underfoot, no warm glow of sunshine in the sand.

This was somewhere else entirely.

The black forest stretched around her as far as she could see. The sounds of animals scraping and chattering to each other mingled with the whisper of leaves on trees. Locusts buzzed around her, suggesting that the night was still relatively young. Though it was warm enough for humidity to cling to her skin, the scene chilled her. She knew this place. It was the forest the Pythia had left her in when she was a girl, expecting her to navigate her way out.

Tara's hands balled into fists. She was no longer a child; she was an adult. She was not abandoned, as long as she had herself to rely upon. And she would find Cassie and get out of the forest.

Something bumped her leg. Tara looked down to see her companion, the lion, rubbing against her side. He yawned; lions weren't nocturnal creatures. In the darkness, his half-lidded eyes shone with reflected light, like coals. His tail swished sluggishly among the leaves on the forest floor.

Tara found the North Star overhead, spied the crescent moon peeping among the trees. She began to orient herself. Remembering the direction the cards had told her to go, she began to walk east, dipping a bit south. The lion padded after her in the woods. Once or twice, he paused to chase something in a sudden burst of energy, but he always returned to her side, flowing along at the hem of her skirts.

She walked for what seemed like hours, until the forest opened into a field. The field was pierced by the pond she'd seen in reality, grown tall with grasses and thundering with the sound of bullfrogs. At the edge of the pond stood the pale form of a young woman, kneeling to drink from the water.

"Cassie!" Tara shouted.

The girl turned, and Tara ran toward her. Grasses sliced into her skirts and cut her legs, but she ignored them, rushing to the girl's side.

Cassie stood in the shallow water by the cattails, looking at Tara with confusion on her face. Tara grasped her bare shoulders. "Cassie. Where are you?"

The girl looked at Tara with a sense of puzzlement. "I'm not sure. I'm running . . . running . . ." She looked up at the bright stars overhead. Tears shimmered on her face. "I killed a man."

"Listen, Cassie." Tara shook her shoulder. "It's going to be all right. Just tell me where you are."

Cassie shook her head, slinging dark hair around her face. "I don't want them to find me."

"No one's going to find you. You'll be safe with me."

Cassie's eyes were black as pools. "Okay. Okay."

Tara patted her cheek. "Tell me where you are."

Cassie bent to the surface of the water. She scooped up the water with her milk-pale hands, poured it into Tara's. Tara struggled to hold the water in her hands, but it slid between her fingers, leaving behind a stone that glittered like a star.

Tara stared at the diamond in her palm, reflecting moonlight into the darkness. Cassie folded her fingers around it, and Tara could feel its cold heat sparkling throughout her palm. The light glowed red through her skin, as if she'd closed her hands over a flashlight. It burned through her fingers in a white haze that obliterated the darkness of the forest and the pond.

TARA OPENED HER EYES TO STARE INTO A LIGHT THAT shouldn't be there.

She blinked.

She was staring into the eyes of an opossum. He sat on his hindquarters less than a foot from Tara, looking up his long, pale nose at her. His whiskers twitched, and he came back down on all fours. Sniffing the ground, the nocturnal creature shambled away into the grass, his long pink tail dragging behind him.

Tara climbed to her feet, but the opossum had disappeared. She was shivering in the warm summer night. She'd been here long enough for dew to gather on her skin, and her shudders shook the drops off, rattling them into the grass.

Frustrated, she turned to go back to the car. The overhead dome light seemed very bright, and she slammed the door quickly to douse it. She cranked the ignition over and pulled the car back on the road. Teeth chattering, she dialed up the heat as far as it would go.

Her headlights bounced down the country road, and Tara wound her way back to the highway. She kept bearing aimlessly east and slightly south, mulling over her vision of Cassie as the Star. She sensed that Cassie would be willing to come to her, but she wasn't able to puzzle out the meaning of her vision. All she could do was follow the direction the cards had given her, and hope.

The Star was a card of hope, of a bright future. She hoped to hell that the Pythia hadn't destroyed that in Cassie's character with that stupid display of violence. It was a card of light in the darkness, of promise. When the ancient oracles looked overhead at the sky, they saw evidence of a higher design of hope. In their eyes, the stars controlled the paths of all the earthly creatures they surveyed.

More than once, Tara's fingers brushed her cell phone. She debated calling Harry to put out an APB on the girl. But she wasn't sure where that would lead. Cassie was frightened, convinced people were after her. If that prediction were confirmed, she'd be even more difficult to locate. Cassie wasn't stupid; she'd been educated to be a physicist, and she'd trained under the Pythia's Daughters. She could certainly find some way to elude the police.

Tara's foot dragged on the brake when she saw an upcoming road sign, and her heart leapt into her mouth. It said DIAMOND—55 MILES, with an arrow pointing south. Tara clicked on her turn signal to follow the arrow.

Diamond was a little town that had built itself just off the freeway. It had a gas station that was closed at this hour, a post office, and a cluster of houses staggering up a hilltop. Tara's eyes scanned the tiny roads winding up the hillsides. Where to look from here?

She idled at a stoplight, considering, when movement caught her eye. An opossum lumbered across the street in front of her, disappearing down a street to her right. Tara followed it to a Dumpster behind a closed restaurant. A car was parked beside the Dumpster under a streetlight.

Tara's intuition prickled. She parked her car curbside, slowly approached the other car. Overhead, a light buzzed and cast blue light through the partially open window. Breath had fogged the glass, but Tara could see the form of a woman curled up in the driver's seat with a backpack in her arms and a dog's head on her lap. With worried brown eyes, the dog looked up when Tara approached.

"Cassie," Tara said softly, not wanting to frighten her.

The girl jumped, reached for the ignition, but caught sight of Tara. Tears shimmered in Cassie's eyes, and she opened the car door. Launching herself into Tara's arms, she burst into heavy sobs. Tara stroked her hair while Maggie circled around them and Oscar poked his head out of the backpack on the front seat.

Cassie's sobs snagged into incoherent hiccups.

"It's okay," Tara said. And she meant it. She'd figure out some way to make things okay. Somehow.

Chapter Eleven

Harry had worn a hole in the carpet pacing when Tara called him in the early hours of the morning.

"I've got her," she said.

"Is she okay?"

There was a significant pause on Tara's end of the line that told Harry what he needed to know. "She's not hurt."

"Bring her here," Harry told her.

"But it won't take the Pythia long to find out where you live."

"We'll figure something out. Remember, we've got Marshals crawling all over us on this case. She'll be safe here for now, until I can find a better place."

"Make sure it's someplace pet friendly. We've got Maggie and Oscar, too."

Harry didn't ask Tara how she'd found Cassie, or what had happened. He knew Tara was busily working her mysterious magick, making intuitive leaps he couldn't follow. Watching Tara work was like watching her walk across an ice-covered lake. He knew he couldn't follow because the ice would crack under his weight, but she seemed to sense some invisible force where the fissures and solid places were. He felt lost in the face of it, like an observer, hoping she didn't fall through.

When sunlight seeped through his blinds, a knock sounded at the door. Tara stood in the doorway, her face blank and unreadable. Her arm was around Cassie, and Maggie leaned against the girl's other side. Cassie had the glazed look Harry had seen far too often on the faces of soldiers. In World War II, they called it shell shock. In modern times, the sanitized term was PTSD: post-traumatic stress disorder. It was still ugly to see in person.

"Hey, kiddo," Harry said.

She blinked at him. "Uh. Hi, Harry."

Maggie wiggled through the door and threw herself down on the carpet. She began to roll on it in an attitude of doggie relief, as if she'd reached the grass of a summer sanctuary. Cassie trudged through the door, and Tara followed. Harry locked the door behind them. He noticed Tara was carrying a squirming backpack. She set it down on the floor, unzipped it.

Oscar wormed his way out and shot everyone in the vicinity a dirty look. He twisted his head around his back to lick down his mussed-up fur, chagrined at being handled like a sack of potatoes.

Cassie sat rigidly on the couch, her hands around her

knees, fingers laced so tightly together that her knuckles were white.

"Are you girls hungry?" Harry opened the refrigerator, trying to inject a bit of normalcy into the atmosphere. "There's coffee . . . and ketchup."

Cassie shook her head.

Tara smoothed the hair out of the girl's eyes, as if she was a small child. "How about I draw you a bath? Then, you and Oscar and Maggie can take a nap."

Cassie looked up in alarm. "You're not leaving, are you?"

Tara shook her head. "No. I'll be here when you wake up. I promise."

"Okay." Tara led Cassie by the hand down the hallway to the bathroom. Harry heard the running of water and the girls' low voices.

Oscar stretched up to claw at the edge of Harry's shirt. Harry patted the cat's head, and Oscar made a disgruntled *mrrrrr*. Harry rooted around for the broiler pan in the bottom of the oven. He set it beside the refrigerator, in the far corner of the kitchen.

Oscar hopped down off the table to stare at it, meowed loudly.

"I don't have any cat litter."

Oscar gave him a dirty look that indicated that he *would* pee on the carpet, if provoked further. *"Meeeeooooow."* The cat sounded positively plaintive. He'd been riding around in a car inside a backpack for twelve hours. He just wanted to take a piss. Harry could relate.

Obediently, Harry dug through his cupboards. He

found a box of stale oatmeal, dumped it into the pan with a sound like rain. Oscar sniffed at the oatmeal.

"Dude, that's all I've got."

Oscar wrinkled his nose, huffed. He delicately stepped into the makeshift litter box, shoved the oats around. With his back to Harry, ignoring him, the long-suffering cat began to do his business.

Tara returned to the kitchen, watched Oscar scratch around in the maple sugar flavored oats. "Thanks, Harry. For everything."

Harry caught her hand. "What the hell happened?"

Tara pulled up a kitchen chair. "The Pythia happened."

"I thought you said the Pythia wanted Cassie to be her successor," Harry said in a low voice. "Why would she let her get hurt?" He didn't understand the vagaries of Delphi's Daughters, and the more he learned about them, the less he trusted them.

Tara rested her chin in her hand. "The Pythia has odd notions of what constitutes appropriate training for an oracle. A lot of it goes back to the time of Delphi. Then, young women were brainwashed with noxious fumes and fasting to inspire visions and loyalty. Training to be an oracle has always been rough, and I don't agree with the Pythia's methods." Her eyes were unfocused, seeming to see a distant past.

Oscar hopped up on the kitchen table to study Harry's fascinating cat clock. He watched the tail and eyes swish, watched the seconds tick by, entranced.

"What happened?" Harry insisted on knowing.

"The Pythia has been training Cassie in combat. That's

not unusual. But she wanted to see if Cassie would be strong enough to kill." Tara's voice quavered. "That bitch sent a man to attack her at the farmhouse, and she got her wish. Cassie killed him."

Harry rocked back on his heels. Without a word, he reached for his keys on the kitchen counter and grabbed his holster.

"Harry." Tara grabbed his sleeve. "Don't."

Rage boiled in him, an unreasoning rage that he hadn't felt in days, not since he'd beaten the would-be mugger nearly to death. "I'm arresting that bitch."

She shook her head. "It's no use. The body's gone. The Pythia will have covered it all up." Her grip on his wrist was like a vise, and her blue eyes were wide. "Please, Harry, I'm asking you. Don't go there."

"Why are you protecting her?" He blew out his breath in frustration. He didn't understand this infuriating bond she had with this cult, these power-mad women who were clearly out of their minds.

"I'm not protecting her. I'm trying to protect you."

Harry's cell phone chirped, and he grimaced. Glancing at the number, he could see that it was Special Projects. "Li," he snapped at it.

"This is Aquila. You had DOT and Homeland Security looking for a needle in a radioactive haystack."

"Did they find something?"

"To put it mildly. We've got one terminal at Dulles shut down. It's all smeared in cesium and strontium particulates. You'd better get down there and explain what the hell they're looking for."

"Be right there."

Harry snapped his phone shut, looked at Tara. "Will you two still be here when I get back?"

Tara nodded. "As long as you're coming back." Tension was writ all over her face.

Harry blew out his breath. "Okay. I'm coming back."

This time, he meant it.

Dulles was a perfect clusterfuck. Even more so than usual.

Harry elbowed his way through a pissed-off crowd by flashing his creds. Security escorted him through the crowded lines, past the security screening area, where the airport administrator met him. The administrator was a nervous, wiry man dressed in a suit and possessing no sense of humor.

"This shit is smeared all over everything like snot when my kid has a cold." The airport administrator stormed down the crowded corridors with Harry in tow, back to the international arrivals terminal. "International Arrivals is completely shut down. I've got planes stacking up, with nowhere to park them. We're setting up a temporary security area at one of the other terminals, but"—the administrator ducked under some yellow caution tape—"I want to know what the fuck is going on so that I can come up with something to tell the media to get them off my ass."

Past the checkpoint, Harry could see several white-suited men staring into Geiger counter screens like crystal balls. They had DHS—Department of Homeland Security—stamped on the backs of their suits.

The administrator whistled for one of the white suits to come back to them. The suit trundled back to them, and the wearer took the hood down. "It's not bad, really. It's just in a few places."

But the administrator was chewing his lip. "How bad is it? Are we all going to get cancer? Is this a dirty bomb? What's it from?"

"Nobody's gonna get cancer. We're finding a few smears at thirty roentgens per hour. That's about five times the amount of background radiation . . . about what you'd pick up in an X-ray. It's basically harmless. Looks like contact residue. And we don't know what it's from."

Harry shook his head. "We think it's from an irradiated refugee from Chernobyl. Where did you find it?" Harry asked.

The DHS tech handed him a clipboard. "We found it in on the ticket counter, a chair, the men's room. And a whole bunch of other places. This stuff is like talc . . . it smears when one person touches it, then another."

Harry frowned. That made it seem unlikely that prints would be found. "Can you tell how long it's been there?"

"No."

Harry ran back the timeline of the disappearances in his mind. He might not be able to tell for sure when his subject got here, but he knew that he *had* been here. "Can you pull all the passports that went through this terminal from Ukraine and Belarus for the last two months?"

"Yeah." The administrator rubbed his temples. "Do I need to shut down this airport?"

Harry hesitated. "I can't tell you what to do. But I can tell you that we think this guy's dangerous. We don't know what else he's left behind. And if you don't shut down, and something happens, or the press finds out . . ."

The administrator shook his head. "Fuck me."

The DHS tech nodded. "Yeah. You're probably fucked."

HARRY WAS FUCKED. HE KNEW IT WHEN AQUILA WAS waiting for him when he got off the elevator at Special Projects.

"Agent Li," he said frostily. "About that *incident* at Dulles . . ."

Harry swallowed. "I know that our subject was there. We're pulling passports to figure out who he might be."

"Figure this out. Soon." Aquila gave him a look that could shatter steel before he walked away.

Through the glass wall of the conference room, Veriss waved at him. Harry groaned. But there was no use pretending not to see. Veriss stuck his head through the door and called out: "Agent Li, I have some interesting findings for you."

"What've you got? Any new disappearances?" Harry snapped. Veriss had taken over the conference room as his private office: whiteboards were covered with equations and diagrams, and photos of the victims were neatly tacked up on the walls with clear tape. Veriss had probably seen too many cop shows, and Harry considered it all to be for show until proven otherwise.

Veriss bounced up and down on the balls of his feet. "No. But I've combed through all the files of the remain-

ing living Rogue Angel personnel." Veriss showed him
a flip chart covered with names in a tree-like structure.
About a fifth of the names were crossed off. "If I had my
projector, I could show you—"

"Bottom line, Veriss," Harry interrupted.

Veriss pointed to a cluster of about forty names at the
lower end of the chart. "This graph contains the names of
all the known victims, plus a few dozen more. It's like a
large game of Six Degrees of Kevin Bacon."

"What the hell are you talking about?"

"Gerald Frost's secretary was Carrie Kirkman." Veriss
drew an arrow connecting the two with a Magic Marker.
"Carrie Kirkman also worked for Carl Starkweather
from 1991 to 1992." He sketched another arrow. "And
Carl's interpreter was Lena Ivanova. For a social network,
these are pretty strong ties."

"We know this already."

"I was running assignments through the model,
searching for patterns of overlap." Veriss stabbed a key on
his laptop. "I was searching for discrete assignments that
included Frost, Kirkman, Starkweather, and Ivanova. All
of them, at one time, worked on tracking down fuel debris
at Chernobyl."

Harry leaned forward in interest. "Let me see that list."

Veriss punched a key. "There are forty names on the
list."

Harry scanned the list, noted that Norman Lockley
was on it. What the hell did the disguise master have to do
with reactor rods? He didn't entirely trust Veriss's data.
"Why's Lockley here?"

"He helped a couple of scientists who claimed that fuel had been improperly disposed of to defect."

"I thought all the fuel rods were destroyed in the explosion."

"Apparently not. The buildings were scavenged for anything of use, and the other three intact reactors were active for some time afterward. Eventually, they were shut down, and there were some fuel rods that weren't accounted for."

"Did Rogue Angel track down the missing fuel?"

"No, they didn't. They tried, but access was so limited that they were unable to make much headway."

"Give me a hardcopy of this list. We need to re-interview those people."

"Someone stole my printer." Veriss sulked. "I'll have to get someone to print it for me. What are we looking for?"

Harry shook his head. "Veriss, you're not going to be interviewing anyone. Get these people rounded up to bring in here for questioning. If there are any who aren't under protective custody by the Marshals, get them under it."

Veriss opened his mouth to protest. It was clear he thought this administrative work was beneath him.

"Just do it, Veriss," Harry said. He wasn't in the mood to deal with Veriss's fragile ego. He banged out of the conference room before Veriss could argue.

Jesus Christ. Harry rubbed the back of his neck. He never thought he'd be at the point in life where he was blowing off NCTC intelligence and more interested in the predictions of a deck of cards. No matter what happened, it seemed that he—and science—were one step behind Tara.

He reached for the door handle at the forensics unit, noticed a yellow sticky note stuck to the door with a hand-drawn radiation symbol. The note said: *Radiation Danger: Knock First.*

Harry rapped his knuckles against the glass, and Anderson popped out from beneath a counter. She was swathed in a white Tyvek suit, but no face mask. She unlocked the door for him and waved Harry in.

"Do I need one of those?" He gestured at her suit.

"Nah." Anderson waved him off. "You're not gonna spend all day with this stuff. And our samples are breaking down, anyway. They'll be in the lead-lined garbage can soon."

Harry's brows drew together. "What do you mean, they're breaking down?"

"Check this out." Anderson punched a keyboard protected with a clear plastic sleeve. On closer inspection, Harry realized that it was a plastic zipper bag from the grocery store. Harry hoped that was to protect it from coffee spills, but he was skeptical. A monitor flickered to life, and Anderson pointed at a purple-tinted series of lines and dashes.

"What am I looking at?"

"This is an image of the DNA of the unknown subject we got from Carrie Kirkman's clothes, the day we took it." She clicked a mouse sealed in a plastic baggie, and the image was replaced by a similar one that resembled broken bits of string. "This is the same slide today. The DNA has degraded to the point that it's useless."

"That's not supposed to happen. Did the radiation do that?"

"We don't know if it's the cause or a side effect. Same story with the DNA from the scenes of the other disappearances." Anderson clicked through a series of slides. Even a layperson like Harry could see the strings broken and bleeding together. "The DNA of your unknown subject is . . . dissolving."

Harry leaned forward on the counter to stare at the monitor. He thought better of it, brushed imaginary radiation from his sleeve. "What does this mean?"

Anderson pursed her lips. "I think . . . I think it means that your unknown subject is dying."

GALEN HAD ALWAYS KNOWN THAT HE WAS DYING.

They'd told him this since he was a child, but the fact seemed insignificant to him. Remote. Irrelevant.

He remembered sitting on the edge of a cold steel examination table at the Minsk Children's Hospital. Try as they might, the doctors were unable to find anything wrong with him. Unlike the other residents of Minsk Children's Home Number One, Galen was physically perfect. His growth was normal. No tumors erupted from his skin. His thyroid levels were textbook.

A doctor finished feeling the lymph nodes in his neck with cold hands. The doctor scribbled down something in his charts. "Good, good," he muttered. He glanced at the nurse standing beside the drafty window. "Are you sure he's one of the Chernobyl children?"

"He is," the nurse said. "His mother was a nurse who

treated the firefighters who put the reactor fire out. She died right after the accident."

The doctor peered through his square-framed glasses. "And the father?"

"Unknown. But he's a very good boy." The nurse smiled at him. Galen gave a small smile back. He liked the nurses. They always seemed hurried, and tired, but they actually spoke to him as if he existed. The one in the room with him now, Anna, always sneaked him an extra piece of fruit when he was brought in to see the doctor. It was a different doctor every time, but they always said the same thing.

The doctor scribbled something in his chart. "Doesn't matter. He's dead anyway, like the rest of them."

But Galen knew he was different from the others. The nurse got him dressed and walked him back through the hallways of the hospital that smelled like piss and bleach and winter. Children were kept here until they were old enough to go to the asylum. The worst of the worst went there: the ones who had no idea where they were, who weren't able to interact with the world at all. Many simply screamed, their cries echoing from the ward. Yes, these would be going to the asylum, if they survived long enough. Many times, they didn't. Galen stared unashamedly at a child being led by the hand down the hall. He wore a hospital gown, barefoot, with his head shaved. The boy had no eyes, just scarred sockets, but at least he was quiet.

"Don't listen to the doctor," the nurse said, kneeling down to straighten Galen's shabby collar. She kissed his cheek, and she reminded him very much of his mother. His mother always told him that he was special.

"You are different from the others," the nurse said, pressing an apple into his palm. "You are one of the lucky ones."

Galen didn't feel particularly lucky, but the nurse's hope was often contagious. He hurried to eat his apple before they made it back to his bunk at the Children's Home. He didn't want the others to see the apple and take it away from him.

Galen had lived in Minsk Children's Home Number One since his mother died. His mother had been a nurse, too. He thought later that perhaps this was what merited him some of the extra treatment. When the firefighters had been burned trying to put out the fires at Chernobyl, his mother had left in the middle of the night to give first aid. She'd kissed him on the head and gone to help, leaving Galen in the predawn darkness, listening to the Pripyat sirens. She'd come back the next day, exhausted and smelling like metal. She'd lain down on their bed and Galen had curled up beside her, listening to her breathing. She did this every day for a few days, went out to help the men, ignoring the evacuation. They called the men trying to clean up the mess "liquidators." The first time he'd heard the term had been from his mother. He remembered her eyes, wide and haunted, her face pink with the kiss of what he thought was sunburn. She would hold him close to her heart and cry. On the seventh day, she just stopped breathing. Galen had been sleeping with his ear to her chest, and he thought he heard it happen, that soft sigh that simply disappeared.

But he was "lucky." Luckier than the children in the asylum, who would never leave. Like his mother, they would simply disappear. And many of the children in Minsk Children's Home Number One would disappear, too. Galen had known some of the children when he had lived in Pripyat. These children had gone out with him to play in the black rain. Then, they had laughed and splashed and smeared the black mud on each other's shirts. Piotr and Nicholas, who had lived next door with their sister, Sophie, had run their trucks through the mud that smelled like metal, pretending to be soldiers.

No more. Sophie was dead. Piotr's limbs twisted as he grew to grotesque proportions. His right foot was as long as his forearm, the rest of his limbs spindly as matchsticks. The right hand he'd used to dig his toy truck out of the puddles was swollen and pink, fingers twisted like a tree root. Piotr knew that he would lose that hand any day, hid it under the blankets so that the nurses would perhaps forget about it, and no one would come after him to cut it off.

Nicholas, bald and pale, sat on the edge of his bed, without the energy to swing his feet. Dark circles smudged under his eyes, and Galen could see blue veins in his scalp. Nicholas had cancer. Galen didn't know what kind. When he asked Nicholas what kind, the boy would just point to his head. Nicholas never spoke anymore.

But Nicholas and Piotr were like Galen. Orphans of Chernobyl. They were different from the children in the asylum. Nicholas and Piotr and Galen knew they were dying. With Nicholas and Piotr, the degradation could be seen.

But Galen was lucky. He had a bit of hope. He had a bit of hope that he would grow up, that he would have the opportunity to get out of this place. One of the nurses who'd lost her own child was even teaching him how to read on her cigarette breaks, a sure sign someone believed in his future. As he grew older, that benign fate of his made him furious. He watched as Nicholas and Piotr and the other boys and a few of the nurses at the Children's Home vanished. Just like his mother. And the world still moved on. And so did he.

But the doctor's words still rang in Galen's head. He didn't know how he could escape the death sentence handed down to all of them. Like the weight of rain in the sky, he knew he couldn't run from it forever.

But he was determined to make the most of the time he had left. And he wouldn't be alone.

In the shadow of Norman Lockley's house he limped, peering through the blinds at the bored Marshals doing a crossword puzzle on the curb. Once or twice, they'd knocked on the door, and Galen had answered them in Norman's voice. The cells of his body, still working hard to overcome Norman's atrophied muscles, had allowed him to walk, at last. But he still kept the timbre of Norman's voice and part of his lumpy profile. Galen felt his mouth full of sharp teeth, spat one out in the kitchen sink. He picked it up, marveling at it. It was a canine tooth that had belonged to the dog, but laced with the base metal of one of Lockley's fillings. He could feel the dog's primal concerns in his head, a bass note to the wealth of Lockley's information that flooded his brain. Galen opened the refrigerator and stuffed some lunch meat in his mouth to keep the voice of the dog quiet, so he could listen to Lockley.

Lockley had what he wanted. Lockley suspected the location of the remainder of the Chernobyl fuel rods. If he could just keep everything together until . . .

The doorbell rang. Galen limped to the door to peer through the peephole.

It wasn't one of the Marshals. It was more prey.

Galen licked his lips.

Chapter TWELVE

CASSIE HAD eventually fallen asleep, her arms wound tightly around Maggie. Tara lay beside her with Oscar jammed into her armpit, purring like a chainsaw. She hadn't bothered to call the Pythia; Tara decided the Oracle could figure out what had happened on her own. Or not. Tara felt it would be a long time before she would feel like having a civil conversation with the Pythia again. Maybe not ever. She felt her hands balling into fists whenever she thought of the Pythia. Damn, but it had felt good to slug the witch.

She dozed, slipped into a dream.

In her dream, the desert was giving way to scrub forest. The sandy soil underfoot had melted into glass. Tara's lion padded beside her, sniffed at a stand of black grass. The sky overhead was a threatening red, and a warm breeze tangled in Tara's skirts. Grains of sand rattled on the cracked, shiny ground.

Tara looked up. The silhouette of a black tower blocked out part of the sky, the Tower from the Tarot. There was no light inside, but Tara could smell fire and ash. Pine trees grew warped around the foundations of the building, reaching at odd angles with needles fanned like brooms.

A figure was walking toward the building, one she recognized: the figure from the World. Instead of being swathed in the white robes depicted in the card, the Sacred Androgyne was wrapped in a black sheet. The figure walked barefoot across the ground, and he left bloody footprints where the glass cut his feet. Now, he looked decidedly masculine, though the laurel leaves around his temples were wilted and dried out.

Thunder and lightning crackled overhead. Tara called out to the figure. The World turned, cast a cold, gray gaze at her, before continuing into the shadow of the Tower.

Rain plinked down from the sky. Tara held out her hands, felt an oily blackness spattering over her skin. It was the black rain from Chernobyl. It buzzed when it touched her skin, as if it had been electrified.

Tara picked up her skirts to run, to chase the retreating World into the shadow of the building. The dark sheet melted seamlessly into the carbon-black of the Tower, which she discovered was hewn of bits of sheet metal riveted with lead. Tara's fingers scrabbled around the seams, searching for a way in. But she could find no door.

The lion growled beside her, staring up with his glowing amber eyes. Tara followed his gaze, saw the blackened figure of the World silhouetted at the top of the Tower against the red sky. Lightning crackled around him. Tara could feel the buzz of it under her feet, and the hair on the back of her neck stood up.

He was going to jump.

Tara screamed at him to stop. Her voice was obliterated by the crash of lightning as it raced along the ground and struck an antenna on the top of the building. She saw the World falling into that rain-spangled blackness like a falling star.

Her breath snagged in her throat, and she ran to the burning form on the ground. But it did not burn as a body should—the World burned with a heat so intense that it sizzled the rain from her face, drove her back. The form on the ground burned like molten steel, red and white, with raindrops sparking on it. It burned so hot it sank into the ground like an ember.

She knew that there was nothing she could do to save it. Tara could do nothing but watch as the World burned.

Tara woke up, heart stuck like a cold stone in her throat.

Oscar was spread on her chest, trying to keep her from shivering. Tara sat up and extricated herself from the blankets, wrapping her frozen fingers in the cat's fur. Trying not to awaken Cassie, she padded out of the bedroom and closed the door. The cat clock on the kitchen wall showed her that she'd slept through the day and most of the night. Dawn was beginning to redden the horizon. She rubbed her cold arms, plucking at a note on the kitchen table:

Came by to check on you. Didn't want to wake you. Went back to work. Call me if you need me.—H

She glanced over at the couch. Harry must have gotten some sleep here; a wadded-up blanket was kicked over one arm. The manila files that had been spread over the floor were missing.

Without Harry to keep her warm, she settled for the next best thing: a hot shower. She stood under the scalding water, trying to chase the frost from her skin. Her fingernails and toenails had turned black and blue under the chill of the dream. This dream had been more intense than the others; she could still taste the metallic rain in her mouth. She ran the hot water tank cold before she got out. She put her clothes for an extra spin in Harry's dryer before she got dressed and put some coffee on to brew.

She found Harry's television remote buried under a cushion, clicked the TV on. The early news announced that Dulles airport was closed. Tara squinted at the footage of pissed-off travelers, thought she saw some Department of Homeland Security jackets in the background. The newscaster, standing in front of the flight drop-off area, was telling the audience, ". . . low levels of radiation have been detected in the international arrivals terminal. DHS tells us that the radiation levels are benign, but that cleanup will take a few hours. The airport will be reopened then."

The announcer stuck her microphone in the face of a gray man in glasses. The banner at the bottom of the screen indicated that this was the airport administrator. "We do not suspect terrorist activity at this time. We're merely exercising caution. All flights have been rerouted, and we're doing our best to get travelers on their way . . ."

Tara hit the mute button and reached for the phone to call Harry. "This thing at Dulles, is that you?"

Harry groaned over the phone. "Yeah, that's us. We think it's residue from when our subject entered the country, but we've gotta play it safe."

Tara sighed in sympathy. This kind of incident was the kind that could ruin someone's career. She just hoped it wasn't Harry's.

"How's Cassie?"

"Sleeping." She didn't know what else to say, at this point.

"Listen, about our unknown subject . . ." Harry began.

"He's dying," Tara said automatically. Behind her closed eyes, she could see the body burning into the earth.

"Damn. You're good. Forensics says his DNA is degrading at an accelerated rate."

"I think he's going to pull something before he goes. Something big."

"We're narrowing down the list of suspects. I've got FAA pulling passports and Veriss has narrowed down the list of ex-operatives to re-interview. We think all of them worked on finding some missing fuel rods at Chernobyl."

"Okay. I'll let you know when I get something else."

"By the way, I've got a couple of Marshals heading over there in a couple of hours to take you to a safe house. I've told them that Cassie's a relative of one of the agents on our watch list. I'll catch up with you as soon as I can."

"Thanks." Tara hung up. She stared at the receiver, feeling like she was a step behind.

"What's going on?"

Cassie peered out of the hallway. Her hair was mussed with sleep, but her eyes were wide with anxiety.

"I talked with Harry. He's going to be sending some Marshals over in a while to move us."

Cassie's fingers gnawed the hem of her T-shirt. "Where are we going?"

"I don't know," Tara admitted. "But I think it'll be somewhere close. Harry said he'd catch up with us when he could."

"Okay, but"—Cassie gestured to the talking heads on the television—"what's *really* going on?"

Spoken like a true oracle. Tara debated how much to tell her about what was happening, decided that it would be good for the girl to have something else to focus on. "Harry and I are chasing a Chernobyl refugee who's responsible for the disappearances of some intelligence agents. He's been selling their secrets."

Cassie sat down on the couch. "That's what my star chart meant."

"Yes." Tara watched the emotions flicker across the girl's face.

The girl blew out her breath. "Is there anything I can do to help? I mean, I'm not . . . really good at this yet, or anything . . ."

Tara smiled. It would be good to get the girl outside of

herself. Maybe she was more resilient than she thought. "Tell me what the stars have to say."

"Can I cheat and use my computer?"

"You can do anything you want."

Cassie dug through her bag for her laptop, booted it up. The screen glowed blue against her wan face, and she began tapping away at the keyboard. "Okay. This is what the sky looks like for us, right now, behind the blue in a transient chart." She turned the screen to Tara. A circular pie was divided up into the twelve astrological houses, with arcane markings within those pieces of pie. "I'm worried about this." She pointed to a series of symbols.

"What's that?"

"Pluto. It's still hanging out in retrograde, which bothers me, and it will be, for some time. The chart's nearly identical to the chart for Chernobyl."

"Are you thinking that such a disaster could happen here?" Tara thought of the Tower.

"I hope not. There are some differences, though. This is Chiron, the comet, and it's also in retrograde." Cassie pointed to a notation on the chart that looked like a key. "Chiron is the 'wounded healer,' and it's hanging out in Scorpio. It represents a tie to the past, attempting to resolve or assimilate old wounds. In mythology, Chiron was half man, half beast. He sacrificed his life to allow mankind to save Prometheus and allow mankind to use fire."

"Assimilate," Tara echoed. She paused, thinking of the World card. "Hold that thought." She went to get her cards, fished out the World to set it before her. "This is the card I've been associating with our unknown subject."

"Eh. Like the song goes, 'Dude looks like a lady.'"

"Yeah. Maybe he is literally both male and female." The light of intuition began to shine in Tara's eyes. She felt like she was on the right track. "We keep finding multiple sets of DNA at the sites of the disappearances. He's assimilating the others, somehow. Absorbing them and their secrets."

"The moon is in the house of Scorpio," Cassie confirmed. "That's the house of secrets."

Tara pulled the Moon card from her deck, showing the serene moon goddess shining over the land. In Tarot, this was the card of deception. The card she'd associated with Norman Lockley. Her intuition buzzed in the back of her head; this felt significant. She reached for the phone, dialed Harry's number. Before he could say anything, she blurted:

"Harry, I think you need to check on Norman Lockley."

VERISS DIDN'T APPRECIATE BEING SIDELINED BY BLUNT instruments like Agent Li, people who had no understanding or appreciation for his talents. Li was giving him busy work, not giving him credit for what he knew, and what he could discover. Agents could be like that, whether in NCTC, Special Projects, or any other division. They could be arrogant, single-minded, and threatened by knowledge. People feared what they didn't understand.

But Veriss would make them understand. He wouldn't let Li take credit for his leads. Veriss was tired of being "support personnel," of serving behind the scenes while men like Li took the credit for being heroes. Li was busy with that airport debacle, wouldn't notice if Veriss vanished for a couple of hours.

Veriss stood on Norman Lockley's doorstep, rang the bell. He'd crack this case wide open, show them his value.

The doorbell echoed inside the house. Veriss glanced back at the Marshals eating cheeseburgers in their car on the curb. They'd waved him on when he'd shown them his credentials. Veriss didn't get to show his creds nearly often enough, and he enjoyed displaying them. "Give him a few minutes," one of them had told him. "The old guy's slow."

Veriss waited. He heard scraping and shuffling inside. Impatiently, he rang the bell again, rocking back and forth on the balls of his feet and his heels. He was eager to start questioning the guy. Was the guy in the can? What was taking him so long?

The door opened a crack, and Veriss looked down. In shadow, he saw Norman's profile. The old man was in a wheelchair. No wonder it took him so long.

"Norman Lockley?"

"Yes." The old man's voice sounded like gravel in a can.

Veriss pressed his shiny National Counterterrorism Center credentials up against the screen. "Sam Veriss, NCTC. Can I come in and ask you some questions?"

The old man hesitated. Veriss heard the squeak of a wheelchair as the man moved away from the door into shadow.

"Come in," he said. "And shut the door behind you."

The air conditioner was cranked up very, very cold. And all the blinds were drawn in Lockley's house. Veriss's eyes took a moment to adjust to the darkness, sun shadows dazzling his vision. He turned to close the door.

"Could you lock it, please?" the old man asked weakly. "A person in my condition can't be too careful."

"Of course." Veriss glanced at the old man. Lockley's back was to him, wheeling away. The old man wore a blanket around him like a shroud. Bizarre, in summer.

Veriss flipped the deadbolt shut. The sound was deafening in the air-conditioned silence of Lockley's house. No television was on, no radio. Just the sterile hum of the air conditioner and the refrigerator.

Lockley squeaked away into the kitchen. Veriss followed the frail old man, taking his notebook out of his pocket. His list of questions covered the paper from right margin to left. He hoped he'd left enough room to fill in the answers. He clicked his ballpoint pen, scanning the list. He was excited by the prospect of being in the field, of collecting data straight from the source.

"What is it that you do for NCTC?" Lockley asked conversationally. His pronunciation was awkward, as if his dentures were loose.

"I'm an intelligence analyst. I work on analyzing patterns in data networks and predicting future results."

"Interesting. I imagine you see many different things in your work."

"Lots of data. Not to brag, but I'm one of the foremost experts in my field."

"Wonderful." The old man's enthusiasm seemed genuine. "Just wonderful. I'd love to know what you know."

Veriss smiled, pushed his glasses up the bridge of his

nose. "Mr. Lockley, I'd like to ask you about your time with Project Rogue Angel. Some data anomalies have shown up in my analysis. Did you work on recovering the fuel rods from the Chernobyl site?"

"I did."

"Our files indicate that the recovery efforts were unsuccessful. Do you have any theories about what may have happened to them?"

The old man chuckled. "Several."

Veriss looked up from his paper to see Lockley standing before his wheelchair. *Standing.* Before he could react, Lockley lunged forward, thrusting Veriss against the kitchen wall. A spice rack crashed down, the bottles rattling and splitting against the floor with the sweet smell of cinnamon. Veriss flailed in the old man's grip, which was shockingly strong around his throat. He only succeeded in tearing down a corner of the curtains covering the sliding glass door to the patio, startling birds. Daylight penetrated the dark house.

Veriss struggled to breathe against the hands wrapped around his throat. In the light, he could see there was something wrong about the old man. The old man's lips pulled back in a snarl, and Veriss could see a jumbled collection of pointed teeth. Panicked, Veriss clawed at the old man's face. His fingers dug into Lockley's skin . . . and the skin peeled away. Veriss registered that it wasn't real skin . . . It was a mask. Beneath the smooth silicone surface, an uneven mass of lumpy skin was underpinned with warped cheekbones and a melted nose.

Veriss cried out, but the hands around his throat closed

inward. He could feel them digging into his skin, trying to steal his breath. But that wasn't all he could feel them stealing. He could feel those fingers worming into his brain, chewing into his thoughts and rapaciously digesting what they found. All that data he'd carefully collected, all the formulas, all the obscure facts that he'd drawn connections to . . . it was being devoured by this monster. He could feel those fingers sifting through the facts, his memories, his emotions, like a librarian sifting through an old-fashioned card catalog.

The monster drew him into an embrace. Veriss could feel his information, his life force, pouring into the creature. Blood began to gush from Veriss's nose.

I'd love to know what you know. The words didn't come out of the monster's twisted mouth, but Veriss still heard them rattling around the broken synapses of his brain.

HARRY LEANED ON LOCKLEY'S DOORBELL AGAIN. NO ANSWER. He glowered at the dark windows, tapping his foot and jingling the change in his pocket. He had to get back to the airport or Aquila would have his ass in a sling. His boss wouldn't appreciate him doing the bureaucratic equivalent of poking a hive of bees with a stick and running away.

He glanced back at the curb and the U.S. Marshals waved at him from their car. They'd told him that Veriss had gone in to see the old man a few hours ago. Veriss's rental car was still parked in the driveway. Harry was furious. Veriss had no business questioning a source without Harry's say-so. He imagined Veriss and Lockley in the garage, playing with Lockley's disguises. As soon as he got hold of him, Harry was going to jerk a knot in Veriss's tail, send him back to Langley with Harry's shoe jammed up his ass.

Harry stabbed the doorbell again.

Irritated, he strode down the wheelchair ramp and circled around the back of the house. Maybe the old man hadn't heard the bell ringing. Veriss had no doubt heard it and was just being an ass.

Harry clomped through the ornamental shrubs, disturbing some mulch. The old man's bird feeders were arranged on the patio. Startled by Harry's approach, a goldfinch flew away in a rattle of thistle seeds. The feeders were almost empty. The air conditioner was running at high power, leaking water out over the edge of the patio. Harry paused before the sliding glass door. The curtains were drawn, but for one side, where a panel dangled from the rod.

His eyes narrowed. A sign of a struggle.

His hand rested lightly on his gun as he crept to the back of the garage. The door was shut, but the knob was gone from the door. Harry's pulse quickened, and he drew his weapon.

Tara had been right. Something bad was going down at Lockley's house.

Harry gently pushed the garage door open. A wave of frigid air conditioning hit him. Harry listened, heard nothing. He swung inside the shade of the garage, gun lifted.

Lockley's workshop had been tossed. The cupboard

doors stood open, their contents spilling out on the floor. Masks and bits of latex had been knocked around, and brushes were strewn on the surfaces of Lockley's tables. Harry scanned the half darkness. There was no telling in this jumble of materials what was missing and what remained. Broken bottles of paint and fixative gave the air an acrid odor. Harry knelt on the floor. The mixtures were half dry. This tumult had been recent. And frantic.

Harry opened the kitchen door. The refrigerator and the air conditioner hummed. Sweat freeze-dried on Harry's palms, wrapped around the butt of the gun. It had to be in the fifties in here. The last time Harry had entered a house with the air conditioning this low, it had been full of bodies. The assailant had turned up the AC to keep them from decomposing quickly.

Harry's nose twitched. He smelled cinnamon and spices from a broken spice rack. The kitchen had been tossed. A wall of decorative clocks behind the kitchen table had been smashed. Lockley's wheelchair was parked beside the kitchen table, but the old man wasn't inside.

"Lockley?" he called out. If Lockley were still here, injured, Harry was sure that he was armed. No use risking being shot. If an assailant was here, he'd have to get past Harry to escape through the back, or get through the front door and expose himself to the Marshals. If they were even awake. "Veriss?" he said, as an afterthought.

No one answered. Harry edged through the kitchen. No dog came bounding up to him. The kitchen curtains were torn, allowing only a dim shaft of light to penetrate the gloom. Over the sight of his gun, he peered into the empty living room, down the hallway. He nudged the doors open, one by one, checked under the beds and in the closets.

No Lockley. No Veriss. No Diana. Just blood.

Harry snatched his cell phone out of his pocket to call for backup. Maybe when more cars rolled into the driveway, the Marshals would wake up.

He only hoped that the Marshals he'd sent to hide Cassie and Tara were more alert than these.

Chapter Thirteen

The Marshals Harry sent weren't what Tara had expected.

Tara stared through the peephole of Harry's door at the two figures standing in the shade of the entryway. The man on the right was only slightly taller than Tara, a beer belly distending the stylized pattern of hibiscus flowers on his Hawaiian shirt. He wore a ginger-colored beard and sunglasses. The man on the left was tall, lanky, clean-shaven. A cowboy hat shaded his eyes, and he crossed his arms over a corduroy jacket obscuring the bulge of a gun. Both of the men seemed a bit long in the tooth for this to be their first rodeo.

"Hold your creds up to the door," Tara insisted, her fingers sweating on the pistol at her hip.

The man in the Hawaiian shirt flipped his ID out of his back pocket, shrugged. He held it up to the peephole.

Tara couldn't make out much through the fish-eye view, but it looked authentic enough. The lamination was yellowed and cracked with age.

"Now him."

The Cowboy rolled his eyes and reached into his jacket pocket. Reflexively, Tara flinched at the gesture. He pressed his creds close to the fish-eye. He wasn't wearing a hat in his cred photo.

The Kahuna said: "Harry Li sent us. He said that you play a mean game of cards. You, uh, a poker player?"

Tara smirked at the inside joke Harry had planted for her. "Not lately."

These guys looked like the C-Team. No wonder, since Harry had rustled up every other Marshal in the district to babysit ex-spies. Whoever they were, at least they weren't Delphi's Daughters. The Pythia would never suffer men with such questionable fashion sense.

Tara's fingers worked loose the deadbolt lock and loosened the safety chain. She tucked her pistol back in her holster and opened the door. Maggie stuck her nose through the door first. The dog sniffed over the two men like an anteater searching for snacks. Apparently satisfied that she smelled no sign of Delphi's Daughters on them, Maggie turned around and let them into the apartment.

The Kahuna's sandals slapped on the carpet. He gave her a big grin and stuck his hand out. "Hi. I'm Steve Barney."

Tara took his hand. "Tara."

He pumped her hand. "Nice to meet you."

The Cowboy stood in the doorway and nodded. He

scanned the area behind the entryway before crossing the threshold and closing the door behind him.

Kahuna Steve jabbed a thumb over his shoulder at the Cowboy. "That's Steve, too. Steve Moss. Don't mind him. He's pretty quiet."

"Both you guys are named Steve?" Tara lifted a dubious eyebrow.

"Yeah." The Kahuna shrugged. "It happens. There's a team of guys on one Fugitive Investigative Strike Team I worked with who were all named Jeff. They all went by code names to keep things straight."

"You guys don't look like Marshals." In the hallway, Cassie stood with her arms crossed, voicing Tara's thoughts.

"That's the idea, kiddo." The Kahuna made a pistol-bang gesture with his hand and winked.

Cassie froze. Tara saw her knuckles whiten where they were wrapped around her elbows. Tara crossed the room and put her arm around the girl's shoulders. "Let's get your things together." Cassie nodded and scurried back down the hallway to gather up her meager possessions.

The Steves were trading glances. The Cowboy gestured at Cassie with his chin. "The girl's gun-shy." His voice was like gravel.

Tara put her hands in her pockets. "Yeah. Is that a problem?" She didn't elaborate further. This was none of their business.

The Kahuna scratched one of his sideburns. "I hope not."

Tara's eyes narrowed. "What do you mean?" Her voice crackled out with more hostility and force than she'd intended.

The Kahuna put his square hands before him, palms up, in a placating gesture. "Look, we were told that the girl's a relative of a shop guy that had disappeared. And that you work with Harry Li."

Tara stared at the mirrors of his sunglasses, stubbornly refused to answer him.

The Kahuna glanced at the pistol concealed under the hem of Tara's shirt. "Looks like you can take care of yourself. And the little one."

"Do you usually ask so many questions?" Tara lifted an eyebrow.

"No, ma'am." The Kahuna shook his head. "Steve and I haven't been on assignment for a while . . . just trying to get the lay of the land," he admitted.

Tara's mouth softened. "She's the most important person in the world to me, okay? I just need her to be safe." She didn't tell them that, as the future Pythia, she might be *the* most important person in the world, period.

The Kahuna nodded. "Where we're going, I don't think that'll be a problem."

Cassie came down the hallway with her shoes on and bag slung over her shoulder. She dragged Oscar out from under the table and tried to stuff him into the backpack. The cat yowled and squirmed, anticipating another long car ride. The Cowboy took Oscar from her and whispered something to the cat. The cat stopped struggling long enough for him to put the cat in the bag and zip him up.

Tara was impressed.

"Steve's good with animals," the Kahuna explained. "Used to work on a farm as a kid."

Tara wondered how the Kahuna had managed to elicit that information from him. She hoisted her suitcase. Inside, she heard the clink of pet dishes against Oscar's makeshift oven pan litterbox.

The Steves made no other comment about the animals coming with them. The Cowboy took point, leading the way out the door. Maggie trundled behind him, and Tara and Cassie behind the dog. The Kahuna took the rear. Tara could see that, once they were in open air, the men constantly scanned the steps, the parking lot, old habits settling over them. Their hands were loose at their sides like gunslingers in old action films.

Tara smiled. She understood old habits died hard. They became like muscle memory, reflexes that were summoned out of any retirement the brain forced upon them.

The Cowboy led them to a hulking beast taking up two parking spaces. A late-seventies model Ford Bronco sprawled like a brown dinosaur on the fresh macadam. The Cowboy paced around the car, checking for sabotage or door dings, Tara wasn't sure which.

"Company car?" Tara murmured.

"Personal car," the Kahuna said. He popped the door open and ushered the women and Maggie into the backseat while the Cowboy paced the perimeter. It took a hop for Tara to get in, and her jeans squeaked on the back bench seat as she piled in with Cassie. Cassie pulled her feet away from the shotgun on the floorboards as if it was poison, stared out the side window.

The Cowboy slid behind the wheel, banging the door shut behind him. The Kahuna climbed in on the passenger side. The engine started up with a deafening roar, and the Bronco backed out of the parking lot.

"I didn't even know that you could still get parts for these things," Tara shouted over the diesel growl of the engine as it pulled onto the highway.

"EBay," the Cowboy said succinctly.

"They don't build tanks like this anymore," the Kahuna laughed. "This thing has the hide of a rhinoceros." He patted the dashboard, which shone with a glossy coat of Armor All. Tara noted that there was a fracture in the upper left part of the dash that might have come from a bullet hole, but did not mention it to Cassie.

The Bronco rumbled down the freeway for a few dozen miles. Traffic thinned a bit the further south they drove, away from DC and into Virginia. The HOV lanes disappeared, and the Bronco exited on a suburban off-ramp. Strip malls, gas stations, and video stores dotted the landscape.

"Where are we going?" Tara asked.

"You know that we're really not supposed to tell you," the Kahuna admonished. "But, seeing as we're almost there . . ."

"Already?" Tara lifted an eyebrow.

"We're local yokels," the Kahuna explained, as the Bronco tooled down a side street. "The official safehouses are all full with the other relics of ex-spies. Since Agent Li specified that you needed pet-friendly digs, we thought we'd take you home with us."

The Bronco pulled down a side street in the commercial district, into a gravel lot. A two-story brick building was decorated with a sign that said STEVE'S MILITARY SUR-PLUS AND FIREWORKS in block lettering. A smaller sign in the door festooned with iron bars said that it was CLOSED—PLEASE COME AGAIN. The exterior of the building had been painted over in a mural depicting an American flag, the Statue of Liberty, and a saluting cartoon soldier. Tara's eyes flitted to the second floor, where there was a balcony holding a gas barbecue grill. One—or both—of the Steves must live above the surplus store.

"That is, if that's okay with you," the Kahuna said, casting a glance through the rearview mirror at Cassie.

Cassie swallowed and nodded, but didn't say anything. Tara squeezed her hand.

The Steves parked around the delivery entrance to the store. The Cowboy unloaded the women's belongings, while Maggie scrambled out of the car to sniff the dandelions growing in random patches in the parking lot. The Kahuna unlocked the steel door and motioned them inside.

"Home sweet home," he announced, flicking on the overhead lights.

The surplus store smelled of mothballs and gunpowder. Racks of camouflage clothing stood on the floor. The walls were decorated with POW-MIA and American flags, gas masks, hats and patches, plus racks of guns with chains run through them. Green ammo boxes were stacked up against the walls. Merchandise bins held gloves, ski masks, and bundles of socks. Glossy glass cases held what looked like grenades. Tara hoped they weren't live.

Beside her, Cassie stiffened. Her gaze was fixed on the handguns behind the case and the targets pinned up on the walls. Tara heard her breath gone shallow, slipped her hand in hers. The girl's grip was cold and clammy.

"Don't mind the décor. This way," the Kahuna said, pointing up a series of steps.

The women followed the Kahuna up the steps to a metal security door, while the Cowboy stayed behind to lock up. The door banged open to reveal a beautiful industrial loft. The building had been gutted, down to the brick exterior walls. Pipes and ductwork gleamed overhead, lit by skylights set into the flat roof. Sunlight streamed down onto wood floors, illuminating a galley kitchen, a massive leather sectional, and built in shelving that held a television and scores of books. Tara glanced at the titles. Mostly military history, small arms pricing guides, and auto repair manuals.

The Kahuna led them down a hallway constructed of what looked like recycled corrugated steel. Bits of stamping and tool marks could still be seen in the metal. The walls stopped some ten feet off the floor, with light streaming in glass partitions above. Tara squinted at the glass, which had a slightly blue tint, and realized they were windshields from old cars, suspended on wires like transoms.

"Wow . . . this place is amazing," Tara said.

"Thanks," the Kahuna said. "Most of the materials are recycled. The floors are old barn wood, for instance. Got it for free when a farmer tore his barn down in Manassas. Free for the hauling . . . and the sanding, and the polishing."

Tara could nearly see her reflection in the shiny gray wood. "It's beautiful."

"Thanks." The Kahuna beamed. Tara wondered how many people got to see this hidden sanctuary above the surplus store.

"We really appreciate your hospitality. This is really so far out of the ordinary . . ."

"No worries." The Kahuna shook his head. "I hate hotels, but like having visitors." He opened a door at the end of the hall. "You girls can stay here."

The guest room was full of sunshine. A bed dressed in simple linens stood against a wall constructed of what looked like part of a ship's hull. A dresser was festooned with a collection of grinning wooden Tiki gods, and a beaded curtain was strung over the window to the outdoors. A private bathroom extended to the right of the room. Tara crossed to the window, pulled aside the rattling beads. From this height, she could see the river and the masts of boats in the harbor.

"I'll let you girls get settled," the Kahuna said.

"Thank you." Tara smiled at him warmly as he closed the door.

Cassie sat down on the bed and released Oscar from the backpack. The cat shook his fur out in indignation and paced across the bedspread to hop down on the floor. He began to bat at the beaded curtain. Tara began setting up Oscar's makeshift litter box in the tiny bathroom. The broiler pan fit nicely under the sink, and the cat immediately began scratching in his oatmeal cat litter.

Cassie remained sitting on the bed, staring at her hands.

Tara came to her side. "Hey." She stroked the girl's hair. "Are you doing okay?"

"Yeah. I think so." Cassie shuddered. "Just as . . . just as long as I don't have to go downstairs."

"I think that they'll understand."

Cassie looked up at the shifting prismatic rainbows on the wall summoned by the glass beads. "Can we trust these guys? I mean, they seem okay, but . . ." Her shoulder slumped. "I don't know who to trust anymore."

"Let's make sure." Tara tugged her purse to the bed and pulled her cards out of the bottom. She began to shuffle them, as specks of sunshine played over her hands. She asked the cards: "Can we trust the Steves to keep Cassie safe?"

When the cards felt as if they began to stick together, her hands stilled. She pulled the first card off the top of the deck and turned it faceup on the bedspread.

The Six of Pentacles showed a smiling, bearded merchant giving coins shaped like pentacles to two needy figures. He was richly dressed in an embroidered coat and feathered cap—Tara thought immediately of the Cowboy—but his cheeks were ruddy with goodwill. The thick beard reminded her of the Kahuna. Snowflakes spangled the air behind him, suggesting that the cold season was coming, and the merchant's alms were sorely needed.

Cassie inched forward to peer at the card. "What does it mean?"

"The Six of Pentacles is a good card. It means generosity from strangers, speaks of loyalty and good faith." Tara looked up at the cavernous ceiling of the loft apartment.

"We're the recipients of the Steves' goodwill. I don't think that our trust in them is misplaced."

Cassie wrapped her arms around her knees, tucked them up under her chin. "I hope you're right."

"I trust these cards," Tara said, surprising herself. She understood that Cassie's faith in oracles was sorely tested, and she was honored that the girl still trusted her.

"Do you think . . . do you think the Pythia will come after me?" Cassie asked.

"It doesn't matter what the Pythia does," Tara said. "Harry and I will keep you safe."

Cassie shook her head. "I want to know if she's going to come after me."

Tara frowned. She didn't have a feeling for what the Pythia would do. Whatever she did, it was certain to be unexpected. But she wanted Cassie to feel safe, to feel shielded from the knowledge.

Tara smoothed Cassie's hair from her face. There was no use hiding the truth from another oracle. "Okay. We'll ask."

She handed the cards to Cassie to shuffle. The girl's fingers worked slowly over the gilt edges of the cards as she cut the deck and clumsily worked the cards back into a pile. She handed them back to Tara, and Tara fanned them out in her hands.

"Pick three cards."

Cassie plucked three from the fan. "This is interesting. You usually deal them out yourself."

Tara shrugged. "I'm making this up as I go along. We'll see if it yields any useful information."

She turned the three cards over. "These three cards represent you and your present state of mind." The Star card, Cassie's card, showed a young woman pouring water into a dark body of water. Tara bit her lip. The card was reversed, suggesting that that energy had been disrupted, poured out. Cassie had been dealt a terrible blow by the Pythia's training . . . and it would take time for her to heal.

She flipped the next card in the stack over. The Six of Swords showed a man ferrying six swords in a boat to a distant shore.

The third card representing Cassie was the Two of Swords. It depicted a blindfolded young woman seated beside the ocean, holding two swords in her crossed arms, balanced on her shoulders.

"What do they mean?" Cassie asked.

"The Star is the card I associate with you. It's reversed, and it's obvious why: you're emotionally distraught, and your energy is scattered," Tara said. "The Six of Swords is a card of internal and external journeys. You'll eventually move through this to the Two of Swords, which is a card of equilibrium, balanced force." Tara looked up at the girl. "You will get through this. I promise."

Cassie rubbed her dripping nose.

"Pick three more." Tara fanned the cards out again, and Cassie chose.

"These cards represent the Pythia and her state of mind." Tara turned the first one over, where it lay haphazardly across Cassie's cards. The Priestess gazed serenely back at them. She was dressed in heavy robes, a moon crown perched in her headdress. A coy smile played on the Priestess's lips. The Priestess was the card Tara had most often associated with the Pythia, the embodiment of female power, intuition, and magick.

The second and third cards surprised Tara. The Five of Cups showed a melancholy man, head bowed, staring at three spilled goblets. Beside him, unnoticed, two goblets remained upright and full.

The Hanged Man showed a man dangling from a tree branch, tied by his foot. His expression was serene. Still.

Tara steepled her fingers in front of her lips. "The Five of Cups is a card of regret. It suggests that the Pythia is genuinely sorry for what happened. And the Hanged Man is a card of sacrifice, of literal suspension. I don't think that she's going to chase after you. She's going to wait, watch for what you do."

Cassie snorted. "I can't imagine having that much power over her."

"Pick three more cards," Tara said. "These last three will show the relationship between you . . . where you agree, and where you fall apart."

Cassie plucked three new cards from the deck, and Tara turned them over. The Hierophant showed a papal figure seated upon an imposing throne. The Seven of Wands showed a young man fighting off the blows of an oncoming salvo of staves. The Two of Wands showed the same man, dressed in rich clothes, standing on a balcony. His gaze followed a ship coming in on the horizon. In his left hand, he held a staff. In his right, he held a globe.

"The Hierophant speaks of tradition, teaching the way things have always been. In old decks, this card is sometimes called the Pope. He can signify dogma, clinging to outdated beliefs or notions. The Pythia is an old-school oracle. She's been in power for so long, she might have calcified, become too rigid to accept change.

"The Seven of Wands speaks of fighting, of competition."

"I don't want to fight with her," Cassie said. "I don't understand why all this was necessary. What she wants from me."

Tara pointed to the last card, depicting the man holding the globe in his hands. "This is the card of new opportunities, symbolized by the ship coming in. It's a new order, a new day." Tara took a deep breath. "And you'll be the one to bring it to Delphi's Daughters, but only if you want to. You're to be the next Pythia."

Cassie rubbed her nose. "I don't understand why she did this."

"In her own misguided way, the Pythia wanted you to be strong. But she's lost her way."

"I can't." Tears began to glitter on Cassie's eyelashes. "I don't want to be a part of this. I want a choice."

"I understand." Tara rubbed a tear dribbling down the girl's cheek. "You want to make your own decision."

"But . . . what happens to Delphi's Daughters if I leave for good?"

Tara shook her head. "Sometimes, I feel like Delphi's Daughters are . . . an anachronism. A useless throwback to a primitive time, with brutal methods. I often believe the world can spin just as well without them, though they'd never believe it."

Cassie pressed the heels of her hands to her eyes.

Tara grasped her shoulders, whispered fiercely: "She can't make you do anything. You want your destiny to be yours. And it is."

Cassie hiccuped, looked up with eyes the color of sea glass.

For a moment, it seemed as if she believed it.

CHAPTER **Fourteen**

GALEN KNEW his time was running out. He could feel it in his bones and in the blood pulsing sluggishly to the surface of his skin. His skin twitched, attempting to assimilate the new material, the bones and organs of the NCTC analyst. Somewhere in his chest, an extra set of ribs ground and grated against his own. If he was still, he could nearly hear the sounds of the vertebrae in his spine scraping together, reorganizing . . .

. . . if it weren't for the voices in his head. It was like being in a subway tunnel, the voices tumbling over each other and echoing. The growl of the dog, Diana, meshed with Lockley's thoughts about his next creation for a horror film. Lena's voice was faint, barely a contralto whisper below them. He had to focus, focus hard to separate the voice of the analyst, Veriss, from the others. Veriss knew government investigators were closing in on him. They knew where he came from, who he'd been to see.

And they also knew that he was dying.

On some level, Galen had always known his time was measured. The doctors at Minsk said he was doomed like the others . . .

. . . but he'd never really felt it. It seemed a certainty in the distant future, remote. Not like now. Now, he could feel it in his marrow. The children at Minsk had often spoken of what it felt like to have cancer, to know that one's body was poisoned, devouring itself. They spoke of how the marrow in their bones ached, how the blood throbbed painfully through clusters of tumors, tumors growing a life of their own and chewing away at their bodies. They cried, wordlessly, when they could feel their organs dissolving, when they coughed up bits of liver and the bile stung their throats. They left bloody fingerprints behind when their own blood seeped through their skin, like stigmata.

Galen never understood, before. Then, he thought himself invincible.

Not now. Now, he understood. He could not escape his fate.

But he would meet his fate on his own terms.

Galen had ransacked the old man's cache of disguises in the garage the day before, looking for anything he could use. Lockley's voice was still strong enough in his head that he could manipulate the gum aspic jars, the brushes, the cosmetic paints. He knew what to take, stuffed the

items in an old duffel bag. He found the old man's passport and bottles of inks and solvents. He'd taken his time
doctoring Lockley's passport, changing the name to one of
the many aliases he used, one of the aliases he'd reserved
a plane ticket for. He'd left the picture intact. He knew
he could wear the old man's face. His own would be too
disfigured to use for days.

Now, he hurriedly pressed a skin of silicone over his
warped features, to give some semblance of normalcy at
a distance. It was the cast that Lockley had created of his
own face, the mask destined for Halloween.

Jamming one of the old man's straw hats over his head
and donning an oversize jacket from the closet, Galen
stumbled to the back door. He needed to get away from
the scene. He couldn't take Veriss's car . . . He knew that
the men outside, dim as they were, would see him.

He slipped out into the backyard, scaring away the
birds at the bird feeder. They were like the birds of Chernobyl, he thought: wary of humans, sensing that invisible
decay on him and fleeing. He cut through the neighbors'
well-trimmed yards, behind strings of laundry that flapped
in the spring breeze like ghosts. His skin itched behind the
mask, and he scanned the streets furtively. There must be
some means of escape. A bus, a way to flag a taxi . . . ?

His blurry vision snagged on something a half block
away. A delivery truck. Resolutely, Galen limped toward
it as fast as he could. He watched as the driver hopped out
of the cab of the truck, staring at his clipboard. The driver
opened the back door and rolled it up with a sound like

a garage door opening. He scanned the stacked boxes for the one he wanted, the one corresponding to the address on his clipboard. He hopped up into the truck, muttering to himself. He began throwing boxes right and left, searching for the package. He dumped a small, heavy one at the mouth of the truck, discarding it.

Absorbed in his work, the delivery driver didn't notice Galen creeping up the bumper of the truck. Galen advanced upon him, picking up the cast-aside box and swinging it as hard as he could.

The only thing the driver saw before he was knocked unconscious was the address on the package. He slumped over the towers of boxes in the back, blood oozing from a gash on his forehead.

Galen clambered out of the back of the truck. He reeled the back door down, crossed to the cab to climb into the driver's seat. The driver had left the engine running.

Galen peered through the windshield at the road ahead, smiling beneath the silicone skin. He wouldn't run from his fate. He'd run right into her arms: home.

Home to Chernobyl.

THE STEVES WERE GRILLING STEAKS OUT ON THE BALCONY, sending the sweet smell of charred meat drifting through the loft. Maggie sat beside the Cowboy, who was manning the grill, leaning on his knee and gazing up at him with adoring eyes. The Kahuna was proudly showing off his shiny new kegerator to Cassie. Apparently, the Kahuna was into home brewing. Tara had declined, but she didn't feel as if a drink or two would hurt Cassie.

The girl was well over the legal age, and nowhere near the legal limit.

Tara's phone rang at her hip. She stiffened, plucked it out of her pocket to look at the number.

"Somebody wants to get ahold of you, real bad," the Kahuna remarked, his moustache trimmed with beer foam. Her cell phone had been going off all afternoon.

Tara stared at the farmhouse number, grimaced. "Yeah. Too bad I don't want to talk to them."

Cassie hiccuped. "It's okay. You can tell her that I'm safe. But tell her to stay the hell away."

Tara shook her head. "I don't think that's a good idea. Besides which, I'm sure she already knows." She cast Cassie a warning glare, and the phone quit ringing.

Cassie turned to the Kahuna. "One of my crazy aunts."

"Oh," said the Kahuna. He didn't look like he was buying it.

The phone began to ring again. Anger bubbled in Tara's throat. Without looking at the number, she switched on the phone. "Listen, you bitch—"

The Kahuna took a swig of his home brew. "Doesn't sound like one of your favorite aunts."

"She's not," Cassie murmured.

Static rattled at the other end of the line. "Tara?"

Harry's voice.

Tara clapped a hand over her mouth. "Shit. Sorry, Harry. I thought you were . . . um, someone else."

"I don't need to be an oracle to guess who. Listen, I've got a problem. That tip you gave me about Lockley panned out."

"Yeah?" Tara's mouth went dry. "Is he all right?"

"I don't know. I don't think so. He's gone, and there's blood all over the house."

Tara rubbed her eyebrow. "Damn."

"Veriss was here. He's also gone." Harry blew out his breath, and she heard it as a burst of static. "I know it's bad timing, but I need you here to look at this scene . . . It's the only uncontaminated one we've got, and it's a fucking mess."

Tara glanced over at Cassie, stomach churning. "I don't know that it's a good idea to leave her alone."

The Kahuna belched and rubbed his palm frond-printed belly. "We've got this shit under control."

From the grill, the Cowboy gave her the thumbs-up.

Tara frowned. She looked at Cassie. The girl blinked into her beer. "Would you be gone long?"

"I'm not going anywhere," Tara said firmly.

Cassie shook her head. "Harry needs you. Besides . . ." She glanced at the Steves. "I think the Steves are more than capable of keeping my crazy aunt at bay."

Tara's mouth flattened. She was duty-bound to help Harry, *and* duty-bound to see to Cassie's safety. "I know, but . . ."

The Cowboy brought the steaks in on a platter, Maggie trotting behind him. He looked Tara in the eye. "You go on. We'll save you a steak for your dinner when you come back." He looked down at Maggie's big brown eyes. "Assuming this one doesn't eat it first."

He fished the Bronco keys out of his pocket, tossed them to Tara. Tara caught them with her free hand and stared at the key ring. From the ring dangled a silver star inscribed in a circle, shaped like the Lone Ranger's badge.

Or the pentacles in the Six of Pentacles card.

Tara bit her lip. She had to trust the cards, and by extension, trust the Steves to keep Cassie safe in this odd little fortress of weapons, beer, and steak. It was as far as theoretically possible from the Pythia's stronghold of feminine power.

And Tara thought that was a good thing.

"Nice wheels."

Harry strode down Lockley's driveway, nodding approvingly at Tara's parking job. She'd managed to get the big Bronco wedged into the crowded driveway without hitting anything. Tara hopped down out of the tank, had to lean hard against the creaky door to get it to shut.

"Thanks. It belongs to the Steves. The guys you sent for Cassie."

"Yeah, I know." Harry said. He was dressed in a wrinkly, white Tyvek suit. In the sunset, his shadow was long across the pavement. "They're good guys. A little obsessive about beer, but they take work pretty damn seriously."

Tara squinted into the sun at him. "You know them?"

"I ran into them working a case a couple of months back about chupacabras . . ." Harry pinched the bridge of his nose when Tara opened her mouth to ask. She was envisioning a story in which Harry was bouncing along in the back of the Bronco in Texas, somewhere, chasing mutants. "Don't ask. They're trustworthy guys, though.

Besides, they're the only Marshals I could find who were willing to take in a dog and a cat."

"You owe me that story." Her eyebrow crawled up her forehead.

"I promise that I will tell you the story of the Steves and the chupacabras. Honest." Harry made the Cub Scout three-finger swearing gesture. "But I need you to tell me a story about this crime scene, first." His gaze flitted back to the house with the blinds pulled tight across the windows.

"I'll spin the best yarn I can." Tara gestured at his suit with her chin. "What's with the gear?"

"We don't want to contaminate the scene. Or get contaminated by it." He said it in a low voice that wouldn't carry to the neighbors' open windows.

"You found radiation in there?"

"Trace amounts. Nothing serious. But nothing you want to handle and then go licking your fingers." Harry handed Tara a white Tyvek suit of her own. She unzipped it and stepped into the oversize suit, wiggling her shoes into the feet. She felt like a child wearing oversize footie pajamas that her grandmother insisted she'd grow into.

Tara glanced at the cars at the curb. "I thought the Marshals were guarding Lockley, whether he wanted it or not."

"Yeah. That didn't go so well. Lockley refused to let them in, though they did manage to ring his doorbell a couple of times a day to make sure that he was all right. Last time they checked on him was this morning. They said the old man sounded like he was working on a bad cold for the past couple of days. They saw Veriss go in late this morning, but he never came out. There are signs of forced entry in the back."

Tara stared at the façade of the house, zipping up the suit to her chin while Harry fitted a hood and respirator over her head. Everything looked normal. She could understand why the Marshals would think Lockley was simply inside, sleeping off a bad cold. "You mind if I go in and walk around?" Her voice was muffled by the plastic.

"Have at it." Harry's cell phone rang, somewhere under his suit. "Shit." He began unzipping his suit to try and get at the phone.

Tara walked up the front step to the house, peered in through the screen door. The screen was thick enough and the foyer in sufficient shadow to obscure the figures milling inside. Veriss would have come here, and he would not have been able to see much inside.

She opened the door, and a wall of cold hit her. Her brow furrowed. The air conditioner was freezing. Too cold, even for summer. Around her, crime scene technicians crawled over the carpet. Flashbulbs flickered in the gloom like lightning. Tara reached for the light switch inside the door. Didn't work. She looked up at the foyer light fixture. Maybe the bulb was burned out, and Lockley couldn't reach it from his wheelchair to change it.

Tara reached up with a gloved hand, pulled away the clip-on plastic shade. The bulb was loose, turned easily in its socket, and produced a blinding brightness.

"I think there may be prints on this bulb," Tara said to a hovering evidence technician, who scurried away to find a dusting kit.

Tara crossed through the living room. Something was missing. The dog. She stopped a technician taking pictures of the living room.

"Did anybody find a dog here?"

The hooded head shook. Under the visor, Tara recognized Anderson. "No. We found dog dishes, leashes, but no dog." The flashbulb strobed again. "We found parts of the dog, though . . . fur and some teeth."

"Where?"

"Back there. You can't miss it."

Tara turned down the hallway. Through her respirator, she could smell the metallic scent of blood. Red was smeared on the wall, and she followed the direction of the smear to the bedroom.

This place. She knew that this was where the assailant had killed Lockley. The bedclothes were rumpled, not smoothed back, as they had been at Lena's house. That was entirely too much activity for a partially paralyzed man. A stain blossomed across the old man's bed, rust-colored with age. A nightstand drawer was open beside the bed.

Here. Lockley had been going to bed, and the assailant had come down the hallway. She knew that an old shop man like Lockley would be armed. She knelt and sniffed the open drawer. She smelled gun oil, but saw no gun, smelled no residue of gunpowder.

She let herself slip into the dream of the altercation as easily as she slipped into dreams of the Tarot. She imagined Lockley scrambling for his gun, but the assailant had come, anyway. Had killed Lockley in his bed. He'd probably fought off the dog to do so.

But where were the bodies? Tara peered under the bed. The old man's pajamas were wadded in a ball among the dust bunnies, and she saw the dog's collar beside them, smeared in red.

Why strip the man and the dog? It made no sense to peel them, unless he was going to eat them. Tara shuddered, remembering a case involving a flesh fetishist she'd worked many years ago. But fetishists and sadists were typically ruled by their passions. The sense she had of this killer, of the person in her dreams who fell from the Tower, was of a cold, organized killer. A broker of information. And there had been no forensic evidence of semen found at the scenes. He wasn't doing this for thrills. He had a purpose.

Tara straightened, trying to imagine what it would have been like to be the killer. He killed Lockley and the dog . . . and went to the bathroom to clean up. She paced down the hallway to the bathroom, peered inside.

She sucked in a breath that pulled the plastic respirator close to her face. The bathroom was streaked with red, bloody towels congealing in the bottom of the tub like bandages on a clotting wound.

"This is a fucking abattoir," a technician muttered, shouldering past her with sample bottles.

"Is it okay for me to touch?" Tara asked.

"As long as you've got gloves," she said.

Tara stood, blinking, in the cold bathroom light. She saw rusty stains on the sink handles, on the grab bars and the bench in the bathtub. Leaning to peer into the bathtub, she saw the towels covered with dog fur. She picked up a sopping towel and turned it over. It was spangled with fragments of a transparent material, like shed reptile skin or mica.

Her eyes flicked to something shiny in the soap dish. A pair of pliers from Lockley's workshop lay in the dish, denting the soap. Surrounding the pink soap were ivory-white teeth. Some had to be human; they had dental fillings. But others . . . they looked long and sharp, like canines.

She sat back on her heels, understanding striking her like lightning. The confused jumble of chimeric DNA, Lockley's clothes on the floor. The World card, and the Sacred Androgyne embracing Lena. The symbol of Chiron in Cassie's charts, half man, half beast.

This room wasn't an abattoir.

It was a womb. Their subject hadn't eaten Lockley, the dog, and all the others. He'd absorbed them, taken them into himself. It was the only way to explain the lack of bodies. He'd not only taken their bodies, but their knowledge.

He was more than they'd all expected. He was the Chimera the Pythia had warned her about, a creature who consumed his prey, becoming some fearsome amalgamation of those he'd destroyed. He was history moving through the modern era, relentlessly ingesting everything in his path. This man had absorbed Lockley, and Lena, and all the others. The Chimera was more than the sum total of all he'd taken.

Her intuition of the truth crackled through her, from the hair at the back of her neck down her spine to her feet.

She took a deep breath, grounding the awful truth of that knowledge.

Tara backed out of the bathroom, sidestepped technicians coming down the hall. In the kitchen, she spotted Veriss's glasses and notepad on the kitchen floor, being photographed by a tech. She asked permission to touch the notebook, flipped through it. Her mouth thinned, seeing the rudimentary list of questions produced by an inexperienced investigator. He'd come here to prove his own points. She scanned through his list of questions, pausing on one that he'd starred and underlined:

Where are the reactor rods from Chernobyl? Do you know?

Her brow wrinkled. Perhaps Veriss's mathematical theories had led him to something solid. Too bad he hadn't had the opportunity to ask the question.

Tara's gaze flickered to the empty wheelchair on the kitchen linoleum. Lockley had met his end in the bedroom. His wheelchair should be there. The killer had brought the wheelchair here. In the shade of the foyer, perhaps he'd been able to convince someone as naïve as Veriss to come in.

And Veriss was gone. Dead, like the others, she was certain of it. Part of the Chimera.

Tara stepped out of the kitchen into the garage. Lockley's shop was tossed. The Chimera had fled, taking with him whatever he needed to escape. This wasn't the organized, careful cleanup she'd seen at Lena's. He'd been rushed. Veriss had not been part of his plan.

She fingered a smudge of blood on the edge of the table. The Chimera was hurt. Maybe Lockley had hurt him. Or maybe whatever Anderson's DNA expert had predicted was coming to pass: the Chimera was dying.

Tara's mouth thinned. She knew where he was going. Her dream of the Tower had told her that much.

He was going home.

She threaded her way through the house, back out into the front yard to find Harry.

Harry was pacing the front wheelchair ramp, growling into his cell phone. Neighbors were peering through their blinds at the man in the radiation suit. The postman glanced at him, looked at the fistful of mail in his hand. He stuffed it back in his bag and kept on walking.

By the volume on the other end, she could tell Harry was getting an ass-chewing from someone. He glanced up when he saw her, hung up.

"Well?" he said, his tone clipped and impatient.

"Our killer. He's going back to Chernobyl," she insisted. "We've got to catch him. I'll explain on the way."

CHAPTER **Fifteen**

DEVOURING THE deliveryman had been difficult, and he did not finish the job.

Galen had not been much interested in the voices in the deliveryman's head. The deliveryman's memories were of insignificant things: schedules and routes, family birthdays, grocery lists, a beat-up paperback novel stowed behind his seat he was reading on breaks. It was a comforting, banal chatter in his head, bits of ordinary life that Galen had never experienced.

But there were some useful nuggets to be gleaned.

Galen had pulled the truck off the road in a discount store parking lot ten miles from Lockley's house. He'd dug in the cab of the truck for a flashlight, grabbed his duffel bag, and gone to the back of the truck. He climbed inside and shut the door.

The driver lay, still unconscious, on the floor. His

breath was weak and thready, and a lump was beginning to swell oddly on the back of his head. Galen sat back on his heels, swept his light around. At eye level was a box that had originated from Tokyo. Galen considered this, scratching under the mask. He needed to get home. And he knew, through Veriss, that the U.S. government agents were close on his heels. They were watching the airports, scanning for radioactive isotopes at the security gates. He would be unable to pass through security without tripping the Geiger detectors, unable to claim his plane ticket.

There had to be another way.

He stripped the deliveryman of his uniform, cast his clothes away. He pressed his hand to the man's chest, felt his heart twitching under his shirt. Galen closed his eyes. His hand slipped down into the deliveryman's chest, and he felt the heart against his fingers. The deliveryman's memories swept past him like blood, and he learned about the package from Tokyo. The delivery service had a hub at Dulles. Packages went in and out at a frenetic pace, under very little supervision.

Galen smiled.

Under his hand, the heart stilled. The deliveryman's voice drained away, and the air escaped from his lungs with a sigh. Galen pulled back, but his fingers were meshed in the man's ribs just as surely as if they'd grown there. The deliveryman's flesh stretched smooth and flawless over the bones of Galen's fingers.

Galen cast about, dug in the man's pockets. He found a ballpoint pen and a box cutter. Holding the flashlight in his teeth, Galen cut around the perimeter of the man's chest, where he supposed his fingers might be. The cheap blade skipped and nicked bone, and Galen ultimately broke the blade point on the sternum.

But he freed himself. He pulled away a mass of flesh connected to his wrist, hissing. It hurt, but he could feel his cells sluggishly trying to reorganize, trying to shut off blood vessels and reform bone.

Cradling his arm in his other elbow, he bound it in his own shirt. His flesh was lumpy from the other assimilations. He was healing more and more slowly. He scrubbed his tongue across the uneven teeth that belonged to the dog and hadn't fallen out yet. He was disintegrating. But he was not finished. He needed to get home, to complete his mission.

And the deliveryman had provided him a way to get past security.

He dressed slowly in the deliveryman's uniform. The cap made the silicone on his skin sweat, but there was no help for it. He used a bit more glue from Lockley's materials to hold his nose in place. He added the deliveryman's sunglasses, flipped his ID badge around. Passable for cursory inspection, he decided. If anyone were to look at his ID, he'd be found out. With any luck, he wouldn't need it.

Galen found the largest box on the truck, opened it. Inside was a large stuffed toy: a unicorn. He scooped it out and stuffed the deliveryman inside the box. He resealed the tape on the top of the box and stacked others on top. The mangled body would be found, but not right away.

He exited the back of the truck with the unicorn under his arm and headed for the cab of the truck. He saw, across the parking lot, a young girl watching him while her mother unloaded her shopping cart. The mother was distracted, yapping into her cell phone, and did not notice Galen's approach.

Galen walked across the pavement, his gait slow but improving. Without a word, he handed the toy to the girl, who hugged it to her chest and smiled widely.

Pretty child, he thought. Too bad that her world wouldn't last.

Galen climbed back into the truck and cranked the ignition. He drove the truck to the airport, followed the deliveryman's memory to the shipping entrance. He parked his truck at the back of the line, hopped out. Galen lost himself in the bustle of boxes and crates being screened for loading, walked across the tarmac into the open bays where carts waited, heavy with packages. No one stopped him as he walked through the freight terminal to the passenger terminal, wearing Lockley's face and the deliveryman's uniform.

He paused to duck into the men's room. He unzipped his duffel bag in an unoccupied stall. He changed quickly into Lockley's clothes, put Lockley's straw hat over his head. He wadded the deliveryman's uniform back into the bag, slung it over his shoulder. Pausing to admire his reflection in the mirror on the way out, he marveled at his handiwork. Lockley had truly earned his reputation as a disguise master when he'd been alive.

Ambling slowly back into the hallway, he examined the computerized schedules posted on the wall. He was careful to keep his wounded hand in his pocket, away from prying eyes. People flowed around him, ignoring him. Many had recently come from security screening on the other side of the terminal, reorganizing carry-on bags and computers, adjusting their shoes. Galen had bypassed it entirely by entering through the freight terminal, avoided the close scrutiny and Geiger counters that would have given him away.

He saw what he wanted: his flight to Rome, leaving in an hour. He took his time getting to his gate, limped up to the flight attendant's desk.

"I believe you have an electronic ticket waiting for me," Galen said. He pushed a slip of paper containing his confirmation number across the desk.

The attendant punched some keys on her computer. "Boarding's already begun, and all I have left are aisle seats, sir. Will that be all right?"

"Absolutely."

The attendant handed Galen a paper ticket. "Enjoy your trip, sir."

Galen turned his silicone lips upward. "Thank you, miss. I'm sure that I will."

"Where do we find him?"

Stress crackled in Harry's voice as he cradled his cell phone in one hand and sawed the steering wheel in rush-hour beltway traffic with the other. The strobe light perched on top of the car did little to part traffic, and Harry was zipping down the shoulder.

The seatbelt jerked against Tara's shoulder, and she struggled to keep her cards from spilling off her lap. She'd told Harry what she'd pieced together about the Chimera's power, that he was much more than the scientific oddity they'd believed him to be. He was a monster.

Harry didn't dwell on the philosophical or scientific ramifications of what she suggested. Instead, he charged into action to keep the future from unfolding, leaving the sticky questions of the past for later. "We've got three airports in the immediate vicinity with international departures—Baltimore, Ronald Reagan, and Dulles has reopened. Can we at least narrow it down?"

"I'm not the Magic Eight Ball," Tara snapped. "I'm working on it. You know, from a mundane perspective, it might be easier to just detain anyone with a Ukrainian passport."

They were en route to Dulles on the assumption that since the Chimera had been here before, he'd return the same way. But they couldn't be sure. A red string of taillights showed the congested path to the terminal.

Harry covered the mouthpiece on his phone. "I'm trying." He spoke back into the mouthpiece. "Yeah, we've determined that the radiation contamination is specific, from Chernobyl. Scanning those passengers isn't enough . . . Yeah, well, fuck you, too. This is a national security threat, you asshole. You want me to call the press? I'm certainly happy to let them know that the administrator of Dulles International Airport is willing to expose his passengers to some nicely warmed-over cesium—"

She plucked four cards from the deck, muttering to herself and trying to focus. She picked the Ace of Cups, the Eight of Cups, the Six of Swords, and the Fool. The Fool was number zero in the Major Arcana.

"Search for any flight or plane combinations of these four digits: one, three, six, zero," Tara interrupted. Her fingers lingered on the Fool. She'd seen him recently, and was surprised to see him again. Something about the card bothered her, but she couldn't figure out what.

She pulled another card from the deck, the Chariot. It showed an armored man charging forward, pulled by two horses. It was a card of fast movement, of relentless pursuit of one's goals.

"Flights leaving soon," she amended. "Our Chimera is on the move."

Harry hung up on Dulles. "He won't ground any more flights. If we can get a description of a suspect, he'll have the suspect detained. But that prick won't allow any more delays to his fucking timetables. DHS is screening all passengers going through security with Geiger counters; if he's hot, they'll stop him."

"I can't conjure up a description. The cards don't work that way." She showed him the Chariot. "He's making fast progress. I don't think that security has caught him."

"There are four flights leaving in the next fifteen minutes from Dulles with those number combinations," Harry said. "One to Texas, one to Oregon, one to Mexico City, and one to Rome."

"Rome," Tara said automatically. "That has to be our flight."

Harry pulled the car into the passenger drop-off area, left it parked in the fire lane. He flashed his badge and elbowed through the crowd. Tara struggled to keep up with him, swimming in the mass of people. He paused at security to argue with the DHS personnel. Someone recognized him and waved him back. They took off running to the gate from which the Rome flight was leaving. By the departure board, it was taking off in minutes.

Tara scanned the crowd, heart pounding. The Chimera had to be here, somewhere. She had no idea what he looked like—or what he would look like after playing with Lockley's disguises. How would she know him if she saw him? Would he look like the World in her dreams?

They sprinted down the people movers, past students with their backpacks, business travelers with stuffed briefcases, and families with children. Her attention snagged on a familiar face in the crowd. A dark-haired young man in a denim jacket, carrying a backpack, met her gaze. His eyes widened.

Tara recognized him. Zahar Mouda, the kid who had been accused of trafficking in dangerous chemicals. The Fool.

Tara shouldered past the passengers to get to him. She had questions, starting with: *What the hell are you doing outside of detainment?*

Zahar's eyes met hers. He turned on his heel and ran.

Tara chased him, yelling at him to stop. The kid was fast, zagging right and left like a linebacker through the crowded field. Through the gaps in the crowd, she saw him dig a cell phone out of his jacket. He stabbed the buttons on the phone furiously.

Tara tackled him, trying to wrest the phone out of his

grip. They fell down in a tangle of limbs, the phone spiraling away under feet on the concourse. Tara reached for it.

A thunderous boom rocked the terminal, echoed by screams. Dust rained down overhead as the building shook. Tara covered her head with an arm, keeping the other firmly wound in Zahar's collar. She smelled smoke.

It was as she'd feared. The son of a bitch had an ignition device.

Klaxons sounded overhead and emergency lights began to flash. Tara spat hair and dust out of her mouth and shook Zahar's collar. She dragged him away from the stampede of feet, near a drinking fountain.

"What the hell did you do?" she screamed at him.

Zahar stared at her with a belligerent glare. "Revenge. Revenge for what your people have done to mine. I want you to feel what we feel."

Zahar was suddenly yanked out from beneath her hands. Harry hauled him up and slammed him into the wall. "What kind of bomb was that?" he yelled. "What was in it? Chemicals? Nerve agents?"

Tara's breathing quickened.

Zahar spat in his face. "Plenty of things that glow in the dark."

The lights flickered overhead. Tara saw that planes were still taking off behind the glass windows. Tara paused, staring through the glass at a plane taxiing down the runway. Over the klaxons, her intuition was screaming at her. She advanced upon the glass, wiped away the dust to see more clearly. The glass still held some vibration from the blast, quivering under her hands.

Her hands balled into fists when she saw the number painted on the side of the plane: 1860.

GALEN KNEW THAT SOMETHING WAS WRONG WHEN THE plane lurched into the sky.

He'd settled into his seat, beside a woman with a dachshund in a carry-on bag. The dog pressed its nose to the mesh ventilation holes, staring and whining at Galen. Perhaps she could smell some of Lockley's dog on him.

"I think she likes you," the woman in the next seat said.

Galen smiled through his silicone lips, careful to keep them over his uneven teeth.

The pilot was waddling the plane down to the runway, chatting banally about the DC heat and how lovely Rome was this time of year.

From the direction of the terminal, a *boom* echoed. Excited chatter rattled in the cabin. In the middle of the pilot's estimating flight time, the radio cut off.

Galen tensed. Had he been found? Would they stop the plane and drag him away?

The passengers craned over to peer through the windows on the terminal side. Galen looked over the shoulder of the woman with the dog to see a plume of gray rising in the distance.

The pilot's voice crackled over the radio. *"Please stay in your seats and stay calm."*

At the admonishment to stay calm, panic broke out. The woman beside Galen clutched the pet carrier and sobbed.

The plane rolled down the runway and gained speed. In moments, the plane bounced into the air, the landing gear bumping back into the belly of the plane. The plane took a long, curving climb in the sky.

Looking down through the window, Galen could see flames emanating from the main terminal. Fire trucks swarmed into view, lights flashing.

"Oh my God," Galen's seatmate whispered. "What is that?"

Galen squinted at the fire until they'd climbed above the cloud cover. He didn't answer, but he thought he knew: it was someone's revenge. He didn't know who, but someone was taking their own vengeance on the world. He could relate.

He leaned back in his seat. He let the voices wash over him, the mutterings about bombs and fires. The flight attendants trotted to the front of the cabin and reassured everyone that they were safe, that there had simply been some malfunction on the ground, likely in the baggage system. They would be proceeding to Rome on schedule.

Hours into the flight, when the ocean spread out dark and blue below them, information began to trickle in from hushed conversations on air phones: it had been a bomb. Someone had exploded a bomb. A dirty bomb. The news media was reporting that people had been killed, that radioactive material had been strewn all over the airport.

Eventually, the pilot came on the intercom:

"Ladies and gentlemen, as many of you have already heard, there was an incident as we were departing Dulles. There was an explosion in the baggage area, and terrorism is suspected. There is no need for you to panic. We'll get you to Rome, safe and sound. You'll be met by workers from the U.S. Embassy

at the airport, who will be able to put you in touch with your loved ones and provide more information.

"In the meantime, please try to relax and enjoy the in-flight film. Headphones will be offered free of charge. Our flight attendants will be offering a beverage service momentarily . . ."

The woman beside Galen started to cry again. The dog paced in its carrier, hearing her owner's sobs, but unable to console her.

Galen leaned back, pretending to watch the movie. But some part of him thrilled at the undercurrent of anxiety in the air, the raw smell of fear of these insulated Westerners in the face of chaos.

It smelled like home.

"How did you build the bomb?"

The interrogator leaned closer to Zahar than was probably safe. Zahar sat in an interrogation room in a nondescript Homeland Security building, wrapped in a white Tyvek suit and handcuffs. He'd been in custody more than twelve hours, propped up in a chair with no sleep. There were no clocks in the room he was being interrogated in, no daylight to measure the passage of time.

Geiger counters indicated that he was flush with roentgens. Standing too close to him without suitable protection could probably turn an interrogator sterile. There was a stainless steel table between them, but still. The interrogator didn't look worried. He was over six feet tall, buzz-cut, and looked like his chest could deflect bullets.

"Go fuck yourself."

Zahar sprawled insolently in his chair, pausing only to turn his head and cough on his shoulder. He was looking pretty green, and had vomited twice in a trash can. Radiation poisoning was a bitch.

Tara watched Zahar through the one-way observation room glass. His posture was different than it had been when she'd last interviewed him. This was all bravado . . . but false. Tara could see how his foot twitched under the table.

"Why did DHS let him go in the first place?" Tara asked. She folded her arms over her chest. She was wearing a white Tyvek suit, like Zahar, and her skin had been scrubbed sunburn-bright. Her clothes had been taken from her for analysis, and the suit was all that anyone had left to give her. It was too large and pooled at her ankles.

Harry grumbled, picking at the seams of his own plastic suit. "DHS says that they let him go, but were keeping him under surveillance. They wanted to see who he'd lead them to."

"Evidently, they weren't watching him close enough," Tara snarked.

"They lost track of him three days ago. He apparently turned out to be sneakier than they thought. But while they had him under surveillance he made contact with some interesting folks on CIA watch lists. Some of these people were the same people trafficking in the secrets from our case."

"Small world for terrorists."

"Yeah. The preliminary lab analysis suggests the materials used in the bomb were rather unique. A cocktail of cesium-137, iodine-131, and strontium-90, pretty specific to former USSR installations." Harry pinched the bridge of his nose. "This is going to be a massive international relations hairball when it gets out."

Tara leaned forward and stared at Zahar, who was continuing to stonewall the interrogator. "I'd like to try to talk to him."

Harry shrugged. "Can't hurt to ask. Homeland Security doesn't seem to be getting anywhere."

Harry let himself out of the dim observation room. Tara watched Zahar go pale and ask for another trash can. Irritated, the interrogator stormed out. Tara wondered if Zahar was now regretting the radiation he'd managed to slather all over himself in the creation of the bomb. At the time, he apparently hadn't cared enough to take precautions.

The door to the observation room cracked open, and the burly interrogator motioned to her. "Your turn, Dr. Sheridan."

He unlocked the interrogation room door with a key card. "I'll be watching. Just go to the door when you want to be let out."

"Thanks." Tara waited for the green light on the door to blink before she went in.

Zahar looked like a miserable frat boy after a party, cradling a trash can in his lap. He looked up as she entered. Tara sat down opposite him at the table, just as she had days before at the prison.

"Hello, Zahar."

Zahar spat into the trash can.

Tara folded her hands in front of her. "You're not the only one with a nice case of radiation poisoning, you know. By last count, more than sixty people are sick. That's aside, of course, from the eight people you managed to kill with the bomb blast in the baggage area. Twelve more were injured."

Zahar shrugged. "Not as successful as I hoped, but it was pretty good for a first try."

"You're really an amateur, Zahar." Tara kept her tone cold and level. "You detonated it way too soon. Your handlers are likely very disappointed."

"Didn't have much choice. I was surprised to see you there." Zahar's brows drew together, and he wiped his mouth with the back of his hand. "I thought your profile was the reason they set me free."

Tara shook her head. "I knew you were lying. My report recommended we keep you for a good, long time. You got lucky."

"I don't believe in luck," he said, with an edge of arrogance.

"Did you build that bomb yourself?"

"Yeah. It's mine."

"Judging by the amount of radiation you seem to have been exposed to, I would think that's true." Tara stared hard at him. "You were expelled from the university, and everything from your apartment was taken. Where did you get the materials for this one?"

Zahar leaned back, hugging his trash can like a teddy bear.

"There's no point in being coy. You're not ever going

to be released from custody, I can guarantee you. Cooperation might win you a private cell or more immediate medical treatment." Tara eyed Zahar's Adam's apple bobbing up and down. She was pretty sure that Zahar had been given only the minimum amount of treatment required to ensure his survival. His comfort was probably not at issue.

"Medical treatment?" he echoed.

"Looks like you gave yourself a heavier radiation dose than you expected," Tara said, neutrally.

"How much?" His eyes widened in startlement. Without his laboratory, there probably wasn't any way Zahar could have known what he'd exposed himself to.

Tara stared at him levelly. "Where did you get the materials?"

Zahar stared miserably into the murky depths of the trash can. "My handler got in touch with me. Said he had a job."

"Bullshit," Tara said. "I know you were lying about being blackmailed for your sister. Tell me the truth."

"Look, just because I don't have a sister doesn't mean I don't have a handler." Zahar burped. "The guy called me, said he had something he wanted me to build. Had some raw materials."

"Who?"

"I just know him as Masozi. He's the guy who recruited me. Said he had the materials, but couldn't build the bomb. At first, I was just supposed to build it, but then . . ." His shoulders slumped.

"What? You didn't want to be the one to detonate it?"

Zahar opened his mouth, closed it. "I was honored to

do it. You've been oppressing my people for years. We want you to know what it feels like."

Tara looked at him. One part of her wanted to reason with him, to point out the comforts his Western education had provided him, to call him a hypocrite. The other wanted to slap the living daylights out of him. Instead, she said: "Where did the material come from?"

"It was old stuff, pretty substandard," Zahar admitted. "I was told that it was fragments from a dismantled Russian nuclear site."

"How much stuff?"

"About three cubic feet of cesium and strontium." Zahar began to sway "About that medical attention . . ."

"I'll see what I can do," Tara stood up to leave, turning away from the sound of retching echoing in the trash can like the angry ocean in a shell.

Information was a lot like radiation. It was contagious, sticking to things that walked away with it.

And information was what Tara needed most.

She leaned against the back of the elevator cab in the Special Projects building, still in her Tyvek suit. She hadn't been back to the Steves, but she'd called Cassie to check on her. She'd been up all night with the airport debacle, and no sleep was likely to be on the horizon.

Though most of the furor surrounded Zahar, Tara was thoroughly dejected that the Chimera had slipped away. But she was going to correct her mistake. She was going to find him, no matter what it took.

Her fingers tightened around two brand-new presentation flipcharts and boxes of markers. Veriss was dead; he wouldn't be needing them. She needed them more: as an offering to the knowledge gods. She imagined this was the way it had worked with the fabled lynx-eyed librarians back at Alexandria.

Tara's cell phone rang in the purse draped over her shoulder. She'd left the purse in Harry's car when they'd gone chasing after the Chimera. Good thing: her cards would've been difficult to replace.

She glanced at the caller ID. It was the Pythia. This time, she decided to answer. Better to have this conversation well beyond Cassie's earshot. She punched the button to stop the elevator for privacy before she answered. "Hello."

The Pythia's contralto voice was irritated. "I've been trying to reach you."

"I've been busy. What do you want?"

There was a pause. "Well, I was attempting to warn you about a terrorist attack on an airport, but it seems as if you have that well in hand."

Tara made a face the Pythia couldn't see. Had her pride kept her from learning something that could have stopped the attack? She rubbed her temple. Shit.

The Pythia continued. "I know that Cassie is safe, and—"

"Don't you dare try to take her back. Not after what you did."

A moment of silence stretched. "I give you my word as Pythia that I won't. I will not take her back. If Cassie returns to us, it will be of her own accord."

Tara rocked back on her plastic-covered heels, chewing on that. The Pythia rarely gave her word. But when she did, Tara could think of no occasions when she'd broken it. Breaking such an oath would be sufficient grounds for her to step down. And the title of Pythia would be Cassie's. This was no light oath for her ilk.

"How is she?"

"She's been better." Just because the Pythia wasn't physically going after Cassie didn't mean that Tara was going to give the Pythia more information to screw with her head.

"And the animals?"

Tara's heart warmed a degree or two to hear the Pythia ask about Maggie and Oscar. "They're fine."

"Good."

"You know Cassie's safe. You know the dirty bomb exploded. What else do you want?"

Tara heard the staticky sound of the Pythia exhaling smoke over the receiver. "You're going to chase your killer down. Back to Chernobyl. I want to help you. If you will accept my help, that is."

Tara blinked. "What do you have in mind? And what kind of strings are you attaching to this 'help'?"

"No strings. Delphi's Daughters wants this man stopped, as much as you do."

"Like you wanted to stop that child molester Cassie killed?"

The Pythia paused. "I understand that you fail to appreciate my . . . economy of action. But in this situation, our interests neatly intersect. I will make travel arrangements for you and Harry to—"

"Not Harry," Tara said. "Just me." She didn't want to get Harry sucked into more of the Pythia's games. Though the Pythia had promised to leave Cassie alone, she'd made no such guarantees for Tara or Harry.

"All right, then," the Pythia continued smoothly. "I'll provide you with a guide, as well. I'll get the information to you shortly. When will you be ready to leave?"

"Tomorrow."

"Good. I'll be in touch."

The phone went dead, and Tara punched the button to resume the elevator's descent. She frowned at the dark screen of the phone. She didn't trust the Pythia, didn't want to get sucked back into her games. But she didn't really have a choice. The Chimera had to be stopped, or else they were courting more disasters like the dirty bomb explosion.

But she'd do her damndest to keep the ones she loved out of the Pythia's grip.

The elevator doors opened on one of the LOC floors, the floor she'd found Jenny tucked away in her archives with her photographic plates. When she stepped out onto the concrete floor, the motion-detector lights fizzled on, heralding her arrival.

"Hello? Jenny?" Tara called into the gloom. It was past nine AM. The archivist should be lurking around here, somewhere—if she wasn't taking a day off.

A light blinked on in the distance. Tara breathed a sigh of relief. She was here.

The archivist approached, wearing a set of brown coveralls and what looked like welder's gloves. A pair of safety glasses was perched on the top of her head. She assessed Tara's costume. "You dressed for the same party?"

Tara looked down at her Tyvek suit and grimaced. "Let's just say that it's been a thoroughly sucktastic day." She extended her arms with Veriss's office supplies. "I brought you a bribe."

"Oooh. Those are expensive, and Finance never approves requests for those." Jenny picked up the charts and markers, flipping through the pages to make sure they were new. "And what kind of information would you be needing today?"

"I'm taking a trip," Tara said. "To Chernobyl. I need maps of the surrounding area, as good as you can get. I need information on transportation, places to stay, a decent phrase book . . . anything you can find for me."

Jenny's eyebrows lifted. "Your own chain of command would typically provide those to you for an investigation."

Tara shook her head, thinking of Harry. He had his hands full, but she knew that he wouldn't want her to go. Better that he knew nothing. "My chain of command is blissfully unaware of my trip."

"Follow me." Jenny hauled the supplies back to her office. Tara followed, her suit making strange swishing noises. The synthetic material was beginning to itch, and she self-consciously scratched her shoulder as Jenny rummaged around her shelves.

"This is for you." Jenny picked up a cardboard box on the floor and handed it to her. It was curiously light. Tara peered inside. She saw file folders full of papers and more Tyvek suits.

"Protective gear. The kind archivists use for handling hazardous chemicals is pretty low-level protection, but you aren't going to be able to get a full Level A contamination suit on a plane. Well, you could get it on a plane, but it'll probably get stolen long before you get to your destination. Those things are expensive, and worth good money in the underground market. The rest is documentation, stop-off points, and some contact information."

The skin on the back of Tara's neck prickled, and she took a step back. "You knew that I was coming."

Jenny shrugged nonchalantly, didn't meet her gaze. "I got a call earlier in the day that you'd want these things."

"From who?" Tara knew the answer, but she wanted to hear it. Her knuckles whitened on the box.

"From a mutual friend." Jenny set the flipcharts down on the floor, stepped back to admire them. "Amira thinks very highly of you."

That bitch. That bitch was always one step ahead. And Tara could almost hear the click and whir of the Pythia's machinations closing around her.

Chapter Sixteen

"WHAT THE hell happened to you?"

Cassie launched herself into Tara's arms, then pulled back, staring at the crinkly Tyvek suits Tara and Harry were wearing. Maggie sniffed at the plastic. Even Oscar was curious enough to pad across the Steves' living room to investigate. He began to wind his way around Tara's calves in a figure eight pattern, seeming to delight at the static electricity generated by his fur sticking to the plastic.

"Were you at the airport?" Cassie asked.

"Yeah. It wasn't good."

In the background of the house, a news channel could be heard reporting on the dirty bomb explosion. The Cowboy was watching the television with crossed arms, an inscrutable expression on his face. He glanced up to say: "Y'all look like you got into a tussle with some aliens. Hope you didn't get probed."

Harry crossed the room and sank into the couch opposite the Cowboy. "Steve. What's up?"

"You better not be getting radioactive particles all over this new leather couch."

Harry snorted. "You still owe me for getting chupacabra guts all over the interior of a rental car. Don't worry about the fucking particles."

The Kahuna finished locking up downstairs and closed the loft door. A bar towel was cast over his shoulder. "Anybody want a drink?"

"I can't stay," Harry said. "I need to get back and—"

"Bullshit," the Kahuna said. "The Department of Homeland Security looks like they're pretending to have things well in hand." He handed Harry a beer. "Drink up, boy."

Harry stared into the glass. "Have you ever thought that you might have a problem with alcohol, Steve?"

"Have you ever thought you might have a problem with being an asshole, Harry?"

Harry grinned and raised the glass. "Cheers, Steve."

Tara rolled her eyes. She didn't want to imagine the three of them on a road trip involving Chupacabra innards. "You guys mind if I go take a shower?" The Tyvek suit didn't breathe much, and Tara's toes were squishing in sweat. The suit was now covered in cat fur from the knees down.

"Have at it."

Tara plodded off down the hallway. Cassie followed her to the bedroom. "Are you sure you're okay?" the girl asked.

Tara nodded. "Just tired. And you?"

Cassie gave her a weak smile. "The Steves are feeding me well."

"You like them?"

"Yeah. They're pretty funny. And they brew good beer."

Not a resounding endorsement, but Tara would take it. "How would you feel about staying with them for a while?"

Cassie sat down on the edge of the bed. "What do you mean, 'a while'?"

Tara took a deep breath. "This man we're chasing. He's a survivor from Chernobyl—altered into something other than human. The lives he's taking, he's absorbing their DNA and memories. He's a chimera, of sorts." She left out the uglier parts of the absorption of his victims. "He's very dangerous, and he's selling the secrets he's taken."

Cassie paused, and Tara could see her mind working to understand, to make the intuitive connections. "Chiron, from my charts. Half man, half beast. And he's bringing the knowledge of fire to those who shouldn't have it."

Tara nodded. "We chased him to the airport, but he escaped in the bomb explosion you saw on the news. Our Chimera is on his way back to Chernobyl. I need to stop him." Tara looked the girl full in the face. "But I want to make sure that you're feeling safe."

"Feeling safe and being safe are two different things." Cassie wrapped her arms around her elbows.

"I spoke to the Pythia."

Cassie blinked, looked up. She didn't say anything, just waited for Tara to continue.

"She's sworn that she will not come after you."

"Do you believe her?"

"Mostly." Tara spread her hands open. "Once upon a time, the Pythia's word meant something. I hope that it still does. But . . . I think the Steves mean well. I'll ask them to look after you while I'm gone."

Cassie's ears pricked up, hearing the wrong pronoun. "You're not taking Harry." It was an accusation. "I don't think it's a good idea for you to be alone." She said it as if she was declaring judgment on the entirety of Tara's life, not just the case.

Tara shook her head. "No. And I don't want him to follow. He's got enough on his hands here." She glanced past the closed door. "These kinds of incidents—the deaths, the bomb at the airport—are the kind that can ruin a career. Whether he wants to or not, he needs to be here to do damage control." That was only half true. Tara didn't want to tell Cassie that the Pythia was leading Tara to the Chimera's trail.

"You're not telling him, either." Cassie frowned at her.

Tara sighed. "No, I'm not telling him. This is something I've got to do on my own. And I know that he won't like it."

TARA WOULD HAVE PREFERRED TO HAVE SLEPT CURLED UP IN Harry's arms, listening to his strong heart beat inside his chest.

But after her shower, she collapsed into bed. The sunshine felt too warm and she felt too drowsy to resist; exhaustion swept over her. She was barely conscious of the *zing-zing* sound of someone walking into the bedroom in a protective suit. For a moment, a cool shadow blotted out the red sunshine behind her eyelids. The shadow kissed her forehead before she fell into dreams. Perhaps she imagined it. But in the sunshine, it felt real enough.

She dreamed of sunlight, too, gentle heat against her skin. In her dream, she was sitting in the prow of a gondola, gliding across water. The water stretched from horizon to horizon, under a blue sky. Behind her, in the boat, the lion lolled. He occasionally reached over the edge of the gondola to slap at the water. Behind him in the boat were arranged six swords, buried point-down in the hull of the boat. She recognized the card from her deck: the Six of Swords, the card of journeys.

The boat seemed to move of its own accord, as if pushed by an unseen hand.

Tara's brow narrowed. She certainly felt pushed by the invisible force of the Pythia's will. Try as she might, she couldn't see very deeply into the cloudy water. It seemed that shadows roiled beneath, too far below the surface to clearly discern.

In the distance, she could make out a dark line of land. The boat moved inexorably toward it. As they moved close to the dark land, Tara felt the sun grow hotter and hotter on her face. When she looked down, her hands were sunburned. It was as if the radiation extended from the black land growing on the horizon.

The black land filled her with dread. The lion in the boat growled, flattening his ears as the dark shoreline curved into sight. Tara's skin crawled as they approached, and she feared setting foot on that black beach unarmed.

She turned to the back of the boat. No. She wouldn't be unarmed. As the boat was propelled into the shallows, she reached for the swords. She pulled them out of the bottom of the hull, one after the other, slinging them over her shoulder.

Where she wrested the swords out, holes were exposed in the bottom of the boat. Water began to trickle in. The lion growled, clambering to the prow of the boat, balancing with his butt on the seat and paws on the edge. Tara sloshed back, nearly losing her balance with her burden of swords. Where the cloudy water touched her, it felt ice cold, cold as if sun had never touched it. The water pooled and rolled in the bottom of the boat like mercury or some unnatural element that was reaching out to drown them.

Tara twisted around in the boat. The shoreline was almost upon them. Black sand gave way to charred trees, twisted and turned at odd angles. The grasses below them were wild and ragged, blackened under the touch of that relentless, invisible heat that radiated from the land.

Cold water licked at her skirts, and the boat's course began to falter and founder. Picking up her skirts with one hand and the swords under the other arm, Tara stepped off into the water.

The water closed over her and drove the breath from her lungs. She clawed to the surface, but the swords were heavy, pulling her down into the sea.

Something in the water bit her. She struggled, but the creature held her fast in its jaws, dragging her through the shallow water and up into the sunlight, up onto the sand of the shore.

She fell on her hands and knees, dumping the swords before her and gasping. Diluted blood from her shoulder dripped down into the water, staining the swords. Black sand was soft between her fingers, tasting metallic in her mouth. The soggy lion stood over her, tail switching, staring down the beach . . .

. . . where a figure stood at the edge of the forest. In this dazzling light, she couldn't distinguish it.

Tara didn't know if it was blood loss or the blinding brightness, but the image faded, consumed in a roar of golden light.

TARA WOKE UP WITH OSCAR STRETCHED OUT ON HER CHEST, his face buried in the crook of her shoulder and her jaw. The sunlight had faded from the glass beads in the windows, and night had washed in. Cassie lay asleep beside her, and the loft was quiet. She was freezing, despite the warmth of the cat on her and thick covers drawn up to her chin.

Tara disentangled herself from the cat and climbed out of bed. Oscar burrowed under the covers into Cassie's armpit. At the foot of the bed, Maggie looked up at her. Tara could see the questioning whites of her eyes in the dim light. But Maggie didn't react when Tara padded around the corner of the bed and left the room.

The skylights overhead cast squares of lighter darkness on the polished floor. Tara skirted around their edges, made her way to the balcony. She unlocked the door, stepped out into the warmth of night. City lights spread as far as the eye could see, reflected in the black water of the marina. She closed her eyes, feeling the warmth of the deck boards under her bare feet. It was nothing like the scorching heat of the sun in her dream, but it served to chase a bit of the trance-chill from her bones.

She smelled cigarette smoke. Her mind immediately flashed on the Pythia. Her eyes snapped open, and she turned to see the glowing ember of the cigarette in the darkness.

It wasn't the Pythia, though. It was just the Cowboy, sitting in a plastic deck chair in the darkest shade of the building, smoking a cigarette.

"Didn't mean to startle you," the Cowboy said, taking another drag.

Tara relaxed. "What are you doing out here in the dark?"

The Cowboy shrugged. "Light draws bugs." He reached down beside the chair and picked up a thick yellow envelope. "Courier dropped this off for you a little while ago."

Tara took the envelope, stared at it. There was no return address on it from the courier service. She ripped it open. The envelope contained no explanatory note. But it included an itinerary, train tickets, three stacks of foreign currency in various denominations, mostly Ukrainian hryvnia. And flight information for a plane leaving three hours from now from Baltimore. Baltimore was the nearest airport still open for business; both Dulles and Reagan National had closed down in light of the attack.

Her blood curdled. This was from the Pythia. She knew Tara was here.

And she knew Cassie was here.

"That from Cassie's crazy aunt?" the Cowboy's voice issued out from under the brim of his hat.

"Yeah. It's from her. How'd you know?"

"The crazy aunt seems pretty persistent." The Cowboy blew a wreath of smoke in the direction of the water, kicked his boots up on the balcony railing. He had the attitude of a man waiting for a story.

"She's dangerous," Tara said. "But she's promised to leave Cassie alone. For now, anyway."

"Dangerous in what way?" The shadow of the hat inclined toward Tara.

"She's got a lot of money. A lot of power. And a massive network of knowledge available to her." Tara lifted the envelope. "This is proof."

The Cowboy nodded toward the envelope. "What does she want?"

"She wants me to go chase down the man who sold the information that made the bombing possible."

"Deep pockets."

"Yeah."

"You gonna go?"

"I have to." Tara's mouth tightened. "But I don't like the idea of leaving Cassie behind."

"We aren't going to let anyone hurt the little squirt." The Cowboy's hat dipped. "We'll take care of her till you get back."

Tara was humbled. "Thank you. I mean it. I owe you guys . . ."

The Cowboy waved away her thanks. "I've got a

daughter about her age. Fiesty, like her. Takes after the ex, traipsing around third-world countries, looking for artifacts and such." The hat shook ruefully. "I'll watch over her like she was my own."

"Thank you."

"Does Harry know about this?"

Tara bit her lip, stared out at the water. "He knows about the crazy aunt, but he doesn't know that I'm leaving."

"He won't like that."

"Trust me. He doesn't want to get tangled up with her crazy aunt any more than he already is."

The Cowboy shrugged. "That's not what I mean. When Steve and Harry and I were out in the desert chasing those damn critters, he talked a lot about you."

Tara's eyebrow lifted. "Oh?"

"Says you're the most enigmatic, frustrating dame on earth."

Tara snorted. "That's high praise, coming from Harry."

"He loves you, you know."

Tara blinked. She knew it, but it had never been put so matter-of-factly before. "He wouldn't have said that."

"Didn't need to." The Cowboy laughed, stretched out his denim-clad legs. "He loves you, and he's going to be pissed that you left without him."

Tara swallowed. "I know."

"So, where you going?"

"Chernobyl." The word itself tasted hollow and metallic, like the sand she'd tasted on the beach in her dreams. "In three hours."

The Cowboy hesitated, then ground out the red light of his cigarette in his ashtray. "Then we need to get a couple of things for you from the store."

He swung his legs off the railing and headed back into the house. Tara followed him, curiosity prickling as she followed him down the steps into the shop. He flipped on the fluorescent lights, illuminating the mountains of surplus gear in flickering, cold light.

"I appreciate it, Steve, really," Tara said. "But I've been told that this is one of those places where your bags leave lighter than when you arrived."

"I was over in Serbia for a while. I know what it's like." The Cowboy disappeared in the back of the store, began digging around in boxes. "There's no point in packing your gun. That will get taken away from you. You're much better off buying one when you get there."

"I can do that?" That sounded like a certain way to get into trouble with the local authorities.

"If you're discreet. What've you got so far for your trip?"

"A couple of Tyvek suits, some latex gloves. A Russian phrase book."

The Cowboy dumped a black deployment bag on the glass counter, started arranging odds and ends beside it: a compass, what looked like a wallet with straps, and a handheld electronic device that looked like a cell phone.

"What's this?" Tara asked, picking up the device.

"That's a universal portable navigator. It's GPS-enabled, should work anywhere you can get a satellite signal."

Tara pointed to the cheap plastic compass. "Then what's that for?"

"That's what you use if this gets stolen from your bags." A smile played around the Cowboy's mouth. He pointed to the wallet. "That straps on under your clothes, to keep your cash and passport in. Should keep thieves' fingers out."

"Gotcha."

The Cowboy rummaged around in a bin full of boots. "What's your size?"

"Eight and a half."

The Cowboy peered at the tongues of the boots, muttering to himself, until he found a pair of shockingly ugly boots to hand to Tara. "Try these."

Tara jammed her feet into them, wiggled her toes. "These feel good."

"Great." The Cowboy opened a frayed cardboard box and lifted out a face mask apparatus with a tube extending from the nose. "This is a flight respirator. Will do in a pinch in low-level radiation settings . . . which reminds me . . ." He rummaged around under the counter. "Try these on. Nomex flight gloves. Should be pretty airtight." He slapped a pair of gray gloves on the counter. "I know it's here, somewhere . . . unless Steve moved it . . ."

Tara tried on the gloves. They fit like a second skin, much better than the latex gloves she'd gotten at the archives.

"A-ha." He dug out an item that looked like a pager. Immediately, he popped open the compartment and began rooting around for a battery. "This is a personal dosimeter. It detects gamma rays and X-rays. Sometimes they're used by the paranoid in nuclear submarines, mines, nuclear medicine, that sort of thing."

"Okay. How do I use it?"

The Cowboy jammed a AAA battery into the back of it. "Clip it to your belt. It'll chirp when it's accumulated more than ten microroentgens per hour. Or, you can turn the chirp off, and watch the readout, here." He pointed to the window. "Anything over fifty microroentgens means that you should get the heck out of the area."

"Gotcha. Thanks."

"It's not much, but it's all I've got on hand." The Cowboy glanced at his watch. "Better get packed up if you want to catch your plane."

He looked past Tara at the stairs and fell silent.

Tara turned to see Cassie leaning on the banister, dressed in one of Tara's T-shirts and leggings. Tara was startled to see the girl venturing this far into the dungeon of weaponry. She clutched the stair rail and stared at Tara.

"You're leaving now?"

Tara crossed the room, reached out to hug the girl. "It's gonna be okay. The Steves will watch over you."

"I know," Cassie said, bravely. She nodded and tried to smile.

Tara thought she still detected a bit of a tremor in the girl's shoulders when she said good-bye.

At least she could say good-bye to Cassie.

She wished she had that luxury with Harry.

CHAPTER Seventeen

"WHAT DO you mean, she left?"

Harry slapped his hand on his desk. The blow sloshed his cup of coffee on a stack of file folders and caused an agent at the copier to turn around and give him the stink eye.

The Cowboy's voice on the other end of the line was tense. "She left last night for Chernobyl. To chase your suspect."

"Why the hell didn't she tell me?" Harry struggled to keep the anger from seeping into his voice. It wasn't directed at Steve. It was directed at Tara for being a maddeningly obscure and independent oracle.

"From what I understand, the crazy aunt arranged the trip. She didn't want you to get involved with what Cassie calls 'family politics.'"

Harry rubbed the bridge of his nose. He didn't understand that fucked-up tie Tara and Cassie had to the Pythia. He doubted he'd ever understand why they kept walking back into the arms of that monster over and over again. But he didn't have to tolerate it.

"Okay. Thanks for telling me."

"What are you gonna do?" the Cowboy drawled.

"Well, as I see it, I've got two choices, Steve. I can kick back and do nothing, and hope she comes back. Or I can go after her."

"That just about sums up your options," the Cowboy agreed. "The second one would be sorta detrimental to your career."

Harry poked at the files on his desk and glared in the general direction of Aquila's office. "DHS and TSA have taken over the dirty bomber case. I'm just window dressing, at this point." He leaned back in his chair. "Figuring out the route Tara took is gonna be the hard part." He knew that she'd let her cards lead her down whatever dark alley tickled her intuition. And he had no hope of guessing where that would be. Her intuitive processes were opaque and inscrutable to him, like trying to look through obsidian glass.

"You guys will work it out," the Cowboy said.

Harry made a noncommittal noise and hung up.

He'd been busy trying to track down what he could see and understand, from Veriss's point of view. He'd been digging through Veriss's files and diagrams. As near as he could determine, he'd isolated part of the decaying spy network tied to the disappearances. All the people who had turned up missing had been looking for unaccounted-for parts from the Chernobyl plant. Some time after the disaster, the other reactors continued to run, until the last one was shut down in 1999. There had never been a thorough accounting made for that material, and Veriss had been sniffing circles around the folks who had been looking for it.

As he always did, he returned to Tara's line of thinking. She was convinced that their suspect was on the flight to Rome, but they had no proof, just an inarticulate hunch. The plane in Rome was long gone, but Harry was driven to find some overlooked bit of evidence that might show that she was right, that the Chimera really had been there. DHS said there was no way that he could have gotten through the Geiger counters at security, that Harry's fears that the Chimera had slipped through their grasp were unfounded.

Besides, DHS had bigger worries now.

Harry rested his chin on his hand and watched the airport surveillance video. He had obtained copies from Dulles. DHS and TSA were combing the footage for Zahar's movements, but Harry was much more interested in what was happening around the international departures. He scanned the people around the gate for the Rome flight, unsure what he was looking for . . .

. . . until he spotted it. A man in a straw hat and casual shirt exited the men's room and walked up to the departures board. Under the brim of the hat, Harry recognized him. Harry clicked his mouse to freeze the image, zoomed in.

It was Norman Lockley's face. But the guy was walking. Harry struggled to reconcile the two. Shit. It had to be the Chimera, gussied up in Lockley's Halloween mask.

He swore, reached for the phone, dialed the main switchboard. "Get me someone in the Interpol Central Bureau."

He drummed his fingers at the frozen face on the screen, the eerie death mask of Lockley's face. Tara had been right all along.

"Central Bureau."

"This is Harry Li from the U.S. Department of Justice. I've got a problem that may have now become yours."

There was a sigh on the other end of the line. "That's how it usually goes. Hit me."

"We were pursuing a subject for several murders of retired intelligence operatives. We think he found his way to Rome." Harry gave the agent the flight information.

"Do you have a description?"

"I'll send you a photo. The guy appears to be approximately six feet tall, in his late sixties, balding, in a green-patterned shirt and straw hat. But this is a disguise. We don't know what his true face looks like."

The agent paused. "By the airport information I have, that flight has already landed."

"Is the plane still at the terminal?"

"Yes. But the passengers are long gone, disembarked hours ago."

Harry pinched the bridge of his nose. "Can you do a quick radiation sweep of the plane?"

"Do you think it was contaminated by the dirty bomb?"

"I think it was contaminated by the suspect in my case.

He's a Chernobylite, and he tends to leave sticky radioactive particles wherever he goes."

"I'll forward this information to our agents in the field immediately."

"Thanks." Harry hung up the phone and downloaded the picture to send to Interpol. Sweeping the plane for radiation would be confirmation that the Chimera had been there, but wouldn't provide him with information he didn't already know.

A bright yellow interoffice envelope slapped down on his desk. Harry looked up to see one of the women from the LOC standing over him. He vaguely remembered her as the one who'd stolen Veriss's projector. A librarian in Special Projects was bad news. He opened his mouth to say something like: *Hold it right there . . . you need to be searched.*

The LOC woman gave him a dirty look. "You're welcome." She reached over his desk with an insolent gaze, deliberately picked up his stapler, and walked away with it.

"Hey!" Harry yelled. "Gimme that!"

She gave him the finger and kept on walking.

Harry picked up the envelope. There were no markings on it to say who it was from, only his name in cursive writing. He unwound the red cord securing the envelope and dumped the contents out on his desk.

It was a book. *Russian for Morons.* When he opened the front cover, an electronic stub for a plane ticket leaving from Baltimore fell out. The destination was Kiev, with a plane change in Athens. His brows drew together in puzzlement. Had Tara sent this to him?

Harry's phone beeped. "Li," he answered in clipped tones.

"Hello, Harry," a musical voice greeted him.

Harry paused in rifling through the documents. "Amira. You weren't satisfied traumatizing Cassie? Had to go ahead and screw with Tara, huh?"

"I didn't intend to traumatize anyone," the Pythia said smoothly.

"You did a bang-up job, let me tell you. If you ever lay a finger on Cassie, I will personally burn that farmhouse of yours to the ground."

The Pythia *tsk*ed. "I promised that I'm not going to force Cassie to return. And I meant it."

Harry rolled his eyes. "What games are you playing now?"

The Pythia chuckled. "No games, Harry. As I explained to Tara, our goals converge. For the moment."

"What goals?" Harry crossed his arms. "I'm never quite clear on what your goals are, you and the rest of the Amazons on Paradise Island. World peace? World domination? A really good jewelry sale?"

"I don't discuss my plans with outsiders, Harry." The Pythia's haughty tone scraped the receiver. When she said *outsiders,* she made it sound like *dog shit.*

Harry pressed on. "Why did you send Tara to Chernobyl? Alone? This guy is dangerous."

"I didn't send her alone. You got my present just now?"

Harry picked up the copy of *Russian for Morons.* "This was you?" He'd been hoping it had come from Tara, and his heart dropped just a little bit further.

He could hear the huff in the Pythia's voice. "Tara needs you, Harry. Sometimes I don't have the faintest clue why, but she does. Since you have your useful moments, I am sending you along with her. Your paths will cross in Kiev."

"One can't help but feel used when you're involved, Amira."

"I'm not concerned about your feelings, Harry. Or Tara's."

Harry glanced at the tickets. "I notice that these are one-way tickets."

The Pythia snorted. "You have an hour to make your plane, Harry."

She hung up, leaving Harry to stare at the ticket. She could just be screwing with him.

Or it might mean that he wouldn't be coming back.

WHAT DID THE CHIMERA WANT?

Tara stared at her reflection in the black glass of the plane window. She knew the Chimera was going to Chernobyl. The Pythia had sensed it, too. And the Chimera was dying, whether he knew it or not. Was he crawling off to his home den to die alone, like a wounded wolf? Or did he want something more? Something about the situation nagged at her, from Cassie's star charts to her own readings to the Pythia's demands. She felt as if she had a blind spot in her vision, something she couldn't quite resolve.

She glanced sidelong at her seatmate. The old woman in a pink sweat suit was snoring with her mouth open, dentures slipping slightly over her tongue. This flight was full, and Tara would need to be discreet if she wanted to consult her cards.

She picked up her purse and crawled over the old woman to the aisle, muttering apologies. She elbowed her way to the lavatory, closing the door securely behind her. She kicked the lid of the toilet down and spread her jacket on the plastic lid. She dug into her purse, dumped her cards out of the cigarette pack she'd concealed them in. She shuffled her cards, mindful to hurry. Under new security procedures, a flight attendant would no doubt be checking on her if she took more than a few minutes.

Kneeling before the jacket, she began to deal out the cards quickly, in a line of five cards left to right.

"Distant past," she whispered, picking up the card on the far left. It was Death, showing a black-robed skeleton riding through a green countryside on a white horse. Death's horse stepped over the pale bodies of men and women as he rode, and red sunset shone behind him.

On a cursory level, that made sense. If the Chimera was from Chernobyl, he'd have had his fill of Death all around him.

"Recent past," she whispered, picking up the next card. The World, reversed, showed the Sacred Androgyne from her dreams, the figure that fused with everything it touched. Now, Tara understood its significance, and why it was reversed in her reading, giving it a sinister connotation. Perhaps as a result of the accident, as a result of one of the terrible mutations of radiation, the Chimera had become what he was.

"Present." She flipped over the Moon. The shape of a

serene moon goddess's face shone from a full moon. Below her were two pillars, one dark and one light. Wolves lifted their heads to howl at her, and a crayfish crawled from the ocean to gaze at her.

Tara rested her hand in her chin. Before, she'd drawn this card in relation to Lockley, the master of deception. The Chimera was doubtlessly using his talents to escape, the arts of subterfuge and trickery. But the Moon also spoke of the subconscious, of hidden motivations. What else was the Chimera hiding? Were his motives even fully known to himself?

A knock sounded at the door, causing Tara to jump. "Ma'am, are you all right in there?"

"I'll be just a moment longer," Tara called.

She turned her attention back to the cards, turned the next one over. "Near future," she muttered under her breath. This card puzzled her. It was the Ten of Wands, depicting a man whose back was bent under a heavy load of rods he was carrying. The card traditionally represented overwork and exhaustion, but that meaning didn't seem to fit here.

The knock at the door sounded again. "Ma'am—"

"I'll be out in a minute, please." Damn that nosy flight attendant.

Tara flipped over the last card. "Distant future."

Her breath snagged in her throat. The Tower was the structure from her dreams and her earlier readings, struck by lightning. It was the card of ultimate disaster, the one that had come to her to symbolize Chernobyl. Her brow furrowed. But its placement was all wrong here. It belonged in the distant past, the foundation of the situation, not the future . . .

Someone jiggled the door, someone with a key. A man's voice, another attendant, echoed: "You have to get out of there, now, ma'am."

Tara stuffed the cards into her purse. She had enough time to pull her jacket off the toilet and push the lid back before the door folded open.

Thinking quickly, Tara clapped one hand over her mouth and the other around her stomach. She glared blearily at the flight attendants, remembering what it felt like to have the flu and summoning all that misery to her face.

"Oh." The male attendant stepped back, embarrassed. "I'm sorry, ma'am. I thought—" He glared at the female flight attendant, who made a face at him. "Are you all right, ma'am?"

Tara made a big show of leaning over the sink and spitting, as if to remove the taste of vomit from her mouth. "I guess I have no choice but to be all right," she said, grimly.

"I'll take you back to your seat," the female flight attendant snipped.

Tara let herself be led by the elbow back to her seat and climbed back over the old woman in the pink sweat suit.

Tara settled back in her seat. The cards had been burned into her memory, and she closed her eyes, visualizing them, trying to figure out how they were connected. She slid more easily into her dreams now than she ever had before. She knew it was the influence of this new deck of cards, and it worried her. She set the worry aside, let herself be pulled down into the dream, the falling sensation indistinguishable from the feeling of a plane plunging through turbulence.

In her dream, she stood on the black beach with the lion pacing around her. The lion made broad tracks in the sand not so much different, except in scale, from Oscar's footprints in a litter box. He glanced at her with his golden eyes. Tara didn't know yet if he was some type of a spirit guide or, more likely, some partitioned part of Tara's consciousness, her intuition, translated into a symbol by this odd turn her power had taken.

She could feel the heat in the land through the soles of her shoes. She squinted into the distance, at the figure she could see walking further on down the strand. The figure approached, but she knew who he was the instant she spied the sun glancing off his polished armor.

Harry. The Knight of Pentacles. Wordlessly, he walked toward her, visor lowered so that she could not see the expression in his eyes.

Tara reached up and took his face in her hands. "Harry, I'm sorry that I had to leave you behind."

His gauntleted hands remained motionless at his sides. Guilt rippled through her, and Tara's hands paused to finger the scars in his armor. He seemed like such a wordless automaton here, a machine. She had the sensation that he was becoming hollow beneath that armor, that he was losing himself.

She threw her arms around his neck. His armor was scalding hot against her body. She reached up to lift his helmet from his face, but he lifted his hands and held her fast. The segments of his gauntlet gloves began to burn the white flesh of her fingers. She wondered whether this was simply the absorbed heat of the sunshine in the metal or whether it was something more radiating from him. Anger.

The lion paced around her, sniffing the air and growling. From the corner of her eye, Tara watched him walk toward the black forest rising from the beach, away from Tara's guilt and Harry's anger.

Tara took a deep breath. She had work to do. She had to follow her intuition, wherever it led. She disentangled her burnt fingers from Harry's, picked up her skirts, and ran away through the black sand, trying to catch up with the lion.

The lion was easy to follow, luminous gold against the crisp burned grasses and blackened bark. As Tara pursued him, she noticed that green sprouts were beginning to emerge from the rich black dust, the dust that coated the bottom of her skirts. It tasted metallic in her mouth, as if she'd taken a mouthful of iron filings.

The lion led her to a clearing, a familiar one. She recognized the Tower from her cards and her previous dream, black against the blue sky. Even in the daylight, it felt ominous, its hulking, uneven shape blocking out the light. But it was even hotter in the shade of it, looking up at the rusting bits of metal and welds that seemed to hold the ramshackle structure together.

Tara paused, her hand coming to rest on the lion's brow. She understood the meaning of the Tower card. Chernobyl. But why was it placed in the future in her spread? Was it merely the act of traveling there that had brought it into such sharp focus? Or did her reading indicate that a new disaster was on the horizon, something beyond the scale of the dirty bomb at the airport?

Twigs snapped behind her, and Tara whirled. She let out her breath when she saw the Knight of Pentacles clomping through the scorched brush. Harry had followed her here. Or her guilt had.

She stared up at the Tower, trying to understand what the silent lion of her intuition was trying to tell her. A sparrow roosting in a bent crenellation took flight, but fell out of the sky. The bird landed at the lion's paws.

Tara knelt down to pick it up. Its wings were bent, feet stuck straight out. It was suddenly, inexplicably dead. Of what?

She turned on her heel. Could it be the heat, the radiation from this place? She stared up at the Tower. The accident happened long ago, the radioactive elements sealed in sand and concrete and on their way to decaying. The monster slept, degrading quietly. What changed? What had awoken to kill the bird and char the forest surrounding them?

Tara gently set the bird down on the cleanest patch of ground she could find. She had the urge to bury the poor thing. Casting about for a suitable shovel, she found a piece of rusty metal at the foot of the Tower. She plunged the edge of the metal into the earth, scraped it away . . .

. . . and gasped as she burned her fingers on something hot. She stepped back, dropping the makeshift spade. Something glowed below the black earth, seething with an unearthly blue light below the surface. The lion approached the fizzling blue light, sniffed. He paced around it three times, began to kick dirt over it to cover it.

Tara understood. Something was being unearthed here, coming to life that should remain hidden. She cradled her burned hand in her elbow.

The Knight of Pentacles clapped his hand down on her shoulder. He pointed to the edge of the clearing, where something glowed, bright as a star.

Tara started toward the movement, shaded her eyes. She called out.

The movement stopped. Tara squinted into the light. She saw the figure of the World, bent over and broken by a burden it was stealing away. The burden was the same as the card, the Ten of Wands. But the rods glowed the same unearthly blue she'd discovered underground, burning shadows into the World's impassive face. Shadows of wrath.

Tara cried out to him: "Why are you doing this? Why won't you let it be buried?"

The World's mouth twisted. "To show you what we have suffered. And never to let you forget it."

TARA AWOKE WITH A START THAT NEARLY KNOCKED OVER A cup of water that had been placed on her tray table while she slept. The old woman beside her snorted and glared. Tara reached for the water, feeling it wash the cold, metallic taste of the dream from her mouth.

She shivered, wrapping her arms around her. A spidery pattern of frost had formed where her face had been pressed up against the window. Tara wiped it away with her elbow.

She understood, now. Veriss had been on to something. His notes and the Ten of Wands made sense. The Chimera was searching for the lost reactor rods of Chernobyl. He'd figured out their location from draining the minds of the ex-spies, and was going back to dig them up.

Tara pressed her fingertips to her lips. If the Chimera managed to do that, the dirty bomb at Dulles would be child's play. With that kind of materiel, someone could poison an entire water supply, kill thousands. The Chimera's vengeance was revenge on an unimaginable scale. The effects of the information he'd sold would ripple through the world for years. But this—this would be an unmitigated disaster of unimaginable proportion.

She knotted her hands in her lap. Perhaps they'd all be lucky. Perhaps the Chimera was still in Washington, deterred by the men at the airport security gate and their Geiger counters. But she knew, and the cards had shown her, that he had escaped. The Moon was the card of deception. She was certain the Chimera had managed to elude the authorities, had slipped through their net and was headed east.

Tara leaned back in her seat. The Chimera had escaped all attempts to ensnare him. How could she hope to catch him, when she was unarmed, alone, and unfamiliar with the terrain?

The only weapon she had was what she'd brought with her into the forest of her dreams: her intuition.

Chapter **Eighteen**

Tara's journey led her first to Amsterdam, where she changed planes after a long layover to take her to Kiev. The flight to Kiev was only half full, and Tara had the luxury of having two seats to herself. The empty seat beside her bothered her. More than once, she wished Harry were with her.

She busied herself with poring over the maps and other information the Pythia had included in her envelope. From Kiev, she was intended to take a train to Korosten, which was about 150 kilometers via winding roads west of Chernobyl. A handler was expected to meet her there and take her onward to the Exclusion Zone.

The plane descended in a fit of turbulence, passing through storm clouds. As the plane broke through the layer of gray, Tara could see Kiev more clearly. It was a beautiful city: multistory white buildings with golden spires peeking out above lush, green trees. The river cutting through the city reflected the color of the gray sky, crossed by delicate-seeming bridges. Tara hoped to be able to return here and explore. If she got the chance.

Getting through the security checkpoint was at least as much an issue as it would be in the U.S. Tara clutched her Russian phrase book and handed the guards running the checkpoint an envelope labeled in Cyrillic script that the Pythia had included in the packet. A yellow sticky note had been attached to it that said: *Give this to Customs in Kiev*. The guard read through it, gave her package a perfunctory search. Tara assumed it explained she was there for a harmless purpose. Or perhaps it contained money.

The guard with the envelope pointed to Tara's Tyvek suit. He muttered a string of words in Russian. Tara flipped through her phrase book, struggling to keep up. One of the words meant "journalist." Another guard rolled her eyes and waved dismissively.

The female guard searching her purse set a pack of cigarettes aside. Tara held her breath. The pack contained her concealed Tarot cards. If the guard tried to keep them, Tara was well and truly screwed.

The guard put all of Tara's items back in the purse, except for the cigarettes. Tara reached for the packet, and the woman's hand slammed down on hers. "Nyet," the woman said.

Tara swallowed. She had to get her cards back. If . . .

The woman turned her back to Tara and flipped open the top of the pack. Tara assumed she wanted to share her good fortune with her colleagues. But when the guard turned over the pack to tap out some cigarettes, a single card fell out on the table, the Devil.

It was easily the most fearsome card in the Tarot deck, depicting a horned devil, wreathed in fire, with a man and woman chained at his feet. People who were unfamiliar with the Tarot often panicked when they received this card in a reading, assuming it signified pure evil. In actuality, it rarely signified such pitch blackness. It usually drew the reader's attention to self-imposed bondage or limitations. But the guard was unaware of those nuances.

She dropped the pack of cards back down on the table, as if it was hot. Tara scooped up the card and the pack, jammed them back in her purse. The guard wouldn't look at her, instead giving the sign of the Evil Eye at Tara's retreating back.

Tara was a bit startled at the cards' behavior. She'd never had a deck before that seemed to exhibit any . . . volition. And this deck appeared to act in self-defense. She made a mental note to question the Pythia more fully about it, if she got the opportunity.

Tara eventually worked through the security line, was thoroughly patted down. The guards even took the wallet that the Cowboy had given her to hide under her clothing. It felt a bit lighter when it was returned to her. Eventually, Tara was sent on her way. Tara wound through the crowded Boryspil airport, searching for a train terminal. She spent a frustratingly long time studying her phrase book before feeling competent enough to ask a man in a uniform where the train was by pointing to a picture of a train in her guidebook.

He gestured to the far end of the terminal, and Tara nodded. Some of the signs contained a pictogram of a railway, and she was able to follow these to a ticket counter. She pulled another of the Pythia's letters from her bag and gave it to the clerk at the window. Without comment, the clerk issued her a ticket and pointed to a platform down a flight of stairs.

Tara slung her bag over her shoulder and trotted down to the sparsely populated train platform. She glanced at her watch. She had easily fifteen minutes until her train left. Nice planning on the Pythia's part. She walked away from the main platform to a kiosk displaying a brightly colored map and began to study it. It was hard to make out all the lines and connections under the dim, flickering light overhead and bits of graffiti scrawled on the glass cover in Magic Marker.

She was too absorbed in trying to figure out how the lettering corresponded to the words in her phrase book to notice a man beside her. He grabbed her wrist, turned her to face him. He said something in Russian. Tara shook her head, not understanding what he wanted.

The man brushed open his jacket, displaying a gun. His intent was clear.

She stomped on the instep of his foot as hard as she could, kneed him in the groin. She twisted her arm around to pull it away against his thumb, the weakest part of his grip. She tore herself away, but had not taken more than two steps before he caught the back of her shirt, hauled her back behind the kiosk, and slugged her in the jaw. He pulled the pistol out of his waistband, aimed it at her head, gesturing for her to hand him the purse holding her passport, cards, and train ticket.

Tara clenched her fists, ready to fight. She couldn't afford to give up any of the meager tools she needed on her mission. Not to the guard, and not to the mugger.

"Hands off the lady."

Tara blinked. The command came in English. And in a familiar voice.

The mugger turned, and a dark figure reared up behind him. The figure knocked the mugger's gun arm wide and smashed his head into the kiosk. Tara lifted her arms to cover her face as the kiosk glass shattered. The mugger slumped into the maw of the kiosk, teeth of glass piercing his neck and shoulders.

"Come on." She was lifted to her feet by Harry, who was tucking the mugger's gun into his jacket pocket. He steered her briskly away from the kiosk, toward the train that had rumbled into the station.

Harry gave his ticket to the provodnitsa at the door to the car, a middle-aged woman in a navy-blue uniform. Tara had read about the provodniks and provodnitsas in her guidebook—they worked in pairs, and were in charge of the sleeper cars. Tara fished her ticket out of her purse and surrendered it to the woman, who returned a stub to her. Numbly, Tara took it and followed the provodnitsa and Harry into the car.

The interior of the car was brightly painted, as one might find in a home, not the industrial colors and finishes Tara had encountered on the plane. The provodnitsa opened a squeaky sliding door to a small room barely larger than a hotel bathroom. Two narrow couches were piled high with pillows, a small table set between them. Fringed curtains bracketed the train window. This was a luxury cabin, a *spalny vagon*. The provodnitsa ushered them inside, and closed the door firmly.

Harry thrust Tara's hair away from her face. He touched the rising bruise on her cheek. "Are you hurt?"

Tara winced. "No. It's all right. What are you doing here?"

"You mean, after you ditched me in Washington?" Harry's mouth pressed into a hard slash.

"Yeah. After that part." Tara pressed her hand to Harry's chest. "Look, I didn't want to get you involved. The Pythia sent me."

"And she sent me after you."

Tara shook her head and sat down hard on the narrow couch. "She's got you all wound up in her plans, now, Harry." She didn't want that for him.

"Hey." Harry sat down beside her, turned her swollen chin to face him. "Where you go, I go. That's not negotiable."

That had never been the case before. She swallowed. "But Aquila—"

"You don't need to remind me about duty," he said, tightly. "This is a duty of a different kind."

The train ground to a start, the wheeze of the engines reverberating through the floor. The train began to pick up speed, chugging away from the platform. Harry pulled the drapes that smelled like cigarette smoke, and Tara wondered how long it would take before the mugger was found embedded in the kiosk. She forcefully turned her thoughts away, hoping the man wouldn't bleed out before someone found him.

"I take it that your presence here also means you think the Chimera made it at least as far as Rome?" Tara asked.

"Rome and beyond." Harry shook his head. "On the Dulles surveillance tapes, I saw a guy that looked like Norman Lockley on the Rome flight. He wasn't detained by anyone when the flight landed. He just vanished. Radiation sweeps in Rome showed some abnormal amounts of radiation in the interior of the airplane. He was there, but disappeared. Since you were right about that, I've gotta assume that you're also right about where he's going."

Harry shrugged out of his jacket. He was dressed as Tara was, in a T-shirt and nondescript pants. Jeans would have marked them as tourists. He checked the gun that he'd picked up from the mugger, frowned, popped out the magazine.

"What's wrong?" Tara asked.

"This is a piece of shit. A knockoff of a cheap automatic pistol. Cheap Czech ammo. This thing is as likely to jam as it is to shoot." He slammed the magazine back home, stuffed it into his jacket.

"But it's better than nothing at all," Tara said.

"It's better than nothing," Harry agreed. "I guess."

Tara rested her elbows on her knees, tried to ignore the tingling in her face. "I think I know what the Chimera is after."

"The reactor rods from Chernobyl," Harry said.

"How did you—?"

"Veriss was on it. I dug through his research files, found that all the missing agents had been searching for them, at one time or another." Harry shook his head. "Poor bastard should have stuck with what he was good at."

A knock sounded at the cabin door. Harry stood to open it, admitting the provodnitsa carrying a tea set.

"Chai?" she asked.

"Spa-see-ba," Tara pronounced slowly, remembering the phrase for "thank you" from her guidebook.

The provodnitsa set the tea service down on the small wooden table between the bunks. She glanced at the bruise blossoming on Tara's face, then at the bloody scratches on Harry's knuckles. She pulled a plastic bag of ice from her apron pocket and left it on Tara's side of the table without saying a word. She gave Harry a dirty glare on her way out.

Tara gratefully pressed the bag of ice to her cheek. "She thinks you're a violent man."

Harry glanced at the drawn window curtains and stared at his scuffed hand. "She's not wrong, lately."

Tara leaned forward and captured his hand. It felt very cold under hers. "I'm glad you're here."

Harry stared back at her, levelly. Tara could see the thoughts churning behind his eyes, and he didn't move to take her hand.

"Like it or not, you're stuck with me," he said quietly.

"WHERE ARE WE GOING?"

Cassie lugged a cooler down the dock to the marina. Maggie trotted behind her, while Oscar squirmed in the backpack slung over her shoulder. The tabby succeeded in getting one leg free of the zipper and was slapping her on the shoulder with his paw.

The Kahuna was walking beside her. A fishing pole was slung casually over his shoulder, but Cassie had seen him fill the pockets of his fishing vest with at least two pistols and several fistfuls of ammo. It made her nervous.

Ahead, on the dock, the Cowboy was fiddling with some ropes tethering a medium-sized boat to the weathered dock. Cassie knew very little about boats, but this one seemed very ordinary. It had a cabin, a motor, and the words *Starry Night* painted on the side. Someone (the Kahuna, she imagined) had put up a Jolly Roger flag on the front railing.

"We're going on a little trip, down the Potomac," the Kahuna said. She saw he was scanning the dawn horizon behind his plastic shades. At this early hour, there was only a handful of people at the marina: a couple of guys scraping the paint from a boat on the shore, a lady walking a dog, and a couple of drunk college students still stumbling around the closed tiki bar.

The Cowboy whistled, and Maggie jumped into the boat. Her tail wagged, and Cassie could see that she was excited to be around new smells.

Cassie wasn't so sure. "I thought that the surplus shop was the safest place," Cassie said reluctantly.

"Your crazy aunt left a package for Tara last night."

Cassie's heart lurched into her throat. "She knows where I am?" she squeaked.

"Yeah. Tara says she promised not to hurt you, but . . .

Steve and I are pretty cautious. Might be better to be on the move."

The Cowboy reached out from the side of the boat to offer her a hand in.

Cassie swallowed. Tara's cards said she could trust these guys. She trusted Tara, and the cards were an extension of her. Hesitantly, Cassie took his hand and swung into the boat. The cooler came in after her, and the Kahuna brought up the rear. The Cowboy finished unmooring the boat, while the Kahuna headed to the cabin. "C'mon. I'll show you round the good ship *Starry Night*."

The boat's interior was actually much nicer than it looked on the outside. Below deck was a living area with a bar and a bedroom and bathroom, while upstairs was the main control room. The décor—wood paneling and maize-colored shag carpet, a couple of curling travel agency posters of beaches with palm trees—hadn't been updated since the 1970s. Cassie set her backpack down and unzipped it. Oscar squirmed out of the sack and zipped behind the bar.

"It's like a houseboat," Cassie said.

"Yeah. Steve lives here most of the year, until it gets cold. I think he's taken it as far south as Mexico. It's his retirement plan, heading to the Yucatan."

"Stars are real pretty out there," the Cowboy offered. He stationed himself at the wheel, cranked the engine, and began to back the boat out of the slip.

"You guys keep surprising me," Cassie said.

"You like to fish?" the Kahuna asked. He opened the cooler, which Cassie had assumed was full of beer. Instead, it was full of ice, sodas, and white plastic containers. The Kahuna ripped the top off one of the cartons. "Mmmm. Nightcrawlers."

Cassie peered in at the seething mass of dirt and wrinkled her nose. "Um. I've never been fishing."

"We'll teach you. C'mon, this is the best time of day for it." The Kahuna clomped to the deck. He paused to grasp the binoculars dangling around his neck, scanned the receding marina as the *Starry Night* tooled out of the harbor and into the river. By Cassie's eye, they were heading south and east on the Potomac, toward the Chesapeake Bay. The Kahuna seemed to be checking to make sure they weren't being followed, but Cassie didn't ask.

The Kahuna spent the next couple of hours teaching Cassie how to operate a fishing pole, choose lures, and attach bait to the hook. Cassie had a hard time learning how to cast, but the Kahuna was a patient teacher. His only warning was to remember to look behind her before she cast, because he'd accidentally hooked the Cowboy's lip one time while inebriated. The Cowboy had not been pleased.

Determined not to repeat the mistake, Cassie practiced casting until her arm ached and she could pretty much put the bobber where she wanted to in the water. It was a peaceful thing, she thought, feeling the sun hot against her skin and the motion of the waves lapping against the boat. Morning sun glistened on the waves, and it seemed like there was nothing on Earth but the water and blue sky.

She clumsily jammed a squirming segment of worm on her hook and cast the line out. The Cowboy had set anchor, and was busy feeding Maggie and Oscar bits of lunch meat from the mini-fridge under the bar. Cassie closed her eyes and felt the warm breeze skimming across her face. For the first time in days, she was beginning to feel like herself again.

But that illusion was shattered when the Kahuna spoke: "Why is your crazy aunt chasing you?"

Cassie's grip on the pole tightened, and she reeled the line in. She cast it out twice more before answering. "I did something pretty awful," she said. "I didn't intend to, but things went pretty wrong."

The Kahuna nodded. He didn't look at her. He just waited, watching his line.

"My crazy aunt wanted to toughen me up. She hired some guy to break into the house, to see what I would do. Problem was, I had a gun handy."

The Kahuna nodded again. He reeled his line back in and cast it out. "Mind if I tell you a story?"

Cassie blew her breath out, relieved that he was no longer focusing on her. "Sure."

"First time I killed somebody was on my first assignment as a Marshal." He said it as if he was talking about going to the store to pick up some milk. "I was supposed to be picking up a prisoner, Gordy Cohen. Sixty-five-year-old man with fake teeth. He lived out in the boonies, had been cooking up PCP for fun and profit for years. DEA had nailed him on federal racketeering charges. He served time, got out, and violated the terms of his parole. They wanted him brought back in to prove a point.

"So, I knocked on his door to serve his papers. He seemed like a perfectly harmless, if crazy, old mother-fucker. I felt kinda sorry for him. His wife and kids were back in the kitchen, scared of me. I didn't want to scare 'em any further, so I was trying to play things nice. Gordy asked if he could get his coat and shoes, since it was cold out.

"I told him yes. That was my first mistake. Gordy disappears into the back of the house. I wait for him a good couple of minutes, yelled for him. No answer. Then I know I've been had." The Kahuna paused to lick his lips. "I radioed for backup, charged through the kitchen at the back of the house to the garage. I figured he was getting his car ready to make an escape.

"But Gordy wasn't keeping his car in his garage. He had his shiny new PCP lab in there. I remember seeing glass and tubes, knew instantly what it was. But I didn't know that Gordy had booby-trapped his lab. Soon as I opened that door, it blew up like a bomb."

The Kahuna scratched his beard. In the sunlight, Cassie could see pink scars underneath it. "I was lucky, though I would've sworn I was the unluckiest bastard who ever walked the face of the Earth for quite some time after. The explosion knocked me through the kitchen, out through a window. But the blast killed Gordy, his wife, and one of his kids. The other two were crispy critters."

Cassie closed her eyes. "Steve, I'm sorry."

"I thought about quitting after that." The Kahuna's gaze was distant, unfocused in memory. "But then I thought: if I quit, I'd never have the chance to make a positive change in the world. I would just have gone back to selling entertainment centers at my parents' furniture store. I could do that every day for the rest of my life, or I could choose to keep on the path, to make a dent in the world, despite the obstacles. Took me years to get over it, though, to realize that things had to happen the way that they did. If it hadn't been me, it would've been someone else who made a mistake. I really had no choice in it."

Cassie looked sidelong at him. "You're saying you were fated to be there, destined to continue to be a Marshal?"

"Yeah. I guess you could say that I believe in destiny. There are some things that are immutable, and just have to be accepted. Gordy was a bad guy, who was gonna cause collateral damage no matter what." The Kahuna shrugged. "Doesn't mean that I don't feel bad about it. I figure I'm supposed to. That means I still have a conscience. But I realize my responsibility in the situation was limited."

Cassie stared out at the water. "I wish I could feel that way."

"You're still operating under the illusion of free will in all situations. I didn't have a choice when I tripped Gordy's bomb. But I had a choice in deciding whether to throw in the towel. You think you had a choice, in shooting that burglar. But did you, really?"

Cassie was silent.

"Would you have let him attack you, hurt your dog and your cat? Lay in wait for others to come home and hurt them, too?"

"No."

"Then there was no other rational decision. Accept it, and look to the future. Look for the things you can change, where you can do the most good."

Cassie felt a tug on her line, and her bobber disappeared.

"Set your hook with a good, firm jerk," the Kahuna said. "Then reel 'em in."

Cassie cranked the reel to draw the fish in. Her heart was hammering ridiculously fast at the excitement of catching a fish. She reeled the heavy weight at the end of the line in to the side of the boat. The Kahuna leaned over and caught up the line, hauling her prize up for her to see.

The fish squirmed green and yellow in the sunlight, flapping, almost a foot long. Cassie blinked at it, while Maggie trotted over to sniff. "What is it?"

"Could be dinner. Or you could throw it back. But it's a nice perch."

Cassie reached out to catch the line and looked at the fish.

The Kahuna beamed at her. "Life's like the fish. We all have the illusion of choice, thinking we have the power of life and death, every minute of every day. But in all actuality, there's only one answer. One path out of any given situation."

Cassie regarded the twisting fish. "You're saying I don't have a choice as to whether the fish becomes dinner or whether I throw him back?"

"You think you do. But not really." The Kahuna grinned.

"That's kind of a . . . helpless way to look at things."

"Not really. It doesn't mean you don't make an effort,

that you don't struggle. But Philosophy According to Steve means you don't agonize over things you couldn't foresee, that you can't go back and change."

Cassie peered at the fish. "How do I get the hook out of him?"

"Like this." The Kahuna grabbed the fish, yanked the hook from the perch's mouth. The perch seemed to gasp, and a chunk of red flesh was removed from its lip. He handed the slimy, flipping fish back to Cassie.

Cassie leaned over the boat and tossed the fish back. It hit the water with a smack, then disappeared under the murky blue. Maggie put her paws up on the railing and stared over it, dejected.

"So, I didn't make a decision just then?"

"I don't think so." The Kahuna rearranged himself on his plaid lawn chair and cast his line over the rail. "I think you are what you are. And there's no changing that."

Cassie stared out at the water, where the fish had vanished. She wished she could vanish like the fish, disappear off the radar of destiny.

The Cowboy clomped around the deck and began to fiddle with the rope that held the anchor.

The Kahuna glanced at him. "You moving to a better fishing hole?"

The Cowboy shook his head. "Just someplace less crowded." He gestured with his chin to a sleek yacht bobbing along the horizon. "That boat's been following us at a distance for the last two hours. Might be a coincidence. Might not be."

The Kahuna reeled back his pole and grabbed his binoculars. He peered through them. "They're not fishing over there, whatever they're doing." He nodded at Cassie. "Take the animals and get below deck."

Cassie whistled for Maggie, and the dog bounded behind her below deck, to the world of shag carpet. Oscar was stretched out on the bar, giving himself a bath. He looked up at her with an expression of annoyance.

The motor rattled to life. Feeling the pitch and yaw of the boat as it turned, Cassie adjusted her footing. Oscar slid right off the top of the highly polished bar top and landed behind the bar with an aggrieved yowl. Maggie ran to check on him. Cassie didn't get the impression that the *Starry Night* was a craft built for speed. If the boat on the horizon was really a pursuing craft, she didn't hold out much hope the *Starry Night* would escape.

Over the whine of the engine, Cassie could hear the Steves plotting in the wheelhouse cabin: "She still behind us?"

"Yeah. She's pulled anchor and is on our ass. She's faster, and will catch us soon."

"I'll get the guns."

Cassie scrambled for her backpack. She'd had enough of guns, enough of killing. She fished her cell phone out of one of the zippered pockets and dialed the number for the farmhouse.

"Hello?" An unfamiliar voice answered.

"Get me the Pythia." Cassie was surprised at the amount of steel that reverberated in her voice, like a piano wire.

"Just a moment." There was the sound of steps retreating. Cassie imagined the kitchen phone set on the counter while one of Delphi's Daughters interrupted the Pythia's smoke break.

"Hello." The Pythia's voice sounded thin over this long distance.

"You promised not to come after me." Cassie's voice sounded cold, though she sat down on the floor to keep her knees from knocking.

"I promised not to bring you back. I never promised not to watch over you."

"Is that what you're doing—surveillance?"

"It's in your best interest for me to make sure you're safe," the Pythia continued, in a soothing purr. "With Tara out of the country, Delphi's Daughters are simply watching—"

"Stop it," Cassie snapped. "You've done enough."

"I can't. You're the future of Delphi's Daughters." The Pythia sounded uncharacteristically helpless.

"Leave me alone. Leave me alone, *right now*. Or I promise you that I will never come back to you. Delphi's Daughters will be without a Pythia. And they will die out."

The threat hung in silence. Cassie's fingers tightened on the phone. She had the trump card, and she'd use it.

"Now, back off. Back off, unless you want more blood on your hands."

Cassie switched off the phone, hand shaking. She climbed up the steps to the wheelhouse. Footing was treacherous as the boat bumped along the waves. The Cowboy sat behind the wheel, while the Kahuna stood with what looked like one of the Pythia's machine guns in his hands.

"They're dropping back," the Cowboy said, glancing behind them.

The Kahuna's grip relaxed a fraction on the machine gun. His sunglass-covered gaze scraped at the sleek boat on the horizon that was falling farther and farther back beyond the waves.

"Good thing," the Kahuna said. "I wasn't much in the mood to play pirate battles on the high seas."

Cassie cracked a wan smile, shaded her eyes with her hand, and stared at the horizon. She was safe for now. But she knew that she couldn't keep running. Eventually, she'd have to confront the Pythia and her own curious destiny.

Chapter Nineteen

T<small>HE TRAIN</small> station at Korosten was little more than a
platform on the outskirts of a small town surrounded
by farmland. A cluster of low buildings stood outside the
sparsely occupied train station, lit with yellow light from
within at dusk. It was a curiously normal scene, one Tara
expected could have been replicated anywhere in the
midwestern U.S. near any smallish city taken root in agri-
cultural land.

As Tara stepped onto the platform from the train station, she took a deep breath. The air here smelled like
freshly mown hay, a welcome change from the cabin
that smelled like cigarette smoke. The smell of smoke
reminded her too much of the Pythia, and Tara had found
it difficult to doze with her face pressed in a pillow that
smelled like her. But the fresh air dispelled some of her
sense of unease.

Until she saw a vendor with a cart stand beside the train station. An old woman was selling beautiful red tomatoes. Chernobyl tomatoes. Tara could make out the Cyrillic word for "Chernobyl" on the sign. She stifled a shudder, imagining the witch in Snow White hawking her poisoned apples. To her amazement, a man walked by and purchased one.

A woman in her late fifties, dressed simply in casual pants, farm boots, and a white cotton blouse approached them. She was petite, brown hair streaked with silver and cut in a chin-length bob. Her skin was kissed with the wholesome-seeming ruddiness of a sunburn.

"Ms. Sheridan, Mr. Lee?" she asked, in heavily accented English. When Tara nodded, the woman stuck out a hand. "I'm Irina. I will be your guide to the Exclusion Zone."

"Thank you." Tara sized her up, wondering how deeply involved she was in Delphi's Daughters. Was she another oracle, or merely one of the Pythia's many flunkies? And how had she drawn babysitting duty? At least the Pythia had seen to it that they were given a handler who spoke English. Tara was relieved; her attempts to stumble through the phrase book the Pythia had sent were thoroughly pathetic.

"This way." She motioned for Tara and Harry to follow her to a crumbling parking lot outside the station. "I have a car."

Irina's car was a small, subcompact car of undetermined vintage, caked in mud and speckled in rust spots. The interior smelled like mildew, and the windows didn't crank up all the way. But Tara was grateful to have the opportunity to be able to communicate with someone who was familiar with the terrain. Harry scrambled into the back with his luggage, his knees jammed up against the back of Tara's front seat. The car's engine sounded like an overworked lawnmower when Irina started it up.

"The Pythia said you are looking for a man," Irina said, pulling out of the train station and onto a gravel two-lane road. "A man selling nuclear secrets."

Harry nodded. "Yes. We think he's coming here. We think he's from here."

Irina's green eyes darkened. "Ah. Another Cherno-bylite has come home."

"What do you mean?"

Irina shrugged. "Many people fled from the disaster, many years ago, and never came back. But many returned to their roots."

"Why?" Harry asked, leaning forward from the back-seat.

"It is home." Irina gestured out the window at the houses dotting the beautiful landscape. Though many looked as if they'd been abandoned, there were clusters of houses that showed signs of life: cows, chickens, cats roaming the yards. "No one bothers us. Not the state, not the churches. In many ways, it is idyllic." She shook her head. "No one brings their children back, of course, but for many of the older folk, and the folk who have nowhere else, it is something of a frontier. No law."

Tara sat forward in her seat, stymied. "But it can't be safe."

Irina barked a harsh laugh. "'Safe' is a relative term. In the days of the war, people feared the Germans. Now, they fear the invisible. It is much more difficult to fear the invisible, the atom that cannot be seen." She gestured to an old woman turning up soil for a garden. "They tell us that we can no longer eat the apples, the potatoes, drink the milk. We must bury the chicken eggs two feet deep. And people did that, I think, for a time, when the soldiers came and scraped all the topsoil away. But that's no way to live."

"The woman with the tomatoes at the train station—" Harry began.

Irina laughed. "Yes. They are sold and given as gifts to many a hated boss or mother-in-law."

Harry didn't cover up his shock.

Irina wagged her finger. "You will become accustomed to our sense of humor, young man."

Harry sat back in the backseat, muttering: "I hope not."

Irina pretended not to hear him. "It's growing late. I will take you to my house, and then we will go to the Exclusion Zone in the morning. The Exclusion Zone is large—it extends for thirty kilometers around the site of the disaster. We will have much before us, if we are to find your dealer in secrets."

"We were hoping to start as soon as possible—" Harry began.

Irina made a cutting gesture. "It's not safe in the Exclusion Zone at night. There are wolves, looters. We wait until morning." It was clear she would brook no argument.

Irina asked Tara and Harry few questions about themselves, and Tara tried to be as respectful of her boundaries. Still, she was curious when the car stopped outside a small house built not far from the road with a ribbon of a disintegrating gravel driveway leading to it. A garden bloomed in the front yard, thick with the smell of manure. A cow chewed cud from behind a ramshackle fence, in a green field heavy with the tassels of grasses. A chicken darted out from in front of the car, clucking in annoyance. It was a bucolic scene, with dusky mist settling from the sky into the ground.

Tara followed her up the creaking front porch. Tara noted that Irina didn't lock her front door. "You live alone?" she asked, surprised.

"No," Irina responded curtly. "I have a cow, three cats, and seven chickens. That's hardly 'alone.'"

The first floor of Irina's house was a large room. It was filled with a jumble of brightly patterned furniture and quilts, old photographs, and a collection of painted eggs. The far side of the room held a small sink, a stove, and a refrigerator, all probably older than Tara. A pressure cooker sat on the counter with open canning jars, lids, and rims. A shelf held dozens of jars of tomatoes put away for the winter. A cat with one blind eye watched Tara and Harry with suspicion.

"This way," Irina said, leading them up a staircase that hugged one of the walls. Two bedrooms and a bathroom were at the top of the stairs. Irina showed them to a bed tucked under the eaves of the house, covered with a delicately embroidered coverlet. "You can sleep here."

"Thank you," Tara said.

Irina nodded. "As the Pythia commands." Her eyes sparkled in humor, and she shut the door behind her as she left.

Harry paced the length of the room, jingling the change in his pocket. Tara could tell he was impatient to get underway. But the light was falling, and there was nothing to be done for it. Irina was their guide, and they were wedded to her judgment.

Tara dug out the GPS device that the Cowboy had given her. She booted it up, hoping that it would get a signal this far out. According to the device, they were a scant five kilometers from the border of the Exclusion Zone. Close enough to reach out and touch it.

She showed it to Harry, and he emitted a low whistle. "I wonder if those chickens glow in the dark."

Tara dug the dosimeter out of her pocket, switched it on. It chirped like a canary. Harry peered over her shoulder. "That's not good. It says that the background level is thirty two microroentgens per hour. That's four times the amount of background radiation in a normal environment. And we're not in the Exclusion Zone yet."

Tara suppressed a shudder, switched it off.

"Why'd you do that?"

She had trouble articulating it to him. She was so accustomed to dealing with the unseen world and measuring it in her own way that the machine was unsettling. "I don't really want to know. We don't have any choice in this mission. This"—she pointed to the machine—"is just a distraction. I don't want to think of how I've dragged you along after me and exposed you to glow-in-the-dark chickens."

Harry wrapped his arms around her. "Hey. I go where I want, remember? The Pythia can't make me do shit. I didn't come out here out of duty to her."

"You came here to catch the Chimera, I know."

"Partly. But I also came here because of my duty to you." Harry kissed her temple. "I can't let you face the glow-in-the-dark chickens alone."

She sighed, resting her forehead on his shoulder. The Pythia had been right.

She did need him here. But at what cost?

THE COST HAD BEEN IMMENSE, BUT GALEN HAD RETURNED home. He had no desire to escape his roots. Rather, he wished to lie down in them and allow them to wrap around him, digesting him wholly.

His fingers brushed the tall, green grasses splitting bits of pavement. In the ruddy sunset, the land had been painted in washes of gold and red. He stood before the looming Sarcophagus, its shadow driven long by the sun before him. This was the place that had been built to contain the radiation from the failed reactor, a black structure lined with lead and steel. But it was disintegrating; bits of rust showed at the seams that leaked bits of straw from birds' nests. Warped pine trees grew around it, digging their roots into the foundations. It had cost thousands of lives to build this thing, and it was failing. Split seams and popped rivets were visible even from this distance, leaking that prickling radiation into the land.

Galen could hear none of the ghosts that had been sacrificed to build it. He could barely hear the ghosts of the people he'd consumed, and loneliness began to infest his thoughts. But he could feel the malignant power of this place, that splinter of poison in this beautiful land.

And he would begin to dig it out.

His cell phone rang at his hip, and he answered. "Yes."

"The materiel you promised us . . . is it on schedule?"

"Yes. It will be ready on time."

"And is it . . . as potent as you promised?"

Galen inhaled, feeling the metallic buzz of the radiation on his skin and prickling in his lungs. He wore no protective suit here. There was no point. He was dying, and he wanted to take this last opportunity to feel the pulse of his motherland, the force that made him.

"It is," Galen said.

"Good. We look forward to obtaining it."

Galen shut off the phone. He turned back to the truck containing his tools. The truck contained lead-lined barrels, empty now. But they would soon be full, full and taken away. Galen had no hope he would be able to remove all of the contamination. An army had tried, and failed. But he could remove some of it, surrender it to the rest of the world for their wars. What they did with it was not his concern.

Galen slung a heavy tool bag over his shoulder and walked toward the cool shadow of the Sarcophagus. A bit of movement around the edge of the building caught his attention, and he froze. It was too late in the day for stalkers to come . . . Who was here?

But it wasn't people. A thin, gray wolf slunk through the sunshine-hazed underbrush. It paused to look at him. Galen returned its golden stare. The wolf trotted away, leaving him to his task.

A good omen, he thought. *A very good omen.*

"Not a good omen," Irina muttered.

The Ukrainian woman had cracked open an egg into a bowl, was peering into it. Tara glanced up from her perch at Irina's small kitchen table. "What do you mean?"

Irina showed her the small bowl. Blood mixed in with the yellow yolk and white albumen in streaks. "Blood is a poor augur for your quest." Irina took the egg and dumped it out the back door, to the chagrin of a chicken standing outside. She carefully rinsed the bowl and dried it. "They say that we're supposed to bury the eggs at least two feet deep, but . . ." She slung her dishtowel over her shoulder and continued to poke at some potatoes cooking on the stove with a spatula. Tara was used to associating eggs and potatoes with breakfast, but Irina was preparing them for dinner. Tara thought her body was just jet-lagged enough that it made sense, and her stomach growled at the aromas.

"You're an oracle," Tara said. "You're one of Delphi's Daughters."

Irina shrugged. "I'm a very minor oracle. There's not much demand for ovamancers. Except for here."

It made sense. Tara glanced around the living area, decorated with hand-painted eggs in egg cups and wooden holders. "Are these all your work?"

"Yes."

"They're beautiful."

"Thank you. Once, I used to sell them. Still do. But there's not much demand for them anymore. People want practical things, things they can eat or tools they can use. Beauty is a useless luxury."

Tara fingered the scars crossing her arm. She understood some of the sentiment. Irina had loosened up a bit, chatted more now that Harry wasn't in the picture. He was upstairs, fiddling with the GPS device and fussing over the dosimeter. "Why are you here, then?"

Irina's mouth turned down. "Duty. I'm a stalker."

"I read about those," Tara said slowly. "You take radiation readings around the Exclusion Zone and record them."

"Yes. Not that I think that it makes any difference to anyone. I report on containment, on the disintegration of structures, on any deformed animals I see." Irina shook her head. "It's very solitary work."

Tara's eyes roved over Irina's shelves, at the photographs arranged on the wall. Most were black and white. One was a wedding picture, showing a younger Irina with a handsome young man in a military uniform. Others were photographs of the same young man in his uniform, standing before the Soviet flag. "You weren't always alone."

Irina followed her gaze. "No. That's my husband, Pavel. He and I used to live here, in this house, together, before the accident." She poked the potatoes. "He was a firefighter. One of the liquidators sent in to clean up after the accident. The radiation killed him within weeks. He turned black as a husk, shriveled away. Just like the men who fought the fire on the roof of the building, and the men who swam beneath the reactor to shut off the valves, keep the melted fuel and radiation from contaminating the groundwater. Thcy were heroes, and the radiation took them."

"I'm sorry."

She shook her head. "I did my best to try and save him, tried to draw the radiation out with the eggs. I rolled them over his body, day and night. When I cracked them open, the yolks were black as oil. But no oracle magick could help him. He was too far gone.

"I knew that it was coming. But no one would listen to me. None of the party bosses, none of the military men. I saw it in the eggs, saw there was something dark and terrible coming. I stood outside of the building and screamed at the men to stop their experiments. But no one listened to me, to the egg witch." Her hand holding the spatula stilled. "They arrested me, took me away. I failed to stop it."

Tara's heart ached for the woman, for the guilt she must carry with her. "Why stay here, then? Does the Pythia ask this of you?"

"Because it's my duty." Irina's chin lifted. "I am the woman who watches to make sure that the dragon sleeps. I'm proud to do it, and . . . it is a kind of penance, for my failure. It is the last small thing that I can do."

Irina scraped the potatoes onto dishes. "It is a different mentality here, than in the West, I think. We have a desire here to be heroes, to make sacrifices. It's a kind of fatalism, I think, that runs counter to the selfish individualism I see in many Westerners." She handed one of the dishes to Tara. "It is a desire and a privilege to serve humanity. You know what that means, to be an oracle in the service of Delphi's Daughters."

Tara didn't answer, just stabbed her fork into the fried potatoes. When she chewed the bite, she expected it to taste like the poison it had leached from the contaminated ground. Instead, it tasted like a potato, ordinary and buttery.

"Sometimes, it's difficult not to question the ones we serve," Tara said, mildly

Irina cracked a sad smile. "Pavel said that, too. But he still went to fight the fire."

"Are we just puppets, Harry? Or are we invisible heroes, like the firefighters and the liquidators?"

Tara lay on the bed, staring up at the ceiling beams in Irina's house. Harry sat on the floor, one of Irina's maps of the Exclusion Zone spread out before him. He looked up at her with surprise. "What brought that on?"

"Talking with Irina. Thinking about Delphi's Daughters. Thinking about the things that both you and I have lost, serving the government." Unconsciously, her fingers scraped the scars on her arm. "The innocence Cassie's lost, serving Delphi's Daughters. I guess my cynicism tends to get the best of me. When I see someone like Irina unselfishly giving herself to a cause no one remembers . . . I feel sort of ashamed. Selfish."

Harry leaned back against the side of the bed. "I think you've given a hell of a lot in the service of man. You nearly gave your life to stop the Gardener. That's more than the vast majority of people would ever contemplate."

Tara stroked the edge of a scar. "And one of the things I've been trying to learn is not to sacrifice my whole life to him. He hurt me, yes. But I don't want that to control my life."

"And he shouldn't." Harry shook his head. "I've been trying to find that balance for myself, too. How much do I give to the job . . . and how much do I hold back for myself?" He reached up and took her hand. "There's no easy answer. The fact that we struggle with it more than Irina does, doesn't make us selfish."

"I don't know. I just wonder if there are some people, like Delphi's Daughters, who don't have another life, who have surrendered it to the larger pattern. And I don't know if I want to surrender that, to the Pythia or the government."

Harry looked up at her. "You know we could quit and run off into the sunset together." He was smiling, but Tara wondered if he meant it.

Tara's heart quickened. "But what about Cassie, and the cat and the dog . . ."

"With Cassie and the cat and the dog."

"Tempting. But do you think we'd get over the guilt of not properly serving our various masters?"

"Probably not. But that's just who we are. The whole hero gig. Somebody's gotta do it. Whether or not anyone else cares or remembers."

Tara sighed. "Maybe." She was nervous about the hero gig unfolding tomorrow, about what they might find in the Exclusion Zone, about confronting the Chimera. And she was worried about Cassie, who was heroically avoiding the Pythia back home.

Tara leaned over and dug into her bag for her cards. She shuffled them quietly and thought of Cassie. She plucked one card from the deck and regarded it thoughtfully.

The Page of Cups depicted a young woman with her back to the sea. She was holding a chalice from which a fish leapt. Her expression was one of delighted surprise. Tara smiled at it. Cassie was healing in her own way, making an emotional recovery Tara was certain would bring its own fair share of surprises.

Tara turned her attention to tomorrow's task: finding the Chimera. The cards fluttered in her hands, and she thought at the deck: *What do I need to know?*

She drew three cards and laid them out on the bedspread. The first one, the Magician, showed a man in a violet cloak, reaching toward the sky with a glowing wand. The card was reversed. A lemniscate, an infinity symbol, glowed above his head. Tara let her finger linger on the card, considering. The Magician usually represented the act of creation, mastery over the four elements. Reversed, it suggested mental illness, disaster, and an inability to tame natural forces. Her gaze was caught on the glowing wand and lemniscate, and she thought of radiation. This indicated to her that she should not expect the Chimera to behave in an entirely rational way.

The second card was the Hierophant, showing a man in papal robes, seated on a throne. This was a card of duty, of servitude. Tara thought about Irina and her service to a silent goal, and Tara's own confusion about her own service.

The third card gave her pause. The Hanged Man showed a man dangling by his foot on a wire suspended between two trees. The man gazed serenely out into space, as if he had surrendered. Tara frowned. This was a card of sacrifice. Something precious was going to be sacrificed in the confrontation with the Chimera. This, with the omen of Irina's egg, suggested that it could be bloody.

"What do you see?" Harry watched her as she tucked the cards beneath her pillow.

Tara shook her head. "The Chimera's not a rational man, at least, not anymore."

"I can't imagine having experienced this place and still being rational. That's not a surprise."

Tara remained silent. She stretched out on the bed with her head on the pillow. Harry climbed into bed behind her, wrapped his arms around her waist. "What else?"

"We've got to do our duty, to stop him. But it's going to cost us."

Harry rested the top of his chin on her head. "Hey, we're heroes. No less than the liquidators and the stalkers. We'll get it done."

Tara bit her lip. She hoped that the sacrifice would be worth it.

TARA DIDN'T DREAM OF THE HIEROPHANT OR THE MAGICIAN. Instead, she dreamed of the Hanged Man.

Tara crept through the brittle black forest of her dreams, searching for the man with the glowing rods. Her lion kept pace, pausing to sniff the ground. The sun poured down through the blackened trees in luminous shafts, suspending bits of ash that clung to Tara's dress and crept into her lungs. It stained the lion's fur black, as if he'd been walking in oil.

The sun sparkled against something metallic overhead, and Tara stopped in her tracks. She looked up to see a figure suspended on a wire, dangling like a toy on a string. She recognized the armor. It was Harry, the Knight of Pentacles, swinging by his ankle in the stillness.

Tara picked up her skirts and drew her sword to rush toward him. She had to cut him down. But the lion blocked her path, growling.

"Let me through," Tara insisted, shoving at his flank. "I have to help Harry."

The lion glowered at her, roared.

"I have to help him." She had no choice in it. It was the duty of her heart. She couldn't just leave him, no matter how her intuition snarled.

She succeeded in sidestepping the lion, making a break for the tree under which Harry was suspended . . .

In a flurry of blackened leaves, something snagged and lashed around her foot. It yanked her up off the ground. Tara dropped her sword, hand scrabbling in the leaves, but the rope suspending her snapped up into the tree canopy. She shielded her head with her arms as the brittle branches snapped against her. The upward motion stopped with a jerk, and she was left, dangling, suspended by her foot in the tree branches. Just like Harry. Trapped.

Blood rushed to her head, and she felt her pulse thundering in her ears. Tara twisted, trying to reach her ankle to release herself. She only succeeded in turning herself in a dizzying spin that slowed only when she reached her arms out to her sides and concentrated on nothing but breathing.

She looked down. The lion gazed up at her, growled, tail lashing in the black leaves. He'd told her so. She'd failed to listen to him, and now Tara and Harry were both trapped.

And he was not alone. Tara's breath caught in her throat when she saw the engineer of the trap standing at the edge of the thicket: the World, holding a precious, glowing bundle of rods, glared at her with a bottomless expression of malice, like a spider who had just discovered something new trapped in his web.

CHAPTER **Twenty**

"You can wear that, if it makes you feel better."

A chiding smile played at the corner of Irina's mouth as she watched Harry and Tara gather their gear. They'd donned the crisp white Tyvek suits Tara had gotten from the archivist, and clunky boots and gloves from Steve's military surplus store. Respirators dangled around their necks, and Harry had insisted that Tara clip the dosimeter onto her belt, while he held the GPS device and the gun from the mugger. Harry had duct-taped together the seams of the suits and gloves. They looked like low-budget astronauts in a middle-school science fiction play.

In contrast, Irina wore a stained canvas suit and a pair of black boots. Tara noticed she kept these items on the front porch, not in the house. A pair of welder's gloves was tucked into her belt, but she wore no respirator. Just a hat and a dust mask. She carried a Soviet-era dosimeter with a strap that went over her shoulder and a clipboard. A pencil was perched behind her ear.

"You don't worry about the radiation?" Harry asked.

Irina shrugged. "I'll roll eggs over you when we get back, if you want. That removes the worst of it."

Harry stared at her, incredulous.

"She's an ovamancer," Tara supplied.

"Oh, well, that explains everything," snapped Harry. Tara knew he was distrustful of things he couldn't see: intuition, radiation, love. And this case had too many of these elements for him to suffer gracefully.

"They used to tell us that vodka and milk would neutralize the radiation," Irina said. "I don't think I believe that, but it doesn't hurt to try."

"I believe I'll be ready for that drink." Harry shook his head and followed Irina to the same car they'd taken from the train station.

The car turned over, bumped down the vacant roads. They passed no other cars, but Tara saw birds flitting between the trees of the lush green forest intersecting the fields. "The animals . . . have they shown any signs of radiation poisoning?"

"Not as much now as they did. When Pripyat was evacuated, soldiers came and shot as many of the house pets and cattle as they could find. They missed a great deal. My cats are descendents of those."

From the window, Tara could see a long chain-link fence, topped by barbed wire, extending through a field. Birds perched on top of the wire. Harry struggled to roll up the window, but had no success. The sky was gray and overcast, threatening rain. Tara wondered if the windshield wipers on the car worked.

Irina continued. "Birds are a good sign. After the accident, the sparrows were the first to die. They'd fall out of the sky like stones. But they came back, slowly. You'll see . . . nature has reclaimed the land. It's still poison, but it doesn't belong to man any longer."

Irina pulled off the road before a gate. A sign beside the gate in Cyrillic detailed a warning that was almost two feet long. A radiation symbol was prominently displayed at the top of the sign.

"Welcome to the Exclusion Zone," Irina said. She hopped out of the car to open the gate.

"Don't you have guards or something here?" Harry asked.

"The main checkpoints do, to deter looters," Irina said. "But there wasn't the interest or funding to keep them at all the gates. Besides, everything worth stealing is already gone."

That was nearly incomprehensible to Tara. In what kind of world would someone willingly take contaminated property? In a very desperate one, she decided.

They continued down the road, into an abandoned city where trees grew in between blocky administration and apartment buildings. "This is Pripyat," Irina explained. "Most of the Chernobyl workers lived here. They were told they would be able to return, and most left everything behind, expecting to reclaim it later."

A rusting Ferris wheel stood in an empty lot, beside

bumper cars that had been wrapped in fencing wire. "What's that?" Harry asked.

"Pripyat was preparing for the May Day festival. They were forced to leave this behind."

Irina stopped the car before a low, flat building that might have been a school. The skeleton of a swing set still remained beside it. "I need to take some readings. Feel free to walk around. But don't pick up anything on the ground. And don't touch the moss, especially. It seems to hold the radiation like a sponge."

Tara slipped her respirator on and piled out of the car behind Harry. While Irina made some notations on her clipboard, Tara listened to the dosimeter at her waist click. She walked up to the side of the building and peered in, mindful to avoid the toxic moss on the pavement. Inside, she could see desks, moldering books, and even pieces of chalk along the blackboard. It was as if everyday life had immediately been annihilated.

"When were you evacuated?" Tara asked.

"Not for several days after the accident," Irina said, distractedly, as she filled out her forms. "I don't think anyone, not even the party bosses, really knew what we were dealing with. At least, I'd like to believe that."

They piled back into the car and continued down the road, past a field full of rusting cars and Soviet helicopters. "This is a storage yard for contaminated vehicles. They've been pretty well stripped for parts," Irina explained. "I occasionally find something there to fix the car, but not often. I don't like the rats much."

Tara's skin crawled, imagining Irina scavenging the junkyard for parts.

Harry asked, "Where are the highest radiation levels you've recorded? We think our suspect is looking to dig up some old reactor fuel."

Irina frowned, considering. "Radiation is a capricious thing. One house on a street may be within normal parameters, but the one next door might be hot. I've often wondered if something as simple as the color of paint might have something to do with it. You may be looking a long time, if you want to examine all the hot spots. But . . . the most consistently high levels I've found are around the Sarcophagus itself. You might start there and fan out."

Irina drove them another two kilometers to the plant itself. Tara couldn't help but feel a sense of foreboding as they approached. She stopped at a gate on the perimeter . . . This would be one of the official, manned gates that Irina had described. It was on a paved road and had a little guard house with a red-and-white painted stop arm.

"I will ask them if they've seen anyone." Irina pulled the car up behind the guard house. She leaned out of the car and rapped on the window, but no one answered. Her brows drew together. "There should be someone here."

Tara and Harry climbed out and circled around the guard house to the unlocked door. A dead guard sprawled on the floor, wedged between the bottom of his chair and the console.

Irina sucked in her breath and swore in Russian. Tara checked for a pulse, but found none. The man was stiff and cold.

"How long are their shifts?"

"Twelve hours. He's been on since last night." Irina stepped over the guard to the radio apparatus on the small countertop. The aging radio had been cracked open and the microphone ripped out of the housing. "The radio's been destroyed."

"Our Chimera's close," Harry muttered. Tara saw that his gun was drawn, that he'd wrapped his clumsy gloved fingers over it. "He must have brought a car."

"If it's here, we'll find it."

They piled back into the car and idled down the main street of the industrial complex. Irina guided the car down rows of blocky buildings studded with glass and concrete. Some of them had to be administrative and supply buildings, Tara guessed. Some still had electricity: one had a digital sign on the side that displayed the time and radiation levels. They passed one that displayed eighty-one millionths of a roentgen per hour. Tara stifled a shudder. Normal background radiation was supposed to be between six and twelve millionths.

Irina wound down to the reactor complex, behind the peeling red and white paint of a smokestack. "We're coming up on unit four . . . the one that failed. Until recently, the others had still been running."

"Unbelievable," Harry muttered behind his respirator.

Unit four was unmistakable. The Sarcophagus covered part of the white building in a black box, holding in the radioactive debris from the reactor. If the spent fuel from the other reactors was being stored somewhere, this would be a good place to put it, behind this formidable lead-lined casket.

And the Chimera apparently thought so, too. A truck was parked in front of it. Irina parked several meters away behind the edge of a crumbling building to let Harry and Tara out.

"He's here. Can you go get more guards?" Harry asked.

Irina nodded. "I'll have to get to the next town for a radio, but I will bring them." She glanced at the Sarcophagus. "Are you sure—?"

"Yes."

"Be careful." Irina handed them a heavy flashlight through the open window.

The small car buzzed away, leaving Harry and Tara in the shadow of the Sarcophagus. A stiff breeze rattled pebbles across the pavement and bent grasses and warped pine trees. Harry approached the truck, gun drawn. Tara clutched the flashlight like a club as they advanced on it.

The truck was the kind used to transport cattle, with a ramp and slats to keep the cattle from pitching over the sides of the bed. Inside the bed were a dozen metal drums. Some were open, and some were closed. As Tara approached, the alarm on her dosimeter wailed. She stifled it, turning off the volume. A glance told her the background radiation was almost a full roentgen. It vibrated against her hip furiously, like a hornet caught in a jar. Tara could feel the vibration crawling along her skin underneath her suit, the prickle of radiation that felt like standing too close to a stereo speaker.

Harry peered into the cab. "Nobody home."

"It's hot. We can't let him take the truck out of here."

Harry slid into the driver's seat. No keys in the ignition. He reached under the dashboard and ripped the wires out from under it. "It's not going anywhere, now."

The back window of the truck shattered in a hail of glass. Instinctively, Tara hit the ground, recoiling when she discovered that it was covered in contaminated moss. When she lifted her head, she saw a figure advancing upon the truck with a rifle at his shoulder. Her breath caught in her throat.

The Chimera was not the figure of the World she'd seen in her dreams. Instead, he was an angry man dressed in dusty black pants, black T-shirt, and a miner's helmet with a light that flashed in the sunshine. A radiation burn blistered over his skin, turning his angular countenance red and furious.

Another shot slammed into the pickup, and Tara ducked behind the truck's bulk. She gripped the flashlight, crawling around the corner of the truck. She didn't think the Chimera had seen her yet. Perhaps she could circle around . . .

Harry returned fire from the back of the truck. Unfazed, the Chimera advanced. Tara heard Harry swear about cheap ammunition, heard him slam the gun against the dash. The gun had jammed. And the Chimera was coming.

GALEN ADVANCED ON HIS QUARRY, TRAPPED IN THE TRUCK CAB like a bug in a jar. He shouted at the man to come out, banged on the flank of the truck with the butt of the rifle. A man in a white plastic suit tumbled out of the cab, hurled a gun at him, and charged.

Galen was tackled into the metallic-tasting moss. The rifle was trapped between the two men, and Galen struggled to re-establish control of the weapon. The gun fired near the truck, deflating one of the tires in a hiss.

No. He would not allow this interloper to interfere with his plans. For an instant, Galen wondered who this intruder was. He was too overdressed in protective gear to be a stalker, but there would be no one else here . . .

Galen's bare hand clawed at the man's face, knocking the respirator off. His palm made contact with the man's face, a man whom he recognized from Veriss's memories: Harry Li. His hot palm seared into Li's face, feeling the burning of memory there. For an instant, he could hear Li's voice in his head, that churning mass of fear and determination and frustration. He heard Li howling outside him, but heard his voice and memory beginning to leak into his head, like a water tap turned on low. He flashed on a memory of a beautiful, dark-haired woman tangled in sheets and scars.

That memory was clubbed out of him by a blow to the back of his head. Galen reeled back, and was struck over and over by something heavy that slammed his head again and again into the moss-covered ground.

He ripped away from Li, lashed out at the new figure in white who was clubbing the hell out of him with a flashlight. He knocked that peculiarly solid ghost to the ground, against the howl of Li's voice in his ear.

He clambered to his feet and ran, ran to the Sarcophagus.

Overhead, the sky split open, and it began to rain.

"HARRY."

Tara cradled Harry's head in her lap, stroking the side of his face where a handprint-shaped burn bloomed. Rain speckled his cheek. The Chimera had only had the chance to touch Harry for a second before she clubbed him. But the touch had seemed to affect Harry like acid. She shook him, and rainwater sluiced off his suit in runnels to the ground.

"Harry, please talk to me."

He didn't move. He was still breathing. She could feel the rise and fall of his chest under her gloves. His pulse was quick, but thready. What had the Chimera done to him? She cradled his head in her hands, and tears gurgled into her respirator. Had the Chimera sucked Harry's mind dry, like he had the others? Was this the sacrifice the Hanged Man had foretold?

Irina would bring help, soon. But she wasn't going to leave him here, in the puddles and toxic moss. Tara grasped Harry under the arms and dragged him away to a piece of broken concrete that jutted above the ruined lot. It was clear of moss and water, and out of the line of sight of the truck if the Chimera came back, but not so hidden that Irina's men couldn't find him. Tenderly, she arranged his hands on his chest. She was reminded of the Four of Swords she'd seen in her dreams, the knight asleep in effigy.

Tara pulled aside her respirator and kissed him. Underneath his plastic armor, Harry made no move. What had been magick in her dream world was dreadfully ordinary in this one.

But, unlike in her dream world, she wouldn't allow the Chimera to win. Tara's hands balled into fists, and she searched the broken pavement for Harry's discarded gun. She popped the jammed round out of the chamber with some effort, saw two shots left in the clip behind a distended spring. It would have to work.

Squaring her shoulders, she confronted the Sarcophagus. Her white-shrouded feet split the surface tension of uneven puddles as she approached. The shadow of the Sarcophagus loomed cold over her, though straw from bird nests leaked from the seams between its uneven and hastily erected lead plates. The windowless façade was streaked with rust from disintegrating bolts and seams forced open by wayward plants. Rain peppered her radiation hood, and she felt water begin to creep in at the neck, mingling with sweat. She paced the perimeter of it until she found an opening, a ripped panel beside a warped pine tree.

The Chimera wasn't afraid of this place, and she was determined not to fear it, either.

She expected nearly total darkness, waited a moment for her eyes to adjust. It was dark, but light streamed in from split seams in the roof, drizzling water from rusted beams. Stripped electronics panels confronted her, windows pulled open and wires snaking out of steel cabinets. She wound her way around the cabinets, the plastic-draped consoles with silent dials, some scavenged for use elsewhere, leaving gaping holes in annunciator panels. Even here, in the control area, steel had creased and buckled under the force of the explosion. Overhead, rain drummed with a deafening sound.

At her hip, the dosimeter vibrated furiously. Tara ignored it, and tried not to imagine what was in the dust she shuffled through as she made her way through the maze. Spray-painted radiation readings were scrawled along the walls with the dates . . . In May of 1986, the background radiation was .5 roentgens per hour. Tara glanced down at her dosimeter. Her dosimeter crept near 1.0 roentgens . . . suggesting that whatever the Chimera had accomplished here had breached containment.

She swore under her breath, muffled by her respirator.

A rusted, bowed set of stairs extended before her. A padlocked door leading to them had been ripped open, a steel radiation sign curled back like paper. Tara guessed this was the path to the main reactor hall. The stairs were lit by dull yellow emergency lighting. She climbed them with her pistol at the ready, sweat trickling between her shoulder blades. The saliva in her mouth tasted like tinfoil, and she could feel the prickling of radiation along her skin, under her suit. Why any human being would voluntarily go in here was beyond her.

The floor of the reactor hall was filled with nearly two feet of uneven concrete and disintegrating bits of yellow plastic foam, poured in an attempt to reduce contamination. Beyond that, the debris field appeared largely untouched. In the dim yellow lighting, it looked like a scene from an apocalypse: torn I-beams warped around massive slabs of concrete and steel reaching four stories tall. Clay and boron particles dusted over the scene like snow, dropped from helicopters decades earlier. Shafts of light and water from the disintegrating ceiling poured through to illuminate the debris. Overhead, a bird flapped, trying to escape the rain. The weak structure groaned under the pelting of the rain, making a sound like sand dunes sighing that Tara could feel in the soles of her feet.

A shattered window to the main reactor perched on a ruined wall. Tara stood on tiptoe to peer in, through gravel and bits of glass melted yellow and blue. Part of the shell of the refueling station had crashed through that wall and landed on its side. This was where the fuel rods had been placed into the machine. Melted fuel, like frozen magma, extended below it from the sleeves where the fuel rods would have been inserted. She could see evidence of digging here: one of the barrels from the truck, hand shovels, and hastily made reinforcement efforts with scraps of metal.

Tara shivered. It seemed ungodly, the immense scale, the force. Unnatural. Evil.

The movement of a light glimmered on the top of the reactor, swept a beam in Tara's direction. She lifted her gun.

"Chimera. Stop." She didn't know what else to call him. He was as much an abomination as this place.

He turned, regarding her. His rifle was at his shoulder. "What did you call me?"

• • • •

"CHIMERA."

Galen cocked his head, looking at the small woman standing on the catwalk below him. He leapt down, curiosity stinging him as much as the air stung his flesh. This was the only living human who understood what he was. He heard Harry Li's voice buzzing in the back of his skull. He knew Tara. Knew that she was special.

"You know what I am."

"I know you survived this." Her free hand, the one not holding the gun, sketched the devastation. "I know it changed you. And I know it shouldn't have happened."

Galen snorted. "It was inevitable."

"It was human error."

"Human error is inevitable in any endeavor. No matter what the precautions, there will always be an error." Galen took a deep breath, tasting the dust at the back of his throat. His lungs ached. He could feel them burning.

"What are you doing here?"

Galen licked dust from his lips. "Everyone thought this place was dead. All the old fuel melted and hardened into rock, wrapped in lead and concrete. But that wasn't true. I learned from the old spies that this place was being used . . . used to store radioactive debris from other sites, other reactors, other projects. And then forgotten."

"Why not leave it alone? Let it rot here in lead."

Galen laughed. "This place is a cancer. And they fed it, made it worse. I want the rest of the world to experience it, to understand what a fucking mess this is, until someone calls a stop to it."

"That's why you sold the information, the whereabouts of the other nuclear debris."

"There's enough poison for all of us." The cesium in his mouth tasted bitter. The ceiling of the Sarcophagus creaked above him, as if underlining his point.

"And now . . . why get your hands dirty, why dig this out yourself?"

He stared up at the vast, dark ceiling. "I am like the firemen who knew they were dying. I have nothing left to lose. I am rooted to this place."

"I cannot let you go." Tara stared down the barrel of the gun at him. Her voice was short, breathy, as if she were having difficulty breathing through the respirator covering half her face. "You must be held to account for your crimes, for spreading this misery to others."

Galen sighed. The stock of the rifle was pressed to his shoulder, moved with each breath. "I won't go with you."

The look of sadness in the woman's eyes reminded him of the nurse in Minsk who snuck him apples. "I am sorry." She pulled the trigger of the gun.

And nothing happened.

She pulled it again, with the same echoing click.

Galen let loose a breath he hadn't realized he'd been holding, coughed on his shoulder. That was the same piece of shit gun that Harry Li had. Useless. He advanced forward on the catwalk to her. Her eyes widened, and she lifted her chin.

"This is a good death," Galen said. "A hero's death. Unlike the men and women who died here of fire and burns, and who will continue to die here, of cancer . . . this will be quick. No invisible force cooking you alive as you sleep. Just a clean bullet."

His finger flexed on the trigger.

"Harry," she said.

The voice in Galen's head that belonged to Harry Li howled at him. Galen's grip on the gun shook. He saw, through Harry Li's eyes, her scars and her smile. Her strength, how she had survived being buried alive. How she had found him, using her cartomancer's talents. She was like Galen. A monster, in her own world, in her own way. But he could feel Harry's love for her, strong and proximate. Not the distracted wistfulness Carl had felt for Lena. Galen could not understand how Harry had been able to leave her alone, and his fingers twitched. Galen had longed for that kind of love his whole life, that kind of a union, being understood with judgment suspended. But Harry had cast it all away, not realizing what he had lost.

"You're a witch," he said. "A witch who knows something of the horrors practiced by man."

"An oracle. An oracle who knows something of horror," she admitted. The plastic on her respirator flexed and caved inward.

"Tell me something." He licked his sunburned lips. "Will this happen again?"

Tara stared at him with those inky blue eyes. "It might. All I can say is that I will do everything in my power to keep it from happening. There is an order of oracles which tries to keep this from happening—one of the stalkers here foresaw it, but no one would listen to her." She shook her head, sucking the plastic close to her face. "I can make you no clear prediction, only say what I will do."

At least she was honest. Not like those lying spies.

Galen advanced across the catwalk. He wanted her voice in his head, wanted it more than Harry Li had ever wanted it. He wanted hers to be the last voice he ever heard.

Tara's breath rang in the respirator, like breathing into a bottle, but something was wrong. She wasn't getting enough air. She thought the dust might be clogging it, but couldn't be certain. Instead, she tried to answer the Chimera's questions as she stood, unarmed. The air trickled down to a thin wheeze, then nothing. The plastic sucked against her nose and mouth.

She lifted the mask from her face, gasping, inhaling dust and rust and all the breath of the Chimera's world.

She stumbled in the debris, tripping on a piece of steel jutting over the edge of the catwalk. She landed on her hands and knees, disturbing a cloud of dust that washed over her face and hands. Tears stung her eyes.

She heard the Chimera's footsteps behind her, felt the cool barrel of the gun brushing her hair.

She reached for a handful of the stained glass shards from the reactor window, glinting in the weak light. She took them in her fist, turned, and flung them at the Chimera. The Chimera dropped the gun and clawed at his face. The rifle rolled off the edge of the catwalk into darkness.

Tara reached for a piece of cable snaking across the floor of the catwalk. She yanked it free with all her strength.

Tara clambered to her feet, brandishing the ruined cable like a whip. Rain sluiced down from the debris, pooling around her ankles.

The Chimera snarled, his sunburned face a mass of scratches. She lashed the cable at him. It struck him across the throat, and he grasped his neck, which began leaking blood on his filthy shirt.

She struck him again. And again. Rage bubbled in her for what he'd done to Harry, for what he'd done to Veriss, Lockley, and the rest. She wanted to scream at him that the way to stop nuclear devastation wasn't by creating more of it. Just like killing wouldn't stop any more killing.

The cable lashed around his neck. Tara yanked him off his feet, dragged him to his knees on the catwalk. The Chimera wound his hands around the cable, trying to yank the cable from Tara's grip.

Tara moved behind him, wrapping the cable tighter around his neck. With her knee in his back, she grasped both edges of the cable and pulled as hard as she could. Tears streamed down her face as she watched his hands flail. She didn't know if the Chimera held the last of Harry's memory, if he was all that was left of Harry's mind. But he had to be stopped.

The Pythia was right. Sometimes, killing was the only solution.

Something groaned overhead. Tara looked up in enough time to feel flakes of rust falling on her face, like snow. She blinked, seeing a flurry of bird wings flapping in the shadows overhead. A rusted I-beam began to shift loose under the force of water on the flat roof, ripped down in a wash of water and wings.

Tara released the cable and leapt away. The I-beam fragment crashed into the catwalk, severing it and sending it smashing into the debris field. Tara clung to an intact support rail, watching as the girder pinned the Chimera to the pile of rubble like a squirming bug. A plume of dust rose, and settled quickly in the rain that plinked over his skin.

The Chimera reached out for her. In a voice that sounded very much like Harry's, he cried: "Don't leave me alone."

Tara picked her way into the debris field, climbing over bits of split concrete and metal to reach him. He was pinned completely under the beam, only his arm and head visible, pressed into a puddle. Tara tried to shove the beam aside, but it was too heavy for her by several tons.

"Don't leave me," the Chimera whispered again.

Tara sat down beside him in the mud. She put her gloved hand in his, mindful not to let his skin touch her. The killing wrath had drained away, and she was filled with sadness at seeing him, this broken creature, returned to the roots of his demise.

The Chimera's fingers spasmed, loosened. She could no longer detect the shiver of breath in his shoulder. Tara remained there, waiting, until she was certain the last breath had been drained out of him.

She stumbled to her feet and headed for the door. Her vision was fuzzy and yellow in spots, but she was determined to put one foot before the other, coughing into her elbow. She had to get out of here. Back to fresh air and sunlight.

She minced her way down the steps, through the control room, out the rend in the side of the Sarcophagus. She stumbled forward on the pavement, hoping that Irina and her men would be coming soon. Rain rinsed over her suit, and she distractedly wondered if it would rinse away some of the radioactive particles.

She collapsed in the soft moss, looking straight ahead to a monument built at the edge of the administration building, depicting firefighters and liquidators trying to contain the disaster with fire hoses and shovels.

Heroes, she thought, grimly, before she blacked out.

Chapter Twenty-one

TARA EXPECTED to awaken in a hospital.

Not on the bed in Irina's house.

She lay, nearly undressed, on the bed, sunshine streaming in from the window. Her skin felt tight and achy, red as if she'd spent all day at the beach. Her mouth was dry, and Irina pressed a cup to her mouth.

"Drink."

Tara gulped down cool milk that soothed the fire in her throat. Irina sat on the edge of the bed, rolling a chicken egg over her body. She rolled it evenly over her arm, turning it slowly until the shell grew warm.

"What are you doing?" Tara whispered.

"Treating your radiation sickness."

She then removed the egg, cracked it open in a bowl on the floor at her feet. Noisome black fluid oozed out of the egg, flowing into the pool of oily blackness in the bowl.

Tara blinked her dry eyes. She was too exhausted to argue. "How long have I been asleep?"

"More than a day. The guards helped me bring you back here, and you haven't moved."

"Where's Harry?"

"He's here." She offered no additional information.

"I want to see him."

Irina offered Tara her hands to help her sit up. Tara took mincing steps to follow Irina to her bedroom, where Harry lay on her bed. He sported the same sunburn as Tara, but the coverlet had been pulled up to his neck. The mark of a handprint on his face, as if he'd been slapped, was fading. One of Irina's cats kept vigil at the foot of the bed.

"Harry." Tara reached for his warm forehead. He didn't respond. His breathing was regular and even. Tara saw that he had an IV bag full of saline attached to his arm. She turned to face Irina. "What's wrong with him? Why isn't he in a hospital?"

Irina shook her head. "I brought more guards with me, where we found you and Harry. They found the other man dead in the Sarcophagus. I think they decided that he was too contaminated, left him there.

"They summoned a doctor. The doctor said that he had no idea what was wrong with him. They wanted to take you two to Kiev for tests." Irina suppressed a shudder. "I would not let them. I remember what happened to the firemen when they took them to Minsk. Poked and prodded them, put in plastic bubbles. But they were unable to do anything for those men. Better you be here."

Tara pressed her hand to his forehead, stifled a sob. "The Chimera. I think he stole Harry's mind."

"You can heal him."

Tara turned around at the familiar voice. In the doorway, the Pythia stood. She was dressed in a peasant shirt and dark slacks, and she held a bowl of eggs in her hands, hair pulled away from her face with a scarf. Dark circles shadowed her eyes.

And Cassie was with her. Tara's heart skipped a beat. Cassie, dressed in jeans and a T-shirt, elbowed past the Pythia and flung herself in Tara's arms.

"What the hell are you doing here?" Tara said, fury rising in her scraped throat.

Cassie pushed Tara's hair away from her face. "The Steves took me out on their boat, and I was looking up at the stars. I knew there was something wrong. I could feel it." She shook her head. "I called the only one I knew who could help you."

"You called the Pythia?" Tara was too exhausted to argue.

"The Steves wouldn't let me go alone," Cassie explained.

Irina muttered, "They eat like horses."

The Cowboy and the Kahuna poked their heads in the bedroom. "We promised not to let her out of our sight, and I meant it," the Cowboy said.

"Whoa, you're not decent." The Kahuna put up his hand and backed away.

Tara glared at the Pythia. "You told them about Delphi's Daughters?"

The Pythia set the eggs down on a dresser. "For men, they're surprisingly useful."

"She just wanted us to carry the luggage."

The Cowboy rubbed his chin. "We've seen stranger shit. Like chupacabras."

Tara was too exhausted to argue. She turned her attention back to Harry. "How do I heal him?"

The Pythia shooed the Steves and Cassie from the room, shut the door. "Do you still have the cards I gave you?"

"Yes. They're . . ." Tara struggled with the right words. ". . . odd."

The Pythia sat at Harry's feet. "Have you had dreams, visions?"

"Yes. What's that got to do with anything?"

The Pythia sighed. "The Chimera drew away some of Harry's memory, but didn't complete the job. He threw Harry into a coma, in the physical world. Metaphysically, though . . . this means that Harry's spirit is disconnected, trying to find its way back. The cards are a tool to open yourself to the unseen, to the world of spirits and archetypes that moves under everyday reality."

"You're saying I can find Harry and bring him back?"

"Maybe. If he's not gone, already."

Tara's hands balled into fists. She wouldn't allow Harry to be alone again. "Bring me my cards."

TARA SLIPPED UNDER THE COVERS BESIDE HARRY. ANTICIPATing the cold of the trance, she'd wrapped herself in two layers of her own clothes. She'd exiled all the others from the room, had drawn the Knight of Pentacles, the Four of Swords, and Strength from her deck. She placed the cards under her pillow. She put her chin on his shoulder, her hand on his chest, feeling it rise and fall, the hollowness behind it.

"Come back to me, Harry," she whispered, blinking tears into the pillow.

She closed her eyes, willing herself to dream.

Gradually, the sounds of the chickens and the cats and the voices in the kitchen below faded away. Tara felt herself moving through hot blackness, falling into the dream. When she opened her eyes, she was standing at the edge of the black forest. She'd lost something here, she remembered. She had to find it.

She cast around. There was no sign of the man carrying the poisonous rods into the world. She knew that he was inside the forest, dead. But he had taken Harry, and she needed to find him.

She looked down at the lion at her hip. "Show me," she pleaded with him.

The lion led her around the edge of the forest to a clearing. Instead of the black tower at the center, Tara saw a lead-lined sarcophagus, riveted with rusting bolts. On top of it lay the crude figure of a knight in effigy hastily hewn in metal, holding a sword over his chest. Tara walked up to it, pressed her hands to the dark lead. It felt warm, as if there was something inside.

"Harry, are you in there?"

Nothing answered her.

She pushed at the lid of the sarcophagus with all her strength. It was welded shut. The lion put his paws up on the lid and pushed, too, growling with the effort. Tara clawed at it until the muscles in her arms shook and her fingernails separated and bled. She continued to push.

She was Strength. She'd open the jaws of this sarcophagus, no matter what. She felt the ancient power of the archetype sinking into her. It was older than time, old as this land. Its power would outlast the half-lives of the radioactive isotopes, timeless and eternal as the sun.

The metal gave a rusty sigh, and the welds split, allowing the lid to slide to the ground with a crash. Sunlight streamed in, shining on the armor of the knight asleep inside.

Tara leaned into the casket, pressed her bloody hand to Harry's face. She lifted his visor, allowing the sun to brush his closed eyes. She kissed him, willing him to awaken and return to her with all the strength she'd summoned.

TARA AWOKE IN DARKNESS. THE SUN HAD SET, AND SHE LAY IN bed with Harry, a cat curled up at their feet. Her body felt cold as a corpse's. She could feel the chill of the trance cooling her radiation burns. Her skin, where it touched Harry's, condensed like dew.

She lifted her head, scarcely daring to hope. Harry's breath was deep and even. She brushed her lips over his, exhaling a mist of condensation, like a ghost.

His lips parted and his eyes flickered open.

"Harry." Tara pressed her cold hand to his sunburned face. "Do you know who I am?"

Harry reached up to grasp her hand. He kissed her knuckle. "You're loved. And you're freezing."

Tears dripped down Tara's nose. "I thought I'd lost you."

"Nah." Harry stretched, rubbed the side of his face. "I had one fucked-up dream though. Dreamed I was locked in a box."

Tara pressed her ear to his chest, smiling. "I think I had the same one."

"What happened?" Harry pushed Tara's hair behind her ear. "Did you catch him? Last thing I remember was getting slapped around by the Chimera, and . . ." Tara felt goosebumps rise on his skin, and she didn't think it was only her touch that caused them. ". . . I could feel his fingers in my head. It was like . . . like a violation. I know I'm not explaining it well. But did you catch him?"

"He's dead. He died in the reactor room."

"Of the radiation?"

"No." Tara blew out her breath. "I killed him."

Harry stroked her hair. "You all right?"

"Yes. No. I don't know. Irina is treating my radiation poisoning with eggs."

Harry pinched the bridge of his nose. "I don't think that sounds like a good idea. When we get back stateside, we'll get you checked out."

"We've got bigger problems."

Harry paused. "Bigger problems than being crispy onions? I can't imagine."

"The Pythia is here. With Cassie."

Harry froze.

"And the Steves."

Harry sat up in bed. "Somebody's gonna get their ass kicked." His gaze was dark, and he reached for his clothes.

Tara put a hand on his chest. "You can ream the Steves out all you want. But leave Cassie and the Pythia to me."

Grudgingly, he agreed. Dressing quickly, he followed Tara down the stairs to the living area. Irina, Cassie, the Pythia, and the Steves were playing cards on the floor. It looked like they were betting with eggs, judging from the pot in the middle.

"Harry!" Cassie launched herself at Harry, buried her face in his chest. Harry hugged her tightly, looked over her head to glower murderously at the Steves.

"I thought I told you guys to keep her safe," he growled. "Not bring her into a radiation zone with—"

The Cowboy stood up. "When that girl has it in her mind that she's going somewhere, there's nothing stopping her. We're just along for the ride."

"I can't trust you guys to do jack shit," Harry snarled.

"Take it outside, boys," Irina snapped. "No fighting in the house."

Harry disentangled himself from Cassie and stalked outside, startling a chicken. The Cowboy grabbed a bottle of vodka and followed with the Kahuna in tow.

That left the women. Tara stood with her arms folded. "I guess I should thank you for helping Harry."

The Pythia put her cards down. "I will go."

Tara looked up at Irina, standing beside her painted eggs and the picture of Pavel. She'd made so many sacrifices. Tara felt inadequate in her understanding of duty, in her selfishness. She didn't feel like the hero that Irina was.

"No. We need to talk. About Cassie."

Cassie shrank back against the stairs. "Look, I, um—"

"Agreed," said the Pythia, tucking her feet beneath her. "I pushed you too hard, and for that, I'm sorry. But you need to decide whether you want to become Pythia, and soon."

"Why?" Tara demanded suspiciously.

The Pythia lifted her chin. "I have lung cancer."

Tara's jaw dropped. "I'm sorry," she whispered. "Are you—" Her mind churned. She wanted to ask: *Are you seeking treatment? How far along are you? Is it terminal? Why the hell are you telling us now?*

The Pythia waved her off. "I tell you only because my time here is limited. Cassie will need to decide whether or not she wants to become Pythia. If she does, she will need to take over my role, soon. If she doesn't, I'll need to find another." She gazed at the women fiercely. "I will not allow our line to die out."

Cassie sat down heavily on the steps. "Wow."

"If you choose to become Pythia, you will need to commit fully to the mission," the Pythia said.

"And what is that?" Cassie asked. "There's all this nebulous talk about the balance of power, but I don't know what that really means."

"The Pythia serves peace, at all costs, even in ugly ways." The Pythia glanced at Irina. "I never told you this, but you weren't intended to stop the disaster here, at Chernobyl."

Irina's eyes widened, and she blinked. "What do you mean?"

"You never failed. Chernobyl was allowed to happen. It was a factor in the fall of the Soviet Union. Ultimately, that prevented all-out nuclear war."

Irina covered her mouth with her hand and stared up at the picture of her dead husband. Tears leaked from her eyes and a sob caught in her throat.

The Pythia gazed at Cassie. "Are you willing to make those kinds of decisions, to sacrifice the few for the many?"

Cassie stared down at her hands. "I'm not that strong. I can't do this on my own."

"You would have Tara to guide you. A regent, of sorts." The Pythia looked at Tara with a sad smile. "No matter what, Tara's counsel can be trusted."

"And who will become Pythia if I refuse?"

The Pythia shook her head. "I'll choose someone else. Maybe Daria. Or Callista. But they are nearly as old as I am, and they haven't long."

Cassie's hands balled into fists. "I'll do it."

Tension fell in the Pythia's shoulders.

"But I won't do it like you. I won't be cold. I won't be brutal. I'll do it my way. No killing."

The Pythia smiled. "I know you will try."

The men stumbled back into the house. The Kahuna had a black eye, and the Cowboy was limping. Harry's shirt was torn, and he had custody of the bottle of vodka. He lifted it and took a swig.

"Cheers," he said. "To settling arguments the old-fashioned way. With violence."

Irina began to pass out glasses. Harry poured. The Pythia raised her glass.

"To peace. Whatever the cost."